CW00430101

THE ERRANT FLOCK

JANA PETKEN

©2015 by Jana Petken. All rights reserved.

No part of this book may be reproduced, stored in a retrieved system, or transmitted by any means without the written permission of the author.

The Errant Flock is a work of fiction and bears no factual resemblance to the characters or events in the story.

Cover design by Novel Design Studios

Also available from Jana Petken:

The Guardian of Secrets

The Mercy Carver Series:

Dark Shadows, Book 1

Blood Moon, Book 2

Acknowledgements

To my mother, Rena, you are always in my heart.

Also, my thanks to:

Nick Wale, my publicist;

Bob Martin, my proof reader;

Editor, Shellie Hurrle;

And to all those who continue to believe in me, thank you for your unwavering support.

CHAPTER ONE

December 1491

The duke of Sagrat, Luis Henrique Peráto, strode through his castle's hallways with his head bowed in sorrow. Tears slipped from his red-rimmed eyes and down his cheeks. So profound was his rage and grief that he boorishly pushed aside servants and soldiers and subjected those within earshot to mumbled profanities.

His stride lengthened further as he neared the castle's heavy iron-studded doors. At least outside he had some respite from the prying eyes that stalked him every time he left his chambers. There was no privacy within these godforsaken walls.

Tears continued to gather in his eyes. He exhaled a guttural grunt, billowing from deep within his throat, and thought, *I must stop crying.* A duke's tears would be seen as weakness of spirit and a pitiful self-indulgence unbecoming of nobility. No one must know why his heart was breaking. Only God would bear witness to his grief this night. Only *He* would know of his suffering, and He would be merciful.

A thick gold chain at his neck, which jangled against his chain mail vest, secured the long black and gold cloak wrapped around his broad shoulders. The mantle's ermine fur trim swept the ground behind him. It was heavy and cumbersome, but it was a vital item of clothing to combat the coldest winter months, when a perpetual wind seemed to blow through the ancient castle's passageways. This night, there was a luminous sky filled with stars, but it was so cold that breath lingered in the air like a fog.

The duke had a handsome countenance. His long noble nose was perhaps too sharp to be called perfect, but it was as straight as an arrow and was framed by light brown eyes surrounded by thick lashes and arched brows which were unusually feminine. Like most Spanish men, he sported a small bearded peak which dangled off the edge of his chin, and as he neared the castle's doors, he twirled its wiry coils around his finger, as was his habit whenever darkness of mood came upon him.

A group of guards huddled on the ground just in front of the heavy ten-foot wooden doors were flicking smooth stone marbles and laughing at each others' jokes as though they had not a care in the world. But upon seeing their nobleman approaching, they jumped to their feet, clearly surprised and ashamed to be caught neglecting their duties.

Luis, sweeping by them with a contemptuous sneer, halted suddenly and barked an order which left his militiamen with no doubt that he was displeased." Get up off your arses and open the doors for me! Should marauders come to do mischief, they'll find my castle an easy catch with such a slothful, useless bunch guarding it!"

Outside, the paved courtyard was coated with a light frost. Luis lifted his face to the air and exhaled a long steamy breath that lingered in the stillness. Hugging his cloak tighter across his chest, he walked doggedly along the stone path towards one of the wall's watchtowers, cursing God under his breath as he went.

Three more guards on the uppermost part of the battlements, which sat just beneath the watchtower, tossed down their dice and stood to attention with the same surprised and guilty expressions as displayed previously by the guards inside. Feeling his resentment rising further, Luis shouted at them to leave the wall. He rarely ventured outside at night to check on what his militia were doing. Why should he? he thought. That was Captain Tur's job. The lazy whoreson was probably sleeping like a dormouse.

After pushing aside the last man to reach the bottom of the wall's steps, Luis questioned his generosity. The militiamen were rewarded handsomely for serving him. In his opinion, they shouldn't be paid any more money than the other fifty or so castle servants, from swine herder to cook. He had often suggested that to his late father, but the old duke had always maintained that until Spain formed a regular army, privately paid soldiers would continue to be crucial. "There are plenty of good men in this town ready and willing to take your jobs from you!" he blurted out now without thinking.

Climbing the stairs to the top of the wall where the tower stood, he leaned his body against the cold stones and then gripped a merlon block by its outer edge. Scraping his fingernails along its width until they bled, he prayed that this physical pain would ease the terrible ache in his heart. His faith had been tested many times, he thought, but this night God was the cruel hand that had once again deprived him of a living child. If only he could blaspheme aloud or blame someone for his misfortune …

Why did the Almighty treat him thus? Luis asked silently. What deeds of his had been so vile that his bloodline be stolen from him repeatedly? Was it God's will that saw his wife's womb a cursed grave for each of the three infants she had tried and failed to deliver safely into the world? He exhaled, shook his head, and choked back a sob. No, he could not hold the Almighty responsible for this calamity, for that would be heresy. But fault must be laid at someone's door, he then thought, for if no one were guilty, this tragedy would not make sense.

"Bring me the physician!" he shouted down to the guards standing at ease in the courtyard. "Bring him to me now!"

Looking over the top of the wall, he stared into the darkness, grunting bitterly and despising what he saw. Beneath him, a long procession of townspeople were snaking their way up the hill's zigzagged path towards the south-east gate, where the statue of Madonna stood. After they laid offerings at her feet, the people would walk back down to the base of the hill and celebrate Mass in the church of San Agustin.

Focusing his eyes, he now saw hundreds of lit fire torches guiding route of the processional. Buildings, trees, and rocks sitting at the edge of the path were lit up, and even from where he stood, he could make out frosty specks on white granite stone.

The alabaster effigy of the Immaculate Conception, sitting atop a wooden pallet with four tree trunk arms and being carried by six men, was accompanied by priests and Dominican monks singing in prayer. For the moment, their voices were faint, but when they reached the castle walls, their chanting would soar and echo throughout the town below. He was in no mood to listen to their wailing prayers.

A hazy orange cloud sat above the town like a halo, yet eastwards across the plain towards the sea, there was only a mysterious darkness. Luis breathed deeply and inhaled the pungent aroma of smoking wild boar and kid meat being cooked on this auspicious night of sacrifice and prayer. After Mass, those lucky enough to have meat would devour it like a pack of hungry wolves. They would drink the wine vats dry, until their legs no longer held them upright and their tongues slurred with senseless mutterings.

Below him, townspeople sang God's praises whilst he suffered in silence. He knew what they were asking Him for. They prayed for rain to end the drought and to replenish the earth. They also prayed for strong olive trees and vineyards to produce oil and wine. They were asking for healthy vegetable crops after a bad harvest. "Give us a return to prosperity," they'd be crying like sullen children.

He had spent hours this night pleading for the life of his newborn son, which was infinitely more important than their greed and need for self-gratification. God would doubtless answer their prayers … but those of Sagrat's duke? No, God cared not a fig for him or his sorrow.

He spat over the wall, symbolically showering his people with his saliva, and his impatience grew. "Where is the physician? Find him!" he shouted angrily. "Drag him here, if you have to!" He wiped a dribble of spit from his bearded chin and stared again at the crowds below. They were ignorant peasants. They contributed nothing to the world, yet God blessed them with children and grandchildren to carry their names and their bloodlines into the future.

Even the Jews in the Jewry, on the northern slope, were more contented with their lot than he was. Why should he suffer his people's mockery and cruel whisperings? He would kill anyone who displayed the slightest disrespect or mentioned his failure to father a healthy child.

Turning sharply at the sound of approaching footsteps, he scowled and silently studied Saul Cabrera, the Peráto family's physician. His stocky frame, trembling with fear, was hunched forwards, heavy shoulders drooping with shame. Glaring at him, Luis thought that he should feel shame. He deserved to drown in a sea of it.

Cabrera cowered before Luis's intense stare, gripping his black cloak so tightly across his chest that his knuckles whitened. "Your Grace?" he muttered sheepishly.

"Hold your tongue!" Luis wondered why his father had held the physician in such high esteem right up until the day he died. The Jew was a bungling idiot and far too old to treat anyone, let alone the Peráto family. He was finished … He'd never be allowed near the duchess again.

"Leave us!" Luis growled at the guards in the courtyard. "Wait for me inside. And close the doors behind you." When they had left, he shouted, "Cabrera, get up here!"

Luis watched Cabrera wearily climb the stairs. *He's like an old hound fit only for the stock pot*, he thought. His rage rose like a wave. Guilt sat in the Jew's beady eyes and on his trembling lips. It was as clear as the light of day. The decrepit old fool knew he was at fault. His manner only confirmed what was startlingly true; his carelessness had killed the infant. Too angry to speak at that moment, Luis turned his back on Cabrera and stared again beyond the wall. He had to think and to come to a decision.

Jews … What was he to do with them? he wondered. He was a patient and lenient man. He'd fought hard to continue a legacy of easy coexistence with Sagrat's Jewish population; such had been the strength of his word to his dear departed father. Recalling Ricardo Peráto's words, he sneered. The Jews were important to Spain. They were the backbone of the community. Because of them, the kingdom of Aragon enjoyed culture, art, and science. Jews had fought for Their Majesties against the Moors. They helped fund the war, which was more than most of the Valencia nobles had done. His father had never tired of advocating for his Jews.

Ricardo Peráto would be remembered as being a good man, Luis thought, but he'd also been a foolish dreamer, incapable of seeing that having the king's love and a Jewish population did not go hand in hand. He should have set more store in pleasing Rome and the Spanish crown. They saw the Jews as a threat to Christian Spain and wanted them gone, whereas his father had stubbornly argued against that notion, albeit in private.

The kingdom of Aragon had four regions: Barcelona, Zaragoza, Valencia, and Mallorca. Less than one thousand Jews remained in Valencia, and most of them lived in Sagrat. Under his father's rule, they had been allowed freedoms long since denied Jews in other districts. Luis admitted that there was a time when he had agreed with his father's decision to overlook the monarchs' demands for tighter control over the Jews and their monetary possessions. And when some dukedoms and provinces expelled their Jews, he and his father had held fast against the idea, preferring to wait until they were eventually forced to get rid of them. Why throw something away when it was still of use? Ricardo Peráto had questioned.

The time was coming, Luis thought, when Sagrat's Jewry would be nothing but a derelict reminder of what was once a thriving business community. In his opinion, the king and queen were not trying to expel a race but rather a religion. Their obsession with the Jews dismayed him, at times, as did their lack of common sense.

Luis recalled his father receiving numerous correspondences regarding the Jews. The letters had been sent to the realm's principle nobles a few years ago. According to Ferdinand and Isabella, it was their solemn duty to support the Holy Office of the Inquisition, mainly because, in their opinion, Christian lives were being endangered by contact with the Jews. The Holy Office asserted their power by providing that the Jews be expelled, and the King and Queen agreed and further stated that there should be no Jews remaining in any of their realms and territories. They were doing this because of their debts and obligations to the Holy Office, they'd added, despite great harm to themselves.

How noble their words had sounded. And what a righteous declaration they'd made in the last paragraph, which had stuck in his mind: *We are seeking and preferring the salvation of souls above our own profit and that of individuals.*

Jolting himself from his thoughts, he turned to face Cabrera. He felt sick. His heart was breaking, and the Jew standing in front of him was to blame and had to be dealt with. Luis struggled to steady his breathing, but the image of his son's limp body lying in his arms and the physician's guilt-ridden face looking on in the chamber's shadowy corner caused his heart to thump hard against his chest.

Maybe the king and queen were right after all? Perhaps Jews *were* a stain on this town. Still staring at Cabrera, his eyes widened with an even more sinister notion. Did Cabrera purposely harm the infant? It was a possibility. He and his Jewish cohorts had been snubbed. The physician and his friend Rabbi Rabinovitch had held positions on the town council for years, until Christian voters recently dismissed them. Cabrera was wealthy and lived in one of the grandest houses in Sagrat, but his home and the Jewry's very existence were under threat. Yes, he was capable of killing a helpless baby to avenge his humiliations.

Luis's lips pursed in anger. The muscles in his cheeks twitched, and his eyes narrowed to mere slits. Thanks to the dukes of Sagrat, Cabrera had lived a self-indulgent, pampered life, yet three Peráto heirs were dead because of him. The man had the gall to look forward to a rich retirement, but he wouldn't get one. He didn't deserve to live until he was a feeble but contented old man, dying as he squatted over his chamber pot.

"I've been blind, but I now accept the error of my ways," Luis said calmly after the long silence. "I've been a sentimental fool. At my father's behest, I accepted you, honoured you, and allowed you to keep your position even after he died. I've shown you nothing but kindness. I put aside my own grief after your last two failures and gave you another opportunity to prove yourself to me ... and you have failed miserably!"

"Your Grace, I..."

"Keep your mouth still. Your godless religion and your wretched, misguided soul have infected the duchess's womb. I forgave you your ineptness after the death of my infant daughter and for the loss of the babe that dissolved to blood inside my wife's womb. I was a fool to think you loved my family. You with your heretic rituals ..."

"No, don't say that. You will not call me a heretic," Cabrera retorted, waving a bony index finger in Luis's face. "I love God, as well you know. I am faithful to him and to his teachings. I am not a Christian, and I do not adhere to Rome's laws or their definition of heresy. Your own good father understood my faith and accepted it as my right. The death of your child is a tragedy, but—"

"A tragedy ... A tragedy, you call it? My son is dead because of you! Both he and the daughter my wife bore before him drew breath for just a few short moments and then died in my arms. They were delivered by your hand, yours alone ... You have cursed my family, Cabrera. You seek to destroy my line. You hate Christians. Don't deny it!" Luis nodded. He was surprised at just how much he agreed with the conclusion he had just reached. "Come closer."

Watching the physician shuffle hesitantly towards him, he grunted with disgust at the downcast cowardly eyes refusing to look up at him. "Face me, you treacherous bastard. Look at me." With a tight grip on Cabrera's jaw, Luis forced the physician to look him in the eye. "What words of comfort can you give me? How will you defend the indefensible?"

Cabrera's reddened eyes stared unwaveringly. "Your Grace, I tried to save the infant. I used every medical method known to me. I would gladly have given it my own breath. Sadly, I have concluded that your wife's womb may be hostile. It appears to me that it was not able to give proper nourishment to the child. She may never give birth to a healthy infant." He swallowed painfully and then added, "In both cases, the babes were not strong enough to breathe on their own."

"Are you saying that my wife is at fault?"

"Not at fault, Your Grace. No blame should be laid at any door. I believe the duchess lacks strength. She eats like a small bird, pecking at slivers of bread. She told me herself that most food is sinful to the world and that she would rather abstain than eat it. She has an ailment of the mind that must be dealt with, and unless she takes better care, I fear we will see the same result every time she falls with child. Next time will be different. I will confine her to bed, and you must encourage her to eat."

"There will be no next time for you," Luis hissed at him. "Your flesh and bones will be rotting by the time I next plant a seed in my wife's womb. Your breath will leave you this night. It will be ripped from you, and you'll feel my children's pain. And after you are dead, I will hurt your granddaughter ..."

Cabrera gasped. Terror sat in his watery eyes, and his body shook uncontrollably. With clasped hands, he struggled onto his knees. "Your Grace, your grief is clouding your judgement. I know you. You don't mean what you say. You must trust in God. It is through His will that your child died ... I love your family. I have served Sagrat's dukes for thirty years ..."

"You killed my children. All of them!"

"No, no, I did not. I could not save them, but there is nothing I would like more than to see your line continue with strong heirs. Luis, I beg you to listen …"

"How dare you call me Luis! I am your duke!"

"And I am the physician who pulled Your Grace from your mother's womb. I wiped your runny nose and cleaned your bloody elbows and knees when you fell." Still on his knees, he begged again. "My granddaughter is all I have in the world. She does not deserve to be punished for any sin you may think I have committed." Then his feverish eyes widened. "I will have her baptised into the Catholic Church. She will convert and become a good Christian. Her devotion to you and to this town will be unequalled. I give you my oath."

"Your oath means nothing to me, Jew."

Cabrera tried again. "My family has lived in Sagrat for over one hundred and fifty years. I have seen my relatives born and die in service to this town. Please do with me what you will – but do not end my line. Sinfa is a good girl!"

Luis lifted the physician to his feet and pulled him closer to him, until their noses were almost touching. Then he stretched his arms beneath Cabrera's cloak and clasped the neckline of the physician's woollen tunic. Gripping tightly, he pushed the physician towards the wall and then heard the old man's back thump against it. He stared into the physician's eyes, which were welling up with tears. God could not be blamed for his son's death, Luis thought again, but Cabrera could.

With one swift movement, he lifted Cabrera off his feet and swung him up and onto the wall's merlons. The physician's shoulders and head dangled off the outer edge of the wall. One buttock balanced atop a block, a leg hung down the inner wall, and the other was wedged in the crenel between two merlons.

Luis held him there. Should he release his grip on the physician's tunic, he'd plummet to his death, he kept thinking. He wanted him to die and to feel life being sucked out of his body. His pain would ease and grief would lessen if he killed the old man. He just needed a few seconds more to stare at the fear visible on the Jew's face.

Cabrera looked at the precipice that met a rocky floor some fifty feet below him. "Please don't do this … Don't allow murder to corrupt your soul. Have compassion for me!" He attempted to swing the top half of his body upright and grappled with air. In a desperate attempt to find something to grab on to, his arms flailed, but then his hands managed to find Luis's cloak chain. "Dear God, no!"

The back of Luis's neck strained against the force of the pull on his cloak, but he allowed Cabrera's frenzied attempts to cling on to him go unhindered for a few seconds. Gazing into Cabrera's terrified eyes brought Luis feelings of neither pity nor regret. His son was dead, killed by this Jew, his mind screamed, utterly convinced of it … With unflinching eyes, he grabbed three of the physician's fingers and then bent them backwards in a sharp tug. He felt great satisfaction when he heard the bones crack loudly. He wanted this over with now.

Cabrera screamed in agony and loosened his grip on the chain. His tear-filled eyes stared once more at the rocks far below and then went back to Luis, "Murdering me will not ease your grief. May God forgive you," he choked.

At the mention of God, a flash of guilt crossed Luis's eyes, but his voice was soft and steady. "You conspired with the devil against my family, and I will now bring God's wrath down upon your line. You can go to hell and burn there."

Luis held on to the physician with one hand gripping the throat. His free hand pushed Cabrera's legs towards the outer edge of the wall. One side of Cabrera's body balanced precariously in the air, whilst only a buttock and one leg remained on the merlon block and in the crenel. Cabrera's body was as stiff as a poker and as still as a statue. Luis grunted loudly and pushed the body, watching it slip off the wall and plummet down the precipice on its outer side.

Mesmerised, Luis watched Cabrera's body tumble like a straw doll. In the darkness, he was not able to see the figure strike the rocks below, but he heard a loud thud and the sound of breaking bones. Grimacing, he imagined the bloody head looking like a smashed chicken's egg. He shuddered involuntarily and thought that Cabrera deserved such a death.

After stumbling down the stairs, Luis adjusted his cloak's skewed position. Was the physician guilty of the accusations laid against him? Probably not, but the physician had been a religious man devoted to God. His sanctimonious conscience would have found it impossible to keep the infant's death a secret from its mother, her ladies, and the Jewry's rabbi. No amount of persuasion or monetary bribe could have dissuaded him from telling Sagrat's entire population that the heir to the dukedom had died. The old man had to be silenced, and that was the truth of it.

Luis opened the doors and came to stand in front of the guards waiting in the passageway inside. His mind was working keenly and quickly. Grief seemed to be heightening his senses. Looking at the men, he thought, *I need to choose someone I can manipulate; a militiaman who will obey my orders without question or one who will be too afraid to disobey me.* He searched the faces looking at him furtively and discarded those he knew were experienced soldiers. No, a seasoned man-at-arms wouldn't do, at all … He was looking for a fresh face. With a pensive expression, his eyes finally settled on the tallest soldier there. He'd not seen this young man before.

"What's your name, soldier?" he asked gruffly.

"Sanz, Your Grace. David Sanz."

"How long have you served me?"

"Three weeks, sir."

Luis nodded his approval. "Come with me."

The duke walked down the passageway and then turned abruptly back to the remaining militiamen, now some distance behind him. "There has been an unfortunate occurrence. My physician has taken his own life," he told them. "A few moments ago, I watched him jump from the wall. Retrieve his body. You'll find it lying on the rocks beneath the tower. Take him home to his granddaughter in the Jewry ... and treat his body with respect. He was a loyal servant."

CHAPTER TWO

The duke and duchess's private residence inside the castle consisted of six interconnecting chambers guarded by the militia day and night. No one but ladies-in-waiting, the physician, the duke's valet, the chamberlain, and the town treasurer were allowed to enter without a summons, and no one left without the duke's or duchess's permission. The castle's most private areas were known as the solace. They were hidden from view by one set of ten-foot-tall, five-inch-thick wooden double doors at their entrance and another set of similar doors standing at the end of a long stone passageway, which stretched the length of the castle.

David Sanz, standing outside the doors of the chambers, felt an uncomfortable heat on his skin under the door guards' curious stares, and he nervously adjusted his leather sword belt. He wore a loose form of military garb, yet it was an untidy ensemble which had not yet found a cohesive uniformity. It consisted of a hooded white woollen over-tunic emblazoned with a red cross, back and front, with sleeves tight at the top but flaring out widely from the elbows. On his legs were tight hose, red in colour, and covering his feet were mid-calf boots. A sallet helmet sat on his head, hiding most of his thick wavy black hair, which curled up at the edges. The sides were drawn forward at the bottom, covering his cheeks and chin, and the rear was curved out into a flange to protect his neck. He wondered if he should remove it or wait until he was ordered to do so.

He shifted from one foot to another, trying to calm his racing pulse. The burning question in his mind was why *he* had been summoned. The duke had never spoken to him directly or asked for his name before tonight. He couldn't recall a single instance when Luis Peráto had actually looked at him, never mind summoned him. He was the youngest and most inexperienced soldier in a militia comprised of forty men.

David felt his excitement stirring. He'd been reaching for his goals since boyhood. When he had turned twelve years old and was almost as tall as the average grown man, he'd managed to persuade the castle's blacksmith to take him under his wing. To this day, old Pépe was one of the finest sword smiths in Valencia. There was not a blade he could not forge or an axe he could not mould to perfection.

David had gone to Pépe's forge every day for weeks, begging for work, and he'd been sent away with a slap on his ear many times before the old man finally allowed him to watch and learn the trade. David's greatest thrill in those early days was the moment he first used the lifting tongs and forging hammer. On that day, he became a man, and a short time after that, he was allowed to practice the turning of soft iron into steel. He made his first attempts at shaping weapons and tools with the use of an anvil and chisel.

Getting as close as possible to the soldiers, knights, and cavalry who had used the forge's services had been his aim, and he'd achieved it. At the age of fifteen, one of the old duke's militiamen presented him with the opportunity to work in the armoury. He'd jumped at the chance to be around weapons, master swordsmen, buckler men, longbow men, and crossbowmen. He remembered those days well. Every night after the fires had been doused and the forge's stone floor cleaned of metal shards, he'd practiced swinging a blade and shooting arrows. During his training, he'd displayed passion, determination, and a rare gift for sword fighting, and before long, some of the militiamen were offering to parry with him.

They taught him how to hone his skills and the best way to strengthen muscles and build stamina. For years, he worked hard to prove himself worthy of service, and three weeks ago, he'd donned the uniform for the first time.

Even so, he had done nothing to deserve the duke's attention this night, he thought again. There had been no notable act attributed to him. He hadn't committed a crime. His duties were fairly menial compared to those of the cavalry and the master swordsmen. He was a good Catholic and had no foes, as far as he knew.

Casting his mind back to the wall an hour earlier, he pictured the duke pushing his soldiers out of the way and then striding angrily towards the watchtower. The physician also came to mind. What had occurred between the two men? Did the physician kill himself in front of His Grace? What could be so terrible in life that would make a man jump to his death? David also wondered about the physician's physical capabilities. When he'd seen Saul Cabrera, he'd looked like a frail old man, unable to climb onto the top of the merlon blocks without a helping hand to hoist him up. David shrugged. He'd probably never find out what really happened to the Jew.

Staring down the length of the passageway and at the thick stone walls, he reminded himself again of what a great honour it was to be in this part of the castle. The militia was used to defend Sagrat from marauders; quash any civil unrest; guard important caravans loaded with coin, travelling to or from Valencia; and to perform ceremonial duties when dignitaries visited. But only a chosen few stood outside these doors.

Since becoming a militiaman, his duties had been mainly confined to the prison, which stood outside the castle's walls beneath the south-east gate. It was rare to see the light of day when on watch in those miserable dark caves. The building didn't look particularly big from the outside, but inside the prison was a maze of tunnels stretching for almost a thousand paces across the hill's underbelly. After being on duty for days on end, he felt as wretched as the prisoners he guarded. He suffered the same smells, rotten food, and foul and stale air. He barely experienced a moment of peaceful silence amongst the despairing, moaning, crying, and maniacal laughter of those who had gone from despair to madness.

Occasionally, he was allowed out of the castle's bowels to perform other duties, such as tonight, when he'd been sent to the wall. It had felt good standing guard and defending his town instead of transporting its citizens to prison and watching their misery. The militia hated prison guard duties, which were still predominately civilian occupations. There was an unpleasantness in arresting respected businessmen, young sweet-tempered women, and old men terrified of rumours, started by people who had travelled widely. According to some, the Inquisition was coming to the town, and they locked up, tortured, or left prisoners to rot for crimes that didn't even make sense.

David believed the rumours. There had certainly been a noticeable increase in arrests. Townspeople were being detained without charge, and after being incarcerated for weeks and months, they were told to be patient. Be *patient*! David had scoffed at the magistrate's idea of a reasonable request.

The guards knew most of those in the prison cells. There were no strangers in Sagrat, for at one time or another, most people shared a processional line on feast days, a water bucket from the town's well, a cup of wine in the taverna, or a bath in the nearby river.

He turned and stared impatiently at the closed doors behind him, willing them to open. How long was he to stand there with his gut knotted like hemp cord? Yes, he was honoured. Yes, he was excited at the prospect of speaking to the duke. But he'd had such wonderful plans for this night. His watch was coming to an end. At the eleventh bell he'd begin his two days' leave, which he would spend with his parents and brothers.

For the first time in their lives, the Sanz family were going to eat wild boar, thanks to the duke's generosity. Once a year, on the day of the Immaculate Conception, which fell on the eighth day in December, His Grace provided four wild boars to the militia. A lottery was used to choose who got the beasts, but one boar was always reserved for the militia's latest recruit.

David smiled, thinking about his good luck. Being the youngest and newest soldier in the duke's forty-man army had its privileges. He'd been presented with the wild boar this morning, and within minutes he'd sent it home in the back of a cart after paying the driver and promising him some leftover meat.

If only he could see his parents' faces at the very moment the beast arrived at the farm. But it mattered not how long he had to wait here, he thought in retrospect. This night was going to be a grand affair for the Sanz family, with or without his presence. The boar, when cooked, would be shared amongst his mother, father, and two brothers. Every slice of flesh, devoured. Organs would be boiled along with bones to make a thick broth for the coming days. Even the boar's tongue, genitals, and ears wouldn't go to waste.

He felt his belly flutter with pleasure. He was happy. Despite his family's troubles, this was a glorious period in his life. He was nineteen years old, yet he had transformed almost impossible dreams into realities. His hard work and perseverance had led him here. Who would have ever thought that he, David Sanz, would be standing right outside the duke's private chambers? He was the most fortunate of men.

CHAPTER THREE

Luis looked down at his sleeping wife from the side of her bed and frowned. Even in sleep, her flickering eyelids still bore the pain of childbirth. Her olive complexion had an insipid pallor. Damp hair stuck to her cheeks, and every now and then, her breathing was interrupted by a sharp, squeaky moan.

He rarely looked at her for this long or this closely, for she scared him. Apart from needing her to bear him a child, he detested being in the same room as her. He would rather face a snapping pack of wolves than her when she was awake.

She was not beautiful by any means, he thought, continuing to gaze at her. Her black lustrous hair was magnificent, but even as a fifteen-year-old bride, that womanly glory had been dulled by the expressionless face it framed. Her body was pitifully thin, with visible bulging bones at her shoulders, chest, and ribcage. When he held her during lovemaking, she felt like a scrawny chicken that he could easily snap into pieces.

Her facial features were uninteresting. Small hooded eyes bordered a long hooked nose. Her lips, which were full and pink, some might call pretty if she were to smile more often, but in his opinion, they were uninviting.

She was the plainest of women, but that mattered not to Luis. No, it was her morose character and the malignant stares that chilled his heart, and lay heavily on his mind. Saul Cabrera had been right about one thing, he thought. She did have an ailment of the mind, although he had no idea what had caused it or how it could be cured.

He must have been blind and deaf. He had only met her twice before they wed, and he'd thought her painfully bashful at the time. But he couldn't recall any blatant symptoms of madness, and as he'd taken very little interest in her since their marriage, he hadn't really noticed her childish behaviour transform into lunacy.

Were it not for her father, he would have had her locked up, out of sight and out of mind. Her obsession with painted dolls, their clothing, and faces with varying expressions vexed him, as did her refusal to part with them. She slept with them, ate with them by her side, and conversed with them much more frequently than she ever did with people. Her incoherent mumblings, hysterical weeping, and stamping of feet when she didn't get her way enraged him and frightened the living daylights out of everyone around her. The screeching outbursts, for seemingly no reason at all, echoed throughout the castle's halls day and night. She humiliated and belittled him – so much so that he no longer appeared in public with her.

Queen Isabella had chosen Josefa for him. The young girl had not been his choice, and he had freely admitted to his father at the time that in favour of any number of other court ladies, he would have cast her aside in the queen's hallways without giving her a second glance.

Josefa was of good Catholic stock, Luis's father had countered. She hailed from a family steeped in loyalty to the Castile crown. Josefa's father, summoned to Aragon by King Ferdinand from Cordoba, in the kingdom of Castile, had ingratiated himself into a position of power with lightning speed. He was not an ordained bishop, priest, or a member of the clergy, for that matter, but he was a scholar of great note and unlike the old Inquisition, an inquisitor didn't have to be a member of the clergy to hold office. There was nothing that Gaspar de Amo didn't know about canon law, for he had studied it for most of his adult life and was a university graduate on the subject. Luis believed that not even the Bishops' Council in Rome could recite, analyse, and act on Catholic teachings as profoundly well as his father-by-law. His published works circulated throughout the Vatican and were a highly regarded source of reading for Catholic scholars everywhere.

In part, Luis was grateful to have Josefa for a wife. Of course, this contentment had nothing to do with her but everything to do with her father. Some three years earlier, De Amo had been chosen to sit on one of the councils of inquisitors. Thomas de Torquemada, the papal inquisitor-general for Aragon, had chosen De Amo personally, and his choice had been backed by King Ferdinand and Queen Isabella.

Since taking office, De Amo's tribunals had been relentless. Many of Aragon's nobles, from Valencia to Zaragoza, squirmed uncomfortably at the mention of his name, for not even they were safe from his scrutiny. His prowess for obtaining confessions of heresy was widely respected, but many people secretly despised him or were terrified of being in the same room as him.

Angered by previous insurrections by Aragon's nobles and Valencia in particular, he delved deep into the lives of counts, barons, and the aristocracy, who in his opinion did not pay an acceptable amount of reverence to canon law. Humble peasants and townspeople, lax in their public devotions, were also targeted in his incessant need to save souls and bring them back to the fold. But those who suffered the most were the *conversos*, Jews who had converted to Christianity. None of them were protected against accusations made against them … and no amount of bribery could save a man or woman from trial, conviction, and the sentence that came afterwards.

De Amo was an extremely wealthy man. The sovereigns, who had plied him with riches and land, loved him, yet he continued to exasperate Aragon's subjects with unfair sanctions, which included confiscation of property and wealth from accused and convicted heretics. These measures were against the *fueros*, local laws, but De Amo had argued that fueros should not be invoked in order to deliver a heretic from justice. Furthermore, the new Spanish Inquisition had been created by the decision of the Holy See, and any other laws could not override canon law, in his opinion. The monarchs agreed with him on every debate; in doing so, they alienated their noblemen and stoked flames of dissent.

Unlike other nobles, Luis believed that he was safe from the Council of Inquisitors' investigations. De Amo loved his daughter, and she was his only child. Scoffing, Luis thought, *If not me, who else would look after the madwoman lying in the bed?* He was sure that the inquisitor would not want his daughter living with him, for at times, she looked as though demons possessed her. Some might even call her a witch … the spawn of the devil. Would De Amo arrest and punish his own daughter? Would he throw her into a prison cell or have her burned at the stake? No, he would protect her, insisting that she was kept hidden in Sagrat's castle, sheltered by her husband.

He shook his head in dismay. A healthy Peráto child would have further secured his position with his father by law. Having a grandson would have ensured the longevity and prosperity of the Peráto and De Amo families. And for the sake of his grandson, the inquisitor would have been only too happy to prop up Sagrat's coffers.

Sagrat was facing financial ruin because of the previous duke's mismanagement of funds. Had he thought more about his town instead of worrying about Castile, Sagrat would not be facing its present troubles. He'd been one of the few Aragonese nobles to give his financial support to the king and queen's war in Granada, and his generosity had been unwarranted and irresponsible.

Competition with Valencia for trade and fishing rights was fierce. Jewish taxes were diminishing, as each day more of them left the town. Their skills as artisans and leather makers had been critical to Sagrat's financial well-being. But their businesses were now being shunned by Christians trying to force them out. Even the most respectable Jewish moneylenders had lost their trade, because of a royal decree. Why should the Jews stay? They had nothing left and no hope of a decent future.

Josefa stirred and opened her eyes. Her feverish wild stare bore into him like daggers. He sighed involuntarily, lifted her limp hand, and pressed her palm to his lips. "Are you well, my lady?" he asked her.

"Don't touch me. I'm tired," she said, pulling her hand away and tucking it under the covers. "And I hurt down there." She pointed between her legs with her other hand. "Where's my dolly? Where is Pepita? I want her to sleep with me. I want her."

She hasn't even asked about the baby, Luis thought, disgusted. Had she forgotten about it? "Do you remember delivering a son?" he asked her.

"Yes, it was horrible. The old man that was here said it was a boy child... I don't play with boys... I only like girl dollies."

"Are you not happy? Our son is a strong boy," Luis tried again. He choked on the lie he had just spoken, but he needed her to hear him say that they had a fine son. Who knew what her tongue would let slip to her ladies should she know the infant was dead. "Rest a bit longer. You must build strength to nourish him …"

"Where is my dolly?" she said sullenly. "I want her … I want her now!"

Luis picked up the closest alabaster doll and threw it on top of the bed covers. Josefa began to cry. "That's not Pepita! You're a bad man!"

Luis walked from the room, closing the door behind him. *Let her weep. I don't have to listen to her,* he thought.

CHAPTER FOUR

With a pensive expression, Luis sat in a cushioned chair in his office. The past two hours had passed swiftly, and in that time, Cabrera had been disposed of. He and the town's treasurer had been the only other two people privy to the baby's death. Josefa, her ladies, and the guards remained ignorant of that truth, for Saul Cabrera had snatched the babe from the chamber as soon as he'd seen its breath falter. At least he'd done something right, Luis thought.

He studied David, who was standing before him, and tried to get the measure of him quickly. Secrecy was the key to success. Persuading the young man to do his bidding would require a subtle yet decisive approach, and if he refused to carry out the order, he too would have to be killed.

Luis couldn't pinpoint the exact moment he'd come up with the plan, which would see him be the father he was meant to be, but from the instant it had come to mind, he'd known that it was the right thing to do. His heart pounded. It was an ambitious proposal, which would have grave consequences should the man in front of him fail. He knew nothing about Sanz, except that he was a fledgling militiaman. He didn't have time to look into the soldier's life, his family background, or to ponder over his loyalty and ambitions. Time was running out, and all had to be resolved before dawn.

He's a handsome devil, Luis thought, staring at David, and exceptionally tall and broad at the shoulders. He had an honest face, yet he had a steely gaze, which was encouraging. His face, although partially hidden by his helmet, was expressive, even if he was standing as still as a statue. Something about the determined line of his lips and unwavering stare from hooded eyes commanded respect and possibly caution from others. Physically, he had passed muster. This was a one-man mission requiring strength and resolve, and Sanz looked to have both these attributes.

"Remove your helmet," Luis finally said. "I want to take a good look at you."

David did as ordered, placing his helmet under his arm and then straightening his body to attention. He bowed his head, lifted it, and said resolutely, "Your Grace."

Luis nodded. "What are your duties?"

"I attend to the incarcerated in your prison, and on occasion I stand watch in the towers."

"I see. And do you do your job well?"

"I believe so. I have much to learn, but I am already a skilled swordsman."

"Skilled? You seem very sure of yourself."

"I have trained with the sword since I was a boy."

Luis nodded his approval. "I have need of you, Sanz. There is an important matter that must be seen to straight away," he said. "I'm going to give you an opportunity to impress me. Does this please you?"

"It pleases me very much, Your Grace."

"You seem like a man wanting to improve his lot in life. Am I right?"

David nodded enthusiastically.

"Perhaps you see yourself rising in the ranks, broadening your horizons. I know I would if I were you."

"I do, sir. I have spent years learning my craft. You will find no better or more loyal a soldier."

"Those are bold statements. You have not yet proved your loyalty to me."

"I am at your command."

Luis gave a hint of a smile. Sanz looked as if he wanted to weep with joy, and so he should. It must feel like a great honour to be in the duke's chambers. "Tell me, what is your father's occupation?"

"He's a saddle maker by trade, but he has the privilege of farming your land," David answered proudly.

"Which plot does your father rent from me?"

"The one sitting by the river, just before the main fork in the road that leads to Valencia."

Luis nodded, recognising that particular farm. Rising from the chair, he poured himself a goblet of wine. Looking at Sanz, he noticed again how tall the militiaman was. He stood head and shoulders above him.

"Do you love your family, Sanz?" Luis asked.

"I do, Your Grace."

"Do you love God and your duke?"

"Yes, of course. I am devoted to both the Holy Roman Church and to your family."

Luis was thoughtful as he sat back down. Sanz seemed to be gushingly loyal and eager to serve. He was also a new recruit – easy to mould – and easily threatened. He couldn't know for sure if the man could be trusted, but swift measures would be taken if he were to become difficult … He'd do nicely.

The treasurer, Sergio Garcia, walked with a confident swagger into the chamber and stood beside the desk. David was glad for the interruption. The duke's scrutiny about faith and family was worrying. The interview was beginning to feel like an interrogation.

Garcia placed a written document on the desk and asked the duke to sign it. Meanwhile, David took a closer look at the treasurer and realised that he'd seen him before at the prison, inspecting the building works. He was a lofty figure in both height and demeanour, with thinning hair and bright pink skin. His face was puffed up, as though he'd been crying for days, and his deep-set unfriendly eyes were disconcerting in what was fast becoming a tense situation. David wagered that he was no more than thirty years old, but being dressed in black from his tunic to his hose made him appear overly austere for his age.

Luis rose from his chair and then went to stand in front of David. "The lord treasurer will give you orders, Sanz. Carry them out to the letter. Remember how important this is to your family. Don't disappoint me."

David bowed his head. "I won't, Your Grace," he said.

When the two men were alone, Garcia took the bold step of sitting in the duke's chair. David cowered under his piecing gaze and had to look away. The duke's questions about his family and their lives had unnerved him. And being in his presence had been oddly unsettling.

"The duke grieves for his newborn son. He died a short time ago, after living for no more than a few minutes," Garcia said, rushing his emotional words. "I fear the duchess's health will suffer because of his death. Sagrat will also mourn this terrible loss."

"My condolences ..."

Garcia waved his hand to silence David. "The duchess's father will be here within days. This news will deeply upset him. Do you know who he is?"

David hesitated. This man would have to be shown deference, he thought. Garcia spoke as one accustomed to commanding and being immediately obeyed. And he did not seem to be the type of man who would view any disloyalty or disrespect kindly. "No, Your Honour, I'm afraid I don't."

"He sits on the Council of Inquisitors," Garcia told him. "He's a very important man. I can't imagine what he'll do when he finds out that another grandchild has died. I hear he's disagreeable at the best of times ... You are aware that the duke's prison is filling up with heretics?"

"Yes, Your Honour, I am aware, although I don't believe there have been any convictions yet. Most remain suspects, and many have not been charged."

"You disapprove?"

"I am in no position to give my opinion. I am slightly mystified by our justice system."

"You're not afraid to speak your mind, are you?" Garcia said sharply.

"Forgive my audacity." David swallowed uncomfortably. He should have kept his mouth shut.

"My point is that the inquisitor is coming to Sagrat. It is his solemn duty to prosecute suspected heretics on behalf of the Holy Office in Rome and our monarchs. Do you disagree?"

"It is not for me to agree or disagree. I do as I am ordered."

"Good. That's good. There are heretics everywhere. You are also aware of the threat they pose to Spain?"

David's palms were sweaty. His mouth was dry, and his instincts screamed danger. "I don't know ... I suppose," he muttered, not knowing what else to say.

"Oh, come now, lad. Surely you must know that there's a snake pit of Judaists in Sagrat claiming to be good Christians yet practising their old religion's rituals in secret."

"Yes."

"Are your parents good Catholics? Are they faithful to the church's teachings?"

David felt the first ripple of fear shoot through his body. His skin blushed with heat. His legs were trembling. Garcia was testing him, baiting him. Thinly veiled threats were hidden behind every word he spoke. David wondered if they were directed towards him or his parents – and if so, why? The Sanz family were good Christians. They had converted to Christianity three years previously and were still considered new conversos, but they could not be called Judaists.

David was well aware that his father's desire to become a Christian had more to do with renting the farm than for religious reasons. And he'd been proved right. The new duke was no longer renting land to Jews.

His father and mother hadn't broken any laws, religious or otherwise. There were no Jewish Sabbath rituals. They didn't attend any Jewish burials. No animal had been slaughtered in the Jewish manner – not in their house. No Jewish prayers were ever spoken, and the Torah … Well, he didn't know where that book was.

"My family are good Catholics," David affirmed.

Garcia spread his arms in a friendly gesture. "Yes, but it's so difficult to know if that's true, isn't it? I believe you, of course, but words of fealty won't be enough to appease the inquisitor. He's like a dog with a pig's leg bone, so I hear, thorough and determined to get to the truth once he suspects a person of heresy. I've heard that people have died under his torturous interrogations."

"Your Honour, with respect, what has the inquisitor to do with me and my family? Why am I here?" David asked, becoming angry.

"I'll tell you why you're here in a moment. As for your family, they have nothing to do with the Inquisition, at this present time … but it *would* be shameful if they happened to come to the inquisitor's attention in the future."

"My family have done nothing wrong. I can see no reason why the inquisitor would be interested in them."

Stroking his goatee, Garcia said, "One would like to think so. But there are bad people in every town, Sanz. It's quite common nowadays for a person to falsely accuse another of heresy for the price of bread or to settle a feud. Some people enjoy inflicting ill on others. The world has always been this way, don't you think?"

"I assure you …"

"Evil is everywhere," Garcia continued, ignoring David's protest. "Your family are recent conversos, are they not?"

"We have been Christians for three years."

"So you are still adjusting to your new religion?"

"We have adapted well and love Christ."

"Then you must know that to revert back to the Jewish way after baptism brings a heavy penalty – death in most cases?"

"Yes."

"Good, good." Garcia sighed. Rising from the chair, he sighed again, as though he were carrying the weight of the world on his shoulders.

David stood like a statue, afraid to move, speak, or make a noise, swallowing the lump caught in his throat. He watched Garcia take a few steps towards him and then stop. Leaning nonchalantly against the front of the desk, Garcia stared at nothing in particular, but then his eyes bore into David, making the hairs on the back of his neck bristle.

"Sanz, keep this to yourself," Garcia said softly. "The duke is worried. He is a powerful man, but he holds no sway when it comes to Inquisition matters. He won't be able to save any of his townspeople, should the inquisitor choose to investigate all of them … Have all members of your family been baptised? Do they have enemies?"

"Yes, they have been baptised, and no, they have no enemies that I am aware of." David swallowed uncomfortably and felt the first droplet of perspiration roll onto his eyelid. He dared to stare at Garcia and was bolder still when he refused to look away. David instinctively knew that he was facing a malicious character, and he had to admit that he was afraid.

"Your Honour, what are my orders?" he asked, thinking that he had stood there long enough playing a game of cat and mouse, knowing that he was the mouse. Whatever the mission was, he wanted it to begin, just so he could get out of this chamber and away from Garcia …

CHAPTER FIVE

David hurried through the south-east gatehouse and stepped onto the castle's main thoroughfare, which wound its way down the hill, through the town, and towards the open plain, leading to the coast. It was a well-trodden path, uneven with potholes and loose stones, and was treacherous to walk in darkness. But it was the quickest route to his destination.

Feeling nauseated, he rubbed his belly. His legs trembled, causing him to stumble and fall a couple of times before he'd even lost sight of the torchlit watchtower. He cursed inwardly, straightened himself, pulled his cloak's hood over his head, and walked resolutely downhill towards the centre of Sagrat.

His orders raced through his mind and crushed his heart. He'd stepped into a nightmarish world from which he would never awaken … not tomorrow … not ever. There was no way out, he thought. If he didn't carry out the duke's orders, the Sanz family would be arrested by the Inquisition or killed by assassins.

Christ's blessed blood. He'd been in the wrong place at the wrong time this night. God rest its soul, but had the duke's baby died one day earlier or one day later, he, David, would not have come to His Grace's attention. He'd be on his way home right now, looking forward to a wonderful feast, drinking wine, and singing songs with his family, not setting off to steal a child and kill innocent people. He was going to lose his soul to the devil.

Halting in mid-step, he turned to look at the path behind him and then walked on, satisfied that he was not being followed. The duke was a madman, drowning in sorrow but mad all the same. No sane man would ask another to rob a baby from its mother's arms, let alone kill all those who witnessed the act. No decent man could possibly conceive such an idea. He had no great love for Spanish noblemen, ignorant of poverty and suffering, but even they would detest the duke and send him to hell for this atrocity, he thought.

There was no escape from this situation, he kept thinking as he came upon the first street of houses. He could run, but leaving his family behind to suffer the consequences of his actions was out of the question. He could kill himself, but his family would be despised, and the duke might still kill his parents and brothers out of spite.

His family were the most important people in his life. Because of them, he strived to become a better man, a man of substance. Everything he did was for his family's benefit.

He stood at a fork in the road. Tightly knitted streets packed with buildings crisscrossed untidily from the south-eastern part of the hill to the most north-eastern point. He was more than halfway down the hill and now in a heavily populated part of the town. The maze of buildings might have been daunting to a stranger, but David knew every corner of every street in the town.

He held the map that Garcia had given him. On it, streets were denoted by a series of lines and squares brushed onto the paper with black ink. There were also writings. The words meant nothing to David, but he had no need of them. He was only interested in the seven crosses that were marked at various points on the map.

He leaned against a building's uneven wall stones and recalled Garcia's words. "The crosses represent recent male births, as registered by the town's priest, Father Bernardo," he'd said. "It is illegal not to notify him of all deaths and births in the town. It is also against the law not to inform the church and, through it, the duke about any changes in family situations, such as house address or employment. The map integrates Father Bernardo's most recent census report, and it is accurate. As you can see, there are seven crosses signifying male babies, born within the past three days, and the location of their homes. The small lines next to the crosses symbolize how many occupants are in the house. Do you understand? Are you aware of how important this is to the duke?"

David had nodded grimly. That had been made perfectly clear when Garcia had said, "If you don't get a male infant, you may as well throw yourself from the highest part of the wall, like the old Jew, for you won't last longer than a drunk's piss hard-on."

He looked once more at the map and chose a house some six streets away from where he stood. Two of the other houses on the map were closer but had more occupants in them. Three lines sat next to the cross he had chosen, meaning three innocent people would die at his hand. His sadness was unbearable and his guilt insurmountable. His mouth was as dry as straw. Life as he knew it was over. He would never be the man he dreamed of becoming or the good husband he aspired to be someday. From now on, the stain of murder would follow him no matter where he went or how he lived his life.

"Enough. Get this done," he mumbled under his breath. He'd face his conscience later, after he had delivered an infant to the duke.

The street, as well as most of the houses in it, was deserted. By now, the neighbours would be at the town square, in the San Agustin Church, listening to the Mass. Only the infirm, very elderly, and those who had new infants would be at home. It was customary for newborns to remain in quarantine until holy water had been poured over them and they were officially welcomed into the Catholic Church.

He was not sure how much time he had, but when Mass was over, the procession would disperse and the people would hurry home to eat and drink their fill. He would have to make sure he was on his way back to the castle before the rowdy crowd filled the entire area.

He studied the house he'd chosen from the other side of the narrow street. Smoke was billowing from the roof chimney, and an inviting soft glow of light was visible through the numerous cracks on the window shutters. There was a smell of food sifting into the street through the splintered wooden door. The people inside would be just about to eat, were eating, or had just finished their supper.

He pulled the hood from his head and unconsciously ran his fingers through his hair. After crossing the street, he stood for a second in front of the door, listening for a baby's cry or sign of life on the other side of it. Eventually, he heard a man's voice and a woman's soft tinkling laughter.

His knuckles rapped the wood five times. His heart thumped against his chest, and his breathing quickened as he covered his sword and dagger with his cloak and waited.

"Yes?" The young man smiled upon opening the door. "Can I help you?"

David didn't answer. Instead, he looked past the man and saw a baby's crib out of the corner of his eye. He cleared his throat and thought for a brief second that his chest was going to explode, and then he forced himself to look at the young man.

"I am here on the duke's business. Let me pass." Seeing the man's expression change from curiosity to fear, he repeated sternly, "Let me pass."

"What does the duke want from me?" the man asked.

He wants to steal your baby and have you killed, David thought, but instead he said, "I'll answer your questions inside. Make way for me."

"I've done nothing wrong … and I've never seen you before. How do I know you're not a thief?"

Hearing a noise, David turned from the man and looked onto the street. There was no one there, thank God. None the less, he couldn't waste any more time standing on this doorstep, where a neighbour returning early from church might see him. His hand slipped underneath his cloak. He felt the pommel of his sword and drew it from its leather belt with one swift movement, making a loud swishing sound.

"Move back inside," David said, with the point of his blade touching the man's belly.

The man's eyes widened with fear and confusion. He took a few steps backwards, encouraged by the tip of the sword nicking his skin. Stumbling, he halted abruptly as he hit the edge of the bed with the back of his leg. "My wife's just had a baby … Please don't hurt her."

"Be quiet," David told him. Lifting his leg behind him and without looking, he kicked the door shut with the sole of his boot. His eyes wandered past the man. The home consisted of only one room, which reeked of burning pine and eucalyptus logs. A baby slept in the crib.

The new mother, looking weary after just giving birth, cowered in the bed and was already weeping and mumbling. "Please …no," she said, as though motherhood had heightened her instincts. David ignored her and scanned the rest of the room.

An ugly brown curtain running along a rope and stretching from one wall to the other formed a partition. A table and two chairs sat by the window, and a small hearth filled the corner wall at the far side of the bed. A chamber pot half filled with piss sat by the door, as though just about to be thrown outside, and next to it were two dirty plates, an empty cooking pot, and a wooden cup.

"Where is the other member of your family?" David asked the man.

"There is no one else. Our other child died recently."

"Why was its death not registered?"

"She died a couple of days ago, just before my wife gave birth …"

"You registered the birth, did you not?"

"Yes, but …"

"So why did you not register the death?"

"Who are you?" the man demanded. "Why has the duke sent you to my home carrying a sword? What have I done wrong?"

Nothing! David wanted to scream. The young father and his wife had done nothing wrong. They were sacrificial lambs.

"We're good Christians," he heard the man say. "Is this because we weren't in the procession or at Mass? As you can see, my wife's not yet ready to leave her birthing bed … and the baby can't go out. I have nothing to give you but a few maravedis … You won't find anything much of value here. For God's sake, tell me what you want." His words tumbled out in quick succession.

Studying the man for the first time, David guessed he must be about eighteen years old. He was particularly young to have fathered two babies. "Shut up," he said harshly. "Bring your infant to me and don't ask any more questions."

The man hesitated. Confusion and then fear settled in his eyes.

"I said show me the child!" David hissed the words. Had he shouted them, they would not have sounded more fearsome.

The baby was asleep in a crib constructed with both pinewood and tightly weaved straw. The man lifted his infant, wrapped in a patched linen blanket, and then held it in his outstretched arms in front of David.

"Remove the blanket. Show me the babe's sex."

The man wept. The mother, who was sobbing quietly, began to pray. "Please don't harm my child ... Oh, holy mother of Jesus, save us ..."

David looked at the baby's tiny body, confirmed the sex, and that it had not been circumcised. He felt his own eyes well up with tears, and drowning in shame and helplessness, he struggled to breathe. If only God would strike him down where he stood.

The point of his sword was still tickling the young father's belly. He took a step backwards and gestured to the crib. "Put the infant back in there."

When the young father had laid the baby down, he straightened and turned to face David. His eyes wandered to the corner of the room. David sensed that the man was looking for a weapon. For a second, he wondered whether to let the innocent victim kill him rather than go through with this evil ... A thought rushed through his mind. Should he tell the infant's parents to leave their baby and run for their lives? No, for not only he but the entire Sanz family would be punished if there were no dead bodies discovered in this house. He had to stop thinking and act. There was no saving these people. It was much too late to turn back now.

The young father opened his mouth to speak. His words hung in the air as David thrust the sword into the man's belly, running it straight through until it stuck out of his back. Grunting, David pulled the sword out of his victim and watched him sink to his knees between the bed and the crib.

The mother's piercing scream jolted David's calm. He had to shut her up. The man on the floor was in his way. He rolled the body aside with the sole of his shoe and then put his knee on top of the bed. Straddling the mother, with his hand covering her mouth, he wondered if he should slit his own throat. That would be easier than slashing hers. For a split second, he was conscious of her flushed, tear-stained face filled with grief. He blinked the image away, threw his sword onto the bed cover, and reached for his long dagger.

For a brief moment, his hand slackened on her lips. When he heard her moan, his heart broke. He wouldn't look at her again. Reaching out, he felt her face, and then he tipped her head backwards and sliced her throat in a simple circular cut from ear to ear.

His legs still straddled the woman, and his breathing came in short, sharp bursts as he looked dazedly around him in horror. He looked at the dagger, his bloodstained sword, the woman, and finally at the dead man on the floor. He moved to get up, but his legs had become entangled in the bed covers. His frantic efforts to free himself only delayed him further. He stopped moving, looked up, and felt his breath catch in his throat. A crucifix sat on the wall behind the bed. He stared at it for a second and then wept for the first time since childhood.

CHAPTER SIX

David's hands and legs were trembling, but his mind was calmer and clearer. His only job now was to get the baby out of the house and back to Garcia before every street around there was filled with people.

There had been enough valuable time wasted. He couldn't stay here all night, weeping and cursing and apologising to the people he had just murdered. He'd not been able to pull himself out of the blackness. He'd drowned in it, unable to breathe or see a spark of light … He hated himself. He was a monster.

After using the bedcover to wipe the bloody dagger and sword clean, he secured them on his belt. Lifting the baby, he covered its head with the blanket and cradled it in his arm, underneath the folds of his cloak. As he reached the door, he stopped abruptly and spun around. His eyes darted to every corner of the room. The sound had been faint, but he'd heard something.

He laid the baby down again, stood perfectly still, and listened. A child was sobbing. At that moment, the infant stirred and began to wail. He lifted it and rocked it in his arms. His eyes were drawn back to the curtained partition at the far end of the room. He had not taken much notice of it before, for most houses hung linen or hemp sheeting to hide clothes, tools, and cooking utensils.

Drawing his dagger, he tiptoed towards it and pulled back the curtain. Sitting on a narrow cot was a child not more than three years old. David moaned at the sight of her. "Oh dear

God, no." Her legs were drawn up to her chest. Her head was downcast, and her small face was partially hidden between the fold of her arms, lying across her knees. He'd been careless in believing the father, who had stated that the child was dead, but at the time, there had been no reason to doubt him. The little girl had not uttered a sound the entire time he'd been here ... Not so much as a whimper.

Tears gathered in his eyes. "No, no," he repeated in a whisper. "No, I can't. Not a child ... Never!" He knelt down and gently touched the girl's arm. "Shh, I won't hurt you. I promise you that everything will be all right. You have to come with me," he added without thinking.

"No, Papa ... Mama ...," she cried. She lifted her head and looked at David's face, staring kindly into her own. She stared at the baby and then back at David. Teardrops from large brown eyes still sat on her flushed cheeks. Her pouting lips quivered in fear as she continued to gaze at the giant of a man kneeling before her. She sat up, looked past him, and opened her mouth in horror.

Pulling her to his chest, he shielded her eyes from the horrific sight of her parents' bloodied bodies. Again he panicked. What was he to do with her? He couldn't leave her here with all this death and blood. He was supposed to kill her, he then thought. He couldn't take her to the castle or to a neighbour's house, and if she was left to wander the streets, she would be recognised. The duke and his henchman, Garcia, were bound to find out about her, and they would not forgive his disobedience. Dear God, what was to become of her?

The girl was still staring at him. Her teeth were chattering with fear. She would not go with him willingly. He couldn't blame her. He must be a terrifying sight.

"What's your name, little one?" No response. "I'll tell you my name ..."

"Mama … Papa," she cried louder.

David sighed. His mind was made up. The girl might mean his death, but he wouldn't take her life to save his own. "We're going for a walk. Your mama and papa are sleeping. You must be very quiet. We don't want to wake them up, do we?" He smiled.

As he lifted her from the bed, she kicked out with her legs and struggled to release herself from his grip. Her sobbing had turned into a soft whimpering, the heart-wrenching sound of a child too exhausted or too scared to cry. Her tiny hands pummelled his chest, but when David opened the door, she became still and looked curiously out onto the street.

After fumbling with the doorknob but eventually managing to close the door behind him, he hurried from the area, juggling the two babes in his arms beneath his cloak. His muddled mind was filled with questions he couldn't answer and thoughts which made no sense. Guilt threatened to overpower his determination but there was no more time to think or to fill his mind with self-hatred. He had streets to manoeuvre, two babies to keep quiet, and a steep hill to climb.

The Mass was over. Torches flickered, guiding the people leaving the church, which was at the base of the hill. David believed that he still had time to avoid a throng of people, but he could see torchlights already flickering on the same road that he had taken from the south-east gate. He swore. He couldn't go back up the hill the same way he'd come down it. He would meet processionals head-on. The duke had left no time for error, he thought. He must have known this might happen but hadn't cared. Cursing again, he prayed for a life of torment for Luis Peráto.

Hurrying along a street which had a steep upward incline, he tried to picture the safest route back to the castle. He knew this to be a long street. At the end of it, he would have to climb thirteen stone steps, marking the boundary line for this section of the town. Beyond the steps, the hill looked more like a cliff face covered with large jagged rocks. It would be impossible to climb with two babies in his arms.

He stopped, defeated, sick with shame, and mindful of his stupidity. The initial idea of taking the girl home to the farm now seemed ludicrous. He doubted he could take her anywhere. The only way he could get up to Garcia, waiting for him at the north-east gate, was if he left the child somewhere along the way. He'd just have to pray that she'd still be there when he eventually got back to her.

There was a bitter chill in the air. The infant was well wrapped, but the girl had nothing but a fine blanket and nightgown to cover her, and every time she squirmed, her legs dangled outside of his cloak folds. He had to find her some shelter now.

Upon reaching the top of the steps, he searched for the spot where the next section of the town began. Farther up the hill and heading north was the high wall that separated the Jewry from other areas in Sagrat. Behind the wall lived what was left of the Jewish community. Once a bustling neighbourhood of affluent Jews and thriving businesses, it now stood a sad, dilapidated cluster of streets full of abandoned homes and empty shops. It was a prison in all but name, David thought. Christians were afraid to go anywhere near it, making it seem more like a leper colony than a neighbourhood.

First Jews had been forced to wear special badges on their garments, and then the tall, thick walls had come, segregating them from their Christian friends and neighbours. Shame on Sagrat, David thought, and shame on Spain. "A plague on the duke and his bastard lackey, Garcia," he mumbled angrily whilst he was at it.

Swinging open a wooden gate, he entered the Jewry. After only a few paces, he came upon an abandoned semi-demolished house and decided that the building would be as good a place as any to leave the girl. As with most doorways, David had to stoop his tall frame to enter. After accustoming his eyes to the darkness, he looked about him. Whoever had lived there had probably stripped the house bare before leaving. All that remained in the room was an old rag lying on a dirt floor, which had once been covered in wooden boards, judging by a few splintered pieces of pinewood that still remained in places. This must have belonged to an affluent family, for only the very best of houses had a wood covering on the ground.

David set the child down in a corner of the room where the stone wall was still intact. She craned her neck and looked up at his great height with an expression of bewilderment, which David found even more pitiful than her crying. After spreading the fine blanket on top of the dirty ground, he laid the girl upon it, and then wrapped it about her body and bare feet as best he could. For a moment, he sat with her, stroking her hair and soothing her with softly spoken words. Her eyes blinked with tiredness and then drooped with exhaustion.

"I'll come back for you," he whispered when her eyes finally closed in sleep. "I'll take you to a nice warm bed and you'll have some milk … I'm sorry – so sorry for everything."

Blinded by his tears, he left the house, rocking the infant, whose mouth was open and searching for his mother's teat. "Please don't cry," he begged the baby.

The house's wooden door was withered, but he managed to close it behind him and click the latch into place. There were no guarantees the girl inside would sleep on or remain quiet until he got back to her, he thought, but she would be safe enough. She was just a baby and wouldn't be able to leave the house on her own. Leaving the house wasn't his biggest worry, he then realised. If she screamed loudly enough, she'd be heard, causing an onslaught of questions to arise in this neighbourhood.

He didn't regret saving her, he kept telling himself as he hurried on. She had multiplied his problems tenfold, but no, he would rather cut off his hands than harm her. He pushed all thoughts of the girl away. He'd done everything he could, and for the moment, she was in God's hands, not his.

David struggled up an uneven rocky path which began at the very bottom of the hill. From the plain below, this narrow track looked like a piece of white rope wrapped around the entire mound in what seemed like never-ending circles. This was probably the most treacherous route to the north-east gate. He was climbing the steepest part of the hill, right to its crest. It was rarely used by anyone, apart from goat herders.

He set off at a steady pace, but after a while, his breathing quickened and became laboured. He felt as though he were running up the hill instead of walking at a snail's pace, which was all he could manage to do in the dark. His skin was moist, his tunic damp with perspiration, but there was no time to stop and rest. He thanked God that the town was below him, and he believed that no one else would be stupid enough to walk this road at this time of night. The babe slept on, no doubt comforted by his body heat, and he calculated that in less than an hour, he'd reach the wall and gate, his mission completed and the horrific night almost over.

CHAPTER SEVEN

As David approached the north-east gate, he was struck by the eerie silence. Craning his neck, he tried to see the top of the wall. There was no sign of flaming torches, nor was there the glint of a helmet or spear peeking over merlon blocks. Moving on, he prayed that Garcia had dismissed the watch in this area and that he was waiting for him on the other side of the wall.

The portcullis was only partially down, and no guards looked to be in the gatehouse above it. After slipping underneath, he walked through the archway, which led to a Roman courtyard. This was the duke's private sanctuary. No townspeople were allowed to enter the castle through this gate. Bordering the tiled square courtyard were Roman pillars, arched alcoves with white granite benches underneath, and Roman statues, some of which were eroded or damaged. Ancient but still beautiful, they stood tall in the darkness, embodying an earlier era, yet ever present, like timeless guardians watching history unfold. He paused for a moment beside a fountain and marvelled at the beauty surrounding him.

He imagined the infant he held in his arms, playing there under the watchful eyes of nurses and guards. The duke's imposter son was going to hae a life of privilege and wealth to look forward to. He'd be raised ignorant of his ancestry, where he came from, and even his given name at birth. Only three people possessed the knowledge of what had happened this night … Only three.

Dark nagging thoughts pounded his mind. Was he to die? Had the physician been murdered because he also knew the truth? Was he to be thrown off the highest part of the wall or stabbed in the back and share the physician's fate? Why had he not considered this before?

"You're late!" Sergio Garcia's voice snapped as he came out of the shadows.

"I was trapped. The processionals blocked my route. I had to find another way up. I'm here now," David said coldly. He was in no mood to show reverence to the bastard.

"Yes, you are. Well, where is it?"

Flicking his cloak over the back of his shoulders, David revealed the baby, who stirred as soon as cold air touched his face.

Garcia peeled away the blanket and nightgown covering the tiny body, looking closely at the infant's genitalia.

David forced himself to remain still, but he was seething with rage at the callous way in which the treasurer was looking at the infant's sex in the cold air. For the first time tonight, he hated someone else more than he despised himself.

"Yes, it's a boy," Garcia said, as though David didn't already know that. "Show me the infant's house on the map."

David covered the baby, pulled out the map, and then tucked the baby underneath his cloak to keep him warm. In the darkness, it was almost impossible to see anything written or marked on the paper, but the black ink cross and lines denoting where the babe had come from were visible.

"Here, in this house," David said, pointing.

Nodding with approval, Garcia said, "I see it. So we should expect to find three bodies in this home come morning? Tell me about them. How did you kill them?"

David's stony expression was unwavering. All the way up the hill, he had dreaded this question the most. Now he would lose his pride and honour forever, for the moment he confessed to the murders, the duke and Garcia would own him, body and soul. "I ran my sword through the father's gut. I silenced the mother with a cut to her neck, and I suffocated the little girl as she slept."

"Good … That's good. And you're sure you weren't seen or heard?"

"I'm sure."

"Then we will grieve and pray for three of our citizens tomorrow. The duke appreciates their sacrifice."

Sacrifice? The duke was a murdering whoreson, David thought. He wasn't saving the town from some catastrophe. "Only two bodies are in the house," he said calmly. "I removed the dead child and buried her on the hill. I dug deep, and she will never be found. I give you my word that not even a beast will be able to dig up her bones."

Garcia's arm shot out. The palm of his hand connected with David's cheek with such speed and force that he lost his footing and stumbled backwards. David planted his feet firmly on the ground and instinctively protected the infant by placing both arms around his body. His heavy breathing slowed. Were it not for the baby, he would have had his sword out of its belt and into Garcia's chest, damning the consequences.

Garcia's skin reddened. He spread his lips in an ugly scowl, and bearing his teeth, he whispered ferociously. "You're an idiot peasant! You were told to kill all the occupants and leave them where they lay – leave them where they lay! Who are you to disobey His Grace? He'll be furious, and he'll blame me for *your* insubordination."

Good. Let him blame you, punish you, and kill you, David wanted to say. "My apologies …"

"You should have left the dead child where it lay, you fool," Garcia repeated.

Lies didn't slip easily off David's tongue, but he'd practiced his explanation on the way up, saying the words aloud until he'd felt comfortable with the sound of them. Straightening his shoulders, he said, "And how is Your Honour to explain one missing child when there were two in the house? Surely it makes more sense to give the impression that both siblings have been abducted. To steal away one and kill another, at such a young age, might bring even more questions as to the reason the boy child was specifically taken. The townspeople will believe this crime to be child abduction for monetary gain, for this is exactly what I made it look like."

As though feeling David's thumping heartbeat, the infant stirred and began to wail. David rocked him gently whilst trying to control his mounting rage.

Garcia thought about what had just been said. He did not suffer fools and was a suspicious man by nature. Life and people had taught him that no man could be trusted and that loyalty came at a high price. He disliked Luis Peráto and all the arse lickers that surrounded him. The duke was a dim-witted man with the whims of a petted child. Why was he allowing the militiaman to live? He had asked Peráto that question and had not received an answer. Had it been his decision to make, Sanz would have been killed the moment he'd stepped under the half-drawn portcullis with the infant. He'd served his purpose, and now he was a liability.

The duke was a gullible fool and, like most nobles, was self-centred and unable to understand a common peasant's mind. Peráto's views of the world around him were amusing, for the duke believed that his townspeople wanted nothing more from life than to serve him. They were pack mules, born and bred to carry his load, he was fond of saying.

Garcia was a commoner. He understood the common man, his suffering, and his aspirations. He also knew that many Sagratans blamed Peráto for their present misfortunes. Commerce was dwindling under the burden of higher taxations. Work of any kind was hard to come by for even the most gifted tradesmen, yet the duke ignored his people's misery. He was too busy planning a future as Valencia's viceroy to turn his mind to the beggars on the street and the growing number of women selling their bodies so that they could feed their children. Luis Peráto sickened him, not because he was unkind to his townspeople but because he was stupid.

Garcia stared at David, trying to decide whether the man was foolish enough to lie. There was no respect in Sanz's steely gaze. Being struck had not seemed to cow him one whit. If anything, the man was being openly disrespectful. "How can I be sure the girl's dead unless I see the grave and her body for myself?"

"You can't."

"If you're lying to me, it will be the death of you. You don't strike me as a man who wishes to lose his life over a mere child," Garcia said, voicing his thoughts. "Where on the hill did you bury her?"

"Halfway down, at the edge of the crevice, where the soil is deep and the undergrowth is at its thickest. As I said, I took great care to make sure the grave would never be found."

Garcia nodded begrudgingly. He was not going to waste time searching for a grave. "Your reasoning might be sound. Let the people think that both children were spirited away." He nodded again but was still outraged that the common pup in front of him had made this decision on his own.

David waited. His fate was in Garcia's hands now. He either believed the story or didn't and was veiling his thoughts. He wanted to punch the man until blood spouted from his ears. His disregard for the three lives supposedly taken revolted him.

Thinking about the little girl and unwilling to be in Garcia's company a moment longer, he asked. "May I take my leave now?"

"Yes, but go straight to your barracks."

David bowed his head in gratitude.

Garcia held out a purse, heavy with coin. "This is an offering from the duke," he said with some resentment. "Take it."

David felt bile rise in his throat. The duke could shove this coin up his noble arse, he thought. "I'm not a paid assassin. I will not accept this blood money." And he wouldn't become indebted to the duke, who had just ruined his life and damned his soul to the fires of hell. "I have killed for His Grace this night, but only because I'm afraid for my family. I did what I did because he ordered me to, but make no mistake: I am a murderer. I deserve to go to hell, not receive a reward."

"You dare to refuse the duke's kindness?"

"I do."

"You will insult him."

"He'll recover."

For a moment, Garcia was pensive as he stood watching David gently rock the infant, who was opening his mouth and searching for milk.

"Take the purse or not; it's up to you. Your refusal won't ease your conscience, if that's what's bothering you."

"Nothing will ease my conscience, and of course it bothers me!" David hissed at him, and then snapped his mouth shut.

"Sanz, what you did was for the glory of Sagrat. Thanks to you, the duke has an heir. You should be happy that he asked you to serve him." Spreading his arms, he suggested, "The benefits of your actions this night far outweigh any distastefulness involved … surely?"

David refused to answer.

"I'm sure your family will be grateful to have this money," Garcia continued. "I wonder why you're not thinking about their welfare instead of your misguided principles."

"My family's well-being is all I think about," David retorted.

"Then I suggest you take this gift. Life has a habit of giving, only to take away when we least expect it. Fate toys with us. It tricks us into false securities and makes us careless, and then one day it kicks us to the ground. You might have a good life now, but who knows what calamities may befall you and your family in the future. Take the money."

"Your Honour, I will take nothing from you. I'd rather cut off my hand than accept anything from yours." Expecting to be struck again, David tightened his grip on the baby. When no slap came, he relaxed his muscles, and said, "The infant needs warmth and milk. I suggest you look after him or you might be the one with a difficult future."

Garcia's eyes narrowed. "Remember this, Sanz: you're still breathing, but only because the duke ordered me not to kill you," he said with a voice crackling with anger. "For some reason unbeknown to me, he trusts you. Don't disappoint him. If you do, he will crush you and your family like ants – and no one will care but God."

David handed the baby to Garcia. Garcia looked at it for a second and then sneered at David, "You are a murderer. Don't ever forget that. If you speak of what happened here, I will make sure your mother, father, and brothers are locked away for the rest of their miserable lives. I will be watching you, but for now … get out of my sight."

David stood alone for a moment, until his racing pulse had returned to normal. He *was* still alive … but for how long?

CHAPTER EIGHT

Garcia found Luis staring at his dead son, who was lying in a crib. He coughed awkwardly and approached. His eyes then settled on the tiny body covered from head to foot in white linen, with only its face visible. The infant would have to be buried soon, Garcia thought. Best to take it out of sight, and let it be out of mind.

"Tell me you have it," Luis said without turning.

"I do, Your Grace. Here is your son."

With the dead baby forgotten for the moment, Luis turned sharply and gazed upon the infant, who, as though knowing all eyes were upon him, began shrieking loudly. Luis smiled. "The sound of a strong, healthy baby is the sweetest of music to my ears." Taking the baby from Garcia, he cradled it in his arms and whispered soothing words whilst stroking its face. "You have looked him over?"

Garcia nodded.

"He's a fine boy," Luis said.

His eyes watered with happiness. "In the morning, announcements will be made. I want written notices on the church's walls. Father Bernardo must celebrate the baby's arrival with a Mass. Bells shall toll, heralding the news of a new heir."

His worries were over. His father by law, the inquisitor, was going to shower him with gifts and favours. The Peráto line was secure. He could now forget about his mad wife. She could rot in her chambers until she drew her last breath, for all he cared. "Praise be to God. This is a miracle."

Putting the tip of his finger into the infant's mouth, he laughed when he felt soft gums sucking it. "You're strong, my son. But you must be eager to taste your mother's milk." Still smiling, he handed the baby back to Garcia. "Take him to my wife's ladies. It's time to see if the duchess has milk or if her scrawny body can't even produce that. Come straight back. We have other business to attend to."

Luis looked once more at his dead son. He kissed its forehead and then covered its face. After tonight, he'd erase all memory of the dead infant. It would not be baptised, or receive burial rights. He didn't know where its un-Christian soul would go, but he was thankful that *he* wouldn't see it in heaven. He sighed with relief. It had been a difficult and heartbreaking night, but it had ended splendidly.

"So did everything go exactly to plan? I want to know the details," Luis said to Garcia after he'd returned.

Garcia shrugged and spread his arms. "It went as well as we had hoped. All was taken care of, just as you asked. Sanz assured me that no one saw or heard him entering or leaving the infant's home. The mother and father are dead, as is their other child."

"Good."

Looking uncomfortable, Garcia continued. "Your Grace, there is something you should know …"

"What?"

"Sanz disobeyed your orders. He removed the other child's body from the house and buried it on the hill. It was a girl."

"He did what?"

"He thought that two missing children would appear more palatable than one. I'm not fond of the man, but his assumptions have merit."

Luis slumped angrily in a chair. He had specifically ordered that there be no loose ends. "Is the girl dead beyond doubt? Can you give me that assurance?"

"Yes, Your Grace, without a doubt. The militiaman told me that he buried her deep in the ground."

"And you believed him?" Luis asked angrily.

"I had no choice but to trust him."

Looking pensive, Luis said, "We will speak of his disobedience later. Did you give him the coin?"

Garcia shifted his feet nervously. "I urged him to take the purse, but he refused. He's insolent for one so common. He also appeared weighed down by guilt. I worry he might want to confess what he did, and that could prove disastrous."

A look of surprise crossed Luis's face. Sanz had insulted him, shown his disapproval, as though he had a right to have an opinion. "What fool has the gall to refuse my money?" he asked, unable to believe Garcia. "I offered him more ducats than he's probably seen in his entire lifetime. He has disrespected me ... the arrogant swine. Can he be trusted to keep his mouth shut?"

Garcia appeared to be undecided. "You have a son safely delivered to you, and I'm certain there are no witnesses alive to make accusations against you – but no, I'm not sure you should trust him."

"Christ's blood!"

"Your Grace, might I suggest you have him killed? It's the only way to guarantee his silence."

"No," Luis answered, albeit reluctantly. He needed the militia and their loyalty. They still adhered to the oaths of the brotherhood, an ancient close-knit family of men-at-arms, sworn to protect each other above all else. Years ago, they had been all-powerful, managing their own criminal courts and dishing up punishments. In Castile, they were still highly respected and feared. Their fealty to each other was well known.

"No, that would not be prudent," he repeated. "The other militiamen saw Sanz being summoned to my chambers. Even now they will be wondering what I wanted with him. Sanz's death would raise suspicion. There will be enough chaos in the coming days. He lives."

"What about the suspicion surrounding your physician? Questions will be asked," Garcia said.

Luis wagged his index finger. "No. Cabrera was well known and respected, but my militia will not question his death. On the other hand, they will not take kindly to one of their own dying suddenly without proper explanation. I need these men, Garcia. Marauders coming in from the sea are ransacking towns, and there are criminals taking advantage of the monarchs' lengthy absences from Valencia. Sagrat is well defended against thieves running around the countryside, but only because of my militia's presence. Sanz lives ... for the moment."

"Maybe we should have used our mercenaries tonight," Garcia offered.

"And have that thieving scum touching my new son? They'd have the tunic off my back and burn this town were it not for the coin I put in their fat pockets. I could never trust them with such personal matters.

"I specifically used Sanz because he serves me. He is duty-bound to keep his mouth shut. And even if he feels no loyalty to me, he will do what's necessary to protect his family." Luis had thought briefly about this. There was no guarantee that Sanz would keep his tongue still. In an unguarded moment, he could blurt out the truth about what he'd done, whether to his family or, God forbid, to Captain Tur. "I want Sanz's family moved into the town. We need to keep a close eye on them, and

Sanz has to know that we are watching them. You must find a way to make this happen."

"I can't imagine how they could be persuaded to leave their farm," Garcia said, "unless their farm were to burn to the ground."

Luis smiled. That was not a bad idea. "The townspeople will be in an uproar tomorrow when they find out about the infant's family. Perhaps we should add to their burdens and give them something else to think about – a diversion, perhaps."

"A diversion?"

"Yes, more tragedies. What could be more tragic than marauders attacking defenceless homes on the plain before stealing into the town to commit murder? They're known to have ice in their veins. It would not be beyond their dark souls to kill a mother and father and abduct their two children. We need suspects ... or did you not think about that?"

Garcia shook his head and spread his lips in a rare genuine smile. "What an excellent idea, Your Grace," he said.

"Yes, it is. It seems we have need of the mercenaries tonight after all. Make sure they visit Sanz's family first ... but no killings and no wounding. Do you hear me?"

"Yes, Your Grace."

"Are your men close by?"

"Our contact in town is always at hand. I will dispatch him with a message to the mercenary leader immediately."

Luis nodded. "Call them up. Set them to task. I want this business concluded before dawn. Do you understand?"

Sergio nodded and grinned with pleasure.

Luis picked up his dead child and kissed his forehead one last time. "Take it. Bury it and never mention it to me again. I'm going to spend time with my son ... Jaime. He shall be named Jaime.

CHAPTER NINE

It had taken David quite a while to reach his family's home. He'd carried the child in his arms, running part of the way, and she hadn't cried or whimpered for her parents. In the Jewry, he'd found her curled in a ball fast asleep and in the exact same spot he'd left her. The streets were empty. The procession had dispersed, and most of the townspeople were feasting inside their homes. When he'd skirted the labyrinth of streets on the way out of town, he'd smelled food cooking, heard laughter and song, saw smoke rising from chimneys – and a terrible feeling of envy had engulfed him.

Walking across the plain against a strong wind had slowed him down, but thankfully the girl had slept on, apart from a few minutes in an area where he'd stumbled over rocks and she'd almost fallen from his arms. His arms and back were aching. At first her weight had been as light as a feather, but now she felt as heavy as a sack of potatoes. He hadn't slept in almost two days, he realised, and the climb up to the north-east gate was tiring, at the best of times.

David had asked Garcia to honour the two days' leave, previously promised to him, but he'd received a resounding *no*. "You serve at the duke's pleasure. Your life is his, and leave from the castle is a gift, not a right." Garcia was a whoreson, David thought for the umpteenth time. He was probably incapable of feeling a sliver of remorse for his part in tonight's murders. "Keep your mouth shut and forget everything that has happened this night," Garcia had also said. Forget? David thought. Only a wild animal would forget what it had slaughtered.

He kicked a stone and then stumbled with a misstep. As much as he despised the duke and Garcia, even more, he loathed all that he, David Sanz, had become. Had he always been wicked deep down? he wondered. Or had he simply shed some pesky skin tonight to reveal his true character? The duke would ask more of him. It was inevitable, for in Luis Peráto's mind, David Sanz had become an immoral criminal, willing to kill on his duke's whims. He'd sold his soul to the man. Maybe he should have taken the money and been done with it.

David shook his head irately. He was not a henchman, an executioner, or a wicked man. No, he wasn't. He'd spend the rest of his life asking for redemption and proving to God and his family that he was a good man. He'd rather be hanged as a traitor than take another innocent life to satisfy the duke's whims. And then he wondered whether he would live to see the New Year. Or would Garcia have him killed against the duke's orders?

The house and small plot of land coming into view in the distance looked like every other smallholding from Sagrat to the sea, but to David's father, it was a palace. Situated approximately midway between the town and the Mediterranean coast, it was a decent walk to get anywhere, but its location was perfect, for it was one of the only plots to have a direct supply of fresh water from a nearby river.

Luckily, this plain had a predominately straight road running through it all the way to the sea. He could find his way home blindfolded, for there was not a crack in the road, a plant, or a bush that he didn't recognise en route. He'd walked this road a thousand times. His skin had cracked in the baking sun and had been drenched and battered in winter storms. The journey this night, however, had by far been the most difficult and miserable he'd ever taken.

He couldn't help but think again about the money. Deciding not to take it had been an impulsive decision. Had he been too hasty? He was aware of his father's debts. He owed rent and taxes, unpaid these past two months, and he was under threat of eviction. The present drought had transformed the fertile land into dusty plains. The riverbed had crusted over, and it was so dry that weeds and plants were growing through the ground where water should be flowing. Even the hardiest of crops had failed in the dry spell that had lasted for months.

The house was in disrepair. His mother, father, and two younger brothers lived together in two rooms under a wooden and straw roof. The plot had olive trees and a vineyard, which had failed to produce more than a few grapes this year. In the past, David's father had been successful, growing onions, spinach, and asparagus. Striving to survive the drought was an uphill struggle, and each day it became more and more difficult to sustain the family's meagre needs.

David missed his brothers, Diego and Juanjo. They were fine boys, growing into strong men with ambitions. Diego had just turned seventeen, and he was determined to leave the land behind for a life at sea. On David's last visit home, Diego had spoken about a navy with ships that travelled to North Africa and Portugal. There were rumours about vessels being built, sturdy enough to sail far to the East, where new lands were being discovered and fortunes were being made. Diego walked to the sea every chance he got. When he came home, he was melancholic and even more desperate to leave home. He might have asked permission to leave, David suspected, had it not been for the drought, forcing the family to look for other sources of income. He was a loyal lad.

Diego and Juanjo wanted more than a squalid life in feudal Spain, where religion dictated what you were and what you could become. All the two boys had to look forward to each day was the long trek to the pine forests, blistered feet, and aching backs. It was illegal to cut down the pine trees in the upper slopes, which lay half a league behind the town, but the lads took only what they found lying on the ground. At this time of the year, there was a healthy scattering of pinecones. If they were lucky, thick branches felled by wind still held twigs. And pine needles carpeted the rocks and soil beneath the trees. These were gathered and put into sacks, later to be used as mulch in vegetable plots or tied into wands for kindling. They never went home until they had sold every piece of firewood collected. And with their profits, they managed to buy eggs, a small joint of meat (on good days), and wheat and grains to make bread.

David didn't want that life for Diego and Juanjo. He'd not settled for drudgery, so why should they?

He stopped. Next door to the main building was a hut full of straw and farming tools. He looked under his cloak. The girl's eyes were wide open, yet she didn't utter a sound. Was she sick? "I'm sorry. It will soon be over," he told her. "You'll have some warm milk and a nice soft bed, just as I promised."

She stared up at him, and her lips trembled at the sound of his voice. "Mama," she finally whimpered.

He opened the hut's door, set the child on the floor, and then left immediately. Thank God. She wouldn't remember this night, he thought, walking towards the house. He wondered which was the lesser of two evils. Was it keeping his family in ignorance about the murders and the girl or telling them everything? The decision he'd taken was not about evil, he then thought. It was about doing the right thing.

His part in this heinous crime would disgust them – and telling them about it might put their lives in danger. But Garcia's veiled innuendos were more than just threats used to scare him. He was convinced that the treasurer had some sinister game in mind.

He had a duty to warn his family about what might lie ahead. He was already damned, his soul blackened with mortal sin. But had he left the child in the Jewry, the Jews would have been blamed for her parents' death and the disappearance of her infant brother. Had he taken her to the steps of the church, every citizen in Sagrat would have been implicated … No, he thought with his hand on the house's front door, bringing her here and telling his family about her was the only decent thing he would do this night.

He stepped softly into the house. The fire in the hearth still burned with deep red embers in their dying moments, managing to cast warmth and a soft orange glow in the darkened room. He gazed lovingly at Diego and Juanjo sleeping soundly on straw pallets in a corner behind the table. After looking about him, he frowned with confusion, which then turned to anger. The air was thick with the smell of boiled vegetables and herbs. The cooking pans were clean. No remnants of wild boar, cooked meat, or bones of any kind were or probably had been in the house. All that lay on the table were two wrinkled potatoes, a lump of bread, and a piece of crumbling hard cheese, leftovers from the family's meal.

The man with the cart, who had gratefully accepted a coin and the promise of meat, had stolen the boar. He and his family had probably filled their bellies with it and had washed it down with wine. David covered his face with his hands and cursed the man to hell. He'd gut the bastard! He'd rip his heart out and shove it inside his lying mouth …

He turned at the sound of the door's creaking timbers. His father, Juan, stood before him, rubbing sleep from his eyes. Without a word, David grabbed him by the shoulders and hugged him tenderly. "Papa," he whispered. "I've come home."

Juan Sanz, his face leathered with years in the sun, was as tall and as broad as David was. He too was a handsome man, with black deep-set eyes and a mop of bluish-black hair curling at the nape of his neck. But unlike David, he sported an unruly beard, which covered the bottom half of his face.

Grinning now with pleasure, Juan slapped David on the back. "Son, we didn't expect to see you this week. What are you doing here?" he whispered.

David forced a smile, but averted his eyes. "I wanted to see my family, Papa, and I don't have much time … We need to talk."

Juan's smile froze. "Hmm, that sounds ominous. Why so serious, lad? You must be freezing. Have some supper and a drop of wine. I got it for our feast, such as it was."

"I don't have time to eat, Papa. Will you come with me to the hut? There's something I have to show you."

David's brothers, also awake now, stared groggily at their brother. One by one, they rose from their pallets and, still half asleep, stumbled towards David.

"Welcome home," Diego said, putting his arms around David.

"Did you bring your new sword?" Juanjo, standing behind Diego, asked.

"I did, but you mustn't touch it," David said, more harshly than intended. His eyes welled up with love. Crushing his family to him, knowing that they might send him away for what he'd done, was terrifying. His heart thumped like a drum in his chest. He flicked his eyes from his father to his brothers, and then straightened his shoulders. He was running out of time. The little girl was probably freezing and starving by now.

"So tell us, what's so important that you won't warm your bones and feed your belly? And what's this about the hut?" asked Juan.

"Papa, I'll tell you everything when we get outside. Please come with me now."

The boys looked on expectantly. David, walking towards the door, said, "You two stay here."

Juan wrapped a blanket around his shoulders. He shook his head and sighed. "This must be important, son. I can't imagine anyone wanting to walk all this way from town in the middle of the night to pay such a short visit. Are you in trouble?"

"You could say that," David answered grimly.

As they left the house, Juan gestured to his other sons, putting his finger to his lips and then pointing to the closed door that separated the bedroom from the main room. "Keep your voices low. Don't wake your mother."

CHAPTER TEN

Outside the farmhouse, David's nervous fingers fumbled with his hood. Hearing the girl cry, he put his hand on his father's arm, and asked, "Will you listen to what I have to say before you go in there?"

Juan stared at the hut's door and then at David. "What's that noise I'm hearing? Is that a child crying?"

"It is."

Shrugging David's hand away, Juan said, "You had better have a good explanation for this."

Inside the hut, the girl's wailing drowned out David's voice. He lifted the child, but this time, he couldn't soothe her. "Father, what do I do?"

"Give her to me and start talking."

David's mouth opened and then closed.

"David?" Juan said warningly.

"Papa, her life was in danger. I had to hide her ..."

"Stop talking!" Juan put his hand up to silence David and then covered the child's mouth to stifle her crying. "What is that?"

David's open mouth snapped shut with fright. His eyes bore into his father and then he whipped his head around to stare at the door. The sound of hooves thundering across the plain became louder and heavier, and upon reaching the plot, they struck the ground so hard that the hut's wooden walls vibrated.

David gasped for breath. "Dear God, the duke?" he choked. His terrified eyes widened. He looked again at his father, rocking the child and gazing with eyes as big as plates at

71

the door. His father had a right to know why the men had come. He had to explain. "Papa …"

Juan cut David off with a fierce whisper. "Hush up!"

The horses halted, snorting and whinnying with excitement outside the hut. Men were yelling. David pinned his ear to the wall. He couldn't hear their words, just animal-like cries. The first smell of smoke wafted through the hut's walls. David instinctively reached for his sword, but his father swiped his hand away. Then the sound of hooves battering against the ground began again, seemingly scattering in all directions.

Juan covered the girl's mouth with his hand and pulled her closer to his chest. Both men crouched in a corner of the hut, as far from the door as possible. Even from inside the windowless wooden structure, David and Juan could see the bright orange torches and hear the crackling of flames through cracks in the timber slats. Terror sat in their eyes as the horsemen's intentions became clearer.

Juan uttered the word everyone in Sagrat feared: "Marauders … What do they want with us? We have nothing." His panicked eyes looked for a weapon. A scythe stood upright against the wall. He grabbed it and stood up, still trying to silence the girl's weeping with his free hand covering her mouth. "I have to get to your mother and the boys."

"It's too late, Papa. They'll run you through before you get ten paces from here!"

"If I'm going to get myself killed, I'll die trying to save my family! Get out of my way, lad!" Juan whispered sternly.

David's mind was racing. Was his father right? Were they marauders? Was he wrong in thinking they were the duke's militia, his own brothers-in-arms, sent to silence him? But no one knew he was here …

Marauders were not known for being merciful. They usually killed their male victims and took female prisoners to be sold or used. And marauders didn't usually attack smallholdings. They preferred towns with richer pickings or robbing caravans on the coastal plains. It had been months since a band such as this had been anywhere near Sagrat.

He couldn't breathe ... couldn't believe ... God, please not his family!

"They might not be marauders," he said. "Papa, trust me – they might be here because of me!" Grabbing Juan's leg as he stood up, he begged again. "Don't go out there. You will be of no use to Mama or the boys if you get killed as soon as you open this door. Don't move! Papa, sit down!"

Juan stared at David with eyes filled with confusion and terror. His legs buckled, and he fell to the floor, clutching the little girl in his arms. Throwing a scathing look at David, he hissed, "What have you done to us? Isa and my boys are out there!"

David crawled on his knees to a split in the hut's wall where the timber was brittle, causing it to crack. He put his eye against the long narrow opening and gasped with horror. It was impossible to count how many men were outside, and he couldn't see what they were doing, but the bright orange glow lighting up the sky was undeniable. "No ... They're going to burn us out." He grabbed a loose splinter of wood and pulled it, widening the hole. Squeezing one eye shut, he peered through the breach with his other eye. The house was already being torched. He saw flames rising into the air, whipping the walls, and dancing wildly in the strong wind.

Isa Sanz's terrified screams pierced the air, drowning out the crackling flames and, for a brief second, silencing the attackers' screams.

David gripped the pommel of his sword and drew it from its leather belt. His eyes were like slits. Fear was replaced with rage. "No more hiding. I'm going to defend my family!"

His father grabbed his arm and shook his head, horrified. "No, son," he said tearfully, "you were right. We can't get to them … God help us!"

Tears streamed down David's face. "I have to try," he shot back. "Stay here and mind the girl. Promise me!"

"You can't fight what's out there." Juan's teary eyes pleaded again. "They'll kill you. Don't you understand? They're going to kill all of us!"

The smell of smoke as well as burning straw and timbers sifted into the air and through the hut's walls. The marauders were still yelling like animals. David strained his ears. He couldn't hear his mother's voice anymore, and he had not once heard a sound coming from Diego or Juanjo. Were they dead?

The little girl was choking on smoke that she had inhaled. Juan covered her face with his blanket and clutched her closer to his chest.

David's eyes stung, and he coughed uncontrollably. The crackling sound of flames and disintegrating wood was overwhelming. Both men looked upwards and gasped. The hut's roof was on fire. Flames had licked their way through the outer covering and were now inside. David's heart sunk. "The ceiling is going to cave in!" he shouted above the noise. "We have to get out before we burn to death in here."

His father nodded, set the child on the floor, and tried to stand. Coughing, he lifted the child back into his arms and then faced the door, panting as though he had just raced a horse.

David cracked open the door. He looked at his sword, held against his chest with its point raised in the air. His mind's eye still saw the blood on it from earlier, and he inadvertently shuddered. Juan stood behind David, holding his throat, trying to stifle his coughing fit. Tears poured down his face, reddened with the scorching heat. Gripping one of his father's shoulders, David gave it an affectionate squeeze, and then shouted above the noise. "As soon as we're outside, run with the girl! Run as far as you can. I'll try to hold them back!"

The attackers saw David and Juan as soon as the hut's door opened. Surprise crossed their faces, and they halted their onslaught on the property to watch the men stumble blindly into the open. Regrouping, they encircled their kill, shrieking with amusement at the pitiful sight of the two staggering men still unable to focus their smoke-filled eyes. The horses' hooves pounded on the ground, at times a hair's breadth from where David and Juan desperately tried to dodge the jabbing swords pointed at them from all directions.

"What do we have here?" a marauder shouted at David, standing with his sword outstretched. "Go on then, dance for us! Make us laugh!"

David wiped his eyelids and saw the men clearly for the first time. He glanced briefly at each of the assailants. They were not militia but five men he had never seen before. Two of them rode mules whilst two sat on horses without saddles and with thick rope for bridles. Only one of the men, whom David presumed was the leader, had a well-groomed horse, dressed with leather bridle and saddle.

The men continued to toy with David and Juan. Laughing, they mocked David's futile efforts to hold them back with his flashing sword.

David searched his father's face, still reddened from the scorching heat. Juan clung tightly to the child squirming under his blanket. Her face and body were hidden, but her legs were visible, dangling and swaying with Juan's rapid twisting body movements.

His father was looking for a way out of the circular enclosure, but he wouldn't be able to break through it, David thought. The marauders had them penned in, and after they had tired of their game, they would cut him, his father, and the child down. "What are you waiting for, you whoresons?" he screamed at the horsemen. "Do it! Do it! Get it over with!"

The marauder's leader sawed at his horse's mouth with the bridle and brought it to a complete standstill. The other men followed suit. The expressions on their faces grew serious, and the malicious laughter faded.

David took a swift step backwards, and with his sword arm still outstretched, he tried to shield his father. Staring up at the leader, he baulked at the man's arrogant smirk. Who were these men? He panted harder now, convinced that he was in the dying seconds of his life. The horseman continued to stare at David with nonchalant enjoyment. The fire that surrounded them still raged. Sparks flew in all directions, continuing to make the horses jumpy.

His mother and brothers …Were they dead? David wondered again. He grunted loudly. Any minute now, he would die too, but why should he be killed like a cornered animal? "Who sent you? Get down here and fight me, you bastards!" he heard his shrill voice shout. "What are you waiting for? Fight me fairly!"

"Not tonight, lad; maybe some other time," the leader said, still smirking. "We'll meet again!" Pivoting his horse, the marauder rode off with his men following behind him.

David was incensed and his mind devoid of rational thought as he ran screaming obscenities after the horsemen. He sprinted as far as he could, until he was forced to stop because of the searing pain in his chest. Light-headed, he bent over double and panted in short breaths. Finally, after steadying his pulse, he ran back towards the house … It was falling to the ground. The roof was gone, walls were crumbling, and the door had completely disintegrated.

At thirty-nine years old, Juan Sanz had suffered his fair share of loss. But as he stumbled over charred smoking timbers and rocks surrounding his house, he felt like an old man. In so much pain, he craved death rather than suffer his present anguish.

For a while, the fire had burned strong and fast, but a gusty wind was beginning to extinguish its power. He shouted, and his booming voice overpowered the dying flames, still crackling and snapping pieces of wood. Tears ran down his face as he tried to get as close as possible to the remaining structure. He screamed his wife's name. "Isabella ... Isa! Diego, Juanjo!"

Running from the front of the house to the back, not once did he lower his ear-piercing shouts for his family. But although he called for them, he had already concluded that no one could have survived the fire or the marauders' blades. Finally, he sunk to his knees, and his cries matched the sound of the weeping child in his arms.

From out of the darkness, Juan heard his wife's screams for help. Stumbling to his feet, he shook with elation, convinced he'd heard his wife's cries but unsure of where they had come from. "Isa, where are you?" he shouted in every direction. Running towards the open field behind the house, he heard her cries again. At a low stone wall, he saw Diego. Behind him was Isa, propped up against the stones. Her head was bowed and violently shaking from side to side.

Juanjo's limp body lay on the ground. His head rested on Isa's lap, and she stroked his pale cheeks. "Look what they did to our son!" she moaned without looking up.

Drowning in grief, Juan squatted down beside her and fixed his eyes on the gaping hole just beneath Juanjo's left eye. The wound was surrounded by a crimson halo, startlingly bright against his lifeless white skin. His blood had streamed out of him. It had turned one side of his face and neck red, and it had spread all the way down to his chest. "My son," he muttered. "Oh, my poor son!"

Diego's hand grasped a rock. "I'll kill them, Papa!" he cried. "I'll kill them all!"

Juan set the little girl down on the ground and then lifted Juanjo's body onto his lap. Rocking his dead son in his arms, he wept unashamedly, his grief so profound that he was unaware of Isa's loud sobs and Diego's questions about the small child sitting beside him.

"Almighty God, why did you allow this to happen? Oh my lad, my sweet child!"

Isa picked up the little girl and looked at the tiny smoke-blackened face for the first time. "You're just a babe," was all she muttered.

The wind whipped Juanjo's straight black hair onto his face, and it stuck to the blood. Juan pushed it away from his son's eyes and felt his heart crushing with guilt. Three years previously, he and his family had converted to Christianity. He had not been happy about the decision, but it had seemed unavoidable and a justifiable means to an end at that time. The old duke's ruling to evict Jews from farms and smallholdings on Sagrat's land had forced many Jewish friends and neighbours to leave the area. Many had left Spain rather than convert or live in the town, faced with new and unfair laws regarding cohabitation and occupations. No Jew wanted to live in the open countryside nowadays. They were being persecuted just about everywhere. The only safe place left in Sagrat was the Jewry, surrounded by its high wall.

How swollen with pride he'd been, conceited and thickheaded to believe that the Sanz family, who had lived in Valencia for almost two hundred years, would be left in peace just because they had become Christians. The great Juan Sanz had refused to abandon his measly patch of dirt and dilapidated house and had forced his family to become conversos. None of the other family members had wanted to give up their Jewish faith. Isa had fought with him, and his children had not understood why they had to lose their traditions and rituals just to have the privilege of living in an old hovel in a field. "Life was good when we were Jews," Isa had remarked only recently. "We wanted for nothing. Now look at us – we want for everything. We are Christian beggars in a flock we don't belong to."

He hadn't listened to her objections, not in the past and not in the present. The family had been baptised and accepted into the Catholic Church. They'd relinquished their holy book, the Torah; Judaist ceremonies; and diet – and all because he wanted to be a farmer instead of a saddle maker. "I'm so sorry, my son. Forgive me," he begged.

Diego's blackened face was full of rage. "Papa, I told Juanjo to run away from the house. I grabbed his arm and pulled him along, but he wanted to go back and save the mule and goat. Mama was terrified, and I couldn't leave her, even when I saw Juanjo struggling to free the mule's tethering. Then the animal panicked and reared up … Juanjo fell, and the mule stamped on his face and chest. Papa, I couldn't get to him in time. He was a stupid boy!"

Isa said, "Son, those men would have killed you too!"

"Mama, if they had wanted to slaughter us, they would have!" Diego shouted. "Why didn't they kill us?"

Diego was wrong, Juan thought, continuing to rock Juanjo in his arms. The mule didn't kill Juanjo. His youngest son was dead because of the bastards who seemed to enjoy terrorizing innocent people. As he listened now to Diego's crying, he was also wondering why their lives had been spared and, more importantly, why David believed that the attack was his fault.

CHAPTER ELEVEN

Exhausted, David dropped to his knees and crushed his tearful mother to him. Over her shoulder, he saw Diego holding the child and Juanjo lying against his father's chest with his head tilted downwards and his hair blowing wildly in the wind. "No!" he cried out, and then he grew strangely quiet. He stared at Juanjo's wound, sickened by the gaping hole and sight of blood. His brother, sweet Juanjo, who was so fond of weapons and dreams of soldiering, lay dead, bloodied like a boar!

The marauders could have come from anywhere, David thought. They had borne no markings of allegiance, but they'd been well armed, like an army. Why had they not used their blades on the family? They hadn't even bothered to get off their animals' backs to steal meagre possessions. Their sole intention, it appeared, had been to destroy his father's trees and buildings. He looked across the plain in the direction of the town and wondered if the town would be next.

Focusing his eyes on the surrounding area, David saw in the distance two more fires lighting up the sky. "We weren't the only ones to get burned out," he said miserably. He wiped his sore eyes, sniffed loudly, and squeezed his lips together tightly in anger. One thing was clear. He would take revenge on the attackers. His brother's murder would not go unanswered.

Although the flames were still high in a couple of places, Juan ordered the family to move closer to the house. The fire would keep them warm for a while, he suggested.

David and Diego carried Juanjo between them. Juan helped Isa, who was holding the little girl … No one had asked who she was or why David had brought her to them. Isa still wept, and every few minutes, Juan blurted out, "The foolish, brave boy."

David shivered nervously as he watched his mother's efforts to settle the girl, who was gasping in short breaths between loud cries for her mama and papa. He wanted his confession over and done with. But when the child was eventually soothed, it was Juan who spoke, not David.

"We must bury our Juanjo here with a fitting Jewish ceremony. My son should go to God hearing words from the Torah. No one will ever find out."

"We can't," Isa said shakily, tears streaming down her face.

"We can, and we will. He should be buried next to his grandparents in the Jewish cemetery. That's where we should take him."

"But we'll be punished as heretics if we take him to the Jewish burial ground," Isa pointed out.

"I know that, so I'm asking if you will pray with me now. Will you allow me to give him a Jewish burial?"

"We have no oils to bathe him or robes to dress him in," Isa said.

"Then he'll go to God with just our words to guide him. These, and our love, are the only comforts we can give him."

"We have nothing to dig with, and the soil is caked," Diego said.

"We'll find something to cut through the ground."

David had never seen his father look so defeated. Carrying Juanjo to a patch of hardened soil, like deep red clay, he laid him down and then rapped the ground with his knuckles.

Isa shook her head, horrified. "No, I refuse to bury him here. He'll be all alone. Can't we carry him to Sagrat and give him a Christian burial?"

"No. Christians killed him!" Juan exclaimed to his wife. "He's staying here. I will not have a Catholic priest pray over him. These Christians accept us and our conversion and then they slaughter us!"

David, who had been weeping for Juanjo, said, "You're wrong, Papa. Look around you. Do you not see the other houses burning in the distance? Those are Christian houses. Marauders don't care about religion. They save their adulation for gold."

"I'm not convinced, David. Everything is about religion," Juan answered. "One of these days, sneezing in the wrong direction will get a man thrown in prison for heresy. You just wait – not one new converso will be safe in Spain … No, this happened because we were Jews."

David wouldn't argue further. His own nagging suspicions were growing louder in his mind.

"David, go to the hut and look for a pick, axe, or a sickle that's not burnt to cinders. I don't care what you come back with. Just find something we can use to dig deep. And, son, after we've buried your brother, you will tell us who this girl is and why you brought her to my house."

The dying night sky looked even blacker as the bright glowing fire finally dissolved into smouldering waves of smoke hovering above the ground. When Juanjo was laid to rest and prayers had been spoken, the family sat on the ground, shivering with cold and lost in sorrow. For a while, no one spoke. The shock had worn off, leaving only grief. David's cloak was wrapped around Isa's slim body. The girl, shielded within its folds, was once again asleep and blissfully unaware of the horrific scenes she had witnessed.

Diego, dressed only in a nightshirt, did not complain about the biting wind that blew through the thin linen cloth. His eyes were dead, like two black stones, but it seemed that his questions could no longer be contained.

"David, does this little one have anything to do with what happened here? Did you know those men?"

"No, this had nothing to do with the little girl, and no, I've never seen those men before," David answered defensively. Looking at his father, mother, and finally Diego, he wondered if they would ever speak to him again with love in their hearts. He suspected they wouldn't. "I've committed terrible crimes tonight," he began. "I don't expect your forgiveness, nor do I deserve it, but you have a right to know the truth about me ... and this poor child."

CHAPTER TWELVE

When David had finished telling the whole story, he felt strangely calmer. No one interrupted him, although his father and mother's gasps of disgust had made him stumble over his words a few times. Sharing what he'd done had been a bit like confessing to their priest, Father Bernardo, he thought. He wasn't cleansed, and he never would be, but at least he had admitted his sins and was now ready to face the consequences.

"I've told you everything. I am a murderer, and I've put your lives in danger, just by telling you about what I did. Come morning, the entire town will hear about these killings and the missing babies and you will not be able to breathe a word of this to anyone."

Juan's eyes blazed with anger. "What were their names? Do you even know who you killed?"

"No, I don't. I'd never met them before tonight," David said, unable to look at Juan. "Papa, the treasurer, Garcia, hinted about doing terrible things to this family if I didn't do as I was ordered. I was forced to do as I was told to keep you all safe."

At first, shock and anger sat in Juan's eyes, but slowly his expression changed to repugnance. "My youngest child is dead. How dare you talk about us being kept safe!" he snapped at David. He was sickened by what his son had done, yet he was even more disgusted at the duke. A man who orders a slaying is just as guilty as the hand that does the slaying, he thought. The Sanz family had never had much in the way of possessions, but they were good, respectable people. The duke, for all his noble blood, was worse than a bloodsucking varlet living off the poor, and now he had killed the poor for their baby!

"Papa, I'm sorry," David said again.

Talking to no one in particular, Juan said, "We Sanzes have always survived by abiding by the law, not making enemies, and keeping our own council. Before me, the Sanz men were indebted to no one, and even when they were Jews, they enjoyed good friendships with Christian neighbours. My father and grandfather were wonderful leather makers. They produced saddles, bridles, leather belts, and dagger sheaths for noblemen from Sagrat to Valencia. I could have carried on the family business had I not had dreams of farming the land. So I'm at fault too, you see ... I have brought you to this."

Juan closed his eyes, unable to look at his family. He'd failed miserably. His possessions and tools handed down by his great-grandfather had been sold these past three years. Any money he'd put aside had been spent on rent and supplementing income lost because of bad harvests and wrong decisions. And now his eldest son was a criminal, an assassin, and a marked man.

Glancing at Isa, Juan thought, *Her world has just crumbled.* He knew that look on her face. He'd seen it once before, when her parents and sisters left Spain for Portugal. He'd given his solemn oath to her father on that day. "I will care for Isa. She'll never go hungry or want for anything," he'd said with the blustering pride of a young pup. Look what he'd done to her ... to all of them.

Finally, Juan stared at David, who was brave enough to return his gaze. "Don't ask your mother, brother, or me for forgiveness. You'll have to ask God for that favour."

"I won't ask. I prayed it wouldn't be necessary to tell you what I did ..."

"Well, you did tell us, and now we are party to a terrible secret."

"I had to get the child out of Sagrat, Papa."

Isa said meekly, "He did save the little girl, at great risk to himself."

"Does that wash away the sin of murder?" Juan asked her.

"No, of course not, but David would be dead now had he disobeyed the duke."

"You can't know that. Anyway, better David be dead than alive with the stain of murder on his hands!" Juan sneered.

"Juan Sanz, don't you dare wish your son dead!" Isa spat at him.

"I didn't mean it, my love … My apologies, David." Ashamed of his words, Juan squeezed Isa's hand, and then looked tearfully at David. "So what are we supposed to do with the child? We have no home to hide her in. No food to feed her with. We have nothing! We'll have to seek shelter and beg for alms in Sagrat. Do you expect us to take her with us?"

David hung his head. "No, of course I don't. It was never my intention to leave her with you for any length of time. I was going to ask you to look after her until I returned in a day or two. She can't go back to Sagrat, but I have to be back at the castle and in my barracks before my watch begins."

"What about us? What should we do – sit here until we freeze or starve to death?" Juan snapped.

"I'll keep you safe. I'm a militiaman. The duke will provide you with a house. He has to."

"That tick on a donkey's back won't do anything for us!" Juan shouted, scorning the idea. "The man has no morals. His heart is a sewer, and he has piss for blood! Why did he order *you* to kill? Did he see badness in you?"

"I don't know," said David.

"Juan, how can you say that about your own son? He hasn't a bad bone in his body!" Isa berated him.

Juan said. "Isa, I can barely bring myself to look at him. The sight of him makes me feel sick to my stomach."

"Papa, please …"

Juan ignored David. "It galls me to say it, but the real villain is the duke. He ordered the killings and then threatened our family, and that makes him even less of a man than my son is."

"Thank you, Father," David said stupidly.

"Don't thank me, and don't you go thinking *he* will allow you to parade around like a proud peacock in uniform! He'll have you killed, lad!" Juan's eyes flashed dangerously. "You're a fool if you think he won't try to silence you."

"God forgive you for saying such a terrible thing. The duke would never harm his own soldiers," Isa sobbed.

"Isa, are you not listening? Have you not been paying attention. He ordered the slaughter of three of his citizens tonight!"

"I know … I know. I don't know what I'm saying. Oh dear God, what's to become of us?"

Changing the topic slightly, David said, "The duke's physician was killed tonight. He was with the duke at the wall. The guards on watch were told to leave, and when we next saw the duke, the physician was dead. I think the duke killed him."

"That man is the foulest of turds of the lowest scum," Juan said. "He'll burn in hell, but he'll bask in good fortune until he goes there. You mark my words."

Diego who'd been silent until now said, "I'll be truthful, Papa – had the duke ordered me to kill, I would have if it meant keeping you and Mama safe."

"Then shame on you too. We'll never be safe," Juan repeated. "David has seen to that."

"We have to leave Valencia," David said quite calmly.

Juan shook his head violently and threw David a scathing look. "Don't be stupid, lad. We have no ducats or maravedis between us, unless we miraculously find some lying around in these charred ruins. How far do you think we'd get on foot? We have no blankets, bread, or alms of any kind. We have nothing. Your mother is in her nightgown, for God's sake. No, we will not run." He looked then at Diego. "Diego, you are this family's last hope. I want you to leave now. Get on a ship and don't get off it until you're outside this realm."

"No, I'm not leaving you and Mama behind." Diego looked from one face to the other. "No! I've lost one brother tonight. I'll not lose another!"

"You must," David said. "Would you rather Peráto used you as a weapon against me? I can't protect you."

"Diego, listen to your brother," Juan pleaded.

Isa said, "Son, you should go. I fear you'll come to harm if you remain here. Don't worry about Papa and me. We'll get by." She then looked at David. "You have committed sins that will stain you forever, but you're not a bad man. Let the duke believe us ignorant. Your father and I will not breathe a word to anyone about what you did. We'll take this terrible secret to the grave with us."

"Your mother's right," Juan agreed.

"Heed my words, son," Isa insisted. You must carry on and do whatever it takes to make that unholy monster believe he can trust you. And if you think for one minute that your life is in danger, you must run. Don't come for Papa or me. Just leave. Give me your word."

"You have it," David told her.

Diego, who'd been mainly silent, stood nervously and then began to pace up and down. "Maybe I *should* leave. I'll be one less worry for David, I suppose." He nodded, clearly coming to a decision. "I'll take the little girl with me, and when I get to Valencia, I'll leave her in a public place." He looked at David's shocked face. "It's the best we can do for her."

"You'll barely make it to the port dressed like that, never mind Valencia," Juan said.

"There will be carts travelling along the main road, Papa. There always are. Some kind soul will take us."

"My poor children … This poor babe," Isa said, her lower lip trembling.

"Going with Diego is her only chance of survival, Mama," David said.

Juan's eyes strained to keep tears at bay. "Go somewhere where the duke's power can't reach you."

Isa said tearfully, "Your father's right. The duke cannot be trusted to keep his word to David."

"I pray I'd been killed instead of Juanjo," David said truthfully. "Had I died, Peráto wouldn't have a reason to threaten your lives."

Isa rose to her feet and stood over David, hands on hips and with an angry scowl on her face. "You will stay alive, son, if only to repent and make good of your life!" she commanded.

Juan gazed at Isa with pride and love. He'd adored her since she was a girl, and at thirty-nine years old, she was still as beautiful to him as she had been on the day he married her. Her dark flowing hair blew around her head, having come loose from its long plait. Her ash-smeared face didn't completely hide her olive skin or dark blue eyes, almost the same colour as a Spanish summer sky. Her strong cheekbones and defiant pointed chin further enhanced the straight upturned nose and thick lips on a mouth that smiled often. That was a perfect face, he'd always thought.

He knew she was a strong, determined woman. His children had rarely seen this side of her, but he had, many times.

They would leave this place now and never return. He would seek work in Sagrat and protect his family until his last breath. God help them all, he thought. A powerful enemy had pulled them into a web of deceit, and he prayed that at least some of them would survive what lay ahead of them.

CHAPTER THIRTEEN

Sinfa, Saul Cabrera's granddaughter, lived in one of the only detached houses in Sagrat's Jewish quarter. It sat at the end of the street furthest away from the Jewry's wall and looked onto an open patch of ground filled with shrubs and cacti.

After being retrieved from the rocks beneath the wall, Saul Cabrera's body was taken to his home covered in bloodied hemp sheeting. He had lain in the back of a cart driven by two soldiers and pulled by a mule, and his body had travelled through the streets, unnoticed by its neighbours.

Upon seeing his broken body, Sinfa's screams had filled the damp air, and her cries for help brought families in night attire running to her aid. Panic spread quickly. The physician was the Jewry's patriarch, and only Rabbi Rabinovitch held equal power and sway amongst Sagrat's dwindling Jewish population. His death would be a devastating blow to the already beleaguered community.

At first, neighbours cried with grief, but when the reality of Cabrera's suicide had sunk in, many discarded their weeping for harsh, unforgiving words. The mystery surrounding the physician's fatal fall at a time when he was badly needed by the community was bewildering to some, but it also drew stark disapproval from others. He was a man who had everything in abundance, and his suicide had been a most selfish act, some of the neighbours agreed in angry whispers.

Rabbi Rabinovitch assembled a small crowd of mourners in the Cabrera house's spacious hallway. Amongst them were members of the Jewish council, disbanded by order of the duke but still actively meeting in secret on a weekly basis. The council members were worried. Cabrera's power over the Peráto family had managed to hold a couple of unjust laws against the Jews at bay, but most of the town's new legislation had seen the demise of Jewish privileges and station in just about every occupation. Now, with Cabrera gone, they would have no voice and no support within the castle walls. The new duke, they all agreed, would shut his ears to their pleas for equality.

Rabinovitch called for Guillermo, his son. Guillermo held great promise as a future rabbi. He was going to become a very effective spiritual leader one day; he'd been bred for that role. Though gangly with an uncomfortable looking gait, which gave him the appearance of being timid and a bit of a simpleton, he was not shy with his opinions, nor was he simpleminded. He was cunning, with a brilliant head for economics. The old duke had seen great promise in Guillermo's talented mind, for figures and economic management. His Guillermo should be the town's lord treasurer, not that fool, Sergio Garcia, who couldn't count up to ten without becoming unravelled.

When Guillermo arrived, the rabbi took him by the arm and led him to an alcove that sat underneath the stairway of the Cabrera's two-story house. There wasn't much time to talk in private, but Rabinovitch was determined to resolve a very important matter concerning Saul Cabrera's granddaughter, Sinfa. She had made it clear various times that she was not keen on the idea of marriage with his Guillermo. She would find the idea much more appealing now, he thought, for without her grandfather's protection, life in the Jewry would become difficult for her.

"Look around you, Guillermo. Just about every Jew in Sagrat is here, either outside or inside this house. There are so few of us left in the town, yet we are all here united in grief. I fear that soon only conversos will remain in Aragon, pretending to be good Christians but wishing they were still Jews. I wonder if, in a hundred years from now, Sagrat will remember that we, the Jewish nation, ever existed here." Rabinovitch grunted angrily. He had watched hundreds of Jews turn their backs on their religion, but whilst some scorned it in public, they continued to practice it in secret.

"Hypocrites, Guillermo. We are surrounded by back-stabbing, lying cowards," he said, voicing his thoughts. "I recall a time when these streets were not separated from each other by walls and when your grandfather and his father lent money to Christians from here to the sea.

"I will never forgive that young upstart in the castle for taking away your chance to be Sagrat's treasurer. Luis Peráto is not half the man his father was. Now, *he* was a duke. The last time I spoke to Cabrera, he told me that the duke was struggling to find enough coin to send to the king in Granada."

"No doubt blame for the duke's financial troubles will be placed at the Jewry's gates," Guillermo said.

Rabinovitch nodded. "I agree, son. Cabrera's death will spell trouble for all of us. I swear he was the only reason we still have roofs over our heads and money in our purses. We must prepare for the worst."

"Do you think he killed himself?"

"No, I don't think he did. I can't imagine any earthly reason why he'd throw himself off that wall. But if for some reason he did end his own life, it was because he'd lost his wits." Rabinovitch hid his grief. Saul Cabrera had been his closest friend since boyhood. He needed to cry just as much as Sinfa did, but he didn't have that comfort.

"There are some important matters that you need to attend to, my lad," he said, putting his sadness to the side. "I want you to make sure that Sinfa Cabrera agrees to marriage before the end of the day. She won't refuse you. Not after this."

"Father, don't you think she should have time to mourn before I ask her again? She has refused me twice now. How do you suggest I persuade her when she's made it quite clear she's not interested?"

"Do you love her?"

"I'm fond of her. I've known her all my life. I used to wipe her runny nose and chase her down the street to pull her hair."

"Well, that's good enough. Love is sometimes an impediment anyway," Rabinovitch said, discarding Guillermo's statement. "You and she are firm friends. Friendship is better than passion, which burns out and leaves resentment in its wake. Don't ever wish for the love of a woman. Ask for her respect. That's all that matters.

"Sinfa is far too haughty for her own good. She's thinks she's independent, but that's easy to say when food and clothing are being provided. Her days of looking down her nose at you are over. She's alone now and must turn to someone for protection. That somebody should be you...Did you know the Cabreras never paid any taxes or rent?" Rabinovitch asked.

Guillermo nodded. "I did know this. You've told me many times about how lucky the Cabreras are."

"The man was hording money in his house for years."

"Well, it won't do him any good now, will it?"

"No, no, it won't." Rabinovitch watched the small gathering waiting patiently for him to join them. They would want to hear that everything would be all right and that nothing would change. But life would not be the same, for with Saul gone, the duke would no longer have to honour his promises to his late father.

CHAPTER FOURTEEN

Sinfa Cabrera was inconsolable. Her neighbours in the Jewry did everything they could to comfort her, but they asked each other what they could do to ease her pain. Saul Cabrera, her grandfather, had been the duke's physician, and he'd just thrown himself off the highest part of the castle wall. She would never recover.

She mourned as she sat by her grandfather's body, which lay on the floor. She was accompanied by the shomerim; watchmen selected to accompany the remains until burial. Volunteers from the chevra kadisha, the holy society, were charged with caring for the physician's dead body. It had been cleansed, bathed, and had received the tahorah ritual, or the pouring of water, as it was commonly known.

The body was completely covered in white linen shrouds, and bandages hid his badly damaged skull and face, leaving only one eye and part of a cheek visible. His injuries were horrific, and although Sinfa was sickened at the sight of him, she insisted on being present for every ritual.

At seventeen years old, Sinfa was headstrong, and she'd refused to accept the soldiers' explanation regarding her grandfather's death. He'd gone for a walk and must have decided to visit the watchtower, they had told her. Perhaps her grandfather was sad? He took his life in a moment of madness, one soldier offered.

"Perhaps he was sad? He took his own life in a moment of madness?" she now said, angrily repeating the soldiers' words to Rabinovitch. "I will never believe that. It's not true! Yayo suffered his fair share of sorrow, but he was not an unhappy man, nor was he a sinner. The duchess is due to give birth. He told me only yesterday morning that he was thrilled at the prospect. He would never deny God's goodness in this life … How am I to bear this?"

Rabinovitch stroked his white beard, shook his head, and then spread his arms wide. "I don't believe your dear yayo threw himself onto the rocks either. Anyone who ever knew him well would say the same. He practiced medicine to save lives. He was proud of you and looked forward to seeing you settled with my Guillermo. He would never take his own life, under any circumstances. But this is how it appears, and we must believe what we're told."

"No, I won't, and you shouldn't either!" Sinfa was horrified.

"We must."

"What do you think happened to him?" she asked him, wiping tears from her cheeks.

"I have no idea, child. We may never learn the truth. God only knows what dark forces are at work in this town. We are in dire need of his guidance and protection. Our troubles are grave, herded into this walled corral like goats and treated like the dirt Christians tread upon. Life has turned sour for us, Sinfa. It will be best for everyone if you don't upset anyone up at the castle with your questions."

Sinfa shook her head. She had so many questions, and she would ask them. "I must seek an audience with the duke. Surely he will afford me that favour? Yayo was with the duke and duchess all day yesterday. Maybe someone saw what happened to him before he fell. Perhaps there's a witness that has not yet come forward. I have to know."

Rabinovitch again spread his arms in a gesture of helplessness. "Sinfa, as always, you are stubborn and determined to get your own way. But listen to me child, I've spoken to the council. We think it best if we bury your yayo quietly and without any fuss – and let that be the end of the matter. He goes to the grave a sinner against God. Many are angry with him, and some refuse to see him go to his rest because of what he did."

"But it's not true! How can they think that?" Sinfa insisted. "Will he be afforded a eulogy?"

"No, I'm sorry. I can't give him that. He murdered himself, and all his good deeds in this life have been wiped out. We should leave now for the cemetery. It's time for you to say goodbye to him."

"He didn't sin. He didn't," Sinfa mumbled under her breath. From where she sat, she could see the crowd of mourners in the hallway. They were whispering. They probably wanted to put her yayo in the ground as quickly as possible to hide his black stain. Their lives were dark and dreary, but without her yayo's devotion to them, their world would have ended long ago.

She was furious. Already these people seemed to have forgotten how much Saul Cabrera had done for them. He was the only one who had managed to persuade the duke not to demolish the synagogue. Yayo's voice was what stopped the Christians from taking an entire street of Jewish houses for themselves before the wall went up. He had even given coin and alms to some Jews who had lost their businesses.

"Look at them out there. They look as though they're ashamed to show their faces here, instead of being honoured to be in my yayo's house," she said, motioning towards the hallway. "They have more to worry about than his offence against God. Who will look after them now? You?"

"Be quiet!" Rabinovitch said scathingly. "You must behave with dignity. Don't meddle in problems that don't concern you. It's time to get off your high horse and realise that without my family, you will have no decent life here.

"It's been decided. Guillermo and I will move into this house with you. You and he will be married immediately, and you'll have his protection. No one else will marry you … Now, cover your head properly. It's time to go. Cry your tears and mourn your yayo, like a good granddaughter."

Sinfa released a throaty sob. Her large green eyes flashed with defiance, but she wouldn't say another word, lest she anger the rabbi further. She flicked errant tendrils of her long black hair behind her ears and tightened the shawl about her head. For now, she would have to listen to the old man and keep her thoughts to herself. But when her grandfather's burial ritual was completed, she would tell Calvo Rabinovitch a few truths.

Walking to the cemetery, she told herself that she would survive this tragedy. She didn't need a husband; she needed her grandfather. She wouldn't want for money either. Her grandfather had a hidden treasure. Over the years, she had watched the pile of coins grow until it could no longer fit under the wooden slatted floorboard in her sleeping room. It had to be moved to a bigger hole underneath the hallway floor, covered by a carpet. "This is for the storm that's coming," her yayo had told her every time he added coin to the pile. And he'd always insisted, "If we are forced to leave, we will not go hungry, nor will we have to beg like dogs from Christians." She'd always thought it strange when he talked about a Jewish expulsion when it was obvious to everyone that the duke relied on his medical skills and his wise council.

She didn't need Guillermo's or the rabbi's protection. Contrary to what they thought, she was quite capable of getting by on her own, with all the coin she needed to weather any storm. She was going to the castle. She'd demand an audience with the duke and a proper explanation of what happened to her grandfather, and that was that!

CHAPTER FIFTEEN

It was still dark, and the church bells had just chimed six times. The forty militiamen stood in line in the barrack's courtyard, which was situated near the gatehouse on the castle's north-east corner. Their swords were sheaved in thick leather belts. Each man had a dagger tucked into his waistband and ten of them also held longbows, which rested upright on the ground, casually held in their hands.

David looked at the men's faces, turning bright red with cold, and wished he could feel the same way he had yesterday morning, when he had not a care in the world and was looking forward to a grand feast of wild boar with his family.

Although his expression was passive, it hid the tumultuous thoughts and feelings that were overwhelming him. News about the previous night's attacks on farms, his brother's death, the young murdered couple, and missing children would come soon. The men were going to be shocked and enraged, and he would have to appear as though he were learning the details for the first time. Displaying grief for his brother, Juanjo, wouldn't be difficult, he thought, for he was in terrible pain and needed to weep.

During the night, guards had spotted one fire burning on the plain; that much he had heard. It had probably been the plot nearest to the castle, which lay in its line of sight. His father's farm and the other casualty of the attack would not have been so easily seen, as both of these plots sat farther to the east, on the other side of a thick wooded area. No one had been dispatched to investigate, however, and as far as he was aware, none of the soldiers with him had been informed about the reason the farmhouse had gone up in flames.

His chalk-white exhausted face fought to hide the anguish he felt. On his return to the barracks, he'd had just enough time to wash the smoky grime off his skin before the other men awoke. Luckily, apart from the two night guardsmen, no one had seen him come in. The guards had not asked him any questions, nor would they say a word to anyone about seeing him. Soldiers often slipped out to see their wives during the night or to poke a lover or an easy wench. This was forbidden, but there was a close companionship within the ranks, and their allegiance to each other was at times stronger than their loyalty to the duke.

Orders were about to be issued for the day. David's eyes followed the militia's captain, Vicént Tur, nervously pacing in front of a castle door. What news would he give the men first? David wondered. Tur's face looked tense. He was not known for good humour or an easy smile. His conversations were usually conducted in monosyllables, with yes and no answers, and he rarely used full sentences. But this morning, he looked as though he would strike a man for so much as farting in the line.

Paco Morales, standing next to David, nudged him, and as though reading David's thoughts, said, "Tur looks as though he's just drunk piss for water."

David had a fondness for Paco, who had guided him through his first weeks in the militia. Some considered his lively character annoying. David thought him amusing, yet at times he was overly curious about everyone else's business … He certainly wasn't boring.

"Maybe he should drink a bucket of wine and make love to his wife," David said, shrugging.

"He should be so lucky on both counts," Paco chuckled. "I don't think he's seen underneath his wife's dress for years, and he doesn't drink wine, not since he got rowdily drunk last year and spent three weeks in prison strapped inside an empty barrel with his head sticking out of the top like a chicken. That had a terrible effect on him... He's turned to God –goes to Mass every morning and confession every couple of days. It wouldn't surprise me to learn that he's leaving the militia and entering a monastery. "

David studied Tur with fresh eyes. "Is that why he always looks so sullen – because he's turned to religion?"

"I don't know. Maybe God doesn't pay Tur any more attention to him than his wife does. All I know is that he was much happier when he was falling down drunk in front of the church instead of kneeling down in prayer inside it," Paco offered with a grin. "This is an important day, my lad. That's all I know. The duke finally has an heir, and apparently there are going to be big celebrations. Good days are coming to Sagrat. I can smell them."

How wrong Paco was, David thought, shifting his feet from one to the other to stop them from becoming numb. He continued to watch Tur whispering to one of the men some distance away and shuddered, feeling that someone had just stepped on his grave. Dear God, what he wouldn't do for some hot broth and the heat of a blazing fire to thaw his bones. Tiredness was making him shiver. He'd freeze his arse off before the inspection happened.

David turned his thoughts again to the previous night. After Diego had left the farm with the little girl, David had persuaded his mother and father to come back to Sagrat with him. Their languid steps had eventually reached the San Agustin church in the town square, after it had been decided that they should throw themselves at Father Bernardo's feet and beg for help.

David had left Juan and Isa on the church's steps, afraid of being seen and later questioned about why he'd been at the farm. He wondered if the priest gave his parents shelter and alms. Of course he did. It was his job to care for his flock.

The sight of Diego, head hanging and walking across the plain with the child in his arms, had broken David's heart. He would probably never see his brother again. His lasting memory of him would be that of his half-naked body and bare feet stumbling in the darkness, his torn nightshirt billowing in the wind.

He would never stop worrying about him. Where was he now? What did the future hold for him? A ship's captain might not employ a man that looked like a beggar without means to clothe himself? But Diego was a clever boy, David reminded himself. He was astute, and underneath the grime covering his body was a handsome man with a beguiling smile which could charm the most reluctant birds off a tree. He was going to survive and flourish. He, David, had to believe that.

At least there was comfort, knowing that the little girl was alive. He prayed for her survival and for her future, but part of him wished he had not saved her. He hated himself for even thinking that, but he also knew that she was the reason he'd been compelled to tell his family about the murders. His father's words would be like pig's dung on his boots, going with him wherever he went. "After we reach the church, I don't want to see your face again. You have shamed me. I have lost three sons tonight because of you. Damn your soul to hell." Not many words, David thought, but they had been powerful and painful to hear.

CHAPTER SIXTEEN

David was jolted from his thoughts by Tur's shrill orders to come to attention. Looking up, he saw Garcia appear. Steeling himself to stand with a blank expression, David steadied his pounding heart and tried to cull his hatred. He should have known this was going to happen. Before any questions could be asked, Garcia was here to lie through his teeth about the previous night.

He studied Garcia from out of the corner of his eye and inwardly cursed him. The treasurer seemed to wear a constant sneer on his mouth, as though measuring another man's worth and finding it lacking. He was a festering boil, born of a whore who had probably never known the name of her baby's father. He was a sinister force, more powerful in nature than the duke was, and he was certainly capable of sending men to the farms to destroy and kill.

After talking to Tur, Garcia came to stand centre front of the line. Cocking his head to one side, he listened to something Tur was whispering in his ear, and then he looked at the soldiers standing in the front row.

"David Sanz, step forward!" Captain Tur shouted.

"What have you done, lad?" Paco whispered hurriedly.

"Nothing," David mumbled as he left the line.

Standing before Garcia, he felt compelled to give him a courtesy bow of his head. But David's only thought was that his fellow militiamen would now share his grief, and he was glad.

"I must have words with you, Sanz," Garcia said in a flat, unemotional voice. "Follow me."

When Garcia, Tur, and David were out of earshot of the other men, Garcia wasted no time. "I've just been informed by Father Bernardo that your father's farm was attacked by marauders last night. It seems that your brother Juanjo was killed … You have my condolences."

An anguished roar left David's mouth. He bowed his head and then covered his face with both hands. Condolences? The whoreson wasn't sorry. Swaying with a rush of blood to his head, he conjured images previously pushed away. The full force of grief and guilt finally surfaced. His brother's lifeless body and the dead couple he had sliced open with his blades … His father's disapproving face and his mother's tears …

The sound of muffled weeping escaped through his fingers. "Oh … dear God … no."

"You have my condolences, Sanz," he heard Tur say.

Lifting his head, David ignored Tur and instead stared at Garcia, who flinched under the penetrating gaze.

"I can assure you that we will find out who did this to your family. We never know when tragedy will strike, do we?" Garcia said, and his left eyebrow rose in a sinister arch.

David gasped. The bastard was taunting him! He *had* ordered the attack. The maggot's guilt was as plain as the reddened cheeks under his shifty eyes. David's hand went instinctively for his sword, and it rested on its hilt for a few seconds, until he came to his senses and dragged it away.

Garcia looked at David's weapon and then lifted his eyes to stare at David with a belittling smirk playing on his lips.

David was lost in rage. Scowling angrily, he willed Garcia to sense his thoughts and to feel his fury. If he could end the whoreson right now and give his mother the revenge she craved, he would find some peace, he kept thinking. He'd accept any punishment for the pleasure of killing this pus from the fattest whore's pox! "Where is my family?" he muttered.

"Father Bernardo is looking after them," Garcia said. "You mustn't worry about them. They will be given shelter in the town."

"Thank you, Your Honour."

"No need to thank me. It's our duty to care for Sagrat's townspeople."

"Might I return to the line now?" David asked politely.

"Yes, but before you join the ranks, I wonder if I might ask you about your other brother … Diego? I believe that's his name. Father Bernardo told me that he was not with your parents. They don't seem to know where he is. I find that strange."

David let out a painful sigh. "I haven't seen my brother for over a month but there is nothing strange about that. Diego is a wanderer. If my mother and father don't know where he is, it's because he probably took himself off to look for work and has not yet returned. He often does that."

"I see. Well, if he returns, you must inform Captain Tur." Looking at Tur, Garcia added, "Perhaps you could find Sanz's brother a position with the militia … if the lad needs a job?"

"Yes, Your Honour. If he's half as good a swordsman as Sanz here, we'd be lucky to have him," Tur answered, albeit reluctantly.

David appealed to his leader. "Captain, will you allow me to go to my parents?"

"Later," Garcia answered for Tur. "Captain Tur will need all his men today."

David's body shook with rage from head to toes. He was safe for the moment. His presence at the farm the previous night was still a secret. Garcia hadn't been told. He prayed that would remain the case.

In his mind, he gathered the images of the marauders' faces and tried to recall the smallest of details. It had been dark, but the fire had lit up the area and he'd had a good look at them. He didn't think he would be able to recognise any of them if he passed them in a street, but their leader's face, pitted with deep red scarring from his left eyebrow to his cheek, was unforgettable.

"Soldiers!" David heard Garcia shout. "Her Grace has been safely delivered of a son. This is a great day for Sagrat and for her people."

Lies, lies! David wanted to scream, as he listened to the men's exploding applause.

"If only our lives were filled with joyous moments and empty of sorrow. Sadly, God tests us, for with gladness comes dismal news," Garcia continued when there was silence. "It's been many months since our port was last attacked and looted by marauders, and even longer since bandits caused mischief in our town, but last night Sagrat was once again violated by scum who came in the night like quiet demons."

He pointed to David. "David Sanz has just been informed that his family's home was destroyed and his young brother murdered by swine! But his family were not the only victims. Two other farms were also burnt to the ground." Garcia stared at David, taunting him once again with his eyes.

The men looked at David, and while many muttered their condolences, others were intent on questioning Garcia.

"How could we not know about this attack?" a soldier shouted.

"Who was attacked? When did this happen?" another wanted to know.

Tur's voice boomed above the noise. "Let the lord treasurer speak!"

David held his breath. *Tell us about the murders,* he thought, staring boldly at Garcia. *Explain why only one home in this entire town was attacked.*

Paco placed his hand on David shoulder, but David barely noticed. His mind raced. Garcia was going to say that the marauders killed the young couple and stole the children. It all made sense now. The marauders had set the fires so that the people would believe that the various crimes were connected. Feeling as though he was going to collapse, David then remembered to breathe.

Garcia continued. "After burning homes on the plain, these evil blasphemers stole into our town and murdered a young couple and abducted their two babies from their home."

The men gasped with shock. Garcia allowed a moment of rage to settle in the militiamen's minds and then continued with dire warnings.

"We must be extra vigilant, for we may have slave traders in our midst. And they will strike again and again, as is their way."

Shame washed over David, but with it came relief. Garcia had shifted suspicion away from anyone living in Sagrat and on to faceless marauders who had plagued Valencia for years. He looked at the stunned faces around him and listened to the rising tide of voices that were interrupting Garcia again. Never had he witnessed havoc in the ranks. He glanced at Garcia, who seemed to be satisfied with the militia's reaction.

At last, Tur told the men to shut up.

"We must find the bastards and bring them to justice!" Garcia shouted as the noise died down. "And when we have them in our grasp, we'll cut off their balls and their rods and hang them around their throats like necklaces! Men, your duke demands that you hunt the vermin from here to the coast, to the north, and south of the port ... Find these stolen babies and bring them home! Garcia stopped talking for a moment to look at the soldiers' faces. "Bring these whoresons back alive," he continued, "and we'll watch them roast like pigs!"

CHAPTER SEVENTEEN

Luis stood in front of the blazing fireplace in his chambers, rubbed his hands together, and smiled with satisfaction. After spending an hour with his new son, he had concluded that being a father was the greatest achievement a man could attain. The baby was everything Luis could have wished for. He had drunk his fill of a noblewoman's milk, and he was no longer a peasant's son but a true Peráto of noble lineage and rightful heir to the dukedom.

Luis had not been able to get the physician's words out of his mind. "Your wife is not strong enough to nourish a baby," the Jew had stated. Well, the old man had been wrong, for one of Josefa's ladies had informed him that the duchess's breasts flowed with milk and that she had successfully satisfied the baby's hunger on her first attempt. His wife had become a valuable cow, but her worth to him ended with her ability to feed the baby and breed more sons.

He tried unsuccessfully to push Josefa from his mind. A frustrated sigh left his mouth, and he grumbled as the first tinge of annoyance blighted his perfect morning. God's grief in heaven, the woman irked him to distraction. She was a mother, for God's sake, and had no need of dolls when she had a living baby. He had pointed this out to her after she had roughly discarded Jaime Gaspar in favour of a wooden effigy lying on top of the bed. In response, she had screamed at him to remove the baby from her sight.

Her ability to care for the infant was doubtful. She obviously didn't like him, but that mattered not. No, the less the mad creature had to do with the baby, the better. He would send for two wet nurses. They would nourish him and keep him safe.

God never gave his people overflowing cups of joy, he thought. Instead, he gave sips, leaving his worshipers with a perpetual thirst for contentment. If the Almighty had provided him with a sane wife and good mother for his son, he would be satisfied and would ask for nothing more. After all, he was not a greedy man.

Shrugging, he cast all thoughts of Josefa aside. Today was going to be pivotal for the town and for his leadership. There were loose ends to tie up regarding the infant, and his arrival would not be fully celebrated until the previous night's acts of violence had been put to rest and were forgotten.

Luis nodded to Garcia, who was skulking at the office door, and gestured to him to enter. When seated, he looked briefly at the treasurer's face, and seeing his grandiose smirk, he relaxed his muscles. "I take it by your satisfied expression that all went well this morning," he said. "I hope so, Garcia. I'm unwilling to hear bad tidings of any kind today."

"I believe Your Grace will be pleased. As you said last night, it's not important what the townspeople think. What matters is your militia's loyalty."

"Do I have it?"

"You do, Your Grace. If anything, their respect for you has grown. The cavalry has been dispatched to hunt for marauders, and there is not a man amongst them who's not seeking revenge."

"Where are your elusive mercenaries? Where do they hide?"

"That I don't know. Our man inside the town won't tell me where their hideout is situated. They're like ghosts. They disappear once they get paid and reappear when I summon them," Garcia said, handing Luis a document to sign. "Here is the payment order for the mercenaries' activities last night."

Luis, grumbling impatiently, snatched the document from Garcia's hand. "Why do you insist in giving me these accounts when only you and I know about my personal funds? The money is not coming from the treasury, is it?"

"No Your Grace."

"Then I don't need to see any more figures. I trust you. If I didn't you would not be standing in front of me."

It was probably better if Garcia didn't admit to knowing where the marauders hid, Luis thought as he casually scanned the document. He'd never been comfortable discussing them with his treasurer. "I have shamefully come to rely on the mercenaries' talents," he said absently.

In the past six months, they had successfully managed to rob two heavy-laden caravans headed for Valencia, carrying coin and gold. One of those caravans had come from Sagrat with tax revenue earmarked for the monarchs' coffers. Two militiamen had been killed in that ambush, but their deaths had been worthwhile sacrifices for the good of the town's finances … He'd felt no guilt then, and he still didn't. Why should the king and queen have the bulk of what the town earned? He had much more need of the money, and after all, it was his to begin with.

He wasn't sure if he liked Garcia having so much influence over the marauders. They obviously thought highly of him. Why else would they come running every time he summoned them?

Sitting at his desk, he realised that there was a lot about Garcia he didn't know. He'd been scribe to a noble family in Valencia. That was true, for Count Javier Castro Ortega, a Valencia noble, had recommended Garcia for his present position. Yet the man was still a riddle to be solved.

"There must be no doubt in my soldiers' minds that marauders killed the couple and abducted their children. I will not tolerate a single rumour or theory that doesn't point to the bandits. Can you assure me that this will be the case?" he asked Garcia.

"I can, Your Grace."

"And what of Sanz? Does he pose a threat or not?"

"He might." Garcia cleared his throat and then nervously scratched his head. "Your Grace, unfortunately there was a small setback at the Sanzes' farm. One of the sons, Sanz's younger brother, was killed as a result of the attack."

"What! Died, you say? I said no killings!"

"I can assure you that the marauders didn't touch a hair on the lad's head. Father Bernardo told me that the boy was kicked by the family's mule and died of injuries to his face. It was an unfortunate accident."

"What do the marauders say?"

"I have not spoken to them. I thought it best not to seek them out until the dust settles."

"Christ's blood! I want Sanz's loyalty, not his hatred, you fool. Tell me, does he or doesn't he suspect us of the raid?"

"I believe he does … No, I'm convinced of it. I gave him reason to suppose it could have been us, just as you asked."

"Good, then we will have his silence. He'll be shitting fear until the day he dies." Luis   looked at Garcia's frowning face. "You disagree?"

"I still don't trust him. Last night I saw insolence in him. This morning I saw anger. When I told him about the attack on his home, he went for his sword. His hand rested on its pommel for just a second, but I saw the hatred in his eyes when he touched it. He's not a meek man, and I strongly suspect he's not as loyal as Your Grace believes him to be … Forgive my outspokenness."

"Carry on."

"These tragedies will not be forgotten. The townspeople will grieve but they will eventually get on with their lives, of course. But I suspect that David Sanz will continue to be a problem. If he loosens his tongue and speaks out about this, only a handful of people will believe him, but it will only take one other person to begin a rumour about your son's origins to spark flames of accusations … It will not be easy to silence tongues once this fire is lit. The effects could be disastrous."

"What do you suggest?" Luis asked.

"You must have Sanz killed – and soon. You'll be making a big mistake if you don't get rid of him."

Luis closed his eyes in contemplation. He knew Garcia was right, but his father's words of advice sprang to mind every time he thought about getting rid of the militiaman: "Remember, son, your militia will protect you. They will fight for you and be loyal to their last breath. But harm one of your men and you will lose them all." He opened his eyes and found Garcia's beady eyes staring at him. The man revolted him at times. He needed to be put in his place.

"I pay you well for your services, do I not?" Luis asked.

Garcia's eyes widened with surprise. "You do, You Grace."

"Then why do you insult me?"

"Insult you? Never!"

"I disagree. My son's baptism ceremony should be my only concern, yet you've given me other worries to deal with. You have neglected to carry out my orders. You failed to dispatch messengers to Valencia with invitations to the infant's celebrations. The inquisitor will arrive at any moment, and I have still to receive your estimate of how much the prison's extension has cost me.

"I told you to deal with the physician's granddaughter, yet she still lives in that grand house with hidden money, which should belong to me! I have mourning townspeople to care for. My people will want answers and justice for the murders and abductions, and they will need my support and my promise to keep them safe. Yet I cannot send anyone to burn at the stake for last night's crimes ... Tell me, Garcia, why must I have the troubles of the world on my shoulders whilst the only thought you seem to have in your head is your desire to kill David Sanz? Do you think I'm a soft-bellied simpleton?"

"No Your Grace ..."

"Don't interrupt me! Look at you, a wax-nosed commoner daring to tell me who I must kill and what I must do instead of solving my problems, which are many!"

"I have not had time to attend to the town's affairs. I've been busy with other business of late ... I brought you the infant," Garcia responded, throwing Luis a look of sullen defiance.

Luis grabbed the edge of the desk and then punched it with his fist. If only he didn't need the an, he thought. He'd been impulsive getting rid of his father's allies on the town council. He'd been tired of old men continually telling him, "This is not how your father conducted his business." He had wanted a fresh face, someone who would be loyal to him and not to his father's ghost. Garcia was unscrupulous and his criminal mind was exactly what was needed.

Rising from his chair, he strode angrily towards Garcia. His open palm shot out so fast that it caused Garcia to stagger backwards when it connected with his cheek. Luis looked at his stinging palm, walked back to his desk, and sat down. He felt better. Garcia would now think twice before answering. Who did he think he was, an equal?

Garcia lifted his hand and massaged his wounded face, and then he lowered his eyes. "My apologies, Your Grace," he mumbled.

"You will never again mention my son's origins. If you so much as speak his name to me I will have your tongue cut out, your hands bathed in boiling oil, and your testicles fed to the pigs. Are we clear?"

"Yes."

Nodding with satisfaction, Luis said, "My business with Sanz and his family is over. He proved his loyalty, and he and his parents *will* be left in peace. I will hear no more about your petty desire to end his life or your opinion on this matter. My people will demand justice for these murders, and I need you to make sure they get it, without pointing your finger of blame at Sanz."

"But how will they get justice, Your Grace?"

"Find a way to give it to them! Do your job! Remember, Garcia, there are many men in this town who are more capable than you are and more willing to serve me. You are not infallible, and I would sooner run you through with a sword than any one of the soldiers, who guard me well."

Garcia bowed his head

Luis gave him a scathing look and then dismissed him with a wave of his hand. "Get out. Go do my bidding."

"Juan Sanz owes rent and taxes to Your Grace. What should I do?" Garcia asked tentatively as he was leaving.

"Forgive him his debts. Let him love me."

CHAPTER EIGHTEEN

Soldiers were dispatched to the Jewry. David lagged behind the others, not wanting to accept their condolences or listen to what they'd like to do with the whoresons who had killed innocent townspeople. As they marched in a two-by-two formation through the streets that led to the Jewish quarter, David questioned the need to demolish the perfectly good house that had belonged to the now-dead physician. Throughout the town, entire families lived, ate, and slept in one room. Destroying a property was wasteful and foolish.

His eyes were glazed with tiredness, but as the men picked their way through the narrow streets, they didn't miss the throng of people who had gathered in and around the area where he had murdered the couple and stolen the children. David stared at the grief-stricken frightened faces and wondered if the victims' family were amongst the crowd. He would like to throw himself at their feet and beg their forgiveness, he found himself thinking. Instead, he peeled his eyes away and concentrated on his footing and the duty he was about to perform.

At the very front of the line, Garcia sat like a proud cock on his horse, and every now and then, he turned to the soldiers with a portentous glare and gave them a telling-off for walking too slowly behind him.

Paco, who was a few steps in front of David, slowed down until David was in earshot. "You need to pick up the pace, my lad, or he'll have your hide."

"Let him try."

"David, I could weep for your loss, but I'm sure the lord treasurer cares not a whit." As though a thought had just struck him, Paco then asked, "Why is he coming with us? He doesn't usually get his hands dirty when we're evicting people."

"I don't know. I've never been to a Jewish eviction," said David.

"Did you see what happened to the old physician last night?"

"No, I was with you," David reminded him. "I heard what you heard and saw what you saw."

"Do you think he jumped? You know, killed himself?"

David shrugged. The duke's rage the previous evening had not been missed by anyone, David believed, but no one would dare speak of it aloud, nor would his men want to believe that he had killed his own physician. "We don't get paid to think or to ask questions that don't concern us. Anyway, what does it matter? If he jumped, he's dead, and if he was pushed, he's still dead." The previous night, David had thought about the old physician on the way back to the town with his parents. The duke killed the Jew, he had concluded. He pushed Cabrera from the top of the wall.

Paco asked one hurried question after another. "Why did the duke summon you last night? What did he have to say to you? He looked angry about something or other. Do you know what? Was it you?"

Looking horrified, David retorted, "No! Why should he be angry with me? He didn't even know my name until last night. God only knows what goes on in a duke's mind. I doubt Luis Peráto has a care in the world compared to those of us less fortunate. He wouldn't know real worries unless they jumped up and bit his noble arse," David said, becoming irritated.

"But why did he order you to follow him? What did he want from you?"

"Paco, can you not still your tongue? Do I not have enough to think about without your interrogation? Leave that to the inquisitor when he arrives. The duke welcomed me to the militia – that's all." Though David regretted his harsh words, he didn't offer an apology. Instead, he wondered how many more times people would ask the same questions of him today.

"You shouldn't be here," Paco said, interrupting David's thoughts again. "You should be with your family ... My condolences. Tur's a swine for making you march up and down this hill today – and so is that arrogant Jew sitting on the horse."

"What Jew?" David asked.

"Garcia."

"He's not a Jew," David said.

"He might not be now, but he must have been at one time. Look at him. You can tell a league away just by his hooked nose and shifty eyes. Anyway, as I said, you shouldn't have to be here. You should be getting ready for your brother's burial."

David managed to stifle a sardonic snigger which would have been hard to explain away had it emerged from his mouth. He wanted to tell Paco that he'd tramped up and down this hill so many times in the past twelve hours that he was having difficulty marching with blistered feet. He'd also like to break the news that his brother was already in an unmarked grave on the plain and that he, David, had recited Jewish prayers before putting Juanjo in the ground. Imagine, David thought, if he were to tell Paco that.

He glanced at Paco, who was waving to a friend. When they had passed the man, he said, "I'm a converso. I was a Jew, and I don't have a hooked nose or shifty eyes."

"I won't hold that against you," Paco said with a grin. "You're a handsome lad, Sanz." And with that, they marched on in companionable silence.

David's axe struck the house's wooden floor with more force than any other tool being used by the soldiers to destroy Saul Cabrera's house. In his imagination, he saw every blow strike the duke, Garcia, and the scar-faced marauder.

Glancing every so often at Garcia, he was disconcerted to see the treasurer staring back at him. Paco's question surfaced. Why *was* the treasurer here? And why was he intent on having every single wooden plank in every room raised from the ground?

The soldiers had begun their work in the opulent family room, removing or destroying every piece of furniture, decoration, and ornament beyond recognition. David had noticed the rich tapestries, glass and gold goblets, fine lace curtains, silk cushions, and luxurious couches the minute he'd set foot inside the home. He had never seen such wealth, not even in the duke's private chamber.

Beside him, soldiers looted what they could carry. They hid small objects underneath chain mail vests and tucked them inside their tight red hose. Larger items were thrown into the cart which had followed them from the castle, carrying tools. Paco, who was fervently thieving alongside the rest of his comrades, laughed at David's shocked face and then told him off for being a naive, raw recruit who had much to learn.

"If we don't take the stuff, the neighbours will, and why should they have anything when we're doing all the hard work?" Paco explained.

David grimaced with the effort it was taking to wield the axe. His muscles were aching, his mood was as black as the inside of a wolf's mouth, and his thoughts were constantly returning to his homeless parents and his dead brother. "All we're doing here is destroying lives. I wouldn't call that worthwhile work or a mission deserving of this treasure," he said bad-humouredly.

CHAPTER NINETEEN

The sun had risen, and unlike the previous day, it was beginning to cast warmth into the air. The clear blue sky and bright sunlight hurt Sinfa's tired eyes, and she shielded them with her head shawl, drawing it down as far as the tip of her nose. She shivered, muttered insults under her breath, and swore to despise most of her neighbours for the rest of her life. Then she smiled gratefully at the handful of faces waiting for her to lead the procession back to her house and vowed to look after them until the ends of *their* lives.

"Most of my grandfather's oldest friends and neighbours have refused to give him the burial he deserves," she said to those brave enough to stand with her. "We know he didn't end his own life, and I promise you that I won't stop looking for answers. Someone will eventually tell me the truth."

"You'll never find the truth," her neighbour Rebecca said sadly. "I doubt you'll even get to speak to the duke. He's got no time for us Jews now."

Sinfa sighed, too tired to argue. She looked once more at the grave and scowled. It had been dug some distance away from all the other tombs in the graveyard, signifying that Saul Cabrera had been given a sinner's burial and would lie in the ground in shame, for all to see and for all eternity. There had been no eulogies or praise for the man who had devoted his life to caring for others, and Rabbi Rabinovitch, who had stood just outside the graveyard gates, had left before the first handful of soil was thrown onto the body. "I'm ashamed of my own people for believing such nonsense," she said, turning away from the grave.

The small group left the graveyard and walked in silence towards the Jewry. For the first time in her life, Sinfa was alone. There would be no outpouring of kindness or offers of charity from the Jewry's streets, as her grandfather would have wished. She'd seen nothing but disrespect from those who had lined the way with their backs to her grandfather's burial procession, and she knew exactly what she'd be walking into when she got home.

An unladylike grunt left her mouth. Rabbi Rabinovitch and Guillermo were traitors. They were a couple of backstabbers who had showered her with sympathetic words and were then too afraid of public opinion to be seen at the graveside with her. They'd be waiting for her, like a couple of vultures picking bones. They wouldn't be too ashamed to demand her inheritance and her property. Guillermo would seek her hand, even though he loved another woman and had hidden that from his father for more than two years. "You're getting nothing from me," she mumbled under her breath, "not even my friendship."

Sinfa's thoughts were interrupted by loud crashing noises coming from the Jewry. Her belly twisted in a knot, and heat coursed through her body. Many times she'd watched and heard Jewish properties being knocked down after their occupants had left or died. Her grandfather had told her once that this was the duke's way of making sure no other Jew ever moved into Sagrat or a vacant house. "If they get rid of Jewish houses, they get rid of Jews," he'd stated.

The Jewry was an ugly neighbourhood now. Its buildings were desecrated, with some dangerously clinging to weakened foundations caused by untidy demolition in connecting houses. They were pulling her house down, her instincts screamed, and by the time she got home, everything of value would have been taken or left in ruins.

She broke into a run, forgetting mourning traditions and ignoring how she must look with her dress revealing bare ankles and her head shawl wrapped around her neck. It couldn't be her house, she tried to convince herself. It was a beautiful building ... Why would they destroy such a landmark?

As she ran, she saw images of all she owned being smashed into the ground, but these images disintegrated as another dreadful thought came to mind. Fear and panic spread through her and left her legs shaking. She looked towards the far end of the Jewry's wall and gasped when she saw the plumes of dust rising above it. They were going to find the money. The house would be ripped apart, and they'd come across the sacks of coin in the shallow hole in the hallway! "They can't have it," she groaned. "It's mine ... Oh dear God, they mustn't find it!"

Sobbing, she ran through the Jewry's open gate and passed the marketplace and fish market, which opened only on Fridays. She inhaled the smell of fresh fish brought from the port and felt nauseated as it filled her nostrils. A small queue of people stood patiently waiting for their turn. Sinfa knew most of the women there and glanced fleetingly at the faces as she bolted past them. Angry voices shouting after her all the way down the street upset her further, and she choked loudly on a cry that ripped from her throat.

"Don't run! Has your family not shamed us all enough?" She heard various versions of such things being screamed at her. She ran on, remembering that today was the start of Shabbat. Her public display of grief would not be tolerated tonight, but she would grieve all the same, she thought defiantly.

The house's ornate front door was already lying on its side against a neighbouring house's wall. A couple of soldiers stood outside beside a cart loaded with the house's valuables. Pieces of furniture were stacked in the street, the neighbours greedily eying them, probably hoping that the militia would leave some behind. Window shutters were smashed and unhinged from their brackets. Cracks zigzagged across the entire length of the house's front facade, and half the street was covered in a cloud of grey fog.

She ran into the dust-filled house panting for breath and with her mind frozen in fear. Her black gown was dirtied at the hem, lightened by dust, and half covered by a shawl trailing on the ground. But the dress was not as untidy as her hair, partly secured in a coiled braid but with so many loose tendrils hanging around her face and down her back that it looked like a wild horse's mane.

At first, she stood in the centre of the hallway with a sense of helplessness and resignation, in the same way she had seen evicted neighbours do before her. But when her eyes began to sting and fill with grit, she felt the full force of her rage rise to the surface. She had to protect what was rightfully hers. This was barbaric. It was a sin!

Her eyes flashed dangerously at the soldiers on their knees, pulling up the floorboards and seemingly uninterested in her arrival. The noise was deafening, so loud that she could barely think. She stared at the ground and then glanced at the stairs leading to a second floor. Just in front of the arch under the staircase was the money, every real, maravedi, and ducat her grandfather had ever saved during years of service and hard work. They would be upon it within minutes. It would be a grand day for the duke's coffers, she thought.

"Get out! Leave my house immediately!" Her eyes narrowed. She couldn't let them take it. She'd be destitute. "You have no right to do this!" She heard herself scream the words, and instead of shutting up, she found her protests growing. "How dare you destroy the physician's home on the very day he is buried! Have you no decency? Stop this at once or I'll flay the lot of you!"

"Silence!" The roaring voice came from the doorway between the family room and the hallway. It was so gruff and loud that it made Sinfa jump and halt her ranting and raving. She stared at the appearance of the stocky dark-haired man dressed in black finery and with a condescending smirk on his flushed round face, and she took an involuntary step backwards.

She flicked her eyes from soldier to soldier, frozen where they knelt and stood, with tools unmoving, but she was far too angry to feel afraid of what they might do to her.

"Who are you to silence me in my own home?" she shouted at Garcia.

"Who are you to order the duke's men out of here?" Garcia parried back.

"I am Sinfa Cabrera, and you are trespassing. This house is under the protection of the duke, and I live here with his grace and favour."

"Is that so?" Garcia sneered. Walking across the hallway, dodging men and holes of deep red soil, he came to stand only inches from Sinfa's face.

Sinfa felt the heat of his breath on her skin and recoiled at his nearness. Her throat was dry and filling up with dirt and wood dust. She coughed nervously in the strange silence that seemed to be lasting forever.

"So you think you have the right to live here after what your grandfather did?" Garcia asked. "Do you honestly believe that any good Catholic nobleman would allow his property to be despoiled by the family of a self-murderer?"

"He didn't kill himself, Your Honour. It wasn't suicide, and I'll tell the duke that if you take me to him," Sinfa retorted.

"You, see the duke? No, wenches like you don't stand in the presence of nobility."

"Don't you dare call me a wench – and don't presume to speak for His Grace. My grandfather was a loyal servant to the Peráto family. I don't believe the duke thinks his physician capable of such a terrible deed, and you can't tell me he does. Anyone could tell you that my grandfather wasn't physically able to get up these stairs without hanging onto both banisters, so how do you think he managed to climb onto the top of a wall that was probably just as tall as he was? The soldiers lied, and you're lying too!"

Sinfa glanced Garcia's arm just as it shot out, but she was too slow to react. The blow to her head forced her neck to twist to the side. It was such a jolt that she thought she might have broken it. Straightening herself, she stared at him with tears in her eyes and said, "Only cowards hit women."

The next backhanded blow to her face knocked her off her feet. She felt her body falling to the side but was too unbalanced to right herself in time to stop herself from falling over. Looking up dazedly from the floor, she saw a soldier standing over her and blinked away her tears. His eyes shone with sympathy and kindness. He helped her up, and she thanked him.

Staring again at Garcia, she knew all was lost, yet she was not ready to give up. She looked at the soldiers. They were scowling with disapproval at the man who had hit her. "You have already destroyed this house, but by law everything inside it is mine. You have no right to take my belongings," she said respectfully. "May I ask Your Honour to leave me alone for an hour so that I can collect my possessions? After that, you can finish your destruction of a perfectly good home. I won't protest further."

Garcia laughed and wiped the trickle of blood running down the side of her mouth with his thumb. "No, you'll leave now," he told her. "I don't have time for any more of your nonsense. Go on – get out of my sight."

At last, Sinfa's tears flowed, along with her disgust for the man whose name she didn't even know. "You're a swine! I'll take my complaints to the highest office. I'll see you lose your position for this injustice!" Her chin jutted in defiance, but she knew she must be looking like a pathetic child, with tears running down her cheeks and barely able to see through the curtain of hair covering her face. She ran her fingers through her heavy mane and pushed it away from her forehead. Staring once more at the soldiers, she was comforted by the pity present in their eyes. "The duke won't be happy about this," she said as a last-ditch effort to save her inheritance.

Garcia took a step forward, grabbed Sinfa's arm in a tight squeeze, and pulled her towards him until her face was inches from his own and their bodies were touching. "Who do you think sent me? You're a stupid Jew. Do you think the duke cares about you and your kind? He wants to cleanse this town. You're an infestation, and if I had my way, I'd wipe your Jewish arses on the floor and throw the lot of you all into the pigpens as fodder!" He looked then at the soldiers and seemed to be enraged even further at the contemptuous stares that met his eyes. "What are you all gawking at? The spectacle is over. Get back to work!"

Garcia's scowl deepened as he met David's eyes. If there was ever any doubt of Sanz's hatred towards him, it had just been removed with that cold, threatening glare, he thought. If he could disobey the duke's order, he'd kill the bastard where he stood. He'd give anything to watch the impertinent upstart take his last painful breaths, with all his secrets dying with him … But he would leave that pleasure for another time.

"You, Sanz, take this girl to the prison. Throw her in the coldest, dampest cell and let her calm her temper," he ordered. He looked again at the other soldiers. "She threatened me. You all heard her call me a swine, did you not?" He waited. There was no response. "Well, speak! Answer me, you good-for-nothing goat pokers!"

"Yes, Your Honour. We heard her, Your Honour. Yes …" Slowly and one by one, the soldiers gave in.

Looking at Sinfa, Garcia said. "Wench, you want a roof over your head? Well, you can have one, with the duke's compliments. You can rot, stink, and eat pork. How would your impertinent mouth like that, eh?" He smirked at her reddened face and swollen lip, glad to be seeing the back of her.

CHAPTER TWENTY

David steeled himself to enter the house but couldn't quite urge his body to move towards it. He stood on the other side of the street, in the exact same spot as he had on the night he'd first laid eyes on the young couple's home, and he cursed Garcia with every breath he took.

Watching the people in the street staring into the house through the shuttered window reminded him of pilgrims visiting a shrine. Women arrived with woollen blankets, bread, and steaming cooking pots exuding smells of kid meat and vegetables. They knocked on the door, and he saw his mother's tear-stained face.

The mood in the street was sombre, but it was also tinged with fear and anger. Every face held shock in red-rimmed eyes and half-open mouths. It was as though they still couldn't quite believe what had happened to the young family. People here would only find peace when someone had been punished for a crime that sickened and terrified them, David thought. Therefore, it would be only a matter of time before the duke and Garcia found it necessary to sacrifice an innocent man to appease the town's need for justice. It would be an easy task for them to pick someone at random, torture him, and extract a confession, for when prisoners suffered the agonies inflicted by a skilful torturer, the vast majority said exactly what the interrogator wanted to hear.

It wouldn't be him. No, they wouldn't accuse him of anything. If he faced a public death, and it would have to be a public spectacle, he would scream the truth about the crime to every citizen before the executioner had time to shut him up.

The duke wouldn't risk pointing the finger at him. No, if they were planning to kill him, they would be thinking about a more subtle murder. He'd be taken somewhere outside of town into the mountains or maybe to the densest area of the forest. His body would never be found. He'd be a good meal for the wolves.

Death terrified him. Any man who said he wasn't afraid of it was a liar. He'd woken up that morning grateful to be alive but wondering why Garcia hadn't finished him off yet. He'd go about his business today thinking that it might be his last. The next time he got into bed, his dagger would be in his hand. He probably wouldn't have a peaceful night's sleep ever again.

He straightened his shoulders. What was wrong with him? His brother had died trying to save his father's property, yet here *he* stood, unharmed and wallowing in self-pity. Garcia was a bully, but like all bullies, he was also a coward, and like all cowards, he would prey on the helpless and run from the strong … The whoreson didn't have permission to commit murder, for had the duke ordered an assassination, he, David, would already be dead.

At last, David found his nerve and walked towards the house, passing men and women who were visibly shaken by what had occurred two nights previously. He said good morrow to them and walked on, focusing his eyes on the door. A man put his hand on David's arm and tutted disapprovingly. "How could anyone want to live in a blood-filled house? I wouldn't live there if they paid me a bucketful of ducats," the man said.

"I hope you lot find out who did this," a woman said.

"You'd better. If you don't, this town will never recover," another person added.

David nodded. "We will. Go back to your business. Leave these people in peace." Even with his glaring disapproval, those who were already standing seemed determined not to move. There was nothing he could do, David thought, apart from appealing to their consciences. "I've come to visit my parents. There's nothing to see here," he told the neighbours again. "Go on now. Go back to your homes and let my mother and father grieve for their youngest son … and thank you for your kindness," he added, recognising the women who had brought blankets and food.

"I don't want you here," Juan told David, grabbing his boots and then sitting on the edge of the bed to put them on. "If you don't go, I will."

"I'll leave Papa. I just want to make sure you're both all right."

"Do we look all right? Do you see what you've brought us to? Your mother is wiping blood from the wall and the floor!"

"Hush, you foolish man!" Isa snapped. "There are people right outside the door. Do you want the whole town to hear you?"

"I want him gone," Juan told her in a quieter voice. He's not welcome here."

"He has my welcome, and by God, he'll have yours too. When are you going to stop being angry with him?"

Juan grumbled, "Not for as long as I take breath."

"You're taking breath now because of him," Isa retorted. "We'd be dead with our throats cut if it hadn't been for his sacrifice."

"His sacrifice? What about the poor souls he killed? What about their sacrifice? And how do you know we'd be dead were it not for what he did?"

David said, "I'm sure of it, Papa."

"Did you hear that, Juan? He's sure, and I believe him. He's our son ... and he's the only one we have left," Isa said, now sobbing.

David went to the window, putting distance between himself and his father. The closed shutters allowed only narrow ribbons of light to enter. It was a dreary day, and had the focus of the townspeople not been on the murders, everyone would have been talking about the possibility of rain.

He turned to face the room. Candles flickered in the corners, casting shadows of his parents' forms on the walls. The cot and partition curtain had disappeared. The little girl's straw pallet was also gone, and even the pots and pans, chamber pots, and a small pile of clothes that had been there had been removed.

"Papa, I'll find you another house. You can't live here. I can afford to pay your rent until you get on your feet. I spoke to the blacksmith. He'll take you on. He knows you're a good saddle maker, and he's happy to let you use an empty space in his workshop."

"I don't want your help." Juan's voice was defiant, but his eyes lit up at the prospect of work.

David continued, spurred on by his father's thinly veiled interest. "Papa, there are rumours up at the castle. They say the inquisitor is coming. He'll bring men-at-arms, horses, and mules. They'll use the blacksmith, and you'll get plenty of commissions for bridles and saddles, purses, and travel chests ... There are vacant houses on the other side of town. I've seen them. I've already asked about the rent."

"I said I don't want anything from you!" Juan hissed loudly. "I will find my own way and look after your mother without your money or your council."

David recoiled at the forcefulness of his father's words.

Isa, now fully weeping, lay on the bed and pushed her face into the new mattress.

"You see what you've done to your mother?" Juan said angrily.

"I'll leave. I'm sorry, Mama."

Isa turned her head and sat up. "You're not going anywhere." She looked at Juan with eyes blazing with anger. "You always were as stubborn as a hot fly, Juan Sanz, but this time I will be just as obstinate. I miss my Juanjo and Diego. I might die of grief … It's suffocating me, and I can't breathe! This is our only son, and you love him, as much as I do. We are a family, and only as a family will I survive this terrible time." She choked back her tears and swallowed painfully.

Crawling across the bed to where Juan sat, she put her arms around his neck and kissed the top of his head. "My love, if you send David away, I will leave with him," she warned him gently. "Now, you listen to me. If there's a job for you with the blacksmith, you must take it and be thankful, for I won't forgive you if we starve because of your selfish pride. I don't want to live here. I've cleaned every bit of this place, and I still see and smell death and innocent babies – and that little girl's terrified face when Diego took her to God only knows where! I can't live here, so if David says he can help us, then that's what we'll let him do."

David, still standing by the window, watched his father's hand stroking his mother's arm, which was still curved around his neck, and asked, "Papa, will you forgive me?"

Juan sighed. "I'm your father, and I would die for you. I love you son, but you must ask God for forgiveness, and I must ask yours for the terrible words I've spoken."

Relieved to hear his father's kind words, David asked, "Did Father Bernardo send you here?"

"No, he looked after us," Juan said. "He gave us and another family broth and bread as well as these old clothes. We were told to wait until the council found us somewhere to live. The lord treasurer himself came to the church and settled us and two other families. He asked for our names, told us not to worry about our debts because the duke had forgiven them, and then he gave us his condolences. He insisted on bringing us right to this door. He then came inside and ordered his men to remove the previous owners' belongings."

David scoffed at the duke's generosity regarding the unpaid rent on the farm.

Isa said, "We accepted gratefully, son. Garcia doesn't suspect us. He asked about Diego's whereabouts. Your father told him that your brother had joined a ship's crew some days ago and that he wouldn't be coming back."

"I wanted to kill the bastard for putting us in here," Juan spat. "Does he mean to watch our every move?"

"I don't know, but we have to presume that is the case," David suggested.

A loud rattling knock at the door and raised voices outside stopped the conversation. Juan got up from the bed and cracked the door open to see what the commotion was. A man and woman, both about his age, stood surrounded by an even larger crowd of people than were there before David arrived. The man's face was drained of colour. The woman's swollen eyes looked as though they hadn't closed in days.

"You have a soldier in there with you?" the man asked Juan.

"Yes, he's my son. What's this about?"

Pushing past Juan, the man and woman stepped inside the room. Juan quickly closed the door, barring the onlookers, and turned to face the strangers.

The man's arm was around the woman's shoulders. The woman's arms were clasped around his waist. "Look at my poor daughter's house," she sobbed loudly.

The man said, "My name is Eduardo. This is my wife, Alma. This was my daughter's house ... our little girl's." He was crying now as well. "Her name was Elena, and her husband's name was Adolfo. The children were named Angelita and Matias."

Alma pointed to Isa. "You're sitting where my Elena sat three mornings ago, feeding her infant. I was here with her. I had brought her some potage. I thought it would do her good."

"Our deepest condolences, Alma," Isa said tearfully.

Looking at Juan, Isa, and David in turn, Alma sniggered contemptuously. "Condolences? What kind of people are you? How could you come to live here when my family's blood still stains the walls and their murderers are still at large? You're worse than vultures picking at flesh! My child is not yet cold in her grave ... You shouldn't be here. No one should live in this house!" Alma was crying breathlessly.

The man said, "This is a disgrace. It's disrespectful. Can you not see what this is doing to us? We've lost everything!" His wild angry eyes flicked from left to right. "Are we not to have their possessions? I made the baby's crib with my own two hands. Where is it? My wife here sewed every sheet and blanket and all the children's garments. What have you done with their personal belongings?"

Juan said awkwardly, "Your family's possessions were taken away by the lord treasurer. We had nothing to do with their removal ... He told us we had to live here. You see, marauders burned down our house, and our son was killed."

David saw the man glaring at him and thought he should say something, but he found it difficult to find words of solace when he was the cause of everyone's grief. He wanted to tell

Eduardo and Alma that their infant grandson was alive and well at the castle and that their granddaughter was with Diego, far away by now.

"No decent Christian would live here now. You lost your son, but we lost our family and you're making yourself at home as though they never existed!" the woman shouted at Isa.

Upon hearing his mother crying loudly, David finally found his voice. "That's enough. I can't even begin to imagine the pain you must be feeling, but please don't take your anger out on my parents," he said. "Can you not see my mother and father's sorrow? They too have lost a child. Their home has been destroyed. They have lost all their possessions, and they were forced to live here against their will."

Juan asked gently, "Do you really think we would be here if we'd been offered any other roof over our heads?"

David said. "We'll find the culprits. Every militiaman who can be spared is out looking for them. They will face justice soon enough."

"No one will tell us anything!" the man snapped. "The duke sent his condolences, but when I went to the castle to seek an audience with him this morning, he wouldn't even see me." He asked David, "Are you searching for my grandchildren? They might have been taken to the port. Is your cavalry looking to the north or towards Valencia? If the scum manage to get our little ones into the city, you'll never be able to find them … Why have you not caught the swine yet?"

Alma said, "Angelita has the curliest of hair. Matías, the baby, is marked by God. He has a deep red patch in the centre of his back. It's shaped like a fig. Please … please find them. I know they're alive!" And she wept again.

"Eduardo, Alma, you have my oath," David said. "We won't stop looking. We're searching as far and as wide as we can. Every soldier in Sagrat wants justice for you. We're using all our resources. We'll give up our night's rest to hunt these monsters, if that's what it takes." David hoped his words would appease them; however, he was sadly mistaken.

"This house is evil now," Eduardo said. "Nothing good will come of you living here. Best you move out and leave it to the devil." With this parting shot, Eduardo took Alma by the arm and left.

David felt his lungs being crushed by guilt.

Juan sat back down on the bed and held Isa in his arms.

CHAPTER TWENTY-ONE

David picked his way through the streets, feeling a bit better now that he'd seen his parents. At the distant sound of thunder, he looked up and saw that the sky had darkened further. From his position halfway up the hill, he could just about make out the sea in the distance; above it, a sheet of black clouds was sweeping across the heavens and heading towards the town. They would see a good downpour at last, he thought.

As he turned a corner, a biting wind whipped back his cloak. Grabbing its edges, he pulled it tighter across his chest and was immediately reminded of the young Jewish woman he had escorted to prison the previous day. She'd be freezing in that cell. Some of the prisoners incarcerated during the winter months died of the cold. No visitors were allowed, and basic items, such as blankets or combs to untangle hair, were denied. Comforts such as hot broth and freshly cooked meat never reached the incarcerated, unless they were wealthy and could pay for those privileges.

The Jew, Sinfa, had left him with an ugly feeling of shame. Garcia had struck her as though she were a mule that needed to be beaten when stubborn. Yet neither he nor any other soldier present had found the courage to stop the treasurer. The young woman had courage, David thought. She'd bravely stood up to Garcia, with chin jutting out in prideful defiance and her mouth full of protests. She'd been humiliated and scorned just moments after burying her only family. She'd lost everything in that house, yet she had looked almost regal.

He felt as though they shared a strange alliance. Her grandfather and Juanjo had both been victims of the same crime, perpetrated by the very men the townspeople were supposed to look up to. The duke would more than likely leave Sinfa Cabrera to rot inside those freezing walls, for he would not want to be reminded of her again. Garcia would make sure she was severely punished for her outburst against him. She had called him a coward. God help her, for he supposed that would be unforgivable in Garcia's mind.

Walking along one of the wider streets, David spotted a mule and cart. It stopped outside a house. He caught up with it, paying no heed to the driver, who was piddling up a wall. But then the man turned and climbed up into the driver's seat. David saw his face. His mood darkened once again. Striding angrily towards the cart just as the man was about to drive away, David caught hold of the mule's reins. Seething, he said, "Remember me, you thieving bastard?"

There was no recognition in the man's expression, but David was still convinced that it was him. "You took my boar and left my family with nothing to eat, you spawn of a whore!"

The cart driver's face turned bright red, but even under David's intense scrutiny, he refused to admit his guilt. Instead, he seemed deeply offended at the very suggestion.

"Get lost. I don't know what you're talking about. I never stole anything from anyone," the man grunted angrily.

Flashes of David's mother's meagre table with nothing but bread, cheese, and two wrinkled potatoes came to mind.

"Get down from there before I drag you off your high-and-mighty position and set you on your arse. Down – now!"

"Look here, soldier. I don't know you. I've never eaten a wild boar in my miserable life. If only me and my motherless children were so lucky."

For a second, David wondered if he had made a mistake. Then the man smirked and David remembered the same toothless, rotting gums of the man who'd sped away with the boar in the back of his cart. His rage came upon him from nowhere, and his self-disgust rose to the surface.

Gripping the driver's breeches, he pulled them with such force that the man tumbled off the cart and onto the ground. David reached down and picked the thief up by the tunic collar. He was so enraged that he smashed his head into the man's face. As he recovered, he stood back and was satisfied to see the man's bloodied lips.

Pulling the man towards him until their noses were almost touching, he then threw the thief against the side of the cart's straw wall and threatened through bared teeth, "Don't lie to me. I know it was you."

"Get your hands off me. I don't know you!" the man insisted.

David's fisted punch broke the man's nose on contact. The thief moaned as blood poured from both of his nostrils.

Without hesitating, David clenched his fists again and swung a crippling blow to the man's belly, and then another to the face. The cart driver bent over double and gasped for air, and then he straightened his body and swung his arms up to cover his face with his hands. "Don't … don't hit me again," he cried like a squealing piglet.

David heard the man mumbling through his swollen lips, but all he could think about was the boar. There just might be some left. His mother and father could do with a piece of meat or even unpicked bones to make broth. "Where is it? Where's the beast?"

Panting with breathlessness, the man stuttered, "I-inside me … Nothing left of it. You won't get it back … unless you eat my shit."

David felt an overwhelming urge to hit the man repeatedly, but he suddenly became aware of the commotion behind him. Turning, he noticed the crowd of people encircling him. He faced the thief, who was clinging on to the side of the cart for dear life, and hit him again, this time across the top of the head.

"If I ever see you near the barracks again, you'll find yourself in prison with your hands cut off," he said. "I hope the meat putrefies inside your belly and your arse shoots fire!"

"Give me your name, you bastard. I want your name," the thief shouted, gripping his sore belly.

A woman standing with her arms crossed and looking furious said to the thief, "I know who he is, Moniño. I know his mother. His name is Sanz." And then she wagged her finger in David's face. "You're a big bully. Go pick on someone your own size," she said.

"I'll get you back for this, *soldado*! I'll remember your name – you see if I don't!" David heard the thief shout.

Walking up a steep incline, David laboured to catch his breath. He hadn't slept properly for days. He was tired, yet his body radiated with energy. He wiped the sweat off his face and strode on until a thunderous noise stopped him in his tracks just as he reached the final bend before the prison. Feeling as though the ground were moving beneath his feet, he turned and gasped at what he saw. Coming up the road behind him was a procession of horses, mules, men-at-arms, carriages, a golden cross as tall as a house, and the Inquisition's seal of cross, branch, and sword imprinted on flags. The inquisitor had arrived.

CHAPTER TWENTY-TWO

The inquisitor, Gaspar de Amo, arrived in Sagrat with all the pomp and ceremony of a monarch. Accompanying him were scribes, a theological assessor, public prosecutor, a civilian guard who policed the legal proceedings, a receiver dealing with confiscated goods, a magistrate responsible for administering sequestered properties, a messenger, and a physician.

Inquisition volunteers were also in the entourage, swelling the inquisitor's ostentatious convoy further. These included representatives of ordinary civil jurisdiction, consultants, a torturer, and familiars, who were an armed troop of twenty men, and Gaspar de Amo's protection against would-be assassins.

Being elected to one of the five royal councils which followed the Holy Office had allowed the inquisitor immense power and latitude in all decisions concerning Inquisition arrests, preparations for judgement cases, and verdicts. The old Inquisition, which had lasted almost two hundred years, was all but obsolete in Aragon. Under the control of bishops with little zeal, it had run its course and depleted its resources. The inquisitor believed, however, that this new Inquisition age, encompassing both Castile and Aragon, was one that would succeed beyond expectations and last for a thousand years.

In the past few years, an uncomfortable and at times confrontational debate had simmered between Pope Sixtus IV and the Spanish monarchs. After nine years, De Amo could still recite every word written in a papal letter to the Spanish bishops. It had been blatantly insulting:

In Aragon, Valencia, Mallorca, and Cataluña, the Inquisition has for some time been moved not by zeal for the faith and the salvation of souls but by lust for wealth. Many true and faithful Christians, on the testimony of enemies, rivals, slaves, and other lower and even less proper persons, have without any legitimate proof been thrust into secular prisons, tortured and condemned as relapsed heretics. They have been deprived of their goods and property and handed over to the secular arm to be executed, setting a pernicious example and causing disgust to many.

Nonsense, De Amo thought now, just as he'd thought nine years ago. Rome had wielded too much power over the Spanish sovereigns, and he'd worked tirelessly on King Ferdinand and Queen Isabella's behalf to shift the Inquisition's authority over to them. He was satisfied with his efforts and of his years of devotion, for after trials of strength with the papacy, the advantage finally turned to the Spanish monarchs.

The defence of the faith and the battle against heresy were now the responsibility of the court, with powers delegated by the papacy but answerable to the civil authority, which appointed its magistrates. The inquisitor strongly believed that Valencia would be a blessed quest to fulfil the dreams of many, for with God's good grace, it would be united in faith and worship. No longer would its territories have to endure the evils of Judaism in silence, and Jews would never again corrupt the minds and souls of weak Christian converts. Soon their dwindling number would be thrown out of Spain for good.

In the past two years, he had rounded up and imprisoned hundreds of suspected heretics. He had executed ten, or was it twele? Many had told him that his work ethics were excellent.

His prisons in Zaragoza and in the city of Valencia were full. He'd augmented revenues for the Inquisition by arresting persons of high standing and thus had been able to sequestrate enough of the detainee's possessions to pay for their upkeep and food. That was not lust for wealth, as the pope had stated; it was just good business.

A short time ago, he had tried a man for heresy and had found him guilty. He would always remember that particular interrogation, for under torture the accused had admitted to declaring in public meetings that the Inquisition fathers were carrying out their trials and executions on rich people as much for taking property and money as for defending the faith. He'd also said that the goods were the heretics, not the men and women so charged. The impudent bastard would spend the rest of his life in prison for those heretic statements!

Looking out his carriage window and seeing Sagrat's castle for the first time, he thought about the imprisoned errant flock of heretics and Judaists spread across a hundred leagues and determined that every decision he'd made thus far had been the right one. It had taken him a long time to obtain Thomas de Torquemada's permission to hold an auto-de-fé, Spain's biggest public display of faith. Sagrat, he thought, would be the perfect town to put on such a solemn occasion.

He ran his fingers across his rosary beads and began to pray. He was not clergy, and he had not taken holy orders, yet prayer brought him clarity and comfort. Every day he fought the elation of pride and the sin of vanity. He was, he kept reminding himself, an instrument of Rome and her Catholic teachings, which of course deserved all the glory. But even so, what harm could it do to recognise that he had done a truly magnificent job in bringing poor misguided souls back to the Catholic Church? Soon the people would witness his good works for themselves, and they would see that a heretic could travel only two paths: one to redemption and the other to the fire.

From inside the carriage, he watched his familiars roughly manhandling the townspeople off the thoroughfare. The onlookers' faces, which were filled with curiosity, amused him, for he knew that their initial interest in his cavalcade would turn to fear. He had witnessed this in every town and city he'd been to. He doubted these people had ever seen the full force of an Inquisition's power in their lifetime. The old duke of Sagrat had managed to hold the Holy Office at bay, but only because he had generously ploughed the king and queen with money and bribes. Soon, these people would take measures to hide their heresy, just as the people of Zaragosa and Cataluña had. But they would be unsuccessful.

This town, with more Jews than any other in Valencia, was rife with contaminated Christians and those who feigned devotion to the one true faith. But he would catch them all out because his job was to instil fear and surprise in the faithful, and he was very good at it.

Coming to the kingdom of Aragon had not been an easy decision for him to make. He was well aware of the long-standing hatred between inquisitors, noblemen, and aristocrats. There was not a man in Spain who had not heard about the inquisitor who'd been murdered in Saragoza. He felt sick thinking about the sainted man who had died at the hands of heretic bastards. Cannon Pedro Arbués was a martyr. He had gone to Teruél, a town high in the mountains, to save souls, and upon his arrival, the municipal magistrates had forced him to leave the town. The municipality was excommunicated from the church for their insolence, of course, but *he* would have taken matters much further than Arbués had he been the inquisitor.

Teruel should have been a warning of what was to come for the canon, but even if he had heeded the threat of plots against him, he would still have continued with his sacred duty, thus was his devotion to the Holy Office.

Six years had passed since Pedro Arbués's death. Before his brutal murder, he had survived two assassination attempts. He'd even worn armour and a helmet in an effort to protect himself. Unfortunately, the paid assassins knew this, and when they struck him with a dagger, it was with perfect precision, just below the helmet and above the collar. *What better way is there to show God love than being slaughtered whilst kneeling in prayer to Him?* De Amo thought.

A surge of resentment rose. It hardly seemed fair that the grand inquisitor, Torquemada, had 250 men-at-arms to protect him and he had but 20.

Making sure his armour was properly secured, the inquisitor pushed his helmet down until it completely covered his neck. He too was forced to wear a chain mail vest and iron helmet hidden beneath his hooded cloak. There was no shame in taking precautions, he continually told himself. And once he got everything under control he would have no need of such attire...The people of Valencia would have a rude awakening soon, for he had no intention of taking a soft approach or dying at the hands of Judaists or noblemen who were still stirring up trouble in this region.

CHAPTER TWENTY-THREE

Luis stood up and kicked the front of his chair with his heel in a childish tantrum. "He's here? How close is he?"

"Within the castle walls, Your Grace. He'll arrive at your doors within minutes," Garcia answered.

Staring past Garcia, Luis said, "I shouldn't be surprised. But today of all days! I'm not ready for him. I need more time to deal with this sewer of troubles. You were supposed to have dealt with them before the inquisitor's arrival."

"I am …"

"If that's so, why is the council still talking about the murders and abductions? We supplied witnesses testifying to having seen marauders running from *that* house. Why do they doubt the testimonies? Well, what do you say?" Luis paced up and down the room. "For God's sake, say something!" he shouted with annoyance at Garcia's hesitance.

"Your Grace, the council doesn't answer to me, and I can't answer for them. I've told you what I know," Garcia said calmly. "The members of your council are suspicious. They cannot understand why only one street in the town was targeted … and why that particular home. Some of them believe that the assailant must have known the victims. They are asking the magistrate to investigate further. You can refuse to accept their decision to pursue this. As duke, it's quite within your right."

"I do refuse! By God, I do. I'll have them all locked up as heretics if they don't drop the matter. My word should be final, not theirs. How dare these commoners muddy waters best left calm?" His own council, men chosen by him, had the gall to make decisions without him being present, he thought. He'd have their hides. "What else did my *loyal* council of men say?"

"They were disappointed to see the militia coming back empty-handed. The people need answers, Your Grace. When the bodies of the man and woman were buried, their families and just about every able-bodied person in Sagrat attended the funerals, bleating like a flock of lost goats and demanding culprits. Might I suggest you allow this futile investigation to go ahead? Send your soldiers to every house in Sagrat. Let them search for the two missing children. They'll find nothing, and the council will have no need to examine the case further."

Luis was not happy with Garcia's answer. His suggestion didn't give him any comfort or solution. "My son will be baptised within days, and I want the people's joyful faces, not their sorrow or suspicions ... No, this investigation will not go ahead. I won't allow it to interfere with the inquisitor's arrival or my contentment. God's grief, the people are so intent on finding murderers that they've stopped coming forward to denounce heretics. Gaspar de Amo will not be pleased to find an empty prison."

"It's hardly empty," Garcia said in a condescending tone. "There are over twenty prisoners incarcerated, and even with the prison's recent extension, it only has the capacity for seventy people. If I might be so bold, finding heretics is the inquisitor's job, not yours. I wouldn't worry about that. Your prison will be full within days, judging by the size of the inquisitor's entourage now approaching the castle."

True, Luis thought. Maybe when the inquisitor began arresting people en masse, the townspeople would forget about the murders. Garcia had said something hopeful at last. Looking at him, Luis shook his head, still disgusted with the council. "I'm not happy. I'm about to see my power and influence in this town shrivel like a bull's balls in winter. I will have no say in the Inquisition's policies, and now it appears I have no mandate over my council. You need to find a suspect … some wandering vagrant. A drunk, perhaps."

"I would advise against that."

"Why?"

"Your Grace, the people won't believe that one man caused such mayhem."

"Then what do you suggest?"

"That we simply allow the council to proceed."

"I'll damn my soul to hell rather than allow a common herd to tell me what should be done!" Luis shouted petulantly.

Garcia sighed. "Your Grace, you really must leave now if you want to greet the inquisitor's caravan."

Luis was relieved that the old duke wasn't alive to see his town's chaos or the arrival of the inquisitor. He'd always wondered if his father had secretly plotted with other Valencia nobles against the Holy Office and the monarchs. Many of his father's old friends were rotting in prison or had been exiled after losing castles, lands, fortunes, and even the tunics on their backs. But Luis suspected that dissension against the Inquisition was still present in the shadows. *Stupid men,* he thought. *Those rebel nobles should be more like me, keeping my mouth shut and living a good life.*

"What of the physician's granddaughter?" Luis asked Garcia as they walked through the castle's hallways.

"She is incarcerated, Your Grace."

Luis was pensive for a moment and then said, "Good. Leave her there until I find forgiveness in my heart for her grandfather."

"What of her impudence towards me? Should she not be punished for that?"

"Being in my prison is punishment enough. Did you find the hidden money in Cabrera's house?"

"Yes, and it was a goodly amount."

"Did you add it to my pile?"

"I did."

For the first time that day, Luis laughed. "At least Cabrera had something of value to leave me. What fool tells another where his coin is hidden?" He remembered well the discussion he'd had with Saul Cabrera. It had begun on the day the old duke died. Luis had asked Cabrera about his granddaughter and whether she would be well taken care of should anything happen to him. Saul had gushed with pride and had been quite happy to divulge the whereabouts of his life savings.

Luis altered the position of his upturned peaked hat and the feathers stuck on top of it. He looked noble, and he would be a regal host. Now his only task was to please Gaspar de Amo. Pleasing him and getting money from him was all that mattered. He stopped in his tracks. What would please his father-by-law more than a public execution?

"Garcia, contact the mercenaries. Ride with them and find men to burn for the murders. I've come to a decision. I will not let the council or the townspeople spoil my son's baptism or the inquisitor's visit. Don't come back to Sagrat until you have suspects in custody."

"I think you're making a big mistake," Garcia said.

"And I think you are overstepping your position. Don't question my decisions. This is what I want; and by God, this is what I'll have! Leave me. You shall fix this outstanding inconvenience, my lord treasurer, or you'll be finished in this town."

CHAPTER TWENTY-FOUR

David gazed at the young woman through the cell's bars. She was a rare sight in this place. She was not the only woman presently incarcerated, but she was probably the most innocent, the others having been locked up for crimes of debauchery, theft, and adultery.

Sinfa, lying on the dirt floor in a corner, had her face turned towards the wall and her body curled, with knees at her chest. She would not be allowed to see anyone, David thought, continuing to watch her. Prisons were secretive places, barred to anyone but guards, attendants, and authorities. Conversing with prisoners was frowned upon. Visitors were not allowed, and unless food and water were being delivered, the incarcerated remained in permanent isolation. David had no valid reason to go inside the cell to speak to the Jewish girl, for the civilian men, paid by the magistrate's office, attended to the prisoners. But he felt it his duty to protect her and to tell her that she had not been forgotten, at least not by him.

Looking along the passageway, he saw Paco. He sat with his legs up on a tabletop with his arms crossed over his chest, and he was fast asleep, judging by the sound of his snoring and lightly bobbing head. David smiled. Paco wouldn't stir unless a rock fell on top of him. Turning the iron key, David pushed the creaky cell door open, entered, and then closed the door behind him.

Sinfa turned around to face the door. After sitting up, she put her back to the wall, pushed her hair from her face, and squinted in the flaming torchlight. "You were the one who brought me here," she said pitifully to David.

David stood perfectly still and then slowly removed his helmet. "Yes, I did. I'm not going to hurt you. I've brought bread." Watching her stare at the bread with greedy eyes, still flashing with the anger he'd seen when she'd been arrested, he got the impression that she was trying to decide whether she wanted to accept his gift or not. "Pride is a lost cause. You have to eat if you want to survive in here," he said forcibly.

"I would rather have my freedom," Sinfa said, still eying the bread, "but I'll take it and thank you all the same."

"Here, take my cloak too. It's freezing in here."

Scowling now, she said, "You threw me in this cell. What do you care if I'm cold? No, I don't want it ... I would rather freeze to death."

"And I would rather you lived." Without waiting for permission, David put the cloak around her shoulders and reminded her, "I'm a soldier, and that means I have to follow orders, even the ones I don't like. I can't give you back your freedom, Sinfa, but I can make sure you get enough to eat and drink. I'll do what I can to help you. I give you my word."

"Why are you being so kind to me?" she asked suspiciously.

Because I know that your grandfather was murdered by the same man who wants you to rot in here, he wanted to say. Instead, he told her, "You shouldn't be here. This is an injustice."

Between tears, Sinfa agreed. "I don't know what I did wrong ... There have been no charges laid against me. I'm innocent. That man should be in prison for hitting me."

"I know that."

"You do?"

She stood up and took a few hesitant steps towards him. "Would you deliver a message to Rabbi Rabinivitch? Everyone in the Jewry knows who he is," she said. "Ask him to plead with the duke for my release. The duke will listen to him. I know he will. Would you do that for me?"

The duke was a whoreson, and he wouldn't order her release, David thought. And Garcia would do everything in his power to keep her locked up, without allowing her the right to a defence lawyer. "I'll see to it," he said.

Watching her standing there sobbing and chewing at the same time, he wondered what else he could do for her. She was headstrong, and haughty for one so young, yet she looked like a frightened child who needed her mother's arms around her. "I'll come back with more food, and I'll bring you a blanket," he said awkwardly. "Keep the cloak around you. No one needs to know who gave it to you. It's going to rain today, and the temperature in here will drop further. Eat the bread I brought you, and don't refuse anything that's given to you, not even pig's meat. No one will be cruel towards you as long as you don't insult the attendants. Keep that in mind." With that said, he left with the sound of her weeping ringing in his ears.

Boots thumping, men's voices, and the sound of iron grating as it was dragged along the passageway floor startled Paco and David, who were ladling thin gruel into their bowls. They stood, and looking in the direction of the noise, they saw the first of the Inquisition's men-at-arms in the dim light. Wearing chain mail vests, white tunics with a single cross painted on them, red cloaks with the Inquisition's emblem sewed onto the left hand, and shining helmets, they looked like foreign soldiers. Drawing their swords, David and Paco placed their feet in an offensive stance, and eyed the strangers.

"Identify yourselves!" Paco shouted in an unnecessarily loud voice.

"Lower your swords!" one of the men-at-arms shouted back, even though he had come within arm's length of Paco and David.

David studied the man, trying to ascertain if he was comrade or adversary, friendly or aggressive. Looking past him, he saw five or six other men crowding the narrow passageway. "Well, who are you?" Paco asked again.

Puffing up his chest and looking offended at not being recognised, the man standing slightly in front of the others retorted, "You should know who we are. We're the inquisitor's familiars. My name is Raul Dávila. Who's in charge here?"

"I am," Paco answered gruffly. "This is the duke of Sagrat's prison. By whose authority do you come prancing in here unannounced?"

"The Holy Office of Rome and the Inquisition," Dávila said with great pomp. "The inquisitor, Gaspar de Amo, has already presented his credentials to your church and secular authorities."

Paco glanced at David and then stared again at the man. "Familiars? Why do they call you that?"

"Our job is to know everybody's business, including yours."

Paco coughed uncomfortably. "So what can we do for you?" he asked with a bit more respect.

"You can do my bidding. We're here to inspect your prison. For a start, I need a list of your provisions and prisoner names."

Dávila's words were interrupted by the sound of men groaning and heavy objects rattling and banging loudly against the walls.

"Make a path for them," Dávila said to the men directly behind him.

David and Paco exchanged another glance. David suspected that Paco was thinking exactly the same thing that he was. It was blatantly apparent that they had just lost control of the duke's prison.

Devices and furniture filled the guard post area. Tables, chairs, ropes, chains, and empty buckets were set down first. Two torture contraptions being carried by six men followed, but they were left farther down the passageway.

David opened his mouth and shuddered with repulsion at the sight of a long wooden framed device with chains and handles at each end. "What is that?" he asked Dávila.

"We call it the rack."

Paco, looking just as curious as David, asked, "What does it do?"

"The heretic lies on the top of the wooden framed mattress. The prisoner has his hands and feet tied or chained to these rollers here, at one or both ends. Then our torturer turns the rollers with a handle, which pulls the chains or ropes a bit at a time and stretches the heretic's joints. Sometimes they're pulled out of place. I once saw a torturer continue to turn the rollers until the accused man's arm was completely torn off."

David felt sick. Paco's face was drained of colour, and Dávila looked as though he had enjoyed shocking them.

"Your inquisitor hasn't wasted any time in bringing his playthings, eh?" Paco said, clearly trying to inject a bit of humour into the man-at-arms' tale of torture.

"He's not my inquisitor. He's Aragon's inquisitor."

"My apologies," Paco muttered.

Accepting them, Davila continued. "You'll give me and my men a tour of the prison, and when we've finished, we'll need access to your keys. Show my man here a list of your prisoners' names and tell him what crimes they've committed. You two can stay at your posts until the Inquisition formally takes over ... Who are these people?" he asked, pointing to three prison attendants cowering in a corner.

"They attend to the prisoners' needs. Our prisoners are mostly petty criminals. Only a few stay here long term," Paco said. "I doubt the Inquisition will be interested in them."

"These attendants can go home. They won't be needed here anymore. As for the prisoners, the inquisitor is interested in every crime committed, whether they are sins against neighbours or God. All criminals have affronted our Lord and his church in some way or another. The inquisitor will decide whether the convicts are innocent or guilty."

David was beginning to feel uncomfortable in the presence of men who had not once parted their lips in a smile. Thinking about Sinfa, he said, "We have a Jewish girl incarcerated. What will happen to her?"

"Our inquisitor has no interest in Jews. They have never been baptised; therefore, they cannot be called heretics," Dávila said. "He cares only for his Christian flock. Your magistrate can deal with her as he sees fit."

David decided not to press the matter further. Taking a step back, he leaned against the wall with a passive expression. Listening to Paco and Dávila discussing what should be done first, he wondered what *would* happen to Sinfa. And what was going to happen to Sagrat and its people?

CHAPTER TWENTY-FIVE

Garcia stood with hands on hips and glared at Tur in a challenge of wills. Tur threw Garcia a thunderous look and then raised his harsh-toned voice. "What you are asking is out of the question," he said.

Garcia was livid. He would have liked to strike the bastard and wipe the insolence off his mouth. But Tur was a consummate swordsman, a hard man who did not take kindly to having fun poked at him or orders thrown at him by anyone but the duke. A corpulent man, his head seemed far too big for his body, and his ruddy face and coarse brown hair that fell about his ears made him look like a rough mountain goat herder. He was probably the only man in this town that Peráto would call indispensable. He would have to be handled very carefully.

"I don't have time to stand here debating with you, Captain," Garcia said. "Give me the horse and prison cart or I'll report you to the duke for your impertinence."

"You say the duke knows about this?"

"Of course he does. Why else would I be here?"

Still looking unhappy, Tur expelled a heavy sigh. "Then I should send my men with you. Surely you're not thinking of detaining the suspects on your own? You need the cavalry. This is what they've been trained for."

The last thing I need is the militia by my side, Garcia thought. He could just picture the scene and what he would say to the soldiers when he found random victims foolish enough to be wandering about in the dark: "Arrest these men ... They are completely innocent, but they look as though they will confess to murders, abduction, and mayhem at the drop of a hat."

"If I had any need of your men, I would have asked for them," he told Tur with a slightly calmer voice. "The suspects are being held at the port by people the duke trusts. He wants this handled quietly. The inquisitor has just arrived, and the duke doesn't think it fitting to interrupt his papal mission with the thunder of hooves galloping down the hill after murderers. The scum will not be dragged into town in chains, escorted by your cavalry and knights … and you will speak to no one about this until I return. Do you understand me, Captain?"

"Yes, I understand, Your Honour."

Garcia climbed onto the prison cart, much like any other cart that trundled through the streets but with a wooden roof and bars on each side and back. Glaring once more at Tur, he said, "Just make sure you're here when I return with the suspects. You can have your moment of glory then. I'll hand them over to you. You can escort them to the prison, and afterwards you will tell your men to spread the word to every house and hovel in this town. Don't disappoint me, Captain." He slapped the reins and drove off.

Still muttering angrily under his breath, Garcia cleared the last of the streets and headed onto the open plain in a northward direction. He was furious. The duke's foolish and inconvenient plan to hold a public execution to appease the townspeople was the whim of an overindulged and naive nobleman who was too stupid to realise that he was putting his own aristocratic arse in danger by pursuing this matter.

Garcia had asked Peráto one simple question before he'd left: "How will I convince the militia and the town council that I was able to find, overpower, and incarcerate murderers on my own?" The bastard had answered, "This isn't my problem. It's your problem."

Garcia looked skyward. Fast-moving black clouds filled the heavens, whipping up a strong wind which caused the rain to fall in horizontal sheets. He bowed his head against the cold torrent of water and pulled the top of his hood down onto his chin. "May God damn you to hell, Peráto. Looking for men to burn in your town square is a waste of my valuable time," he mumbled under his breath.

After travelling half a league to the north of Sagrat, Garcia jumped down and led the mule and cart up an incline. When he got to the top, he once again took the reins and drove the cart as fast as he could, finally reaching a rocky plain heading inland towards the mountains.

Halting, he tied the horse's reins to the wooden shaft at the side of the cart and walked towards a crevice. Stopping just before he reached it, he cast his eyes over the area. He lifted his arm and waved it in the air. Men were watching him. They were probably hiding behind rocks on the higher ground in front of him and inside one of the many deep cracks in the ground, running like veins.

The mercenaries' leader, Alejandro, had chosen a good hideout, he thought. The terrain was wild and virginal, as though man had never claimed it or tamed it. The rocky valley leading to the base of the mountains inland was overgrown with prickly cacti, tall grass hiding deep potholes that could swallow a horse and rider, and shallow hills that were like gentle waves, obscuring the inland pathway he had just taken.

Cautiously walking through waist-high weeds and taking care not to kick or trip over hidden rocks on the ground, he eventually reached the crevice he was looking for. He raised his hands in the air again for good measure and called out his name. "Sergio Garcia. I'm here to see Alejandro!" This was the third time he'd come here, and he hated this part the most. Some of the mercenaries knew him, but there was always the chance that one of them could get trigger-happy and fire a longbow dart without asking questions first.

A man's face appeared at the crevice's lip. He held a crossbow pointed at Garcia's head.

Looking at the arrow's tip, Garcia forgot his fear and said impatiently, "It's me, you fools. Didn't you hear me shout?"

The crevice was shoulder deep and about three feet wide. Holding on to the banks, Garcia jumped into the centre of the crack, and sidled awkwardly to an opening farther along. He looked down at a hole, which was just wide enough to allow an average man's body to slip through it, and sighed with relief when he saw a rope ladder attached to a large rock. Good, he thought, at least there was a proper ladder in place. The last time he'd been here, all he had to grab on to was a rope.

Garcia was not afraid of Alejandro, but he was mindful of the marauder's hardened criminal mind and penchant towards violence. Alejandro could never be fully trusted, Garcia had remarked to Peráto when the duke asked him what he thought of the thief. But he did seem to be a strong leader, and he had a reputation amongst his men for being fair when sharing bounties.

A man stood at the bottom of the ladder. He nodded in recognition but said nothing to Garcia. Both men walked a few paces until they reached a low-hanging rock. Garcia got onto his knees, grunted with disgust, and then followed the mercenary. The narrow low narrow ceiling cavern was the most awkward part of the caves to manoeuvre. The iron cold rocky ground underneath Garcia dug into his thin hose, ripping them at the knees and cutting his skin. He could feel every stone, hard and unyielding, bruising his legs and palms. His grunt of displeasure was audible. How anyone could live like this, he'd never know. These men earned a decent living stealing from others, yet they chose to live like animals underneath the ground. What was the point of having coin if not to use it whoring, drinking, and living comfortably in a fine home? Garcia had always wondered.

The man finally spoke. "Alejandro is up ahead. He wasn't expecting you."

So what? Garcia thought. He had money for Alejandro. He didn't need an invitation. "Just hurry up. I've got an urgent job for him," he told the man.

At the end of the tunnel, a large opening appeared. The moment he entered the high-ceilinged cave, Garcia heard the sound of running water coursing down the rocks. It had been a while since rain had soaked these walls, he thought. Only once before had he seen the reservoir fill with such a tide of water. No one knew how deep the underground lake was, for no man had ever touched the bottom of it with his feet. It was ironic, he thought. All this fresh water lay under the ground, yet Sagrat had suffered a drought. Shame the people didn't know of its existence.

A boat was anchored at each end of the waterway. Garcia got into one of them and sat down, looked at his bloodied legs, and grumbled to himself. As the man rowed, he went over his plan again. On a wet day like this, there would be a greater chance of finding drunks and vagabonds at the coast than anywhere else he could think of. It was already mid-afternoon and would be dark within three hours. They would strike when darkness fell. He cursed the rain again. He couldn't go back to Sagrat empty-handed, but it wasn't going to be easy finding victims when everyone was probably scurrying for shelter under roofs.

After getting off the boat, Garcia had to climb a small incline before reaching the entrance to the largest cavern. Inside, oil-lit torches and soft glowing campfires sat on shiny flat rocks which looked as though they had been polished. Around him, shadows stole across the walls, nebulous and eerily unfamiliar. Scattered throughout the cave were conical pillars rising up from the floor, and above his head, other pillars reached down from the ceiling like long arms fused into the stone.

He blinked, adjusting his eyes to the brighter light, and then he scanned the enormous space, big enough to fit more than one hundred grown men. He walked past two men sitting by a campfire, and they nodded to him in recognition.

"Where's Alejandro?" Garcia asked.

"Walk on. He's in the next cavern," the man told him.

Nodding his thanks, Garcia took a step, and then he stopped with a thought that had just come crashing into his mind. He could order Alejandro to perform, not one, but two tasks. The duke and Alejandro didn't know each other, and they would never meet. It was the perfect opportunity to get rid of a problem that was plaguing him, and Peráto would never have to know anything about it …

CHAPTER TWENTY-SIX

In the port of Sagrat, Diego Sanz huddled beneath an awning dipping in the middle with the weight of rainwater. What in God's name was he doing here? he asked himself for the umpteenth time that day. He should be in the city of Valencia by now, sitting in front of a fire in a taverna, heating his bones with a rich wine, a bowl of fish broth in front of him. He would have found work within hours of arriving in the city, for the only thing he'd heard people talk about in the past few days was how important Valencia had become.

People's lives were going to change for the better in this new era of commerce and discovery, they had all agreed. King Ferdinand had granted licence to Valencia's first real port only this year, turning the city into a busy trade centre. There were rumours of great construction sites being built at the edge of the sea to house ships undergoing reparations. He'd also heard that there were plans to build an entirely new fleet of vessels which would be sturdy enough to sail to the other side of the world.

He could have boarded one of the many ships at anchor. He would have accepted even the lowliest of jobs. He wasn't daunted by tales of sickness in the galleys, where men rowed until they dropped like flies. A life at sea was what he wanted and what he would have eventually.

Looking about him, he realized what a small and insignificant place this was compared to Valencia. Sagrat's port was nothing more than a fishing enclave holding a dozen or so small vessels that fished the waters between the mainland and the island of Mallorca, to the east. The boats were not suited to deep open waters and tended to cast their nets no farther than two leagues from the shore. It held no mysteries or adventures. It had nothing to offer other than a scattering of houses bordering the shoreline. Made of wood and stone, they were sturdier than the houses in the town and housed families who earned their living catching and selling fish, lobster, prawns, oysters, mussels, and eels to neighbouring towns, specifically Sagrat and its castle.

Fishermen here had laughed at him when he'd asked for a job. These men had fished all their lives and been forced to give up their boats because of a drop in demand. "It's the monarchy's fault," a man he'd met earlier this day had stated. "The kings are to blame for our hardships. They've scared most of the Jews away, and they were our biggest customers. They give Valencia money to enhance its port, but they forget about us poor fishermen. Our old boats are no match for the bigger vessels in the city. They can get to deeper waters and haul as much in a day as we can in a week. We'll be lucky if there're any fish left around here soon … or customers to buy them."

Diego wiped his wet face and grumbled. There was no real shelter here. The wind was picking up, and the rain was lashing down and hitting him from all angles. He looked out to the thunderous sea. Lines of tall waves with white crests visible even under a black sky were coming ashore one after the other and crashing noisily against the stony banks. White salty sea foam, spraying into the air like giant snowflakes, settled on the ground for just a moment and were then dispersed by rainwater. Boats were being pummelled against rocks, and they made loud snapping noises as timbers split and broke. This was one of the worst storms he'd seen in years. Some of the boats would be lucky to remain afloat.

Standing up, he wrung the water out of his robe's hemline. Thank God he'd found that convent, he thought. The nuns had saved the little girl and had rescued him as well. At the time, he'd not been too keen on wearing monk's attire, but the robes had given him a decent covering for his head and body and had probably stopped him from freezing to death in his night tunic. Diego would never forget the sisters' kindness or their shocked faces after he'd begged them to take the small child crying in his arms.

It was rare for a parent to abandon a child. Children were precious to the Valencian people, who would rather starve themselves than see their sons and daughters want for anything. At first, the sisters had been reluctant to take her in, but they'd relented after he'd spun a heartbreaking tale about the death of his young wife, no other family to help him, and his inability to care for a daughter because he had no work. *I'll come back for her within a period of four weeks*, he'd told them, knowing he probably never would.

Diego walked into the taverna, stood just inside the door, and looked about him. Stepping aside, he let three men pass him on their way out, nodding to one of them. Disappointing, he thought. He knew that man. He might have been kind enough to offer him a pitcher of ale. He pulled his soaking wet hood off his head, closed his eyes for a second, and bathed in the lavish heat emanating from a blazing hearth fire. The smell of freshly cooked meat gave him a heady feeling. He shifted awkwardly from one foot to another, sniffing the air like a dog, and followed the path of a platter of pork and potatoes being served by a wench.

At last, his eyes found Javier Ubeda, a fisherman Diego had known since boyhood. Grinning with pleasure, he called out and walked towards Javier's table, laden with bread, cheese, a carafe of wine, and a fine joint of kid meat.

Javier sat with a friend who seemed to eye Diego's robe with both curiosity and humour. "You're not a monk, are you?

Where's your bald patch?" he asked, pointing to the crown of his head.

"A monk! Who, this strapping lad?" Javier said. "Rafael, this is Juan Sanz's son Diego. They've got a farm on the plain. I've known his father for years. Diego here wants to be a fisherman. Isn't that right, lad?"

"I do, now more than ever. Our farm got burnt by marauders a few days past," Diego told him. "Juanjo was killed."

"So it was *your* brother?"

"He died trying to save our mule," Diego said in a cracked voice. "We never did find that cursed animal."

"We heard about the fires and that a boy was killed. You have my condolences," Javier said.

Nodding his thanks, Diego said, "I suppose you heard about that family in Sagrat too?"

"We did, and there's not a person who's been able to find rest since it happened. It's not right, I tell you. People are scared to go to sleep without putting daggers under their pillows. Imagine an entire family being wiped out on the same night. They'll never find those babies. No, they'll be dead and buried or long gone from here by now. It's a sad time we're living in."

"We're living in dangerous times," Rafael added, "and the king doesn't seem to care. He's too busy conquering Granada from the moors with his Castilian wife to worry about us poor *Valencianos* and our troubles."

"What's the duke doing about those murders in the town, lad?" Javier asked Diego. "I heard he sent the militia out and they returned with not so much as a whiff of the culprits. He needs to do more. His soldiers are no good to man or beast, if you ask me. All they seem interested in doing lately is arresting people for no good reason. They should be defending the likes of us, for we can't defend ourselves."

"I'm sure they're doing all they can," Diego answered lamely. "David's in the militia now. Did you know that?"

"Your elder brother?"

Diego nodded.

"Well, tell him from me that the people here are scared. Did you hear about one of our carts being robbed?"

"No."

"It was robbed of its fish – bastards! Fish! Only the foulest turds of the lowest scum would do something like that. It happened the morning after those terrible murders." He gestured to Rafael. "We think the thieving swine are local. Don't we?"

"Got to be," Rafael agreed. "The attacks are becoming more and more frequent, and the robbers seem to know exactly where and when to strike. They're not pirates. We would know if they were. We don't take our eyes off the sea. If a tick on a fly's back floated in, we'd see it ... My deepest condolences, lad. Your parents must be devastated, losing a son like that. Here, eat with us. Warm your bones."

Diego's eyes brightened. His belly rumbled at the thought of food coming his way. "I think I will," he said.

CHAPTER TWENTY-SEVEN

The taverna's door burst open and banged loudly against the wall with a gust of wind. Antonio Marsal, a local man, staggered inside like a drunk, with glassy eyes and his tongue sticking out of the side of his mouth with exhaustion. His hands, pressing against his belly, were covered in blood and rainwater, colouring them pink. His ripped tunic looked as though a wolf had mauled it. His hair, bloodied and matted, dripped rose-coloured water onto his face, which was creased with pain, and into his wild, feverish eyes.

Not looking at anyone in particular, he moaned words like a Latin hymn and made no sense at all, until finally he managed to utter a few brief sentences. "I'm dying ... Help me ... God, help me!"

Many of the revellers were already on their feet. Some were shouting questions, others rushed towards him, and there were those who seemed to be rooted to their seats in violent shock.

"They took them ... Stop them ... Get them back!" His outstretched bloodied hands grasped the shoulders of the first man to reach him, and then his legs buckled.

"Lay him down!" someone shouted.

"Who are *them*?" another asked.

"Please save them ... Outside ... You have to save them. Marauders." Antonio's hoarse voice was almost inaudible.

Diego watched the commotion and listened to the enraged voices soar with questions: Everyone wanted to know who did this to Antonio. Finally, a man whispered into Antonio's ear and then put his own ear to Antonio's lips.

"The port has been attacked! It's the marauders! They've got Miguel and Ignacio!" the man who'd just spoken to Antonio shouted. "They're at the back of the tavern!"

Javier, running towards the door, yelled over his shoulder, "Well, what are you all waiting for? The whoresons are not getting away with this!"

Rafael and Diego joined the group of men heading for the door. Outside, they saw nothing but sheets of rain and mist coming in from the sea, but as the group strode farther along the street towards the corner of the building, a militia prisoner cart came into view. Striding towards it, they heard a faint high-pitched scream and horses whinnying, above the noise of rain battering the ground.

The men from the taverna broke into a run. Diego surged onwards with the group until those at the front halted abruptly. From his position near the front, he could make out two men being dragged by their underarms onto the back of a cart by two cloaked men whose faces were hidden beneath masks of linen cloth. Then two riders brandishing swords appeared from nowhere. Their horses, panicking at the sudden appearance of the crowd, reared up. One of the riders lost his grip on the reins, and the horse, upon feeling itself free, struck out with its forelegs and then pounded the ground with its hooves.

"Let them go, you bastards!" a man from the taverna screamed at the abductors.

Some of the men picked up stones that were scattered on the ground, and others advanced on the cart, getting within arm's reach of the horsemen.

Undaunted by the crowd of men, the riders moved forward, slashing the air with their swords and panicking their horses even more by sawing harshly at the animals' mouths.

"If any one of you throws a stone and so much as grazes me, you'll find your guts cut out and your entrails lying on the ground!" one of the horsemen hissed loudly. "These men are being arrested on the duke's orders for the recent murders in Sagrat!"

The group's collective courage disintegrated at the mention of the duke's name, and instead of advancing, they halted abruptly and then retreated in fear.

Diego pushed his way to the front, enraged at the attack he was witnessing so soon after his brother had been killed. For the first time, he got a good look at the riders' faces. Staring at one of them, his jaw dropped. He recognised the man … He'd know that scarred face anywhere.

"They're not militia! They're marauders!" he shouted over his shoulder. Turning to the crowd behind him, he yelled. "The whoreson is lying! Come on!"

Diego couldn't believe what he was seeing. The men from the taverna were standing like statues, allowing their friends to be abducted by criminals. He was baffled, for in his mind, if all of them moved forward together, they would be able to pull the riders to the ground, disarm them, and then get the prisoners to safety.

"Are you going to let them get away with this?" he shouted again. "Your friends are innocent! If you let these bastards leave here, you'll never see Miguel or Ignacio again!"

Amidst the chaos, the two cloaked men inside the cart's cage had managed to secure their prisoners and reach the driver's bench.

Miguel and Ignacio lay on the cart's floor and were strangely silent.

The scarred marauder sneered at the crowd and then cackled loudly just before he gave the order to the cart driver to move along.

Javier joined Diego at the front of the line. "What are you, a bunch of old wives?" he shouted at the other men. "They're getting away. For God's sake, we have to stop them!" From somewhere in the crowd, a stone was thrown. It hit the scar-faced man on the shoulder, and some of the men in the crowd gasped when he urged his horse towards them.

"I'll rip your bellies open if you hit me again. Take another step forward and it will be your road to hell!" he cursed, with his sword in the air.

The cart, having been stuck for a moment in a mud puddle, managed to move at a sloth's pace until it picked up speed on the road leading out of the port. The feeble-looking group dropped their stones and watched the cart's fading torches dimming with each turn of the wheel, and as the reality of the situation struck the men, they began to trade insults. Diego listened. Their condemnation of each other seemed to be an attempt to cover their own guilt, he thought, feeling ashamed.

"There were fifteen of us for God's sake. We should have stopped them," one man accused the rest of them.

"Stopped them with what ... stones? They had swords. Or were you too busy hiding at the back to notice the blades pointed at us?" another retorted.

"That cart bore the duke's crest, and that's a fact. If we had seized Miguel and Ignacio, we'd all be hanged for treason before the week was out. Did anyone think about that?" another man asked.

"You're all a bunch of goat shaggers," an elderly man said, obviously disgusted. He then went home.

Back inside the taverna, Diego tried to hear what was being said above the noise of what seemed like a hundred angry men screeching like wives, all at the same time.

"In the name of God Almighty, shut up! Let Antonio speak before he takes his last breath!" Javier ordered.

Antonio lay with his head on a man's lap. His grey pallor and bluish tinged lips left no doubt that he'd be gone within minutes.

"They were just sitting there waiting for us to come out. They grabbed the three of us. The cart had the duke's seal."

"We know. We saw it, Antonio," Javier said.

"Miguel and Ignacio … didn't stand a chance. They were in front of me. I tried to fight one of the bastards off, but he got me with his sword … I ran."

"You did well, my friend," said Javier.

"Did you save them?"

"No, we were too late."

"I'm dying. Get me a priest!" Antonio, coughing up blood, weakly gripped Javier's hand, and whimpered. "Oh God, I'm not ready."

The voices grew louder again. Javier raised his hand and silenced them. He looked again at Antonio's gaping wound. "You're dying all right. Someone, go get the priest!" he shouted without looking up. "Antonio, if he doesn't come in time, confess your sins directly to God. That should be enough. We won't listen."

Shortly after, Antonio died.

CHAPTER TWENTY-EIGHT

The prisoner inside the cell was slumped against the wall as though he'd not moved since being thrown there. David lifted his torch to get a better look at the man, who raised his arm and shielded his eyes from the sudden burst of brightness. The suspect was elderly, feeble with age and skin hanging over raised bones. His tunic, in rags, hung loosely on his frame, barely covering his ribs, looking like waves on his chest. His bald head was lined with deep gashes. Dried blood stained his skin, and the first sign of yellow pus seeping from the wounds was already visible.

The man's frailty should leave no sensible person in doubt of his innocence, David thought, for he was not physically capable of carrying out the crimes he'd been accused of. The duke probably wouldn't care about such details, however. The people demanded justice for the young family's killers, and Peráto, it seemed, was determined to give it to them by the foulest of means. Unless God granted a miracle, the poor creature in the cell would be sentenced as quickly as the law allowed and, along with his companion, who was locked up farther down the passageway, would be brutally executed in a grand public exhibition.

When the men had been brought in, both had borne the marks of heavy fists on their bodies. Broken jaws, eyes swollen tightly shut, and plumped-up lips had given their faces a grotesque appearance. The bones in their cheeks were shattered. They would not be able to utter a word in their own defence, such was the extent of their injuries. This was not the work of the militia, David thought. It was not their way to beat up suspects ... The men had been deliberately and viciously silenced.

He thought back to the previous night. Captain Tur and two other militiamen had brought the prisoners in. After they'd been locked up, Tur had deposited the arrest warrants, signed by the duke. He'd said very little about the men's capture, but before leaving, he'd been emphatic in his condemnation. "These are the murdering turds who killed an entire family and your brother, Sanz. Never have I arrested such repugnant scum."

David's thoughts were grim. He was the repugnant scum, not the broken man he was looking at. He didn't want to serve in the militia anymore. He'd sooner kill the duke than serve him. His dreams had been soured and his ambitions sunk in a sea of guilt.

From within the passageway's shadows, Paco watched David looking fixedly through the opening in the cell door. He had noticed a drastic change in the young militiaman. He was not the same enthusiastic man with dreams of becoming a knight. His eyes were haunted, as though all he saw reminded him of some terrible occurrence. David had every right to grieve for his brother, Paco thought, and to be furious at the attack on his family's farm, but his expression was not one of sorrow or anger, and his mood was not so much sombre as tense. No, there was more than just Juanjo's death on David's mind ... Perhaps the Jewish girl had put some spell on him. He seemed taken by her.

Paco had served Sagrat's dukes for over twenty years. He'd been but a lad of twelve and, unlike David, had begun his soldiering life as the militia's lackey. He'd been no more than a messenger, a barracks boy who had emptied the soldiers' piss and shit buckets and seen to the disposal of the waste. He'd never been happier than the day the garderobe had been built. The antechamber, with its long sitting bench with holes where men could shit and pee until their hearts were content, and not have to get rid the waste themselves, had been a glorious sight to him.

In the early days, he'd not been given a sword but a broom, a polishing rag, and a few clips around the ear when he'd not cleaned a pair of boots properly. Those days had been hard, but now he had a wealth of experience and keen instincts that only years of service could provide.

He'd only ever known Valencia. He had fought in no major battles and had never travelled outside the kingdom. His mind had not been weighed down with grand ambitions or dreams of adventure. Marriage to his childhood love and a flock of six children, arriving one after another before he'd reached his twenty-fifth year, had been fulfilling enough for him. He loved Sagrat and its people. He never grew tired of gazing at its mountains and fertile plains or walking along its busy streets, which were vibrating with vegetable traders, urchins, fish sellers, gossiping wives, and artisans. But he was now seeing his town becoming mired in ugliness and evil and those around him complicit in dark secrets and lies.

Paco's eyes narrowed in contemplation. He didn't believe in coincidences. All the events in the past few days were connected. He didn't know how or why, but he was convinced that David Sanz, Captain Tur, and the duke had a lot to do with what had happened in Sagrat.

The duke killed the physician. He and every other soldier who'd been on watch that night knew it was no suicide. The Jew's granddaughter had been unjustly treated – this he also knew. David had not returned after the duke summoned him. Where did he go? Why would he not talk about his audience with Peráto? Why was his farm raided only hours later? Tur had lied about the capture of the two murder suspects. He would never have allowed his men to beat prisoners to a pulp, nor would he scream a suspect's guilt so profusely. But if Tur didn't seize the two men, who did?

Lies and secrets surrounded him, Paco thought again, but he would keep his suspicions to himself. Fear kept men's tongues silent, and he was no different from other common men, afraid of the nobleman they served and the religion they worshipped. His lips would be sealed, but his eyes would be wide open and his mind would stay keen. He would feign ignorance, but he'd dig a spoonful of dirt at a time until he uncovered the truth. He'd do this because he loved his town.

"I'd kill them myself if I got half a chance," Paco said, startling David. "Move away from the door. Don't give him light from your torch. Let him squat in darkness."

"They haven't been found guilty yet," David complained. "The magistrate hasn't even been to see them."

"You've got a lot to learn, my lad. We live in an age where guilt or innocence is determined by public opinion and the Inquisition's whims," Paco said. "They're as good as dead. They'll be lucky if they see another night. Can you not hear that mob outside? They've been at it since last night, crying out for blood and demanding public executions."

"There will be a trial, won't there?" David asked.

"Probably, although I doubt it'll take the magistrate long to deliver a verdict. There's a powerful thirst for revenge in this town. There are men outside from the port protesting the prisoners' innocence, but they might as well complain to the boil in the crevice of my arse. The duke wants this over with, and he's not going to listen to anything that might delay a burning. You keep your mouth shut, David – do you hear me? If Tur comes back here, don't mention the prisoners' injuries or even speak the word innocent. All we've got to do is make sure those murdering whoresons stay alive until it's time for their execution."

Paco pushed David out of the way and looked at the prisoner. This man didn't murder anyone, but he would keep that thought to himself too.

CHAPTER TWENTY-NINE

Gaspar de Amo stood at his daughter's bedside, masterfully hiding his disappointment and sadness in front of her ladies. His beautiful daughter had succumbed to the same brain disease that had struck her mother down when Josefa was just a child. He knew this to be true, for it was startlingly apparent not only in her gaze, for the most part lacking in emotion, but also in her childish manner. She was incapable of grasping the reality of adulthood, he thought miserably. At eighteen, she had not matured in the three years since he'd last seen her. In fact, if anything, her condition had worsened. She barely recognised him and seemed to have forgotten the first fifteen years of her life, when he had cared for her, doted on her, and groomed her for marriage. It was as though he had never existed in her life.

Her brain was being infected, eaten away by God only knew what, and the sickness would eventually kill her, just as it had her mother at a young age. Gaspar shook his head in dismay as he rocked his grandson in his arms and watched his daughter pull the comb through the horsehair wig on a doll's head. He gestured to the infant and, with his arms outstretched, said, "You have to feed him, Josefa. He needs his mother's milk."

The duchess, who was sitting up in bed, pulled the covers up to her chin, pouted moodily, and glared at her infant son. "I don't want to feed that baby. He bites me, and it hurts. Let someone else feed his greedy mouth. I have things to do. I have to finish brushing my dolly's hair, and then I have to dress her in her finery."

The inquisitor looked around the chamber, shocked at the sight of so many wooden and alabaster effigies dressed in the finest garments made from the best of materials. He wished he could throw them all into the fire, shake sense into his daughter, and snap her out of this malaise. But she would scream if he touched her roughly, and she wouldn't stop screaming until she exhausted her voice.

He tried again. "Daughter, you finally have a child, but he'll not grow strong unless you care for him. Look at him. Is he not wonderful?"

"He's not mine. He's a boy child. I like playing with my pretty dollies. And he has no hair. I hate him … I'm going to sew a new dress for Isabella." She lifted one of the dolls lying on top of the bedclothes and gave her father a radiant smile.

"I wish to begin my mission as soon as possible. There is not a day to waste," the inquisitor told Luis later in Luis's office. "I am ready to use all my talents and guide your lost sheep back into the fold."

"My lord inquisitor, it pleases me to hear that. My builders have worked hard to ready the prison. I'm sure you'll be satisfied with their progress. You will have my complete cooperation."

"I have already presumed that. But before we discuss the Inquisition, I want to talk to you about my grandson's baptism. Having heard of the evil infecting your town, I took the liberty of cancelling the grand occasion you had planned." De Amo watched Luis's face redden with anger, but his mind was set. His daughter was much too fragile to be seen in public. People would laugh at her, and she would embarrass him in front of men he might have to interrogate one day.

"But I have invited half of Valencia's nobles," Luis said angrily.

"And I have sent a messenger informing the invitees of your noble sacrifice. I believe a more private ceremony in your private chapel would be in order, in light of the town's sombre mood ... Come now, Luis, surely you don't want to appear insensitive?"

"No, of course not," Luis said, apparently seeing reason but unable to hide his resentment. "However, I do believe my son's baptism would have brought much-needed joy to the town. The people deserve to meet their duke's heir. What will they think if I don't celebrate?"

"It matters not what peasants and commoners think. This town is a black pit of sin. This is a time for pious reflection and mourning for your congregation, and you must lead by example."

"Yes, my lord."

Nodding his approval, De Amo said. "There's one more matter to do with your son. He shall be called Gaspar Luis Peráto De Amo."

Luis's face turned purple. "I am his father. I have named him, Jaime."

"And I am the inquisitor, and it pleases me to give him *my* name."

"It will be an honour to give my son your name, my lord inquisitor," Luis said like a sullen child.

In part, Gaspar was disappointed in Luis's answer. Peráto was a weak leader, just as he'd always suspected. Had the infant been his son, he would not have given in so easily to the question of baptism and name.

Turning his thoughts to other matters, he said, "After my grandson's baptism, I will expect your townspeople to come forward with the names of suspected heretics. News of your physician's suicide, murders, houses being burnt, and children going missing, has been running rampant in Valencia. The evil one is present here, and I intend to strike him down before he desecrates Sagrat ... and you along with it."

"God will praise you."

"God praises all pure souls and those poor misguided errant sheep who find their way back to Him through His Holy Inquisition."

"Praise be to God," Luis added.

During an uncomfortable silence, Luis poured them each a goblet of wine. When he sat back down, De Amo said, "I have other news. I have chosen your town to represent the very greatest of events. There's no town in the realm of Aragon and Valencia more in need of a public cleansing, don't you think?" The inquisitor gleefully watched Luis's eyes widen with fear. It would probably take the fear of God to make Luis the competent duke, he was supposed to be, he thought.

"I have been given permission to hold an auto-de-fé here in Sagrat. Thousands will attend. They'll come south from Zaragoza and north from Alicante to witness God's hand at work. I've invited every nobleman from here to the borders of Castile. I plan to bring over one hundred tried and convicted heretics from across this realm to Sagrat. After Mass, they shall be sentenced in your town square in front of the multitude, performed by Bishop Hernandez, a friend of mine.

"But you, Luis, must not expect your own people to go unpunished for their heretic acts. Should sinners not come forth voluntarily, their punishments will be harsh. Those found to be wanting in faith will not be spared. I will not display favouritism towards you. You do understand this?"

"I do."

"Are you sure?"

"Not entirely," Luis said honestly. "I don't have experience in these matters, but I imagine people might be afraid to come forward voluntarily."

De Amo laughed. "My boy, you are missing the point. The Inquisition is designed to cause fear. The purpose of the trial and execution is not to save the soul of the accused but to achieve the public good and put fear into others. Fear is a most useful deterrent." Noticing Luis's nervous ringing of hands and shifting feet, he asked. "Is there something wrong?"

"Forgive me for asking, but who will pay for this grand spectacle? Sagrat may not be the best choice."

Gaspar lifted an eyebrow. Insolent pup, he thought. Who did he think was going to pay? "Why, you will pay, of course. Your money will be used to entertain nobles and clergy after the ceremony and sentencing. You don't want to shame the house of Peráto, do you?" Unmoved, he watched the colour drain from Luis's face. Sagrat was a wealthy town. The duke just didn't want to spend his money. "You can't expect the Inquisition to pay? We spend more than our coffers receive. This is a great honour for your town."

"Yes, and I am truly indebted to you. But the Jews are leaving, we've lost trade, and then there's the drought and a war that's draining my treasury ...," Luis hurriedly tried to explain before being interrupted.

"You don't think the king and queen's holy war in Granada deserves your coin and the offerings of every noble in the kingdoms of Aragon and Valencia?" The inquisitor blurted out, shocked at Luis's complaints. "For ten long years, they have fought the Moors and their Nasrid dynasty, who have kept us out of our rightful territories. Ferdinand and Isabella are about to take the Alhambra and Granada. At last, all of Castile will belong to God and his true worshipers. I also have it on good authority that every last Jew in Spain will be expelled within months. Soon all of Spain will be united in one faith. Our monarchs are doing God's work, and to criticize their demands for money is heresy!"

"Yes, it is indeed a g-glorious mission ... set by God himself. I will, of course, support the Holy Father in Rome and

Spain's monarchs," Luis stuttered. "You will have a magnificent show of faith in my town. It will be a day never to be forgotten. The Holy Inquisition and its guests will have every facility at its disposal. I won't ... I will not disappoint you."

Gaspar watched Luis grapple for words. He was a transparent man, not clever or cunning like his late father. He didn't possess ambition, apart from his need to be admired and respected by his peers, but he was Josefa's protector and had the good grace not to mention her illness. "Your offer is graciously accepted," he said.

"Lord Inquisitor, there is another matter which may require an urgent response from the Inquisition."

"You may speak freely," the inquisitor said. "We are family, after all."

Luis nodded. "As you know, a great evil has been done in my town."

"Yes, the family with the children."

"That's right. My men have arrested two suspects connected with the murders. It was fortuitous that they were caught whilst trying to flee the port by boat. Witnesses have come forward to testify to seeing these men with the two missing children. Unfortunately, since being spotted, they seem to have killed the poor babes and buried them somewhere. They deny all involvement with the crimes, as of course they would, but the evidence against them is overwhelming."

"And what is your problem?"

"The magistrate insists on a public trial, but that could take weeks," Luis told him.

No, De Amo thought, a trial that went on for weeks would not suit his plans. "The townspeople cannot set their minds to confessions of heresy when they are filled with terror and rage. I would hate this matter to interfere with my auto-de-fé. Perhaps if the Inquisition were to preside over this trial, we could avoid prolonging its agonies?"

"My thoughts exactly," Luis said.

"In which case the Holy Office would be most pleased to attend to this matter. There's no sin greater in the eyes of God than murder ... Are you convinced of their guilt?"

"I am."

"Then I expect these men to confess by the end of the day, and if they are found guilty, there will be no mercy."

"And might I expect a speedy resolution ... for the sake of the people?"

"If my magistrate believes the witness statements to be in order, you can expect a swift verdict from me. But you and your magistrates will determine the sentence. Is that clear?"

"They will be executed as soon as possible, of course," Luis said resolutely.

"Then we are agreed on this matter."

Luis nodded gratefully. "We are indeed."

CHAPTER THIRTY

It was not yet dawn. David walked out of the prison and manoeuvred his way through a throng of people seemingly undaunted by the steady downpour that was drenching them. He calculated that possibly one hundred townspeople or more had gathered. They were no longer shouting or threatening to storm the prison, David noted, but neither did they seem in any hurry to leave the area surrounding it.

Some of the crowd sat in empty carts. Others sheltered together in groups under awnings and in doorways. A line of militiamen and Inquisition men-at-arms, dressed in full armour with weapons at the ready, barred the prison's doors like a wall, and a couple of the soldiers greeted David as he walked past their line.

Going deeper into the gathering, he felt his arm being pulled and heard voices shouting in his ear, asking questions he didn't want to answer. Who were the murderers? they wanted to know. What were their names? Had they been interrogated yet? Would they be executed soon? David ignored them, until one voice called out his name. David turned sharply. Standing before him was Eduardo, the lost babies' grandfather. David swallowed painfully and nodded in recognition.

"Eduardo, how are you fairing?" he asked.

"My wife is sick, but I hope to take home some good news. Is it true that you have the men who killed my daughter and her family?"

"We do." David felt as though he were suffocating. A large crowd had gathered around him, clinging to every word. "The two men will face justice. I hope this brings you and your wife some comfort. That's all I know, Eduardo." Not wanting to say more, David strode away from the crowd.

Behind him, he could hear Eduardo shouting. "Did you hear that? The murdering turds will be going to hell this night, and I'm not leaving until I have seen their blood run out of their bodies!"

David walked hastily down the hill towards the Jewry, leaving the people behind, and tried to focus on all he had to achieve before going back on watch. He hadn't forgotten about Sinfa or about his promise to seek out Rabbi Rabinovitch on her behalf. The noise of the crowd, gruff voices of Inquisition men-at-arms, and the rough handling of the two men incarcerated for the murders must have terrified her. She had been in the back of his mind even during the commotion following the arrival of the two prisoners. She was never far from his thoughts.

David knew the rabbi he was going to visit. For years, the Sanz family had attended the synagogue and all Jewish ceremonies. When David and his brothers were babies, the rabbi had officiated at their circumcisions. He'd also been present at the burials of deceased Sanz family members. During the Jewish festivals of Yom Kippur and Rosh Hashana, the Jewish New Year, the rabbi had always made a point of going from house to house, preaching the importance of being Jewish and urging people to hold fast to their religions. That period in his life seemed so long ago now. He was a Jewish outcast, a convert who would not receive a warm welcome when he turned up at the rabbi's door.

David had asked himself a few times why no one from the Jewry had gone to the prison to enquire about Sinfa's welfare. She was suffering terrible indignities, yet he'd been at the prison for the best part of three days and not one living soul had asked if she was alive or dead.

Recognition crossed the rabbi's face. "I know you. You're David Sanz, Juan Sanz's lad," he said sullenly. "What do you want?"

David stood awkwardly, like a scolded boy, at the rabbi's door. He straightened his shoulders and removed his helmet. He didn't have time to feel guilty about not being a Jew anymore. In his mind, he was neither Christian nor Jew. His soul was lost, and when he died, it would go to the same place as all other evil souls, regardless of religion.

"Sinfa Cabrera is in prison. She needs your help," he said. "You must plead her case to the duke."

"I know where Sinfa is, but I cannot plead for her. The duke won't see me. I ... I tried, but he won't give me an audience."

"You must try again," David insisted.

"I can't, I tell you. Sinfa has caused her own downfall, and she must suffer the consequences of her actions."

"Is this how you protect your people? You leave them to rot in a stinking prison when they have no business being there in the first place? Is this how you fight for the rights of Jews?"

The rabbi's face reddened. David couldn't decide whether Rabinovitch was embarrassed or angry, but either way, he would not back down. "Are you turning your back on her?" he asked.

"I will never turn my back on Jews! I have given my life to this community. Can you and your family say the same? No, you became Christians because of your father's earthly ambitions ... for a piece of dirt! You're all traitors, every one of you. Don't you dare come here and tell me what I must do. I officiated at your mother and father's wedding. I walked with your grandmother to the burial ground when we laid your grandfather to rest – and with your father when he laid *her* to rest."

"That's all in the past. I'm here to discuss Sinfa."

"I can do nothing for her. I no longer have the duke's ear or his favour."

David didn't know whether to feel pity or anger. After Cabrera's death, all Jews were probably feeling vulnerable. "Just tell me that you have tried. Let me go back to her with news that you have not forgotten her," he urged.

"I told you that I did try. I sent my son to the castle. When the soldiers saw a Jew coming, they refused to let him through the gatehouse."

"Your son is not the Jewry's rabbi. You are, and you still command respect, even at the castle. You can't give up so easily," David said curtly.

Poking his head outside, Rabbi Rabinovitch looked left and then right, checking that no one was listening to the conversation. "You listen to me, you impertinent young pup. I have almost two hundred souls in this Jewry. We are confined by walls and marked as undesirables by these badges they make us wear on our sleeves. My people are terrified to leave the neighbourhood. They are afraid to complain to the town council when they lose their businesses. We no longer speak to Christians and Moors, who were once our friends, lest we are accused of corrupting souls. We are cornered like rats, with no safe haven in Spain to run to.

"I loved Sinfa's grandfather like a brother. I weep for him and tire of the accusations against him, for I know they are not true! But I cannot put my people's lives in danger because of a silly girl's temper tantrum. I will remain in the shadows until the duke forgives Saul Cabrera. Eventually, Luis de Peráto will look favourably on the Jews, just as the old duke did, and in the meantime, I will pray for Sinfa. She will be freed eventually."

"Freed eventually," David repeated angrily. "Is this what you tell yourself to ease your conscience?"

"I can do nothing ..."

David took a step closer, disgusted at the cowardice and fear on the rabbi's face. "You don't deserve to be rabbi of this Jewry. You have condemned a young woman to death."

Dismayed and angry, David left the Jewry. Having only a couple of hours to spare, he quickened his pace. He wanted to take his parents to see a house. With two bedrooms, it was much bigger than the hovel in which they now lived. It was unoccupied and sat in the same street as Paco's family home. Getting his parents out of their current situation was a priority.

There was good news. His father would work at the blacksmith's premises. His mother would sew and mend tunics. She was an excellent seamstress. Life would be kinder to them, and when they were settled, he, David, would find some measure of solace for the terrible crimes he had committed.

He halted at the sight of a young boy with watery eyes, red cheeks, and a runny nose. Dressed in rags, he was surrounded by firewood and sitting on the ground outside a hovel.

Memories surfaced, and David's eyes welled up as images of his brother Juanjo drifted through his mind ... Juanjo, with his filthy face and hands and his proud cockish stance when he arrived home after collecting and selling bundles of kindling ... His mouth spread in a grin from ear to ear whenever he brought home bread and, on occasion, a cut of kid meat or a couple of fish for their mother. Juanjo had been a dreamer and never happier than when he was regaling the family with his fantastical stories and imaginary adventures. He would have become a good man, David believed, maybe even a great one.

David sniffed and then grabbed his purse, which was tucked into his leather belt. "How much do you want for a bundle, lad?" When the boy told him, David handed over the coin. "Do you live here?"

The boy nodded.

"Well, if you're going to sit here and wait for Sagrat to wake up, you should get yourself a woollen blanket. Your mama won't be happy if you catch cold, will she?" David smiled, ruffled the boy's hair, and picked up the tied bundle of thin branches.

Behind him, he heard the grating hiss of a sword blade being drawn from a belt. The hairs on the back of his neck stood up. Sensing danger, he said harshly to the boy, "Go inside your house – now."

He turned around slowly, one hand gripping his sword's hilt, and his eyes widened in recognition. There was no mistaking the identity of the man standing in the middle of the street. The taunting smirk and ragged scar had haunted him for days. He stared into the marauder's eyes and felt a cold rush of fear. The man had come to kill him …

CHAPTER THIRTY-ONE

Candles flickered inside houses. Outside in the deserted street, a heavy downpour battered the earth, watering the soil and turning it into a slushy stream running over David's feet. "You," he said to Alejandro. He drew his sword.

Out of the corner of his eye, he caught a patch of bright red and shifted his gaze from the marauder for just a second. Even from a distance, David could see the horse's white breath leave its mouth and a man wearing a hooded red cloak sitting on its back. David instinctively knew whom the rider was ... Garcia had finally made his move.

"We meet again." Alejandro planted a smile on his face, yet he stood with his arms and legs in an offensive stance. "Do you still want to fight me?"

A deep growl left David's throat, and he unleashed the rage he'd been nursing for days. With the agility of a cat, he moved forward, his flushed face and hooded eyes filled with hatred. Advancing, he watched Alejandro's belligerent smirk being replaced by surprise and fear, and self-belief soared within him. "I'm going to send you to hell, you murdering turd!"

The two men were equally matched in height and build. David's arms, as thick as tree trunks, were taut with solid muscles, strengthened over the years by lifting and swinging bladesmith's tools and, later, swords, longbows, spears, and maces. Energy rushed through him. His desire for revenge dulled his senses. No more hiding. No more fear. He would not die at the hands of this bastard, his inner voice screamed. He'd kill the marauder and piss on his dead body!

David spun around in a complete circle, pivoting on one foot and with his arm in the air, gaining speed and momentum. Drawing back his elbow slightly, a movement needed in order to obtain the best line for his thrust, he faced Alejandro and then lashed out with his sword. At the first clash of steel, David felt his sword vibrate and bend against the heavier and larger claymore blade. He stumbled backwards but quickly regained his footing in time to deflect Alejandro's swift slashing parry. Using that sword, the bastard would likely tire long before *he* did, David calculated, but there was a possibility that his own sword would bend and break under the weight of the thicker blade.

The two swords struck at an alarming speed. Alejandro was a superb swordsman, David kept thinking, and he was quick on his feet. The street had a steep incline. David knew that if he took his eyes off his opponent for even a second, he would die. Alejandro held the higher ground, which gave him a huge advantage. He had strength, skill, and a tactical mind, but after every clash, David searched for weaknesses.

Watching moments of tenseness in his opponent's hands and shoulders, David managed to gauge when Alejandro's next strike would come. He was also noticing that just before Alejandro struck, he glanced in the direction he was going to move. David was aware that he was defending rather than attacking. This was clear because he had lost ground and was moving backwards down the incline, sliding in the mud as though he were skating.

Every time he jabbed, Alejandro blocked and then struck back twice as hard. David's sword hand was becoming painful, and for a brief second, he saw his death.

The crashing sound of steel on steel grew louder as the thrusts intensified. Both men were panting and grunting like beasts. The rain blurred David's vision. His sodden cloak was heavy, making it hard to dodge, twist, and turn. But neither the torrential rain nor exhaustion deterred him or Alejandro from trying to inflict a fatal blow.

For a brief second, David took his eyes off Alejandro and saw people coming out of their houses. He couldn't stop now, he thought. *He dies or I do.* The thought of death energised him. Raising his sword, gripped now in both hands, he groaned loudly and rained it down in an attempt to slice into Alejandro's shoulder and render his arm useless.

Alejandro ducked and deftly moved out of the blade's reach. Then, with his arm outstretched, he swung his body around at the hips in a half circle and pivoted back until he faced front. His claymore flashed with speed through the air, slicing into David's forearm.

David lost all feeling in his hand. His sword fell from his grasp, and he groaned in disbelief. Looking down, he saw it hit the ground, and sink into the mud. He panicked. The marauder's sword would cut him down by the time he reached his weapon. Without thinking, he lunged forward and threw a punch. His fist connected with Alejandro's jaw. Stumbling backwards, Alejandro slipped in the mud and fell onto his backside.

Getting back up, Alejandro's sword was forgotten for the moment. Both men traded blows. David, losing all strength in his wounded arm, felt Alejandro's fist raining onto his face and tasted blood spraying from his nose. He fell to his knees, rolled over in the ankle-deep mud, and reached his sword. After grabbing it, he tried to stand, but twice he slipped on his thinly soled boots, which were seeping in water.

Panting, he looked up and saw Alejandro standing above him, sword in hand and swinging it high above his head ... Inexplicably, he held it there, and then he harassed

David with childish giggles, false lunges, and feints, as though savouring the moment just before going in for the kill.

David's eyes bored into Alejandro, and then sensing the exact second of the strike, he rolled his body twice, ending up a few paces from where the sword's tip landed.

For just a brief second, Alejandro stood looking down at his sword sticking in the slush. Grunting angrily, he flicked his eyes to David, painted in deep red mud, almost the same colour as the blood dripping from his arm, and struggling to get to his feet. Clearly losing his enthusiasm, Alejandro jerked his sword from the dirt and moved to strike David again.

David, now back on his feet, panted with exhaustion. His sword did not feel as comfortable in his left hand as it did in his right, but he'd learned to use both over the years. *Don't give up!* his mind screamed.

The two men glared at each other. A handful of men stood watching from a safe distance. Women who had come outside were told to get back indoors. David braced himself and planted his feet in an en garde position. Alejandro struck first. David blocked but felt his feet slipping again, as he was forced to take another couple of steps backwards. He would die now, he thought. His wounded arm was heavy and limp. He couldn't hold the lower ground any longer, and he couldn't beat the marauder with only one functioning arm.

He glanced at the onlookers, and then he stared directly into Alejandro's eyes. "Get this over with," he panted.

Alejandro nodded. "It will be my pleasure," he answered.

With a grunt, Alejandro swung his sword. David's body swerved, evading the weapon's tip by a hair's breath, and then he too struck with every bit of strength he had left.

Neither man saw the onlooker with a thick log in his hand advancing towards Alejandro from behind. When he thumped the wood against the back of Alejandro's skull, shock and surprise crossed both the sword fighters' faces.

David, a spectator now, gasped at the ferocity of the strike. Alejandro staggered towards David with the force of the blow. His pupils rolled upwards, and then he dropped like a stone to the ground.

Holding the sword limply in his left hand, David advanced on Alejandro, whose unsteady legs were slipping and sliding in the mud as he tried to stand. The neighbours' angry shouts halted David.

"That's far enough, lad! There have been enough killings in these streets of late!" the man holding the bloody log said to David.

David looked briefly at the onlookers' furious stares. The battle with the marauder was over, he thought. The people had saved his life, but they probably wouldn't think twice about wrestling him to the ground if he tried to carry on with the fight.

Alejandro had managed to get to his feet after struggling with his heavy muddied cloak. The back of his head was bleeding. He touched the wound and then looked at the blood on his hands. "You were fortunate, but this is not over. You hear me? This is not over!" he shouted at David.

"Off with you!" the man with the log said to Alejandro. "Don't show your face in this street again."

"I'm coming for you," Alejandro told David. He then turned his back on the crowd and strode away.

"I'm here, you bastard! Come and get me!" David retorted to Alejandro's retreating form.

Filled with hatred, David watched the marauder trample through the mud towards the end of the street. When Alejandro reached the corner, the horseman in the red cloak appeared, riding a horse and leading another. After Garcia handed the reins of the spare horse to the marauder, David returned

Garcia's stare. He was too far away to see the treasurer's expression, but he didn't need to look into Garcia eyes to know that they were full of hatred. The feeling was mutual.

Turning around, he stumbled through the clustered group of men.

"Who was he?" the man with the log asked him.

"A thief probably. I've never seen him before," David lied. "I thank you for saving my life. I'm indebted to you."

The men went back to their houses, but the man with the log remained.

"Lie to me if you will but have a care, lad. The man you were fighting was no thief. He was a skilled swordsman, and he wanted to kill you."

David nodded. "Yes, I know, and I wanted to kill him."

CHAPTER THIRTY-TWO

David sat bare-chested in the only chair in the room and grimaced with pain at the first touch of the damp rag on his wound. The muscles in his cheeks were taut. His skin was the colour of cold white ash. Droplets of sweat had settled on his forehead, and his eyes were still full of rage.

His mother wept and his father cursed the duke and Garcia to hell, but all David could think about as his mother bathed his injury was how lucky he was to be alive and not lying dead on the muddy ground in a nearby street. He'd been so sure of his skills when he'd faced the marauder. His anger had been so intense that he'd felt invincible. The images of Juanjo's ripped face and his mother pleading for revenge should have been enough to spur him on to victory through rage alone, but in truth, his rage had probably been the cause of his defeat.

"They won't stop. They'll come after me again," he said to no one in particular.

Juan's forehead was furrowed with worry. His hair was untidy and looked as though it had not been washed for weeks. "I agree," he said grimly. "Give me your sword, son."

"Why do you want his sword?" Isa asked, frowning.

"I'm going to heat it in the fire and burn the wound."

"No. I'll use a needle and thread. I'm going to close the slash," she told him. "Fetch me a bunch of comfrey or elm herbs. They'll ease the pain … And bring some dried figs for the infection. Knock on every door until you get them. Hurry."

When Juan left the house to look for the herbs that Isa requested, she rinsed out the rag and then hunted for a needle and thread. "There's nothing of any use in this house," she grumbled after a few minutes. "I'll be back as soon as I can. Keep your arm still and don't move from that chair."

David stared unseeingly at the hearth and the softly glowing fire within it. First his mind was filled with thoughts and regrets, and then it was filled with images of swords sparking together as though they would ignite. Even now, he heard the echoing, ringing clash of steel. He touched his painful jaw and felt the marauder's fist raining punches on his face. He still tasted the thick mud that had splashed into his mouth and slipped down his throat. Finally, he saw his own image, carelessly dropping his guard and exposing his arm to the marauder's blade.

Isa had meticulously ground the elm herbs to just the right texture and had placed them inside the open wound. When she had sewed the final stitch, completely closing the gaping slit, she smothered the stitches and the surrounding area with powdered figs and then bound the arm in a linen rag. She had given David comfrey herbs for the pain before she'd begun her ministering, insisting that he chew them and then swallow them with his saliva.

Juan sat patiently, knowing that interfering in the healing process would mean a tongue-lashing from Isa. He had never had such dark or dismal thoughts. What could he say or do to help his son? he kept asking himself. David could live in the prison. He would be safe there. But he couldn't stay there forever, shutting himself away just to stay alive.

"Listen to me, David. We will survive this," Juan finally said. "As soon as we have enough money, we'll leave Sagrat, and if we have to, we'll cross the nearest border and get out of Spain."

"Leave our country?" Isa said, looking horrified. "And go where?"

"To another country," Juan said. Looking about him, he added, "Pack what little we have. We're not spending another night in this hovel."

The sudden sound of men shouting filtered into the house through the shutter slats. Juan instinctively grabbed the poker lying at the side of the hearth. David got to his feet and with Isa's help put on his tunic and chain mail vest. Picking up his sword, he said, "They've come for me."

"How did they know you were here?" Isa asked, clearly panic-stricken.

Juan said, "I suppose he was followed."

The door rattled with heavy knocking. Juan, Isa, and David stared at the vibrating wood.

Tears were streaming down Isa's face. "Oh God, no … David, hide. Please hide," she begged.

"There is no hiding place, Mama," said David, still looking at the door.

"By order of the inquisitor, come outside immediately!" a shout rang out.

The Inquisition? What new gloom was this? Juan wondered. Would they drag David away like a criminal? "Son?" he said miserably.

"It's all right, Papa."

Juan opened the door and stepped into the street. David put his helmet on and followed his mother, who had covered her head with a thin blanket.

The torrential downpour had eased but still fell in a soft misty spray. Men, women, and children had already gathered outside, bunched together and looking terrified.

Juan put his arm around Isa's shoulders and held her to him.

The men-at-arms, or familiars, as they liked to be called, had become a common sight in Sagrat. Two of them stood apart from the crowd, dripping water from their hair and armour, but neither seemed in any hurry to announce the reason for their summons.

One of the inquisitor's men held a piece of parchment that was getting wet, and he tried to shield it with his cloak. Juan stared at them, and he realised after a moment or two that neither man was paying attention to anyone in particular.

David, standing much taller than the rest of the neighbours and dressed in a soldier's uniform, stood out amongst the others, yet they never looked at him. They seemed more intent on making sure that all the neighbours were present. Juan choked back his tears. The men were not here for David.

"What's going on?" Juan whispered to a neighbour.

"I don't know, but I wish they would hurry up and tell us. We'll all be drenched if we stand here much longer," the neighbour grunted.

Standing behind his parents, David felt his heartbeat ease into a steady pace. Filled with relief, he could only guess that the neighbours were going to hear a decree which would involve the entire town.

Finally, one of the Inquisition men-at-arms read from the wet document. "By order of the Holy Office, Pope Innocent IV, and Their Majesties King Ferdinand and Queen Isabella …" He paused for effect. "The townspeople of Sagrat will, without an exception, attend High Mass this coming Sunday morning at the tenth ring of the church bell. Those who are able-bodied and do not attend will be punished!

"On completion of Mass, you will remain in the church and thus hear the edict given to you by the inquisitor, Gaspar de Amo. This town and its people living therein are now under the protection of the Inquisition and its canon law … That is all. Go about your business!"

After the familiars had left, Juan, Isa, and David huddled around the hearth.

Isa, holding Juan's hand, asked, "David, do you know what this edict will say?"

Shaking his head, David said, "I haven't heard anything about this High Mass, but I have seen instruments of torture at the prison. The inquisitor's men speak of heavy duties to come and the prison overflowing with heretics. I fear the inquisitor is weaving a web. He is the spider, and we are his flies."

David wanted to tell them about all the other dismal chatter he'd heard at the prison. The terms Judaists, heretics, errant flock, confessions, and punishments were in every conversation, as though his town had already been found guilty of breaking every religious law ever invented by man. If he survived Garcia and his marauder, he would see some very dark days. No one would be safe from the inquisitor, he thought, no one.

CHAPTER THIRTY-THREE

David unlocked the cell door and entered. The putrid smells that hit his nostrils were   overpowering, worse than any he'd ever experienced before. The pungent odour of rotting pork lying on the dirt floor, which a couple of hungry rats were gnawing, made him gag. The stink of shit and pee running through the overflowing sewers and seeping up through the ground was heightened further by the stench of animal waste that had been thrown into the underground drains by the townspeople.

Rainwater dripped from the rock ceiling onto the ground, making a rhythmic popping sound and causing puddles to form in various areas. This was the first time David had seen the effects of wet weather inside the prison. He'd never noticed before how porous the granite stone was, how soggy the floor was, or just how inadequate the stone ceiling was at keeping out the rain.

The cells on this side of the prison formed part of a labyrinth of small caverns built into the hollowed rocks beneath the castle's ground. Each cell had been modified with bars and stone walls to keep them enclosed and secure. In David's mind, this part of the prison was suitable only for the rats that scurried across its floors. It had probably existed as a prison during the Roman occupation. There was certainly evidence to support this theory, for Paco had pointed out to him Latin writings on some of the walls. They should have filled the entire area with dirt when the last legion left Sagrat, David thought.

Huddling in the corner of the cell with her knees at her chest and her arms wrapped about them, Sinfa looked hopefully at him.

"Did you speak with the rabbi?" she asked with a hoarse voice.

David nodded. What could he say to her? He couldn't lie, give her false hope, or make promises that he couldn't keep. He could only give her bad news and hope that she would listen to his advice and see sense. He stepped closer and held the torch higher to brighten the space around her. She looked pitiful, he thought. Her gaunt face was filthy, and her hair hung limp and knotted around it, looking like a black hood. Her dress had torn just under the bodice. It was filthy, and there were probably enough bugs on it to chew off a mule's ear.

David cleared his throat, feeling childishly uncomfortable at the sight of her bare skin.

"Did you speak to Rabbi Rabinovitch or not?" she insisted.

"I did at length, but it seems your rabbi is too afraid to speak out on your behalf. You won't get any help from the Jewry. You must find your own way out of this."

Her loud sobs filled the cell, drowning the noise of the dripping water and squeaking rats, which began scurrying away in fright. He wanted to hold her. No, he wished he could take her by the hand and run with her to safety.

"Convert. Throw yourself at the mercy of the inquisitor," he begged her.

"I can't ... I can't ... I'm a Jew. I'll go to hell if I convert," she said, gasping for breath. "Oh God, help me! I can't bear this another day!"

David got down on one knee and lifted her chin in his fingers. Her blackened face was streaked with white lines on her cheeks, where tears had washed away the dirt. "Listen to me. We are but flesh and bones housing souls, and whether they be Christian, Jew, or Muslim, it makes no difference to God. I believe that every soul will travel to heaven or hell together

216

after our bodies die. Being Christian will not change who you are. I should know. I'm the same person now as I was when I was a Jew."

"You were a Jew?"

David nodded.

"I can't. I will shame my grandfather's memory if I abandon my beliefs."

"No, you won't. He would not want you to suffer in this foul cell. The duke and his treasurer, Garcia, will not set you free, Sinfa. Your own people have abandoned you. If you refuse to eat the pork that's given to you, you'll starve; then you won't have the strength to fight the diseases that must be lurking in this cell. You will never feel the sun on your face or breathe in fresh air. You will be in this place for years … Please heed my words."

He could stay no longer. Rising to his feet, he urged her one last time. "You will have one opportunity to speak to the inquisitor before you are forgotten. Just one."

"What do you mean you didn't get a good look at the man's face?" Paco insisted again. "You were stabbed in the arm, for God's sake! You must have seen your attacker."

David had spent the last hour trying to convince Paco that the wound on his arm had been caused by a thief trying to rob him of his purse. The rag covering David's injury had not managed to stop a small amount of blood from seeping through onto the thin linen tunic's sleeve, and Paco's inquisitive character would not let go of the matter.

"As I said, I was taken by surprise. The attacker slashed my arm, and by the time I turned to face him, he was already running off down the street. That's all there is to the story."

"Christ's blood, I've never met such an unlucky man. First your family's farm gets burnt and then your brother gets killed, God rest his soul … and now you get stabbed with a dagger. David, you need to pray more often. You're cursed!"

David almost smiled at Paco's earnestness. "I do have good news. My mother and father have moved out of that terrible house. I helped them move into the house in your street, the one you told me about."

Paco smiled. "It will be good to have you as a neighbour, David."

"You say that now, but I warn you, Paco. If you bother my mother with questions as you do me, she'll give you a tongue-lashing."

Paco laughed. "I hope not, lad. I get enough lashings from that wife of mine."

David sighed with relief when one of the inquisitor's men-at-arms arrived. He hated lying to Paco.

Unlike the other familiars who had taken over the prison, this one was dressed in a partial suit of battle armour and looked as though he was going into battle. On his head, he wore an armet helmet. David had only ever seen a few of these, when he'd worked for the blacksmith. It was rounded at the top, like a bowl. It enclosed the man's entire head and had hinged cheek plates, which the man had folded backwards. His gorget plate covered his neck and upper breast. David looked closely at it in the torchlight and noticed the Inquisition's crest engraved just beneath a cross. He was fascinated with the amount of protection the man was wearing, from the bands of plate at his shoulders to his schynbald plates covering his shins.

"I'm surprised you can get up and down our great hill in that lot. Are you expecting an invading army?" Paco asked the man.

For the first time in days, David wanted to laugh. Paco would never learn to separate his thoughts from his tongue, he thought. One day his friend would get himself into trouble with his humour, which didn't amuse everyone he met.

The familiar said sullenly, "Have you seen the hordes out there? We are prepared for anything, and you should be too. The inquisitor will arrive with the duke shortly, so best you tend to your business instead of sitting around like a couple of spent whores."

David stood up and then looked at Paco, who still remained firmly in his seat with a furious scowl on his usually placid face.

"We have not been outside this prison for more than an hour or two in the past three days," Paco said, refusing to stand. "We have not slept, eaten a decent meal, or sat on our arses for more than five minutes at a time. We live in filthy squalor not fit to house my goat, and we're going blind, for lack of daylight. So I'll thank you not to come prancing in here looking like a plated hog and giving opinions on what we should be doing with our time. State your business with us, soldier, familiar, or whatever you like to call yourself, and be done with it."

David felt a rush of respect for Paco. He was the militia's jester, never taking anything too seriously, always with a joke and a prank on hand when watches were tedious and long. Today, however, he was seeing Paco in a different light.

Looking at the man-at-arms' reddened face, which looked like a slapped arse, he asked, "What do you want?"

"Have the two prisoners that were brought in last night been prepared for interrogation?" the man-at-arms answered, throwing a contemptuous look Paco's way. "The inquisitor will arrive shortly with his entourage."

"We'll do that," Paco said.

David turned his thoughts to the task at hand. He should have checked on the prisoners' state of health various times, but he had not. Instead, he'd hoped that the next time he entered their cells he'd find them dead of their injuries. He was ashamed for thinking that, but death for them now would be much better than what was to come.

Thinking about having to face the accused, knowing that they were innocent and that he was guilty, sickened him. What a coward he was. His hands were trembling, and his legs could hardly hold him upright. He wasn't sure if his body shook because he was terrified of what was about to happen or if perhaps he was overcome by shame.

The thought of being sentenced to death twisted his gut and made him want to shit on the floor there and then. Imagine it, he thought, being tied to a stake and burnt alive; or being choked to death by a heavy rope and left dangling in the air; or hung, drawn, and quartered, watching pieces of his body being cut off whilst he still breathed … And worst of all, standing in front of the townspeople as a repugnant man who'd perpetrated the worst crime in Sagrat's history. He'd be pelted with stones and cursed to the fires of hell before he took his last breath. He should tell the truth and save his soul and his sanity. It was what any decent man would do. But he wouldn't. He didn't have the courage to face a town spewing hatred at him or to face a gruesome death. He was a disgrace, and he always would be.

CHAPTER THIRTY-FOUR

Torches standing in each of the four corners lit up the windowless chamber. On the ceiling, a candleholder with several branches cast long shadows and looked eerily like arms reaching out to those sitting beneath it. Thick iron-hinged rings with chains and shackles attached were hammered deep into the stone walls. A row of chairs was in the centre of the room, and behind them sat two scribes at desks overflowing with parchments, files, books, inkwells, and quills.

David and Paco dragged Miguel, who was barely able to stand, into the room and shackled him by the hands and feet whilst two Inquisition men-at-arms did the same to Ignacio. When the accused were secured, David and Paco took their places at the door and waited for the trial attendees to arrive.

David had already seen the town's prosecutor and his assistant enter. They'd been weighed down by documents. He'd also been present when the defence advocates had insisted on speaking to the accused men. Their job would be difficult, David thought, for both suspects were unable to speak or supply witnesses on their behalf. He wondered if justice would prevail here today, and if by some miracle, the two men would be set free due to lack of evidence. No ... There would be no justice unless he confessed.

The duke, town magistrate, Father Bernardo, Garcia, the inquisitor's magistrate, and two leading councilmen entered the chamber and took their seats. Captain Tur, one of the last men to enter, stood next to David and Paco. His face was drained of colour. He looked sheepishly at the prisoners, and then his eyes settled on the hard, cold floor.

"They're a horrible sight, Captain, are they not?" Paco whispered to Tur. "I'm surprised they managed to put up a fight and that you found it necessary to beat them into submission."

"Hold your tongue, Morales, and mind your business," Tur told him. "I'll not have you questioning me about mine."

A burning heat engulfed David's body. His chest felt tight, and his throat was as dry as an old wench's mossy cave. Swallowing painfully, he stared at Garcia with unmasked defiance. Then, at the mere thought of the fight with the marauder, his wound started stinging. If it got infected, he might lose his arm, he thought. Damn Garcia and all the devils in hell if that happened.

He wasn't afraid, and he wanted Garcia to know. He intensified his gaze. He was   wounded, but he was still alive and so angry that he would fight anyone else the whoreson sent and probably enjoy thrusting into him. He smirked, lifted his wounded arm so that Garcia could see it, and then watched with pleasure as the treasurer's eyes narrowed to angry slits.

The bastard had suffered defeat. He was probably livid and feeling humiliated. He wished his thoughts could reach Garcia's ears. They would hear him say, "I'm still posing a threat, you turd from a pig's arse. I'm ready for you and any assassin you care to send."

David shifted his eyes to the duke, whose forehead glistened with perspiration. Feeling a measure of satisfaction, he concluded that although the duke and Garcia had marked him for death, and that had been made painfully obvious, he saw fear in their eyes. In all likelihood, he would die at their hands or he'd be stabbed in the heart by their lackey, the scar-faced marauder. Yet at this moment, he felt strangely unafraid of them. The duke might be giving the impression that he was a mere interested party in this trial, David thought, but he was probably sitting there bum wetting himself and terrified of the truth coming out.

Luis shifted nervously in his chair and stared straight ahead. He could feel Sanz's eyes on him. The man had not stopped staring at him since the moment he'd walked into the chamber. If it were anyone else, he'd order him removed for his audacity. David Sanz was a loyal soldier, Luis had told himself repeatedly since *that* night, yet there was an absence of respect in his bold glances. Maybe he now wanted the money he'd thrown back in Garcia's face, Luis thought. He was probably as greedy as any other man was. Perhaps he was thinking of confessing to the inquisitor about the murders. Luis was surprised to find that he was strangely unafraid of that happening. There was not a man in the world willing to go voluntarily to the stake, not even a self righteous scum like Sanz.

Luis flicked his eyes over David and shivered as though a cold breeze had just enveloped him. Sanz was still glaring. He glanced at Tur. He'd speak to his captain about Sanz. He'd have him confine the man to prison duties on a permanent basis … No, that wouldn't work. No matter where Sanz was, he would continue to vex. Garcia had been right all along, although he'd never admit that to the treasurer's face. David Sanz would have to die.

Looking at the prisoners, Luis squirmed at their ugliness, yet his mind was not entirely focused on them or on the trial about to take place. He inadvertently grunted in anger. He'd been hoping for financial aid from the inquisitor but instead De Amo had demanded money. What an effrontery. The inquisitor could buy Sagrat's castle and still have enough coin left over to live comfortably. His father-by-law's arrival had been disappointing, Luis thought miserably. He'd given the

Inquisition every courtesy: residency in the municipal palace, a new prison, complete access to the townspeople, and accommodation for a large entourage. Yet he, Luis, had received nothing but disrespect in return.

He'd never forgive his father by law, he decided, watching the inquisitor enter the chamber. The future duke of Sagrat had been baptised in the castle's cold, damp chapel without one person of note being present to witness the occasion. The infant hadn't even been given the name originally chosen for him. Gaspar Peráto, as he was now called, was not a good name. To make matters worse, he, Luis, was stuck with a madwoman for a wife, yet her father had not had the good grace to compensate him for the inconvenience or even mention his daughter's insanity ... And now Sagrat was going to lose money to feed the inquisitor's vanity in a grand auto-de-fé.

Sighing, Luis closed his eyes. Ugliness surrounded him. Everywhere he looked, the malicious eyes of greedy, power seeking varlets met his. He was being bombarded with problems, and they were ruining his happiness and his plans.

"Who deformed the prisoners' faces?" the inquisitor barked at Luis in front of all those present. "How can they confess to me when they have no voices to speak with?"

"My lord inquisitor, I believe Captain Tur may have been overly zealous when capturing the accused," Luis answered with an equal amount of disdain. "According to him, the prisoners were armed and put up a fight. They are murderers and had to be subdued. Isn't that right, Captain?"

Tur nodded. "Yes Your Grace," he said.

The inquisitor continued to stare at the two mangled faces kneeling in front of him. He despaired at Luis's lack of common sense. A soldier under the command of a nobleman would never strike an accused unless his master gave him permission to terrorize the common man. This was a clear sign of bad leadership, and the fault lay on Luis's shoulders, for it demonstrated that Sagrat's militia had no respect for their duke.

De Amo faced a conundrum. He was obligated to follow canon law to the letter, for it sat at the core of all Inquisition procedures. Suspects could only be arrested after the Holy Office's magistrates and a theology expert had seen conclusive evidence against the accused. But in this case, a civil authority, not the Inquisition, had collected and perused the testimonies. Naturally, the suspects were to be presumed guilty, and the onus would fall on them to prove their innocence, but how could these men defend themselves, he wondered again, if they couldn't even open their mouths?

His sole task was to obtain an admission of guilt and a penitential submission, but achieving this would also be impossible. During every trial, scribes meticulously documented accusers' statements and suspects' words as well as records of the prisoners' treatment whilst in custody. The prisoners also had the right to question evidence against them, and if it were to be found lacking, the suspects were usually set free immediately. Interrogating and issuing a verdict on both men together in a single day would also be frowned upon, for by law, every Inquisition prisoner must have the right to a full investigation over a period of days, weeks, or even months.

Taking a moment to look at the witnesses' written statements, he wondered how he could justify such a speedy trial. Under Inquisition law, it was not necessary to reveal the names of accusers to the accused. Nor did he, as inquisitor, feel it necessary on this occasion to investigate the witnesses' truthfulness. All five testimonies seemed to agree on facts, the time the crimes took place, and who had been responsible.

When he'd arrived at the prison, he'd been shocked to see hundreds of people gathered outside, weathering the damp and cold. Their calls for the suspects' execution had been heartfelt and desperate. High Mass would take place in two days. He needed the townspeople's undivided attention, and he wouldn't get it if the case against these two men was not resolved.

He comforted himself. His real work would begin after Sunday's Mass. These two men were obviously guilty, and the charges against them didn't require a lengthy investigation. No one would know that Inquisition procedures fell short on this occasion. God would forgive him, he believed. *He* would be satisfied to see the two murdering whores go to hell.

The inquisitor regarded Miguel and Ignacio, and for a moment, he felt pity. His stiff pristine white collar and cuffs, black robes, cap, and cloak, were in stark contrast to the men's half-naked bodies, which were covered in bruises and blackened with dirt. The prisoners were on their knees, craning their necks and moaning with pain.

De Amo stepped forward and touched both prisoners' heads as though he were blessing them. He felt one of the accused tug the hem of his robe. He looked down and saw the man's broken fingers. He shuddered and shifted his gaze to the other man, who was clasping his hands in prayer. His eyes, blackened and bloodied around the edges, held a terror that Gaspar de Amo had seen previously on heretic's faces. But even he, a hardened interrogator, found it difficult to look at him.

"I believe I am ready to begin," he told all those present.

CHAPTER THIRTY-FIVE

De Amo nodded to his magistrate and then to the defence advocate, who looked almost as terrified as the men he was there to defend.

"Magistrate, present your evidence and accusers' statements," the inquisitor ordered.

Vicent Arguti stood, bowed to the inquisitor, and then picked up one of the many documents lying on his tabletop. He cleared his throat. "My lord inquisitor ..." Then addressing Luis, he said, "Your Grace, Miguel Ferrer and Ignacio Ruíz are accused of murder, kidnapping, and fire-raising. The deceased persons in this case – Adolfo Marsal and his wife, Alma Casellas – were found brutally stabbed to death in their house. Upon hearing the victims' terrified screams, three neighbours were awakened, and they took it upon themselves to investigate. In the street, all three neighbours saw the aforementioned men running out of the victims' house with an infant and a small child in their arms. The witnesses have since formally identified the accused.

"Furthermore, on that same night, three smallholdings were burnt to the ground on the plain lying east of Sagrat. A boy, Juanjo Sanz, was killed during one of the raids. Witnesses have come forward, and all, without fail, have identified the two present suspects as being the perpetrators of these horrific crimes.

"On the morning following the vicious attacks and murders, His Grace's militia were dispatched to hunt and capture the murderers. When Miguel Ferrer and Ignacio Ruiz were eventually seized, they were found to be in possession of an infant's blanket." Arguti held up the blanket covered in blood.

All those in attendance crossed themselves and gasped in horror.

The two accused men shook their heads. Tears ran down the cheeks of one, whilst the other grunted incoherently at the magistrate.

"Reliable witnesses have testified that this is the blanket belonging to the murdered infant, Matias Marsal Casellas. Unfortunately, the militia were unable to find the infant's body or that of his sister, Angelita, Marsal Casellas.

With a wave of his hand, the inquisitor gestured to the magistrate to sit back down. Looking at both of the accused, he said, "I don't want to prolong this trial. It is quite clear that multiple witnesses have identified you both and that you are guilty of these atrocities. I could stand here all day and read witness accounts, but for your sake, I would much rather forego this lengthy process and hear your confessions now. Taking a step closer, he added, "I cannot save your souls, for they are beyond redemption, but I can show you mercy with a prompt death."

Miguel hung his head. Ignacio grunted and shook his head violently. The inquisitor raised an arm and then snapped his fingers. The masked torturer, who until now had stood behind Inquisition men-at-arms, stepped forward. Knowing what was required of him, he gripped Ignacio by the arm with his gloved hand and dragged him to his feet.

"Ignacio, are you ready to confess to your terrible crimes against man and God?" De Amo asked Ignacio, not unkindly.

Ignacio groaned like a whimpering wounded beast and shook his head.

"You killed five people. We have proof," De Amo told him. Your advocate sits here unable to defend you against the barrage of evidence that we have presented. Why do you prolong your suffering? Surely no physical torture can compare to the anguish of a tormented soul. God cannot show you mercy if you don't unburden yourself of these terrible sins. You understand that it is my sacred duty to hear your confession and bring you back to the faith?"

Ignacio's glassy eyes stared at him; he looked like a small child not understanding a word that he was hearing.

"You need only nod your head and this will be over."

Ignacio let out a desperate moan. Saliva dribbled down his chin, and his head drooped. The inquisitor gestured to the torturer, who tilted Ignacio's head back, forcing him to look up.

Bending down, the inquisitor looked into Ignacio's eyes and said patiently, "Would it not be better for you to get this over with? You have caused great suffering, yet I am giving you the opportunity to find rest."

Ignacio shook his head and then bowed it again until it hung limply.

De Amo had seen this gesture of defeat many times. It usually meant that the prisoner was ready to make a confession. He didn't want to torture these men. They would not survive any of the inquisition's methods, and there would be no justice for the townspeople if he burned dead bodies. "You killed five people. You murdered them! You took the lives of innocent babes ... You must confess before you face the eternal flames of hell!"

Ignacio looked at each face in the room as though searching for one single ally. Raising his eyes, he stared now with terror at the masked torturer. Tears poured down his face. Mucous dripped from his nostrils. His lips trembled, but he couldn't seem to open them. He could only manage to whimper.

"Will you now confess to God?" De Amo asked him again.

Ignacio nodded.

There was no point in going through any more Inquisition requisites, the inquisitor thought. He would have a just confession as long as the accused nodded his head at the right time and the scribe noted the gesture in the records.

"Did you, Ignacio Ruiz, murder five innocent people and set unlawful fires that resulted in the destruction of properties?"

Ignacio stared into De Amo's eyes and then nodded his head.

"Are you confessing?" the inquisitor asked once more, to make sure everyone else could see Ignacio nodding in answer.

Ignacio nodded.

"Is the confession recorded?" the inquisitor asked his scribe.

The scribe said, "Yes Your Excellency, every gesture."

Miguel was pulled to his feet. He was in an even weaker state than Ignacio, and the torturer had to hold him up with both arms wrapped around his chest.

"Miguel Ferrer, are you ready to confess to the murders?" the inquisitor asked.

Miguel gasped for air and then released a loud sob.

"Nod your head. Did you kill those people?" the inquisitor urged him.

Miguel tried desperately to open his mouth.

"Don't try to speak. You'll only cause yourself more pain."

Miguel nodded.

"Are you confessing?"

Miguel nodded again.

The inquisitor sighed with relief. He did not normally conduct his business this way, and he had found it distasteful. "Did you all see their confessions?" he asked the seated men.

"I did," Luis answered. "They are both guilty."

The others nodded in agreement, and then each man said, "Yes, guilty."

De Amo sat down. In capital offence cases, the Inquisition generally handed convicted prisoners to the civilian authorities for sentencing. The Holy Office did not involve itself with the issuing of death sentences. "As we are all agreed, I will now abandon the prisoners to the secular arm. The Inquisition has done its duty," he said, and then he sat down.

For a moment, there was a silent pause as each man in the chamber came to terms with the verdict. David stood rigidly to attention, eyes boring into the prisoners. Paco inadvertently shook his head in a gesture of disgust. Captain Tur continued to stare at the ground as though daydreaming. But the council members, clergy, and Garcia nodded their heads in satisfaction whilst looking at the duke, who would now decide the convicted prisoners' fate.

Luis stood and then went to stand next to De Amo's chair. Facing the council, he said, "The sentence must be death for both men. What does my council say?"

"I agree, Your Grace," the town magistrate said with enthusiasm.

"They must be executed immediately," Garcia said. "If we don't carry out the sentences this night, we will have civil unrest. All hell will break loose."

The other councilmen agreed. The monks nodded. Father Bernardo, the only other clergyman present, had not yet spoken.

"What say you, Padre?" Luis asked him.

"They have been convicted of such evil crimes that I cannot even think of a suitable punishment. They have inflicted injury on so many lives in this town, and in my opinion, they should be mutilated and their parts fed to the pigs."

"No, not mutilation," Luis said hurriedly. "These men will suffer the agonies of fire. They will be burnt alive. There will be no garrotting beforehand. I want the townspeople to hear their screams when the flames lick their skin. Every last man, woman, and child will attend, without exception," Luis said enthusiastically.

The council nodded in agreement, and Father Bernardo asked, "May I give them God's forgiveness before they die?"

"You may, although I don't think God will listen to your absolutions," Luis told him.

CHAPTER THIRTY-SIX

Darkness had fallen, and the rain had stopped. The streets, with a thick layer of mud still wet and slushy, were lined by a crowd of people carrying lit torches all the way from the prison walls to the town square.

Inquisition men-at-arms and the duke's militia, stationed along the route from the prison to the edge of the town's plaza, formed a barrier between the thoroughfare and the throng of people waiting expectantly for their first glimpse of the condemned men.

Two soldiers, pounding heavy drums with their fists, led the execution procession. Father Bernardo and two other priests from San Agustin carried crucifixes and were followed by two Dominican monks from the nearby monastery. The prisoners, lying in the back of a cart, were chained together by iron links attached to neck collars. Their wrists and feet were also shackled, and every time the cart hit a stone or bump in the road, the men groaned in pain. Two knights flanked the cart, and behind it marched the duke, Captain Tur, and the town council members in a solemn line.

Over centuries, executions had taken place on the outskirts of town. But such was the ferocity of these crimes that the council elected that it should be held in Sagrat's centre so that people would always remember it whenever they passed by the church or sat gossiping on the steps of the municipal palace.

When the procession reached the town square, La Placa Del Rey, two militiamen took up positions on top of each pyre, which was almost as tall as an average man. The stakes, wedged in the centre of the pyres, had been hastily erected and were visible from every corner of the square and surrounding streets.

There had not been a burning in Sagrat for over ten years. The people, mesmerised by the sombre beat of the drums, the sight of the stakes, and then the arrival of the prisoners, stood in morbid stillness, until some gasped with shock when Miguel and Ignacio were pulled off the cart and dragged across the muddy ground on their bellies towards the pyres.

A few of the duke's soldiers, holding lit torches which would ignite the fires, watched in silence, but some of them couldn't resist throwing a disapproving look the duke's way.

Miguel and Ignacio reached the foot of the stakes. At most burnings, the condemned prisoner was tied and bound to a high ladder lying on the ground. After the heretic had been secured to it, it was lifted by ropes until it stood vertically. With the prisoner facing the fire, the ladder was then lowered again onto the mountain of burning kindling, where the prisoner died almost instantly. Not so this night. It seemed that Miguel and Ignacio were to be given a slower and more painful death.

Standing on top of the pyres, militiamen holding the chains connected to Miguel and Ignacio's iron neck collars tugged continuously, until the condemned men began climbing over the wood pile. Like a couple of reluctant mules, they tried to take steps backwards instead of forward, with their heads jerking against the collars around their necks.

Both prisoners fell and, unable to stand up again, were dragged the rest of the way on their stomachs, groaning in agony as their bodies became entangled in the jagged twigs. The crowd watched as the men's skin was ripped, scratched, and stabbed. But inch by inch, they continued to move upwards towards the wooden stakes.

Some of the onlookers looked away. A few people with weak bellies tried to leave the town square, but soldiers blocked their way and ordered them to remain. Only the murdered victims' family, given a place right at the front of the crowd, openly displayed exuberance for the proceedings.

A stone flew through the air, hitting Miguel on the back of the head, and then another and another, until both men were pelted on every part of their bodies. Angry voices from within the crowd rose above the sound of beating drums. Captain Tur called for order, but the shouts of the people grew even louder, until a man's anguished scream shocked the crowd into silence.

"Where are our grandbabies? Give us peace!" Eduardo, the missing children's grandfather, sobbed. "Tell us where you buried them!"

Surrounded by the people's fury, David felt his gut wrench. He stood at the foot of the stake, light-headed and convinced he was going to vomit. Desperate to tell Eduardo where the babies were and scream his sins aloud, he forced his eyes to close and set his lips into a tight line. He could save these men, his scrambled mind screamed. All he had to do was confess. He was going to hell and would suffer all its agonies, but before that, he could do at least one good thing before the devil took him. He could return the babies to their family and bring the duke and Garcia to justice. He could do those things were he not a coward, unable to even let himself imagine the horror of flames engulfing his body …

His eyes snapped open at a lull in the shouting. Turning to face the stake, he watched his fellow militiamen unshackle the prisoners and shuddered at the sight of their almost naked bodies and torn skin. Thick ropes being coiled around Miguel and Ignacio's foreheads, necks, and bodies left them standing rigid, like soldiers to attention, against the smooth poles. God help them. God help them! his mind screamed.

Jumping at a sharp pain coursing up and down his wounded arm, he looked down to see fingers digging deep into the linen bandage and the emergence of fresh blood surrounding the open wound. Tugging his arm free, he looked back up, and scowled at Garcia, smirking with pleasure at the pain he was causing.

"You should be up there, Sanz. I'd pay with my own coin to watch you burn." Garcia tilted his head and whispered into David's ear, "It would give me pleasure to watch you squirm in agony."

"And it would give me even greater satisfaction to see you standing up there next to me," David hissed back.

"You are not long for this world." Garcia grinned maliciously and then walked away.

Father Bernardo and two other priests from the church of San Agustin went to each pyre in turn, holding crucifixes in the air. After making the sign of the cross and uttering prayers that no one could hear, Father Bernardo turned his back on the prisoners and then walked towards the church, followed by the duke, Garcia, and the town's civil authorities.

"Empty the buckets of pig fat onto the pyres," Captain Tur ordered his soldiers. The logs and kindling were wet from recent rains and the pig fat would help ignite them.

After the pyres had been doused, David was ordered to put the flame to Ignacio's pyre. Frozen with dread, he hesitated. His mind scrambled to think of a way out of the horrific nightmare he'd found himself in. For a second he envisaged the two prisoners getting loose from the ropes and running to safety. Gripping the lit torch so tightly that he thought the wood would snap, he found he couldn't move his arm or take a step forward. It was as though some invisible hand were holding him back. His teeth were chattering. His ears heard the sound of drums and people's voices shouting at him to hurry up and light the fire, yet he still couldn't do his captain's bidding.

"In the name of God, man, give it to me!" Tur's gruff voice snapped.

David, dazed, handed Tur the torch and then hung his head, lest anyone see his tears.

"Lift your head and behave like a soldier. Every man in this cursed town is looking at you," Tur said.

Slowly David raised himself to his full height, stood to attention, and nodded. His head was pounding as though it were being struck with hammers. Tur shouldn't have to light the fire and damage his good conscience, David thought, ashamed. "My apologies, Captain," he said.

"Are you ready to follow orders, Sanz?" Tur asked, not unkindly.

David nodded again. "Yes, Captain." Looking up at Ignacio's terror-stricken face, he mouthed, *Forgive me*. Then he lit the kindling.

CHAPTER THIRTY-SEVEN

Miguel and Ignacio appeared to have been overcome by smoke before the first flames licked their feet. Their flesh, now peeling off their bodies like slices from tender joints, fell onto the flames, making the odour of pig fat and smoke even more pungent and the sight horrific. For anyone in close proximity to the fire, it was becoming increasingly difficult to breathe. It was also dangerous because of the sparking wood flying perilously far from the pyres and into the crowd of people.

Even though the bodies were still burning, the militiamen no longer stopped the townspeople from leaving the square. Eduardo and Alma, electing to stay, were surrounded by their family members, who were standing in a clustered group and staring unflinchingly at Miguel and Ignacio's charred remains.

Paco approached David, sitting alone some distance from the stakes. Placing his hand on David's shoulder as he sat down on the muddy ground, he asked, "What did the lord treasurer whisper in your ear?"

"Nothing. It was of no importance," David answered.

"David, I am your friend, but I will hammer down this wall you've built around you until it cracks. I'm weary of your lies and secrets."

"Not now ... Please, Paco, not now," David said impatiently.

"Yes, now. I've been watching you. You lit the flames on those pyres, but I suspect you knew those poor bastards were innocent, just as I did."

"That's nonsense!"

"Is it? Then why do I see more guilt and fear in your eyes than in any prisoner we have locked up in our prison. Who are you afraid of?"

Shrugging off Paco's hand, David tried to rise to his feet.

"Sit down!" Paco exclaimed, tightly gripping David's arm. "You're not going anywhere until I get the answers I'm looking for."

"I've got nothing to say. Let go of my arm."

"Sit or I'll hold you down by the tip of my sword."

David swallowed painfully. His throat felt as though it were filled with bone-dry straw, and it tasted of burnt meat. He didn't think he could talk to Paco even if he wanted to. Sitting back down from his half-risen position, he decided to let Paco have his say. What did it matter? He wasn't going to tell the truth anyway. "Get on with it," he said hoarsely. "What do you want to know?"

"I want to know why you were summoned by the duke on the night the physician died."

"You've already asked me about that. I told you—"

"You lied. I have served in Sagrat's militia for over twenty years. I hold a higher rank than you, yet no lord or master has ever given me so much as a fleeting glance. Not even Captain Tur crosses the threshold to Peráto's private chambers. I spoke to the guards who were on watch at his doors that night. They told me you were inside with the duke for a long time. What did he want from you?"

David held his tongue.

Paco tried again. "I watched the lord treasurer approach you tonight and whisper something in your ear. I saw the loathing in your face. What did he say? Why do you hate him?"

"I don't hate him."

"More lies. I sensed the hostility between you and him. You either think me stupid or blind."

"I think you are an astute man," David said sincerely.

"If that's so, you'll not be surprised to learn that I also think you've played some part in this shameful travesty of justice. The town was cursed the night the physician fell off that wall … the same night you were summoned and hell spilled onto our streets. I'm not asking anymore. I demand answers or I swear to God Almighty that I'll take my suspicions about you to Captain Tur."

David's sharp intake of breath was audible. Panicking, he averted his eyes. Paco *was* astute, which meant that his suspicions could run deep. He wouldn't give up until he was satisfied. He would chip away until he got to the truth. "Will you give me leave until we've finished here?" David asked.

Paco nodded. "Yes, but when we leave this square, you'll spill your guts to me," Paco warned him.

CHAPTER THIRTY-EIGHT

The militia had been given strict instructions to keep the fires going until every piece of human bone had been incinerated. Just before dawn, the last flickering flames simmering within the pile of ashes died. David tried to concentrate on the job of clearing the mounds of ash. First the men had to douse the debris with water, and then they would shovel it onto the back of the cart.

When the area had been cleaned, the cart was driven away. David and Paco left the square and began picking their way through the deserted streets towards the prison. Walking briskly, David braced himself for Paco's interrogation. A devoted militiaman, Paco was also loyal, persistent, and above all honest. He and his family would be relatively safe as long as he remained ignorant, David believed, but the moment the truth came to light, his sense of duty would compel him to seek justice against the duke and everyone else involved in the terrible crimes that had been committed.

Battling with indecision, David gave Paco a quick sideways glance. Should he keep his mouth shut, share every detail, or omit certain facts? Would it be better to say that the little girl and the infant were dead or that they still lived? Could Paco be trusted to keep his mouth shut? What would he do when it was confirmed that the wrong men had been executed? Would his disgust outweigh their friendship?

David, jolted from his thoughts by Paco's sudden grip on his arm, halted in mid-step.

Gesturing behind them, Paco raised two fingers in the air. "There are two of them," he mouthed.

David pricked his ears but heard nothing. Regardless, he followed Paco, striding towards the end of the street. Turning a corner, they slipped simultaneously into the first shadowy porch and pressed their bodies against its inner wall. Then, with hands on the pommels of their swords, they listened and waited.

Panicking and feeling a sense of doom, David flexed his muscles and tried to slow his breathing. His sword arm would be ineffective, he thought. He would be of no use to Paco. The wound had started bleeding again after Garcia's rough grip had ripped some of the gut stitches out. If he was forced to wield a weapon now, he would tear the skin further. "Paco, if they're armed, we should run," he whispered urgently. "This is not your fight."

"Hush." Paco put his fingers to his lips and shook his head.

The two figures wearing dark cloaks with hoods pulled over their heads walked briskly past David and Paco's position but then halted abruptly, as though they were lost or looking for something.

David, standing rigidly against the wall, silently urged the two men to turn around so that he could see their faces. His chest felt as though it might explode. In his growing anger, he hoped that one of them was the marauder, coming back to try to finish the job. What life was there to be had when he was constantly stalked by fear and threat of death, he thought. Best to die fighting with what little honour he had left, and if he could inflict pain on the whoreson, all the better.

With no swords in sight, Paco leapt from the porch and lunged at one of the men with such force that both tumbled to the ground. David, right behind him, pounced on the other man and after a brief tussle pushed him roughly against a wall and pinned him there with his elbow.

"No, no, David! Son, it's me … Papa," the man in David's grip gasped hoarsely.

Open-mouthed, David whipped the man's hood off. Still unable to comprehend what was going on, he flicked his eyes to the figure on the ground, being held down by Paco's dagger, tickling his throat. "Hold fast, Paco!" he said hurriedly. "That's my brother, Diego."

Paco's bewildered eyes widened and then bore into Diego's face as though he were looking for a resemblance to David. Finally, he withdrew his dagger. "Get up, you fool. You almost got yourself killed! Why were you following us?"

"I can probably explain that …," David began.

"You had better." Without waiting for the explanation, Paco glared at David's father, Juan. "Sagrat is on high alert. This is no time to be wandering the streets in the middle of the night, stalking militiamen like a couple of thieves or paid assassins. Don't you know what's been happening in this town?"

"Enough, Paco," David said.

"No, David, not enough! Had they come across any other soldiers but us, they would be on their way to prison for questioning. Or they would be dead!"

"We weren't stalking you. We were trying to catch up with David," Juan said unconvincingly.

Diego's eyes were as big as plates. Standing on shaky legs, holding the nicked skin at his throat, he panted for breath. "We went to the prison … but the soldiers wouldn't let us see you."

"That's right," Juan said. "And when we got home, we found our street crawling with militiamen. They forced us to go to the square, even the neighbours' children."

"Instead of shadowing us, why did you not approach us before we left the square? You didn't do a very good job of it," Paco said, clearly still angry.

David was no longer listening to Paco but embracing Diego. He was overjoyed, yet his heart thumped anxiously. He had so many questions for his brother. Where did he go after the fire at the farm? Was the little girl well? Where did he leave her? Why did he decide to come back to Sagrat?

"For the love of God, will someone tell me what's going on?" Paco whispered furiously.

There was no way out of this, David thought. He had to talk. "Paco, I'll answer all your questions. I'll tell you everything," David said.

Juan put his hand on David's arm. "David, no. Please, son, don't," he warned him.

"I must do this, Papa. I can't lie to him any longer. He already suspects me."

Juan's panicked face paled. He opened his mouth to protest, but David raised his hand to silence him.

CHAPTER THIRTY-NINE

Paco had listened to the entire story in stunned silence. Sitting beneath a tree with David, Juan, and Diego on the outskirts of town, his expression had held a mixture of anger and shock, but he'd also been pleasantly surprised to learn that the infant and little girl still lived.

After a long discussion about the situation, the whereabouts of the girl child, and what they could do to keep David safe from another attack, Juan and Diego went back to the house they'd just rented near Paco's home. Paco and David set off for the prison.

"David, the duke is destroying his own town," Paco said as they approached the prison walls. "The man I pledged my sword to – the noble lord entrusted by the king and queen to protect his people and lands – is killing his own citizens? The bastard ... No more ... I will serve Peráto no more. I'll live to see the man stripped of his title and his miserable life!"

"The common man has no weapons to fight his master. We do his bidding or die," David said, miserable.

"You might be right. I can't help but think that our beloved Captain Tur has also been swept into this mire of dung. And him, a man who prays in the church every day for absolution! He took the credit for the capture of Miguel and Ignacio. He brought them to the prison, yet he wasn't even at the port, according to Diego. I suspected he was lying. At the trial, he looked as though he'd just been kicked in the gut by a mule and had the wind knocked out of him."

"You think he is obeying the duke and Garcia's orders too?" David asked.

Paco nodded. "Yes, but he's probably not a willing participant. I know him. He's a good man."

David wondered what Paco would have done. "Would you have killed those people?" he asked, needing to know.

"I would have carried out my orders, same as you. I would have tried to protect my family, just as you did," he said honestly. "You have to understand, lad, that we militiamen are no better than pack mules in our nobleman's eyes. We serve him until we drop. We carry his heavy burdens and protect his castle and his coin. We do not retire until we are too old or too infirm to be of use. The only difference between us and the mule is that the mule's flesh gets eaten after years of gruelling service.

"To disobey the duke's orders is to sign one's own death warrant. We're fodder in his eyes, used to feed his whims. Nobles, my lad, have absolute power over their lands because they demand absolute obedience and loyalty. And make no mistake – these men of privilege and wealth may talk with fancy tongues and wear fine robes, but they are amongst the biggest thieves and murderers that God ever created.

"Peráto killed his physician, David," Paco continued, becoming more irate. "I knew that man. For years, he walked the castle's hallways as regally as a noble himself. Yet the duke probably didn't think twice about murdering him … So, lad, what do you think would have happened had you disobeyed him? I'll tell you what would have happened. You and your family would be dead and buried by now, and another militiaman would have been appointed to carry out His Grace's hellish orders in your stead … That person might have been me."

"I obeyed. I did as commanded, and the duke still wants me dead. His word means nothing," David said angrily.

"I agree. That's why the duke no longer has our allegiance. Saving the people of this town is all that matters now … and somehow, with God's good grace, we will succeed. We have to."

Looking at Paco, David wondered how he now viewed *his* future. He knew everything there was to know, yet he was still willing to risk his life. Why? David wondered. Why risk the lives of his family? It was an important question.

"Don't stare at me sideways," Paco said, as though reading David's thoughts. "And don't ask me again why I've agreed to help you."

CHAPTER FORTY

After the chaotic trial and execution earlier that evening, the prison seemed almost peaceful. David and Paco set to work checking prisoners at random and delivering water to those in need. In this part of the prison, only one familiar was on duty. Sitting with his arms crossed and feet atop an upturned bucket, Raul scowled disapprovingly at David and Paco, who were making far too much noise in the middle of the night.

"For God's sake, can't you two leave the prisoners' well-being until morning?" he finally asked Paco.

"We've got a couple more to do, Raul, and then we'll take our leave. Please accept our sincerest apologies for disturbing your rest," Paco said with a touch of sarcasm, which the man missed or chose to ignore.

At the other end of the passageway, some distance from the guard post, David entered Sinfa's cell. The acrid smell of excrement coming from a pile of straw heaped against the wall hit his nostrils, making his stomach twist and his eyes water. Carrying a water bucket in one hand and an oil-lit torch in the other, he kicked the door shut behind him with his heel and then raised the torch to get a better look at the prisoner.

She tried to sit up, but her thin, weak arms lacked the strength to lift her body off the floor. Her face, white as chalk, and the ripped bodice hanging off her shoulders, blackened with dirt, tore at David's heart, but it also strengthened his resolve. Hardening his thoughts, he placed the bucket on the floor and the torch in the wall bracket.

"Sinfa, stand up," he told her, gripping her arm and lifting her onto her feet.

Sinfa, staggering like a drunk, pushed her knotted hair from her face and then shielded her eyes from the brightness. Struggling to stay on her feet, she looked disorientated. She tried to speak but apparently couldn't. Finally, she pointed to the water bucket.

David shifted his body weight, clenched his fist into a tight ball, drew his arm back, and then swung a punch. After hitting Sinfa hard on the face, he watched her frail body reel backwards until she hit the wall and slid to the ground unconscious. "Forgive me." She might hate him later, he thought briefly. But that had to be done.

"Paco, we've got a dead one," David said, joining Paco, who was still speaking to Raul. "It's the Jew girl. She's stinking and covered in pus boils. We'll need to scrub the cell later. I think she was diseased."

"I suppose we'd better take her away," Paco said to Raul with a worried frown. "Even the dead can spread sickness. You know, I remember a time when ..."

"I don't want to hear another one of your stories, Paco. By the time you've finished telling it, we'll have a plague on our hands. Just get rid of her," Raul said irately.

"Do you want to help us carry the body out?" Paco asked.

"No, why should I? The Jews don't concern me."

Shrugging casually, Paco nodded.

Back in the cell, David picked Sinfa up and threw her limp body over his shoulder. Time was short, David thought, heading towards the prison doors. If she were to wake up before he and Paco got her outside, she'd moan or struggle and he and Paco would be arrested and locked up within minutes.

"Let me look at her," Raul shouted from farther along the passageway.

Paco held the outer doors open. David, who was just about to walk outside, halted. "I wouldn't get too close if I were you, Raul!" he shouted over his shoulder. "She's marked with open sores all over her face and body. She might infect you with her pus."

Holding his breath, David watched Raul take a step forward and then stare for a brief minute at Sinfa's bare thighs and legs dangling lifelessly as she was strapped to David's back. If the man decided to put his curiosity ahead of his well-being, their plan would be shot to hell and he and Paco would be finished. "Well, do you want a look at her or not?" David asked casually.

"Take her – and good riddance!" Raul shouted back.

Outside, David laid Sinfa in a coffin on the dead man's cart. This transport, used by the prison guards to move dead bodies to the graveyard, was no more than a wooden box sitting on a couple of planks of wood atop four wooden wheels and connected to two narrow wooden arms used as handles. It was heavy to pull, even for two men, and it made a loud noise when the badly constructed wheels grated against the wooden base. But they needed the coffin and the cart. Their plan would fail without them.

After clearing the streets surrounding the prison, they stopped. "Do you think it's safe now?" Paco asked David.

Walking to the corner, David looked left and then right. There were no houses in this area, only the long zigzag road down the hill. "There's not a soul in sight," David told him. "I doubt we'll see anyone on the streets until morning."

After hiding the cart and coffin on a grassy bank near their street, David carried Sinfa in his arms and followed Paco through the deserted streets.

Sinfa stirred and moaned softly. Halting in mid-step, David laid her on the ground. Her eyes shot open. Filled with terror and confusion, they bore into David's face.

David dropped to his knees and clamped his hand over her mouth. "You're safe but you must keep quiet," he warned her harshly. "Not a sound, Sinfa."

Sinfa tried to move her head but couldn't. Her terrified eyes darted left to right and then rolled upwards, as though she were trying to take stock of her surroundings.

"You're safe. You're free," David told her again.

She stared again at David, and the hope in her eyes seemed to replace the terror. Finally, she nodded in understanding.

David withdrew his hand. "I'm going to carry you. We're almost there."

"Where ... are you ... taking me?" she asked in a barely audible whisper.

"I'm taking you to my parents' house. My mother will care for you. I give you my word."

Sinfa nodded. "Did you hit me?" she mumbled, and then she closed her eyes again.

CHAPTER FORTY-ONE

The inquisitor rubbed his eyes, turned his head, and stared at the sleeping boy lying next to him. As always, after the sexual act, regret and a measure of guilt struck him, but never enough to replace the satisfaction and surge of vigour that followed lovemaking. He stroked the boy's body and revelled in its youthful contours. He would take the lad again tonight. Today would be momentous, but it would also be tiring, with long hours in contemplation and devotion to duty. Sighing loudly with a reluctance to lose the boy's warmth, he lay for a moment longer.

An inquisitor's life was not an easy one, he thought, and the boy brought him a well-earned respite. Did he not deserve to have comfort in the midst of his gruelling duties? Slapping the boy's bare buttocks, he smiled.

"Get up and see to your business. Bring me food and wine. See to my bath. Prepare my robes for High Mass – and be quick about it. I have God's work to attend to."

Once alone, he picked up his Bible, which had been resting on a table, opened it and read Genesis 3–5 from the Old Testament. "Like God, you will be able to tell the difference between good and evil," he repeated several times. That passage had always held a special meaning for him. The devil had spoken those words to Eve in the Garden of Eden, yet they could have come from God's mouth and could quite easily have been directed towards His inquisitors. He, Gaspar de Amo, had only one mission in life: to know the difference between guilt and innocence, sin and purity, and to seek confessions from lost souls.

He looked at his naked body in the smoky uneven glass mirror, which distorted his form somewhat. His narrow shoulders, flabby arms, chest hanging like two small sacks of wheat, and a large belly which folded over and covered his genitals reminded him of his mortality. He wasn't the healthiest of men, he acknowledged. Cursed with the bloody flux, he had good and bad days. On particularly sickly days, he struggled to leave his daybed, so frequent were the eruptions from his arse and tight knots in his stomach.

Life was too short, with barely enough time to achieve one's full potential, he thought as he tried to reach a boil on his buttock so that he could squeeze it. Sagrat would be the pinnacle of his success and his lasting legacy, for he doubted he would live to see many more years. Here in this town, a statue would be built to honour him. Centuries from now, he would be remembered as the just inquisitor whose fair judgements transcended secular bias and racism.

During his years of service to the Holy Office, he had brought order and peace to countless towns and cities. No longer were there violent acts against Jews and Moors from townspeople who would take justice into their own hands without understanding what righteousness was. Before this Inquisition, townspeople rounded up suspected heretics and brought them before the local lord, but no one knew how they were to be judged or how witnesses were to be heard and examined. The Inquisition had brought order to the proceedings and fair trials for the accused.

The Inquisition was Christianity's most instructive and protective body, gently shepherding its errant flock back into the fold and towards an idyllic world, where only sinners experienced God's wrath and the pure lived blissful lives. The Inquisition was not cruel. On the contrary, it provided a means for heretics to escape death at the hands of inexperienced townspeople and to return to the community.

He opened a wooden trunk sitting at the bottom of the bed and lifted out a leather whip. Kneeling in prayer, he asked God for guidance and clarity of mind. "Let my pain bring me closer to you. Accept my suffering as a testimony of love towards my fellow men and my devotion to you," he whispered.

His mind's eye caught glimpses of the two men burning at the stake two nights previously. He had watched the fires being lit from his sleeping chamber in the municipal palace and had not moved from the window overlooking the square until the bodies had turned to ash.

Shaking his head violently from side to side, he tried to cast out the images. An anguished sob ripped from his throat, his legs buckled, and he fell to his knees. Holding the whip tightly in his hand, he used his free hand to stroke the three arm's length knotted leather prongs one by one. "May I bleed as Christ did for his fellow men," he muttered. "Let this sacrificial deed atone for my sins and lead me to sanctity."

As the first strike of the whip slashed his back, he shuddered with a mixture of pain and ecstasy. Lifting his arm, he coiled the whip onto his back and shoulders and with each lash flogged himself more viciously than the time before.

His body, jerking violently every time the whip dug into his flesh, stung like the kiss of a thousand stinging nettles, yet his mind urged him to continue. During flagellation, he had once crossed the thin veil between two worlds. God had spoken to him, first telling him to punish the heretics who would destroy Spain, and then saying that He and his angels would smite the sinners with rocks from heaven.

"Speak to me, Lord!" he cried out. He *needed* to experience the Lord's presence again. "I do this for you! This is your will!" he exclaimed, vividly remembering God's words in that wondrous vision.

Again he pictured the men at the stake, their rigid bodies tall within the high wall of smoke that surrounded them, their heads exploding with intense heat. "Oh, Lord, it was done in your name!"

Lashing himself harder still, he tasted the blood that was spraying from his back onto his shoulders throat and mouth. His teeth were chattering, yet sweat poured down his forehead and onto his eyelids and cheeks. Conjuring up images of tortured faces, his mind settled on a young woman in Zaragoza whose body had been roped in the torture chamber. Tears sprang from his eyes and coursed down his cheeks as he recalled her agonising screams for mercy.

Thick ropes had been coiled around her body. Between the ropes and her skin was a wooden pole which the torturer turned like a key. With each twist of the wood, the ropes had tightened until they had squeezed her belly so tightly that her skin bled and ribs broke. "I love my people!" he cried. "I am their saviour!"

The whip slipped from his hand. His body keeled over, and he curled himself into a tight ball on the floor. Shivering, he reached out his arm towards the bed and gripped the blanket hanging over the edge. Groaning with pain, he dragged it towards him and pulled it over him. His panting breath was like smoke rising in the cold air, and for a fleeting second, he wondered why he'd not ordered the fire to be lit. "I do what I do to save God's flock," he mumbled. "I am their shepherd. God, grant me Your Grace …"

CHAPTER FORTY-TWO

The church of San Agustin was bathed in light on this last Sunday before Christmas. In the front-row pew, Luis sat with his town council. On the other side of the isle were the Dominican monks and visiting clergy from Valencia.

There were not many pews, and every one of them was filled. Children sitting on parents' laps shifted impatiently, waiting for permission to go outside to play in the town square and eat their caraway seed biscuits, a Sunday treat. In the centre aisle, invalids lay or sat on the floor. Halfway down the church, a throng of people, unable to find a seat, stood in dishevelled lines, ten deep in places.

After finishing his sermon with a blessing, Bishop Sanchez left the pulpit and gave way to the inquisitor.

Gaspar de Amo rose from his throne-like chair and allowed his chamberlain to adjust his cloak before making his way up the spiral staircase to the highest pulpit – the eagle's eye, so called by Father Bernardo.

Looking down at the multitude, he took a moment to search out the enthralled sea of faces waiting, probably wondering and undoubtedly fearful of the edict which he was about to read. From where he stood, he could see over the tops of the people's heads at the back of the church and into the crowded La Placa Del Rey outside. His heart soared. Hundreds of townspeople, unable to find a spot inside, had gathered to listen to him and to learn from him. His mission had begun, he thought, for by the end of this day, many would have already come forward to confess their sins.

There was a hushed stillness, yet the inquisitor, inebriated by power, raised his hand as though he were the pope himself, silencing the masses.

"Children, by the grace of God, the Holy Office, and Their Majesties King Ferdinand and Queen Isabella, I extend a solemn invitation to you the faithful to hear the edict of grace," his voice rang out. "This is your one opportunity to confess all that which blackens your soul.

"Heresy, that most terrible crime, is not only a sin against God. It is also a grave offence against Rome and Spain. A priest cannot give you absolution," he continued, giving his first warning. "Your confessors can, however, refer to me any penitents who have denounced themselves for sins against the faith. I urge you all to think well on this! By self-accusing yourselves, you will avoid the most severe penalty for heresy, which is death!" De Amo paused and allowed the soft rumbling of shocked voices to settle. The people would not be filled with fear were they not shocked at his words, he always reminded himself at this point in the edict. And fear was exactly what he wanted from them.

"Let me remind you that self-denunciation is not enough. You must also denounce your relatives, friends, and acquaintances who have taken part in your reprehensible practices. Those who witness a heretic act and do not denounce the sinner are just as guilty, and the punishment will be just as severe, as though you too have sinned!" Watching confusion and disapproval spread throughout the congregation, he wondered why it was not obvious to the people that their duty to the church far outweighed any loyalty they might feel towards friends or family members.

"Amongst these heretic crimes are any and all ceremonies or meetings where Jewish prayers have been recited or a circumcision has been performed," he continued. "All

Judaizers must be reported, for I repeat, if you do not accuse those heretics, you will be excommunicated and charged by the Inquisition.

"Even those already in the grave should be denounced if it is clear to you that they *were* Judaizers. They shall not rest in peace … Their bodies will be exhumed and burnt, and all remaining possessions will be confiscated!" Again De Amo paused for effect. The church was as silent as a tomb. Only a sea of terrified eyes spoke of the fear he was inflicting.

"You must look for signs. People who refuse to recite the 'Gloria Patri' at the end of a psalm are to be denounced as heretics, as are those who slaughter animals in an unchristian way, abstain from eating Christian foods such as pork, and do not work on Saturdays.

"All who attend funerals must also be vigilant. Judaizers must be denounced if they attend to a dead person whose body is washed in warm water and its armpits and beards shaved when it is wrapped in a new winding sheet, with its head propped up by a pillow filled with virgin earth! If you see that a pearl or coin has been placed in the dead person's mouth, or that the house has been sprinkled with water, then in all probability, you will be in the presence of Judaizers!

"Hear me well, my children. You have been warned! By the grace of God, you are given a period of one month's grace to come forward and …"

A piercing scream coming from the town square filtered into the church and echoed up into the wooden rafters. Seconds later, the sound of men's raised voices, cries of terror, and a chaotic congregation in the square, running towards one of its side streets, managed to halt the inquisitor's edict.

Wagging an index finger at Luis and throwing him a contemptuous look, De Amo shouted, "What is this, Your

Grace? What new calamity has befallen your inflicted sin-ridden town!"

Luis rose from his seat, ignored the inquisitor, and was halfway down the aisle before De Amo had stopped shouting. Barging past people blocking his path, he headed towards the church's doors, screaming with rage at those in his way.

"Murder! There's been another murder!" a man's voice boomed at the church's doors.

Women's screams vibrated through the church. People blessed themselves and cried out to God. Some knelt in prayer, but the majority clambered towards the doors, climbing over pews, which toppled onto the floor. Effigies vibrated, and some fell off the altar. The invalids lying in the centre aisle screeched with horror as the able-bodied ran over their bodies. And in a frantic effort to get outside, they knocked down Inquisition men-at-arms, trying to block their paths.

The inquisitor's mouth opened and then snapped shut after deciding that he wouldn't be heard. Making his way down the spiral stairs, he stumbled and fell to his knees just as he cleared the last narrow step. Kneeling, he attempted to untangle legs from the folds of his robes and inadvertently cursed. "A plague on them all!"

His chamberlain tried to pick him up off the floor. "Get your hands off me, you fool!" De Amo shouted. "Make a path for me! Move this spawn of the devil out of my way!" When he'd steadied himself, he strode onto the dais. "Sit down, all of you!" he screamed.

Having no effect on the people, he left the pulpit and angrily pushed aside worshippers blocking his path to the doors. His rage, increasing further at the sight of his flock following the duke, who had already left the church, caused him to stop in his tracks. If he lost control of the people today, he would never have their obedience, he thought. They would not confess to him if they were not afraid of him.

"Halt!" he screamed again. "You cannot disobey your inquisitor! Remain in your seats. I have not finished! You will be reported to the Holy Office. This is heresy!"

Finally, the people took notice of him. A few returned to their seats and got on their knees to pray, as though their very lives depended on the words they would speak. But most, stunned by the growing chaos outside, seemed determined to find out what was happening and, more importantly, who had been murdered.

"Go back to your seats! I demand your obedience! You will go to hell. I give you my word that you will all see the devil and burn for eternity!" Although de Amo tried again, only a few listened to him.

Sitting down in an empty pew, he covered his face with his hands. This was a catastrophe, he thought. Never had he been so humiliated. Sagrat was a cursed town. The evil one and his legions lurked in every corner of every street. Peráto had caused the flock to scatter, and the opportunity to rein in the heretics had been lost. They would not come back inside the church, not today. "Damn you to hell, Peráto," he cursed under his breath. "You'll pay dearly for this!"

CHAPTER FORTY-THREE

A crowd of people blocked a narrow side street between the municipal palace and the monastery walls. Luis, weighed down by ceremonial robes and cloak, strode into the crowd, which parted at the sight of him and the handful of militiamen behind him. When he got to the street opening, he pushed aside the remaining few people standing in his way and approached the dead body, which was half hidden underneath a cart.

For a moment, he stared at it, unable to comprehend the carnage that met his eyes and who he was looking at. His breath came in sharp gasps. He felt as though he were being punched in the chest. *It isn't possible!* his mind screamed. *How can this be true?*

The acrid stench made him feel light-headed. The sharp metallic odour of blood seemed to hover above the body. Bending over, he wretched violently and clutched his stomach. Wiping the bile from his mouth, he stared dazedly at Tur. "Monstrous," was all he could say.

Standing next to Luis and as pale as a white sheet, Captain Tur said, "The body looks as though it's been here all night, Your Grace. Worms are already feeding on it."

Luis shuddered. "Move the cart away from the remains."

When the cart had been pushed away, Luis covered his mouth and nose with a linen cloth and then took a closer look. Garcia's face, streaked red with blood coming from a deep wound to the head, seemed much less grisly than the lower part of his body, which was ripped open from his chest to his genitals like a gutted goat. His entrails were spread around the body as though they had been placed in a pattern. They had been cut into pieces, and they mingled with excrement, blood, and bodily fluids. A dagger pinned a ripped piece of parchment to Garcia's throat, and written on it was a single word: *Abomination.*

Luis wanted to run from the putrid smell and the revolting sight. He suddenly felt vulnerable, afraid of the people surrounding him and powerless against a would-be assassin who had not been afraid to butcher the treasurer's body.

Forcing himself to look objectively at the scene, Luis noticed two things in particular. Garcia's sword and belt were missing. The killer must have taken them, he thought, for Garcia never left his chambers without being fully armed. His sword, a gift, bore the Peráto crest. The second thing that struck him was the ferociousness of the slaughter. The killer's hatred was palpable. This hadn't been a random or frenzied attack. Whoever did it had taken the time to disembowel and display the treasurer's guts and, in doing so, had publicly marked Garcia as a coward.

Still staring at what was left of Garcia, Luis noticed the glint of a key and chain. He picked it up in his gloved hand and shuddered with revulsion when blood stained it. It was the municipal palace's key to the treasury.

Turning from the body, Luis saw a sea of terrified people. Looking at their faces, his eyes widened with shock. Their blatant insolent stares were directed at him. Why? Were they blaming him for not keeping the town safe? If that were the case, he would lose their respect, maybe even their loyalty. The town was descending into hell! This murder would strike the fear of God into every citizen in Sagrat, and who knew what madness would erupt.

"Go back to the church, all of you!" he shouted harshly over his shoulder. Looking at Tur, he said, "Get rid of this crowd. I don't want anyone else to look at this gruesome sight." Whilst Tur ordered his men to control the crowd, Luis focused on the parchment. Grimacing at the sight of the blood running through the letters, he wondered why anyone would call Garcia an *abomination*. When he had Tur's attention, he asked him, "What Christian soul could do such a thing? What did Garcia do to warrant such a title?"

"I can't imagine. The lord treasurer was not a soldier. He fought no battles. Maybe he had enemies," Tur suggested, looking as mystified as Luis.

"Get a coffin here at once. Remove him, every last bit of flesh and scum."

"Where shall we take it?" Tur asked.

"To the church, of course! Tell Father Bernardo to say a prayer and then bury Garcia immediately. See to this and then report to me. We have a monster in our midst, Tur, and by God, we shall find him."

Unable to breathe in the putrid stench any longer, Luis staggered numbly out of the side street and back into the square. Repeating the word *abomination* to himself, he was chilled by fear. Did someone know about Garcia's part in the murders and about the infant and little girl? Was this revenge? Looking about him at the scared townspeople following him, he wondered if someone might be planning to strike him down, as they had the treasurer. Was the murderer in the square stalking and planning his attack? Who could possibly detest Garcia enough to do *that*? Luis kept asking himself. Not the marauders. No, why would they kill their paymaster? Not David Sanz? Garcia hated Sanz, but why should Sanz hate Garcia? Did Garcia try to kill Sanz, and Sanz got the upper hand? No, Luis thought, the order to assassinate the militiaman hadn't been issued. But then again, Sanz could have done it. It was a possibility.

Overcome by panic, he halted in the middle of the square. Horrifying thoughts were tumbling into his mind one after the other. He couldn't stop them. Had Sanz told someone about the murders? If he had, would he, Luis, be arrested, tortured, and burned by a pack of rabid townspeople? No, he then consoled himself. He was a duke. No commoner would dare accuse a powerful nobleman of wrongdoing.

Thinking again about Sanz, he looked at every man in militia uniform. Sanz wasn't there, but he was a plague on the mind ... The militiaman should have been killed weeks ago. But who would dispose of him now that Garcia was gone?

Coming out of the church and being followed by his familiars and entourage, Gaspar de Amo's face wore a thunderous scowl. He began to stride towards Luis but then halted mid-step and gestured Luis to go to him.

Luis cringed with trepidation. He'd all but forgotten the inquisitor, his edict, and his glorious mission to terrify Sagrat's people. Walking reluctantly towards him, Luis braced himself for De Amo's torrent of insults, and he couldn't help but blame Garcia for causing this entire mess ... Garcia, the man who'd been entrusted to run Sagrat's affairs and finances, and who'd controlled some very dangerous marauders, had been cut into pieces like a carcass. He'd been careless letting himself be killed like that! Luis thought. And now he, Luis, was left staring at a frightening and uncertain future with no one but God to turn to. This was probably the worst day of his life!

Sitting in a pew next to Isa, Juan felt waves of relief wash over him. The information which had filtered through the crowd in the square had horrified and shocked everyone around him, yet his heart had soared with gladness. Garcia was dead, and there was now a real possibility that David would have a future after all.

Upon hearing the shouts of murder, Juan had sat stunned and afraid to leave amidst the inquisitor's threats of death and imprisonment for anyone who dared to move. But his words had been no match for Isa's wretched tears and sobbing voice, saying, "Not David. Not David!" He would have defied God himself to get to his son, he'd thought at the time.

He stood and looked towards the back of the church. There were still about a hundred people standing around. The place was a mess. Some overturned pews had been wrecked, and pieces of wood were strewn on the floor. People were crying with sheer terror. Children clung to their mothers, not fully understanding what was going on but swept up with the adults' emotional reactions.

Voices buzzing like a thick hornet's nest died abruptly when soldiers carried in a wooden coffin. Juan and Isa watched as it was taken to the altar. When it was set down, four of the soldiers left, leaving two behind. Isa held Juan's hand. "What are we to do?" she asked him. "I don't want to stay here with that dead body. The inquisitor has left with the bishop, Father Bernardo's nowhere to be seen, and I doubt the duke will come back. Do we just sit here until someone tells us to go home?"

Juan shook his head. Sinfa, the Jew girl David had brought home the previous night, was alone in the house and very sick. The damage here had been done. Father Bernardo would return any minute to deal with the coffin and remains, and the mighty Inquisition would probably punish Sagrat's people, whether they remained or not. But he would not think about The Holy Office today, he thought defiantly. He was far too relieved. God had finally smiled on the Sanz family.

"Let's go home," he said. "We've been forgotten."

CHAPTER FORTY-FOUR

Isa stopped what she was doing, looked up, and smiled at David. "You can come in when she's finished eating," she said. "Sinfa has been eager to speak with you. She has questions."

Nodding, David looked at Sinfa, who was sitting up in the bed and taking another spoonful of broth. "I have time. I'll wait, Mama," he answered.

He'd been desperate to get there, but circumstances had made it impossible for him to come home any earlier. Reluctant to cross the threshold until there was no more food in the bowl, he leaned against the sleeping room's door frame and felt his heart melt, just as it always did whenever he saw Sinfa.

According to his mother, Sinfa had slept for three days and nights. But she had also been awakened sporadically by nightmares which had left her drenched in sweat and crying uncontrollably. David could only imagine how wonderful a warm soft bed, hot food, and his mother's loving care must have felt to Sinfa after weeks in captivity, sleeping on a cold dirt floor. Garcia's order that she be fed nothing but pig's meat had been carried out. His statement that she would probably starve to death might well have borne truth, for she had refused to touch the meat. David believed that had it not been for the bread and vegetables he'd smuggled into the prison, she would not have survived.

Bathed and dressed in a white linen nightdress, she was already looking better, he thought. There were tinges of pink on her pale cheeks, although one side of her face was marred by bruising that sat underneath her left eye and crept down her cheek. He'd done that to her, but he prayed that she understood why and forgave him.

Sinfa ate very slowly, he noticed. It probably pained her to part her chapped, swollen lips. His eyes wandered to her recently shorn head. It saddened him to see her scabby and reddened scalp covered with a scattering of black bristles. According to his mother, Sinfa's head had been so flea-ridden that there had been no other option than to cut off all her hair, which had once fallen in lustrous waves to her waist.

"It will grow back. I'm glad to be rid of the insects that were nesting in it," Sinfa said matter-of-factly.

Mortified at being caught gawking, David looked to his mother for permission to enter. When she gestured him to go closer to the bed, he asked Sinfa, "Do you feel a bit better?"

"Yes, thank you," she said, but her voice was hoarse and weak. "I don't remember much about escaping from the prison ... I don't know how I can thank you."

"No need," David said awkwardly.

"What's to become of me? Are the soldiers looking for me?"

There was no easy way to tell her that she was dead to the world, David thought. But tell her he must. "Sinfa, you're going to find my words hard to grasp, but I want you to know that I did what I did to save your life. You would have died in that cell ... You did die – or at least the world thinks you did."

Furrowing her brow, Sinfa stared at Isa and then back to David. "But I'm not dead," she said. "Can I go home to the Jewry?"

"No, you can never go back there," David told her emphatically. "The authorities have been informed that you died in the prison. I registered your death in the office of Jewish affairs in the municipal palace. We, my friend and I, took a coffin filled with dirt to the Jewry. We saw your rabbi ..."

Sinfa began to sob. Her eyes bore into Isa and then David. Her confusion was being replaced with shock. She stared vacantly, as though lost in a world of her own. She tried to get out of the bed but it was a feeble effort. "I must go home. No, it can't be … Rabbi Rabinovitch thinks me dead?"

"Yes," David replied. Rabbi Rabinovitch and his son, Guillermo, had cried like babies at the graveside. Their tears had affected him greatly, for they had been genuine. After the burial, the rabbi had approached him and Paco. Appearing defeated, Rabinovitch had stood before them with a bowed head. "You probably blame me for her death, but God forgive me, I couldn't help her," he'd wept. "At least she is at peace. We Jews will soon be thrown out of our own country, and Spain will lose a most worthy race of people. This is a catastrophe … an unholy crime against my race!"

"Rabbi Rabinovitch, Guillermo, and my neighbours? But surely they didn't bury me without my Jewish rites?" Sinfa said.

Her question surprised David. How she was supposedly buried should be the least of her worries, he thought. Presuming she was in shock, he said in a firm voice, "I told the rabbi that you were infected with a disease and that you had died in your cell. The coffin was nailed shut. Paco and I stood outside your cemetery gates and watched your people bury it in the ground …" David paused. She looked devastated.

"Sinfa, you do understand what this means?" he pushed on. "You cannot be seen alive in Sagrat. No one must know you're here."

"But I'm not dead!" Sinfa sobbed, reality finally striking her.

"No, thanks to God, you're well."

Isa, holding Sinfa's hand, shook her head, gesturing to David not to say any more.

David raised his hand to silence her. "No, Mama, she has to know the truth."

Sinfa wept on, but her eyes never strayed from David's face. "My life is over in Sagrat, isn't it?" she asked after a while.

David nodded sadly. "Yes, it's over."

"But you will have a new life elsewhere," Isa said, desperately trying to console her.

"And who will I be in this new life?" Sinfa wept even harder.

David wanted to comfort her, but before he could do that, she had to be aware of the enormity of the situation. "You must understand that my family's well-being now depends on your willingness to stay hidden. You cannot leave this house. You must not look through an open window, stand at the door, or even think about going into the street. If your presence here is reported to the authorities, you, my entire family, and I will be arrested and put to death."

After a while, Sinfa wiped her eyes, and let out a long broken sigh. Nodding her head, she finally seemed to understand. "For how long must I be hidden here?" she asked, sounding calmer.

"A few weeks," David said truthfully. "Maybe longer."

CHAPTER FORTY-FIVE

Walking along a particularly foul-smelling street, David and Paco covered their mouths and noses with their hands and picked up their pace. The pathway between the houses was barely wide enough for two doors on opposite sides to open outwards at the same time. There were no drains or sewers nearby, thus this part of town always smelled of decaying meat and human waste.

The street, sloping downwards towards the base of the hill, sat just a stone's throw away from the town's slaughterhouse and goat pens, which overlooked the cramped buildings. Animal blood frequently flowed down the hill like a stream, forming red puddles in a dip at the base of stone steps bordering the bottom end of the lane. Worse were the animal innards and other unwanted leftovers that were dumped on an embankment at the top end of the alley, forming thick rotting piles which were eaten by stray dogs roaming the area.

Every so often, David looked up at the top floor windows, praying that wives wouldn't empty a piss pot at the exact moment he walked underneath them. It was still early, he thought. Everyone would probably still be asleep after the Christmas Eve processions, Mass, and family suppers, which had gone on long into the night.

This was going to be the strangest Christmas he'd even known. If truth be told, no one seemed to be in the mood to celebrate anything apart from one Mass after the other. The townspeople were no doubt praying for an end to the series of murders, which had left them terrified, and who could blame them?

Sighing with relief when they'd left the stench of that street behind them, David asked Paco, "So how long will these night patrols continue?"

"I don't know. It's unheard of," Paco said.

"It seems a bit harsh not allowing people to leave their homes after it gets dark. There're going to be a lot of unhappy shopkeepers."

"People are scared, lad, and I'll wager they'd rather stay indoors than be in the streets at night. My cousin caught a glimpse of Garcia's dead body. He said it put the fear of God into him. He's convinced that the evil one is in Sagrat."

David had heard similar comments from people who'd been at the High Mass. People were barring their doors at night, afraid to sleep or to be alone in a house. Captain Tur and the militia had relentlessly hunted Garcia's killer, but he was still at large. The soldiers had gone from door to door, questioning people and looking for clues and evidence. New guard posts had been positioned at every entrance into Sagrat. Strangers not known in the town were being interrogated, and every sack in every cart that moved was searched. David wasn't sure what the militiamen were hoping to find inside sacks of wheat and corn, but at least they were being seen doing something.

"It's been a week since Garcia's murder. The militia is on a fool's errand," David said, voicing his thoughts. "They'll never find the person who did it. He's probably long gone."

"I disagree. I think the killer lives in Sagrat."

David's mind had raced all week with questions he was unable to answer. Like Paco, he too believed that there had to be a connection between Garcia's death and the murders that he, David, had committed. He had theories, but they posed more questions than answers: Did someone in the town, apart from the duke, know the truth about the infant? Did Garcia have a disagreement with the scar-faced marauder over money, and was he killed because of that? Or did the duke pay someone to murder the treasurer? That theory was, in David's opinion, the most likely. For a short time, he had even suspected his father and brother, but his father was not capable of murder and wouldn't butcher a body, not even Garcia's. Diego didn't have the stomach to gut a man either. Paco, on the other hand …

David and Paco found Captain Tur in the castle's north-east courtyard. They had news for him, but before announcing it, they took a moment to observe their fellow militiamen trudging laboriously up the stairs to the battlements with arms loaded with weapons.

"Are we expecting a siege?" Paco said jokingly. "What in the name of God are they all doing?"

David was mesmerised. Tur, looking flustered, was shouting orders at the men. There was nothing new about his barking orders, David thought, but one would be led to believe that an enemy army was advancing on the town, judging by the urgency in his voice.

Looking up at the battlements, David saw longbows, spears, pikes, clubs, and buckets of oil being deposited at various intervals on the wall. In the courtyard, militiamen were red-faced, sweating, and panting with exertion as they moved heavy rocks to the foot of the wall's stairs. The duke was afraid, David thought. Perhaps he didn't kill Garcia.

"Why would the duke order the defences to be strengthened?" David asked Paco.

"I'm not sure. Tur must be cursing him. Who does Peráto think he is coming to attack him? No army will be able to scale these walls. The north-east gate is practically impenetrable. It has withstood attempted breaches for the past two hundred and fifty years," Paco said. "The duke's private chambers are in this part of the castle. Maybe he's scared of being bludgeoned to death in his bed. What a favour that would be."

"If that's the case, he didn't have Garcia murdered," David suggested.

"Maybe not ... Or maybe this is a ploy to cover up his guilt."

CHAPTER FORTY-SIX

Luis cradled Jaime Gaspar in his arms and tried his best to soothe him. In truth, the baby's cries were comforting in the midst of Josefa's grating screams and the crashing noise of crockery breaking as it hit the walls, he thought. She was an abomination. Her black soul, straddling hell, was lost to God. She was beyond redemption.

She would never see his son again. He would make sure of that. Whenever the baby had been taken to see her, she had become violent and had threatened to throw him out the window. Even her ladies-in-waiting were terrified of her. She would let no one touch her, and she had not been bathed in days. Soon she'd stink like a diseased old whore whose mossy cave had been poked too many times. And her stench would fill his chambers. Sighing with disgust, he kissed the baby's forehead and then handed him to the waiting wet nurse. "Keep him away from his mother," he ordered.

As soon as he was alone, he locked the door and went into his dressing chamber. A heavy oak cabinet, standing as tall as he against one of the walls, had been there since his grandfather's day. It was a heavy piece of furniture. He broke out in a sweat and strained a muscle every time he had to push it farther along the wall.

Grunting with exertion after moving the cabinet about two feet to the left, he picked up a lit oil lamp and then held it held it in front of an opening in the wall. Totally obscured when the cabinet was in place, the hole was just high and wide enough to allow a man to step through it without having to crouch down. Holding the lamp with one hand and the stone wall with the other, he stepped inside and cautiously descended the stairs, which led to a secret chamber.

Once inside the hidden room, he looked at two leather chests sitting against a wall. They looked the same as the dozens of other treasury chests that had been used to transport money over the years. The duke of Sagrat's crest was embossed on the sides, and the inside frame was made of wood. These chests had been brought here years ago, and they had been empty at the time of his father's death, apart from a hundred or so ducats. But over the past eight months, he and the marauders had worked together to fill them to the brim.

He had given the mercenaries the task of raiding caravans whilst he pilfered Sagrat's vaults with Garcia's help. Little by little and one small sack at a time, money had left the municipal palace and had ended up in these chests, and no one had ever been the wiser. After lifting a handful of silver and gold maravedis, reals, and ducats, he tipped his palm downwards and watched the coins trickle back into the chest, making that wonderful jingling sound that he loved so much.

There still wasn't enough money to buy the political power he needed to become Valencia's next viceroy, he thought on reflection. To have a chance at that seat, he would have to bribe noblemen and council members across the region, for nominations from his peers would be the only way to convince the king and queen that he was the right man for the position.

After pulling one of the chests along the wall, another opening was revealed. Waist high and just wide enough to take a man's girth, a tunnel extended as far as the castle's north-western side, exiting halfway up the shallowest part of the hill. It was the only part of the hill that did not require a defensive wall. There, the castle's back facade was at its highest. There were no windows and no doors. It stood like a giant wall, flanked by battlements on either side.

The tunnel's exterior exit was well hidden within dense vegetation and rocks, and it was covered by a heavy iron grill which could be opened from the outside. It was a sewage outlet of sorts, for halfway along the tunnel, a tributary carrying waste from the barracks flowed into its main pathway.

A short time after Luis had removed the iron grate that cased the opening inside the secret chamber, he heard a man's heavy breathing and the sound of knees and hands scuffling along the tunnel's dirt and rock floor. "You're late," he whispered into the tunnel.

Alejandro crawled out, stood up, and stretched his muscles. Stinking like shit, he grunted with disgust. "Better late than never. Why don't you crawl through that filth the next time?" he said.

"It's been awhile, Alejandro. It's good to see you, my friend," Luis said, giving Alejandro a slap on the back.

"It's been too long, Luis. I was surprised and troubled when I received your message. It's not like you to contact me unless it's absolutely necessary."

"It was." Pointing to a chest, Luis gestured Alejandro to sit. "Are you sure no one followed you from the caves or saw you on the hill?"

"I'm sure."

Nodding, Luis said, "Garcia's dead. Someone cut him into pieces … Was it you?"

Alejandro did not seem at all saddened by the news, but he did appear to be taken aback by the question. "No, I had no need to kill him. He was a useful messenger."

Luis sighed with relief. "I had to ask. I'm baffled by his murder."

"It doesn't surprise me that someone would want him dead," Alejandro said.

"Why do you say that?"

"The man was careless with his tongue. I didn't trust him. I had no way of knowing if I was following your orders or his. He was not fond of you, Luis, and I doubt he was completely loyal. He tried to pit me against you. Said we could take a bigger share of the money and you would never know. Who knows what enemies he had."

"Bastard … Still, his death is unfortunate."

"You have no clues?"

"No, only my own suspicions," Luis said.

"What do you know of a man named Sanz?" Alejandro asked. "Could it be him? Garcia sent me to kill him."

Luis's heart was racing. Garcia … the useless, disobedient fool. Did he tell Alejandro why he wanted Sanz dead or about the infant? No, Luis thought, if Alejandro knew, he would have said something about it. "What did Garcia tell you about the man?" Luis asked.

"Only that he posed a threat to our mission."

Luis felt relief spread through his body. Shaking his head, he said, "If Garcia wanted you to assassinate this man, it was probably because he had a personal vendetta."

Looking furious, Alejandro said, "Garcia didn't tell me that Sanz was skilful with a blade. He gave me quite the dual."

"Why did you not kill him?"

"I could have ended him had a neighbour not split my head with a log." Touching the back of his head, Alejandro added, "It was not the first time I'd encountered Sanz."

"What? What do you mean?"

"He was at one of the farms we torched. He wanted to fight five of us. There he was, surrounded, trying to protect his father and a small girl with nothing but a sword in his hand and hatred flashing in his eyes. I have to admire his fire and passion. He's no coward."

Thoughts crashed into Luis's mind. Shit! Shit and pox! That bastard Sanz was at the farm. His eyes widened as an even darker thought crossed his mind. Sanz had no sister, which could only mean … No, it was impossible.

Luis could barely think straight. All he could hear in his mind was a voice screaming, *The girl is alive! Sanz didn't kill her!* Taking a long breath, he forced his mind to concentrate on Alejandro and the matter at hand. He would think about killing Sanz after Alejandro had left. He would think of nothing else!

Spreading out a map on top of a trunk, he said, "Garcia is a loss, but he was not indispensable. I've had to adjust our plans, but when I tell you about my proposal, I think you'll agree that not only will it work, but also that we'll be even richer than we first anticipated."

"How many days do we have to prepare?"

"Ten."

"Then you had better tell me everything, down to the finest detail."

Nodding in agreement, Luis said, "Prepare well. This is the last time we will see each other until after the auto-de-fé."

After Alejandro left the chamber through the tunnel, Luis locked the inner tunnel's grate and then pushed the trunk back to its original position against the wall. He loved Alejandro better than he loved his brothers. Yet not even Garcia had known about their friendship or that they had even met. Secrecy was their most powerful ally, and it had served them well for the past year.

Before his father's death, Luis had spent a great deal of time in Valencia. He often wondered why he'd gone to a particular part of the city one night. He knew that the very worst of men inhabited it. Overcrowded streets swarming with rapists, murderers, swords for hire, blackguards, and thieves was not a place he would ever want to visit. Not even the Inquisition wished to show its face there. He could only put his exuberant curiosity to explore down to being overly inebriated on grape wine.

Picturing Alejandro's long ragged facial scar inflicted upon him that night, Luis was reminded that he would have died had it not been for Alejandro's timely intervention. He could still feel the excruciating pain from lying on the ground and being kicked repeatedly by three thieves who'd already stolen the clothes from his back. There had been so much blood in his eyes that he thought he'd been blinded. Alejandro, appearing from nowhere, had rushed head down towards the men like a bull, intent on gouging into their flesh. He had fought like a demon from hell, killing two of the attackers and leaving the other on the ground begging for mercy.

CHAPTER FORTY-SEVEN

Walking into the courtyard, Luis was met by militiamen forming to escort him to the church of San Agustin for the Christmas Day Mass. Earlier he'd ordered Tur to have four cavalrymen and eight militiamen ready to move at all times. From now on, he wouldn't leave the castle unless surrounded by battle-ready guards, he'd told Tur. With a killer still at large, he trusted no one but his own soldiers … In truth, he feared David Sanz.

After he'd inspected all the men and was satisfied that he recognised them, he crossed the courtyard towards his carriage. His eyes settled on Captain Tur standing next to the carriage door, and then they flicked to the man standing slightly behind him. Sucking in his breath, he stared at David from across the courtyard. Dressed in full armour and looking like a hardened soldier, he no longer seemed like the wide-eyed apprentice who'd shook like a shitting dog only weeks previously. Was the dog now going to turn on its master? Luis wondered.

At first angry, he now felt a cold stab of fear. Passing soldiers, he absently wished them a blessed Christmas, but in the forefront of his mind, his inner voice was repeatedly screaming *betrayal*! Thinking about Sanz and the child he was supposed to have killed but didn't had kept him awake all night. Feeling the hairs rise on the back of his neck, he shivered and asked Tur, "Why are these two men not on watch in my prison? I need them there, not here."

"Your Grace, it's Christmas," Captain Tur answered falteringly. "A few men have been granted leave. I've been strengthening our defences and using more soldiers to guard the walls, at your request. Your escort is larger than usual …"

"That's not what I'm asking, Tur!" Luis shouted. "I already know what you've been doing for the past three days. I want you to tell me why Sanz and this … this other man … What's your name?" he asked Paco.

"Paco Morales, Your Grace."

"Morales? Yes, that's right. So tell me, why have you and Sanz disobeyed my orders?"

"We didn't disobey you, sir. We were at the prison earlier this morning. We were informed by the inquisitor's familiars that the entire prison is now under the control of the Holy Office," Paco said sheepishly. "We were denied access and told not to return. My apologies. I presumed you were aware of the changes."

Boiling with rage, Luis recalled the previous evening. He'd extended the inquisitor every courtesy, he thought, now resenting every kindness he'd done for the man. His father by law had eaten well, drunk the castle's best wine, and had spent hours tediously boasting about the prison filling up with heretics. He'd even demanded money from Sagrat's vaults to cover the cost of the prisoners' meals and the upcoming auto-de-fé. Yet he'd said nothing about the Inquisition's plans for the prison.

Stepping into his carriage, Luis refused to look again at David. His mood, already gloomy, darkened further. The inquisitor had just humiliated him in front of his men. "What are you standing there for?" he hissed at Tur. "You're coming with me. Move your arse!"

David and Paco sat with their backs against the wall next to the north-east gate and wiped the sweat from their faces. Tur, seemingly blaming them for the duke's foul mood, had ordered them to carry every rock up the stairs to the battlements and not to stop for so much as a sip of water until the task had been completed.

Closing his eyes, David ran his fingers through his damp hair. When was the last time he'd had a proper night's sleep or had thoughts about anything other than trying to stay alive?

"Get on your feet, David. Tur's coming," Paco said, giving David a sharp nudge.

Seeing Captain Tur striding across the courtyard towards him with a thunderous look on his face gave David a nervous jolt. Tur was fuming; that much was clear. But who was he angry with? He could only presume that the captain's meeting with the duke had not gone well and that his anger had something to do with the extra defences.

Tur motioned David to follow him to the centre of the courtyard, and when they had reached the selected position, he said in a loud enough voice for every soldier to hear, "David Sanz, give me your sword."

Paco, who had been a step behind them, scowled with disapproval. "Why do you want his blade?"

"I'm talking to Sanz, not to you, Morales. Take a step back," Tur said, his voice crackling with anger.

David felt as though his lungs were on fire. Looking at Tur, he wondered if all the rage he saw was directed towards him and Paco or if perhaps he was bothered by his conscience. Tur had a sour face, and he always looked irritated, David thought, continuing to stare at the captain. But it was rare to see such anger shining in his eyes.

For a brief second, David looked at the men who'd gathered around, and he felt the horror of public humiliation. If he had support from any of them, they were not showing it. "Your blade, Sanz," Tur said through his teeth.

David drew his sword and rested the blade in the palms of his hands. When a militiaman was asked for his sword, it meant only one thing. He looked at it for a brief second and recalled the day that Tur had presented it to him and welcomed him into the militia's ranks. Reluctantly, he outstretched his arms and offered the sword's hilt end to Tur. "Captain, my sword is yours," he said with a catch in his voice.

Tur also looked at it briefly, and for just a second, David thought he saw a flash of regret cross his sunken eyes. But if he had, it had gone in the time it took a man to blink.

Tur took the sword and handed it to another militiaman who was standing next to him. "David Sanz, your services are no longer required. You are dismissed from the militia," he said piercingly, for everyone to hear.

"Why?" Paco asked again.

Ignoring Paco, Tur continued. "Remove your armour, chain mail, and helmet."

Starting to disrobe, David felt his palms slick with sweat, his fingers fumbling, and his knees nervously knocking together. Aware that all eyes were upon him, he thought he should ask Tur why he was being dismissed. He deserved to know and so did his brothers-in-arms.

Looking up at the watchtower, he fought to keep his fury in check. Until now, he hadn't realised just how much he hated the duke. Standing in the frame of the tower's arch, hands on hips and with a victorious smirk on his face, Peráto seemed illuminated with malicious glee.

Glancing again at his fellow militiamen and noting their sympathetic expressions, David felt the need to speak. Yes, he was being disgraced, but he would not leave this castle like a cowed dog.

Taking off his armour, he asked. "Why am I being dismissed? In what way have I displeased the duke?"

"That's not your concern," Tur answered.

"Then whose concern is it? I'm losing my livelihood, Captain. Do I not deserve an explanation?" David insisted.

"The duke has found you unsatisfactory. That is all I can tell you," Tur said, averting his eyes.

David had expected a change to his circumstances. On the way from the prison, he had said as much to Paco, but Paco had insisted that he'd never seen a militiaman being dismissed. It was unheard of, he'd said. Being a brother-in-arms was a lifelong privilege, and that was why the men in private militias were carefully vetted.

After giving the duke a long, cold stare, David said sarcastically, "Once a brother, always a brother – isn't that so, Captain?"

Ignoring David, Tur said to the men. "Listen, all of you. If Sanz comes anywhere near our gates, arrest him for trespassing. This order comes directly from the duke's own lips. Anyone who disobeys his command will find himself shamed and living outside this brotherhood." Pointing to the men standing closest to him, he concluded, "The four of you escort Sanz through the gate."

With his arms being held and his feet being guided by his fellow militiamen, David set off on his walk of shame to the south-eastern castle gate. However, as soon as the duke and Captain Tur were out of sight, the two men let go of David's arms and strolled beside him in a companionable silence. Their gesture of friendship gave David some comfort.

He couldn't stop thinking that all he'd ever wanted was to serve in the militia. Yes, it was true that he no longer had the stomach to serve Peráto, but still, he felt as though his heart had bottomed out in a pit of failed ambitions. His dreams had ended, he thought, walking through the south-east gatehouse. His employment and income were gone, and he was now more vulnerable than ever to another attack.

CHAPTER FORTY-EIGHT

During Mass earlier that morning, Juan's mind had been filled with dark thoughts of Juanjo, so cruelly taken, and of David struggling to atone for sins. Yet since arriving home, his thoughts had turned brighter and more optimistic. He smiled at Sinfa, sitting on a stool cleaning beans. Her health was improving, apart from a couple of suppurating sores on her lips. She seemed to be coming to terms with her new situation, although her courage probably hid her sorrow. He and Isa had asked her to become their daughter, and she had accepted.

Since renting a room in the blacksmith's premises, his life had improved. He and Diego had more orders than they could handle, for it appeared that the inquisitor's entourage couldn't get enough of his goods. He was doing so well that he'd managed to afford a decent-sized joint of kid meat and a carafe of wine for the family's Christmas feast, and for the first time in a long while, he dared to believe that his fortunes were on the rise.

Stoking the dying fire, he sighed with satisfaction. He had David to thank for much of his new-found success. Whilst on watch in the prison, his charming son had somehow managed to convince the Inquisition men-at-arms that the blacksmith's tannery was by far the best place in Sagrat to purchase leather goods.

Juan couldn't remember his father ever being asked to produce so many tunics, boots, bags, parchments, trunks, and even leather bottles in such a short space of time. And the patrons paid half the money before he and Diego had even started tanning the ordered items. Over the past weeks, he'd deduced that many of the Inquisition men were affluent, not just because of the amount of coin they were willing to part with, but also because some of his customers had asked for their family crests to be indented on new saddles. It was a pity, he thought, looking at Isa's shabby dress. He might have become a wealthy man one day. Isa might have been clothed in beautiful gowns by next Christmas had they not been set on leaving Sagrat.

"Are you going to stare at me and this old dress all day or resurrect that fire? The meat won't boil without a flame," Isa said, looking amused.

Juan smiled tenderly. For all her shabby clothes, she was still beautiful.

"We should have saved some food for David. I doubt he's having a feast up at that prison," Isa said, looking at the empty plates.

"We don't know when he'll be back, Mama," Diego said. "It could be days before we see him again."

"Don't crease your brow, my love," Juan said, kissing Isa hard on the mouth. "It's Christmas. David will forgive us."

"The meat was cooked to perfection," said Diego.

"It was wonderful." Sinfa sighed contentedly.

"It was," Juan agreed. "One more goblet of wine to wash it down wouldn't go amiss, don't you think? I might sing to you today."

"Spare us that torment," Diego laughed.

The banging on the door was startlingly loud. Juan, putting his finger to his lips, gestured for quiet. Sinfa rose quickly to her feet and rushed into the sleeping room. Isa, following behind, opened the lid of a wooden chest which sat against the wall and helped Sinfa climb inside it. Then she gathered up every blanket and piece of clothing she could find and covered Sinfa's body. "It's probably just a neighbour wanting to borrow something. Don't make a sound," she whispered just before she covered Sinfa's head. This was not the first time Sinfa had been hidden, for every time there had been a knock at the door, the family had taken this precaution.

Throwing straw pillows on top of the chest, Isa surmised that the likelihood of a neighbour coming into the sleeping room were slim. A person would be rude to barge into a private chamber uninvited.

Back in the family room, Isa ordered Juan and Diego to remain seated on the floor and then she planted a smile and opened the door.

Her face drained of colour. Heat raced through her body. Having heard stories, there could be only one reason why these men should be at her door.

"What took you so long?" an Inquisition man-at-arms standing on the doorstep, asked. Clearly irritated at being kept waiting outside, he pushed Isa aside and barged into the room, followed by two more familiars and a well dressed, official-looking man holding a ledger.

"Are you Isabella Merendez?" the official looking man asked Isa.

"I ... I am." Isa's eyes darted to Juan. "And who might you be?"

"I am the inquisitor's *alguacil*. Which one of you is Juan Sanz?"

"I am, Your Mercy," Juan said.

Sensing what was about to happen, Isa watched in horror as the alguacil held up a written parchment. She had heard so many tales of Inquisition arrests but had always supposed that the suspects must be guilty of something. The alguacil was becoming well known in Sagrat. He had already detained four other people in this street alone, and God only knew how many others, he had taken to prison. This was clearly a mistake, she thought. She and Juan had committed no crime.

"This is an Inquisition arrest warrant for Isabella Merendez and Juan Sanz. You will come with us."

"No!" Isa shouted. "On what charge?"

"The charges will be read out to you when you have your audience with the inquisitor. That's all you need to know."

Isa's terror-stricken eyes bore into Juan. Pleading with a look, she begged him not to say a word to anger the men. Her throat closed up. Grabbing at it, she fought for breath, and then she uttered pitifully, "No ... Please ... no."

"As long as you come with us voluntarily, we're not going to hurt you," a familiar said, plainly unmoved.

"We have done nothing wrong," Juan finally said.

"That's what everyone says. Take them," the alguacil told the familiars.

Isa heard the order and hurriedly moved towards Juan. Her legs buckled at the knees. Her head was spinning, and the men were blocking her path. "No, no, it's a mistake!"

"If I received a coin every time someone said that, I'd be a very wealthy man," a man standing in the doorway said.

"Who are you?" Juan's voice snapped.

"I am the Inquisition's receiver," he retorted, puffing up his chest and appearing to be angry that Juan didn't already know that. "After you two have been taken away, I will remain behind to take note of your valuables and possessions. If you are found guilty, they will be confiscated."

Dear God, Isa thought. Sinfa was inside the chest. He was bound to look there. "We eat on the floor. We have nothing of value!" she screamed at him.

The alguacil frowned. "Lady, we've devoted enough of our time to your objections. There's no point arguing with us. One way or another you're going to the prison."

Still rejecting what the man had just said, Isa continued to stare dazedly at Juan. "Why are they doing this? Tell them, Juan. Tell them we're innocent."

Juan, looking devastated and defeated, finally found his voice. "We are innocent of whatever it is they think we have done, but we can't fight them, my love. We must do as they say."

Feeling her stomach clench like a vice, she moaned with despair. He was wrong. If the men took Juan and her to the prison, they would probably never get out, she thought. There were rumours about prisoners in Valencia locked up for years without being charged with a single crime. Sinfa had only been incarcerated for two weeks, yet her imprisonment had almost killed her. She had sores and rat bites, and her head had been eaten alive by insects! David rarely spoke about what went on inside the prison, but she knew … and she knew she would rather go to hell.

"No, I'm not going!" she shouted defiantly.

"You're making this difficult for us, the alguacil said tolerantly. "The inquisitor wants to save your soul and bring you back to the flock. Don't you want salvation?"

"God is my salvation!" Isa spat angrily. "I'm a good Christian, and so is my husband."

With his patience seemingly at an end, the alguacil gripped the back of Isa's neck. Pinning her against the wall, with her face squeezed between its stones and his hand, he ordered her not to move.

"Remove your cord belts and tie the husband's wrists too," he told the men-at-arms. "I'm not going to drag the wife out into the street by the scruff of the neck. Not today."

Isa could hear Juan's muffled voice behind her, say, "Get your hands off my wife." She tried to turn around, but when she struggled, the man who had tied her wrists behind her back pushed her cheek hard against the wall and held her there by digging his fingers into her skin.

Out of the corner of her eye, Isa could see Diego, who had come to stand at the door. Tears rolled down his cheeks, but he had the good sense not to utter a protest or get in the men's way. Isa's lips trembled, and she managed to mutter, "I love you, Diego."

Pushed back into the room, Diego was ordered to stand against the wall and not to move.

As soon as her arms were tugged and she was roughly pulled back from the wall, Isa's legs gave way. Facing the door on her knees, she saw a closed cart outside. She wanted to scream *no!* but she was breathless and could only manage to utter choked sobs.

As though her life depended on escaping, as soon as she was picked up off the floor, she struggled to free herself from the man's grasp. But when she saw Juan walking with dignity towards the cart, she realised that only an army could stop this arrest.

Landing with a thud on the carriage floor, she stopped moving and stared longingly at Juan sitting against the wall. His wrists were tied, but he was able to shuffle on his backside to where Isa lay surrounded by her crumpled skirts.

"We can't fight these fanatics, my love," he said tearfully, bending over her. "Struggling against them, screaming at them, and telling them you're innocent, won't help you."

"The duke did this to us because David is our son," she sobbed, her head against his chest. "He will never allow us our freedom. I will never see you again or hold my boys in my arms. I hope they kill me soon ..."

CHAPTER FORTY-NINE

On the eve of the New Year, the same day the curfew was lifted, David walked to the prison. When he arrived, he sat on a grassy embankment opposite the prison doors and waited patiently for the guard watches to change and for a friendly face to appear.

Knowing that it could take months or perhaps years for charges to be brought against his father and mother should have deterred him from continually badgering the men-at-arms for information, but he was determined to break through the Inquisition's wall of silence. He would not give up or succumb to self-pity when his fingers and toes numbed with cold, and the familiars, sick of the sight of him, threw insults and threats his way. Nor would he fixate any longer on the scar-faced assassin, the duke, or his humiliating removal from the militia. His parents' incarceration overshadowed every other trouble that faced him, even the dismal situation at home.

On Christmas Day, David had received the devastating news about his mother and father's arrest. Later he had listened to Diego and Sinfa weeping their way through a story of how the receiver came but a hair's breath away from discovering Sinfa hiding inside the chest. The man had lifted the chest's lid, only to close it again after seeing old and frayed sheets, Diego had told him. And then, deciding that there was nothing worth confiscating, he'd left soon after.

After hours of hearing Diego and Sinfa's tears and incessant questions about what was to be done, he had decided to drink himself into a stupor on his father's wine. Being intoxicated had felt good, he thought now as he watched a cart pull up at the prison doors. For the first time in weeks, his shame had been numbed and his concern for Sinfa diluted. His bleak imaginings of a future without his parents hadn't disappeared like the last dregs of wine, but somehow even the terrible thought of losing them had not been able to take away his languorous mood.

He could do *nothing* to help his family, he'd thought in his dreamlike state. No begging, bribing, storming the prison, and killing every prison guard would secure his parents' freedom. Grief-stricken yet strangely relaxed at the same time, he'd also believed that it might be a good idea to assassinate the inquisitor. If there was no inquisitor, there would be no Inquisition. And then later, in the cold light of day, when his wits had returned, he'd decided that trying to find out what had happened to his parents was better than doing nothing at all.

Watching a vegetable cart being unloaded, he was reminded of the troubles facing him at home. There was no food left in the house and no money left to buy more. He'd not managed to find employment. It seemed that no one wanted to hire a disgraced soldier. Diego, not knowing anything about tanning without his father's supervision, was also out of a job. And Sinfa, poor Sinfa. She too was a prisoner, in all but name.

Shielding his eyes from the winter sun, low in the sky and glaringly bright, he felt his muscles tense. He squinted in the blinding light at the figure of a man walking along the road towards the prison. It was Raul, a familiar who had shared long night watches with him and Paco. Raul was not like the other men-at-arms, who thought they were superior to their fellow citizens. He'd always been sociable.

Looking at the distance Raul still had to walk before he reached the prison doors, David thought there wouldn't even be enough time to ask one question. Deciding to take a chance, he stepped in front of Raul, blocked his path, and brought him to a complete standstill. "Raul, will you give me a minute of your time?" he asked.

"I know what you want, David," Raul said apologetically, "but you know I can't tell you anything."

"I know I shouldn't ask and you're not supposed to tell me, but for the love of God, they're my parents," he said, rushing his words before Raul had a chance to stop him. "I have to know if charges have been brought against them. Please … No one needs to know that we've even spoken."

Raul looked furtively towards the prison behind him and then back to David.

"Please, Raul," David urged.

"I'll tell you what I know and then you should leave. Don't come back to the prison again, for your sake and for theirs."

David nodded in agreement. "I won't. You have my word."

"Your mother and father have been charged with heresy."

"Why?" David already suspected that they would be charged with heresy; otherwise, why would the Inquisition arrest them in the first place? He needed more information, something he wasn't already aware of. "What heresy charge?"

Again, Raul looked about him before he spoke. "Someone has accused them of refusing to accept a wild boar delivered to them on the feast of the Immaculate Conception. The magistrate has an accuser's written testimony. He states that your mother called the pig's meat the devil's poison."

"That's a lie! There was a wild boar, a gift from the duke, but it was stolen from me," David said, stunned.

"I have to go," Raul said, pushing David aside. "I have nothing more to say."

Jana Petken

CHAPTER FIFTY

Long after darkness had fallen and there was not a soul to be seen, David spotted the man he'd punched to within a hair's breadth from death. The street, shrouded in a low-lying mist and so black that even the keenest of eyes couldn't see more than two paces in front of them, was quiet at the best of times. There were few houses or buildings of any kind, and only a small number of neighbours, but it did house a particularly well known taverna of ill repute halfway along its route.

Seeing Moniño stagger out of this particular drinking house didn't surprise David. It was notorious because of its easy wenches, pleasuring men for coin, and patrons who spent their days gambling and picking fights. Frequented as often as the churches, and by the same people, it was also a popular establishment for those who preferred to wash away their sins with a jug or two of wine rather than be absolved by Father Bernardo. It was said that a   good jug of wine could make a man forget even the most serious religious improprieties.

Although the tavern now seemed an obvious place to find Moniño, David and Diego had elected to comb the entire town, sometimes going in circles to recheck those streets wide enough for a cart and mule to pass through, because they'd thought they would eventually spot the thieving whoreson delivering something or other.

Angry at wasting so much of the day, David stroked his beard, still itchy with recent growth, and thought that his time would have been better spent stalking the tavernas all day instead of the streets. A man like Moniño didn't work, he thought. He was a bloodsucking varlet, like a tick on the skin of hard-working people.

Keeping his eyes on the man peeing against the wall outside the taverna, David calculated that his quarry would probably walk up the slope towards the north end of the street. There was a flat grazing area there, and taverna drinkers were known to leave their animals tied loosely to tree branches and bushes, sometimes for the entire day.

There was to be no fighting, no blood, and no death, David had warned Diego before leaving the house. Under any other circumstances, he would care not a whit if the thief was injured, killed, or put up as pickles, but he was their parents' accuser. He was the reason they were in prison, and he was the only person who could get them out of it.

Watching the man from the shadow of an arched entryway, David now thought that inflicting some pain on Moniño wouldn't be such a bad idea after all. The drunken bastard, who seemed to enjoy causing harm to unsuspecting people, would probably not admit to the Inquisition that he had lied about the boar. For fear of being charged with false testimony, an even greater crime, no accuser in his right mind would take back his words. He would cling to them for dear life … But it didn't mean that Moniño couldn't be brought to account tonight. Life was not being kind, good, or just to his parents. In a pig's eye, would he let Moniño off lightly!

David gestured to Diego to cover the lower part of his face with a piece of black linen cloth, the remnants of a man's cloak, which his mother had been sewing for a neighbour. There was no need for Moniño to know who Diego was, David thought, but it would be pointless for him to cover *his* face. As soon as he told Moniño what he wanted, his identity would no longer be a secret.

Standing perfectly still and silent in a darkened corner, they watched Moniño clumsily climb the stone stairs leading to the grassy plateau above. They followed him.

There was no moon of any size or the faintest twinkling star. Whatever was in the black sky was covered by thick clouds. David looked about him and saw no one but their victim, staggering two steps sideways and one forward towards his cart. He gestured to Diego to move forward.

"Stop where you are, you thieving, lying turd," David said, his voice crackling with anger.

Moniño turned in a large circular movement, as though the mere effort was making him lose direction. Swaying from side to side, he looked at David, and then stumbled as he took another pace forward. "Who are you? What do … *hic* … you want?" he slurred. Then he staggered another pace, until his face was only inches from David's.

David was close enough to look into Moniño's eyes, dimmed in the darkness but still visible enough to see that they were red and unfocused. "Do you know me?" he asked with his voice laced with impatience. "Do you remember what I did to you for stealing my boar?"

"Ask him about the accusation," Diego urged whilst keeping one eye on the area.

"Quiet," David whispered.

Moniño giggled. "Get me … to my cart … eh, lads." And then he broke into song.

David grabbed him by the shoulders, shaking him until his head looked like a loose bottle top. God damn him! Shit! A shithouse of shit! The man didn't even recognise him. "Moniño, you accused Isabella and Juan Sanz of not accepting the boar that you stole. Do you remember that?" David insisted.

"Boar? Nice … piggy."

"He won't talk," Diego said, already defeated.

"He will. I'll get what I want from him, even if I have to pull out his tongue with his words hanging from it!" David said, throwing Diego a scathing look.

Moniño wagged his tongue and muttered, "Pull it …"

Letting go of him, David sighed with frustration. "God and his angels have spat on us tonight. You're right, Diego. We're not going to get a word of sense out of him."

"We have to. We can't leave until you scare the life out of him," Diego now insisted.

"Does he look frightened to you? Unless we stand here and wait until the wine flows out of his body with his pee, we're wasting our time. I doubt he'll even remember seeing us. We're going home."

"No, he needs to recant his testimony."

David looked once more at Moniño and then walked away, shaking his head in disgust. "No, we're leaving," he said firmly.

Still unwilling to move, Diego stood his ground and glared at Moniño. "You'll be seeing me again," he warned.

Moniño's mouth spread in a lopsided snigger. Raising his hand, he placed an index finger just underneath his left ear and then drew it along the length of his gullet as though he were slicing it.

At the gesture, Diego rushed forward.

David turned at the sound of Diego's angry gasp but was too late to stop him from pushing Moniño to the ground.

The thump of the thief's skull hitting a rock sounded like the crunch of pig's crackling. David rushed forward and dropped to his knees. The rock beneath Moniño was saturated with blood. Spreading fast, it covered the granite surface and then dripped over the edges. Moniño's eyes were open and staring up to the heavens. Turning to Diego, standing behind him with his mouth half open, he exclaimed, "He was our parents' accuser, you fool! You've just brought hell to our door."

"I didn't mean to do it. He was laughing at us. He *did* know who you were – I swear he did," Diego insisted, but he looked horrified at what he'd done.

Shaking his head in disbelief, David looked again at the dead body. There was no time to think about what had been lost here, he thought. He and Diego needed to flee the area as soon as possible. Looking at Moniño, David noticed a leather string hanging from his breeches. Bending over, he pulled it and found a purse.

After finding four reals, he rose to his feet. Staring at the cart and mule with a pensive expression, he strode to Diego, who was still staring at the thief's body.

"I'm sorry, David," Diego said.

"Moniño was drunk, and inebriated men are apt to fall over," David answered without a hint of pity. "We can't bury him or move his body, but there are no witnesses and no obvious signs of violence or an attack. An accident – that's all this was, an unfortunate accident …"

David stood by Moniño's cart and mule. "Diego, get up there," he said, gesturing to the driver's seat. "You're leaving Sagrat … tonight!"

CHAPTER FIFTY-ONE

The inquisitor's interrogation had started calmly enough, with seemingly innocent questions about Juan's life and that of his family.

"What's your name?" Gaspar de Amo had asked. "Do you know why you have been arrested?"

Juan had answered the questions truthfully. And to the last one, he'd said, "No, I don't know why I am here."

"The Inquisition doesn't arrest people for nothing; you are aware of that."

"If you say so, Your Mercy."

"Are you ready to confess now? You do know that if you tell the truth, you will be treated less harshly."

"You keep saying that, but I've told you that I've done nothing wrong," Juan had repeated. He'd already been interrogated twice before. First he'd seen the alguacil, then the inquisition magistrate, and now he was sitting before the inquisitor. He'd spent hours assuring all of them that he was innocent, yet nobody believed him or didn't seem to want to believe.

He was terrified of being sent back to the cell to be forgotten, but he was even more afraid of the inquisitor losing his patience with him and turning to violence.

He couldn't stop thinking about Isa. The thought of her being questioned like this and living in a cell like his was making him feel physically sick. He'd not laid eyes on her since their arrest. What heresy was she being charged with? And what had happened to David and Diego? Had the Inquisition arrested the boys? And Sinfa ... Did the authorities find her hiding place? Dear God, he would probably never find out. The inquisitor was bombarding him with questions, but he was not answering any of *his*.

"Do you remember what you were doing on the feast of the Immaculate Conception?" the inquisitor asked for the umpteenth time.

"Yes, how could I forget that terrible day? My farm was burned down, and my youngest child was killed."

"And do you now recall refusing a wild boar and saying that it was …" Gaspar de Amo paused and looked at the notes in front of him. "Yes, that is was filthy meat from the depths of hell, fit only for Christian stomachs?"

"No. As I've already told you, I said nothing of the kind, nor was I or anyone else in my family offered a wild boar to eat … I've told you over and over!" What nonsense was this about a boar? He'd denied all knowledge of it repeatedly.

De Amo sighed and looked at Juan in a way that would lead anyone to believe he felt pity. "The Inquisition does not like to rush to judgement," he said. "We prefer the process to be drawn out so that our prisoners can think calmly about their crimes and come to the conclusion that to confess is to cleanse the soul. If you refuse to cooperate, the wrath of God will fall upon you through the long arm of the Inquisition. We are ubiquitous and *very* persistent."

Juan pictured being tortured and shuddered with terror. "I have nothing to say," he said.

De Amo sighed and then closed a thick file sitting on the table. "Very well, Juan. Unfortunately, I have no more time to devote to you, so I must insist that you confess now and not waste any more of my valuable time."

"I have nothing to confess," Juan said again. His hands and legs were trembling. He was worn out after having no sleep and barely enough food in his stomach to keep a bird alive. His voice sounded hoarse from all the denials. "Please … a little water," he begged. He was scared to confess but was also terrified of what would happen to him if he didn't. How could he fight against such a filthy lie? The inquisitor would not divulge the name of the accuser, and he didn't seem to believe in the concept of innocence, only guilt. "In the name of God, have mercy."

"Confess to Judaism, and God will be merciful."

"I will not. To make a false confession would be a sin against God, for it would be a lie."

"So be it." De Amo pushed his chair back and walked over to where the magistrate and scribe sat. The magistrate scratched his head with a quill and asked, "How would you like to proceed, my lord?"

De Amo's expression hardened, and his sunken eyes bore into the magistrate's face. "He's a stubborn one. I have invested enough time in him and his wife. I picked them because of the joint charges. I had hoped to make an example out of them to other husbands and wives," he said disappointedly. "But with the auto-de-fé in three days' time, I don't see how we can give him the time he needs to come to his senses. Send for the torturer."

The sound of the prisoners' screams grew louder with each step Juan took. Shackled at the hands and ankles and pulled roughly by a thick neck chain attached to a collar, he shuffled as fast as he could and tried to keep up with the man-at-arms dragging him along as though he were a mule.

When he was led into the torture chamber, he was left for a moment to take in the scene. A man was suspended by his arms, which were bound at the wrists behind his back, head down, and seemingly unconscious. A woman had her wrists bound high above her head, her feet dangling over a fire and covered in pig's fat. An old man on a wooden mattress was being stretched, squealing like a pig being slaughtered.

Juan, standing as still as a statue, open-mouthed and with tears already streaming down his face, thought that he must be in hell's anteroom. He beseeched the inquisitor to let him go, but De Amo, sitting in a chair on a raised podium, looked to be enjoying himself. He wasn't smiling, but his eyes, fixed on the screaming, demented woman whose feet were being roasted, were filled with perverse gratification.

As he gasped in short, sharp breaths, Juan was led by a man swathed in black from head to foot and wearing a mask to a wooden device which looked like a long mattress resting on four wooden legs. "Welcome to the *toca*," the torturer said.

Juan's chains were removed but quickly replaced by rope. Lying flat on his back bare-chested, hands tied by his sides and feet dangling over the edge of the mattress, he was forced to swallow a long length of cloth. When no more cloth could fit in his throat, water was poured into his mouth, triggering his swallowing reflex. His eyes widened with terror and pain as he swallowed more and more of the material, until he felt it entering his stomach.

The rack was tilted towards the floor, at the top end. Juan stared at the ceiling. For a brief second his feverish eyes saw a bucket, and then he felt splashes of water pouring onto his face.

He was suffocating, drowning, and in agony as the cloth expanded and moved in his belly. He tried desperately to move his head and evade the water that was being poured into his mouth, but his cheeks were locked in someone's hands. He was going to die! He couldn't breathe. His life was ebbing away, and he didn't care. He wanted this pain to stop!

Jolted, he felt the cloth being wrenched from his mouth. What torture was this? What hellish suffering was he enduring? His mind screamed.

They untied him. He sat up, tried to catch his breath whilst enduring sharp pains in his throat, and looked dazedly about him.

"It's all over, Juan," De Amo said, as though he were a friend.

Juan, still gasping for air, looked at the inquisitor. His comforting voice sounded strangely sincere, he thought. But it was the devil speaking.

"No more, please," Juan croaked.

"Are you ready now to confess to your sin? Will you admit to being a Judaist and heretic? Will you allow God to forgive you?

"Forgive … what?" Juan stuttered hoarsely.

The inquisitor's eyes went to the door. Juan followed the gaze and saw Isa being held at the top of the steps, where the entrance to the chamber stood. "No, no, no!" he tried to shout, but he could only manage a hoarse whisper. Not his beautiful wife. They couldn't torture her. She would not be able to endure what they had just done to him!

Her eyes found his. She cried out his name. "Husband, what have they done to you?"

Juan's eyes darted to the inquisitor. "Please don't touch my wife," he said.

"If only you would tell the truth, she might be able to avoid your fate."

Juan looked again at Isa. Yes, he thought. If he confessed to everything they had said he'd done, they would spare Isa. He'd do anything, say whatever they wanted, not to see her suffer. He nodded at the inquisitor. "I confess. I did it," he said. "I refused the boar... I still have a Jewish soul. I wouldn't eat it … My wife had nothing to do with it. She was not at home." He wanted to say more, but he felt bilious and every word tore his throat.

The inquisitor called for the scribe. When he appeared, De Amo said, "Juan Sanz, do you confess to Judaism, in that you refused to eat pig meat because of your Jewish beliefs?"

"Yes … I confess. But you must allow my wife to go home. She's innocent."

"And do you also confess to blasphemy against God and his Catholic Church."

"Yes. I said yes."

"I don't know which of your sins is the gravest, being a Judaist or calling pig meat the devil's poison. Both are grave, Juan Sanz," De Amo said, and then he nodded to the torturer. "Untie him. When you have finished, take Isabella Sanz to the stocks and apply the pig's fat to her feet."

CHAPTER FIFTY-TWO

The cart raced across the plain towards the sea, shaking from side to side with speed, on old unsteady wheels. The mule's heavy hooves, continuing to hammer against the ground, had made enough noise to awaken an entire neighbourhood. But David had chosen a fast pace over a soft and furtive departure from the town, in the hope that they could outrun any militiamen that might be patrolling the streets in the dead of night.

Their destination was a dilapidated old house that sat in the middle of an overgrown field. Diego had suggested it. He had sheltered there for a night after he'd taken the little girl to the convent near Valencia.

Leaving Sagrat with Sinfa and Diego had been an impulsive decision but the right one, David thought. Sinfa had been sleeping like a dormouse when he'd woken her with a rough shake. Staggering with sleep, she'd not even bothered to ask questions but had simply nodded at his order to get up, and then, at his request, she'd hidden under the sheeting in the back of the cart. Diego, saying very little since leaving the dead body on the plateau, seemed to be badly affected by Moniño's death. David, on the other hand, didn't care one whit that the thief was dead.

Isabella and Juan Sanz – two people so full of life, benevolent, tolerant, and placid to the extreme – faced charges of heresy because of a stinking turd who had stolen and then lied, all to fill his belly with meat.

David halted the cart at the river that ran next to the ruins of his father's farm. "Do you want to visit Juanjo's grave before leaving the area?" he asked Diego.

"No, we'd better keep moving."

"David, where are we going?" Sinfa asked him.

"I'm not going anywhere. You and Diego must travel on without me," David replied, and then he jumped down to the ground

Diego nodded with approval. "Help them," he said.

Sinfa was not so easily convinced. Jumping down from the back of the cart, she raced to David's side. Her eyes boring into his were like black liquid pools. David could already feel the void in his heart. Long talks, a touching of hands, and her loving gaze had been his only comfort in the past week. He wasn't sure how she felt about him, but he knew without a shadow of doubt that love had crept up on him like a long shadow at dusk.

"Will I ever see you again?" she asked him tearfully.

"You will. I will come for you in a few days. Diego will look after you." Turning to Diego, he said. "Wait at the place you told me about for as long as possible. The auto-de-fé will take place in two days, and then, with God's grace, I will find out what is to become of our parents. Take these," he said, handing Diego the reals he'd found on Moniño's person. "You and Sinfa should be able to purchase enough food to last you a few days, if you eat frugally. If I don't appear within four days, leave the refuge and head south."

After smiling tenderly at Sinfa, he turned from her and began his long walk back to Sagrat.

The lumpy straw-filled mattress was not particularly comfortable, but after sleeping on a pallet on the floor for weeks, David had slept like a marmot. Waking with a start at the sound of loud knocking at the door, he rose, winched at a pain shooting through his head, and stumbled to the door.

Nodding with gratitude, David accepted Paco's freshly baked bread. "Paco, you're a welcome sight for my tired eyes," he said, biting into the loaf. The sleeping room door was open. He watched Paco cock his head to the side as he stared into the empty space.

"Where is she?" Paco asked, right on cue.

"She's gone. Diego too. They left Sagrat last night after the curfew was lifted." Filling his mouth with more bread, he waited for more questions. This time he wouldn't tell Paco anything. Sometimes knowing little was much better than knowing too much.

"Gone where?" Paco asked.

"North on foot or on a boat … Perhaps south or west or across the mountains. I don't know. They've left, and they won't be coming back."

"It's a fine fix you and your family are in. You're mired in shit, David, and it's the duke's stink that covers you. The militia sympathises with your plight."

David raised a questioning eyebrow and then grunted with sarcasm, "What would any of them know about my family's suffering? Not one man was bold enough to speak up for me."

"Tur's got the face of a raging bull. He told me himself that you were a good soldier."

Waving his hand, David dismissed Paco's pity and soothing words. "So apart from feeding me, why are you here?"

"Tomorrow is the auto-de-fé. You know what that means?"

I do. It means I might see my parents being burnt at the stake because of a pig!" David wanted to shout. "No, I don't. Enlighten me," he said instead.

"They've started building a high scaffold in the Roman theatre, and there are wooden benches in front of it," Paco said. "Heretics are being publicly sentenced. Your parents might be there. It could be the last time you see them."

"Why is it taking place in the Roman theatre?" David asked.

Pago grunted. "Only our duke knows the answer to that question. He and Tur had a   clash of opinions within earshot of the men. Tur suggested that the theatre was too big and too open to control a crowd, saying that it was vulnerable to thieves and troublemakers. He also asked the duke to reconsider leaving most of the men inside the castle's walls during the auto-de-fé. They looked like two goats butting heads.

"The town is filling up with visitors and prisoners from all over Aragon. Builders are erecting pyres and stakes at the edge of town. There's a rumour that the viceroy will attend …"

"None of this is my concern anymore. I only care about two prisoners. The rest of them can go to hell for all I care."

Sighing, Paco said, "I served with you in the prison. You're not a hard man, Sanz, or an uncaring one. Look at you. You're unshaven. You look as though you might have a bird's nest in that hair of yours. And a splash of water on your face might not go amiss. Look for employment. Go to the blacksmith. He might need the help, and you need money. You can't sit here all day burying your head in the dirt."

"I've already been to see the blacksmith. He doesn't want me near his place," David snapped. "You would think I was carrying a hundred plagues. No one in this town wants to employ me. Do you think I haven't tried to find work?"

For a moment, there was a pause in the conversation, and then David said, "I'm going to speak to the duke. I will demand that he use his influence to get my parents released. I will threaten the bastard if I have to."

Paco looked horrified at the mere suggestion. "You'll never get within twenty paces of the castle gates," he said. "Wait until you see what happens at the auto-de-fé. With a bit of good fortune, your parents will receive a light sentence."

"There's no such thing as a light sentence. Anyway, you seem cocksure that my mother and father have committed a crime. As far as I know, they haven't even been charged!" he lied, not wanting to mention his conversation with Raul. "I'm still hopeful for their release, even if you're not!"

"You might be right, but you need to forget about seeking an audience with the duke. Go to the Roman theatre. Support your parents if they *are* being sentenced. And don't do anything foolish."

David nodded. Paco was right. He wouldn't get near Peráto, and he'd be of no use to anyone if he was arrested for trespassing on the castle grounds. "My apologies. I'm in a stinking mood."

After giving David a friendly slap on the back, Paco changed the subject. "We found a dead body on the plateau near La Taverna de Javali. He was no one of consequence, just a drunk who probably couldn't hold his wine."

"How did he die?" David asked, hiding his interest by filling his mouth with the remainder of the bread.

"It looks as though he fell and smashed his head on a rock."

Chewing some more bread, David felt his body relax. Paco hadn't mentioned the word *murder*, and the question of Moniño's missing cart and mule hadn't been brought up either. At least there was good news.

CHAPTER FIFTY-THREE

The sky was cloudless, but it was bitterly cold on this first Sunday of the year. After Mass had been celebrated, all 186 prisoners, flanked by Inquisition men-at-arms, Dominican monks, and the clergy, marched in procession from the church of San Agustin to the Roman theatre.

The men, grouped together and carrying unlit candles, were bareheaded and unshod. Because it was winter, they had been told to wear soles under their feet; however, not all prisoners were in possession of such comforts. The women, also carrying unlit candles, followed behind the men with their heads uncovered and their faces bare. Most of them shivered with cold, for they had neither shawls nor cloaks to cover their scant rags.

David's eyes, darting from one prisoner to the next, were emblazoned with a mixture of hope and dread. He was desperate to see his parents, yet he dreaded hearing a sentence that might see them suffering in prison for years.

When the last prisoner had passed, he ran towards the Roman theatre, which was still some way away from the procession. He would have to look at all the prisoners' faces again as they approached, he thought. There had been too many of them obscured by men-at-arms and spectators jumping up and down to get a decent view.

Every condemned man and woman wore a tunic made with two lengths of cloth, one at the front of the body and one at the back, in the form of a scapular. They were not all wearing identical tunics, David noted, for the colour and cut seemed to vary from person to person.

When the procession approached, a somewhat zealous, pious man standing next to David, clutching rosary beads and muttering prayers, took it upon himself to enlighten the people around him about his experiences as an ardent supporter of the Inquisition.

Introducing himself as Mariano but intentionally leaving out his father's name, he pointed out that he had attended an auto-de-fé in Toledo six years previously. That one had been the first to take place in Spain, and it had involved a procession with over seven hundred heretics.

Paying attention again to the approaching prisoners, Mariano informed the people nearest to him that the tunics worn by the heretics were called *sambenitos*. Those wearing black sambenitos bearing embroidered snakes on the front and with red caps adorning their heads were the heretics who would be executed by fire, either when still alive or after being garrotted. Other prisoners, wearing yellow tunics marked by two red crosses of Saint Andrew and painted with upside-down flames, were to be sentenced to some other punishment which didn't involve death at the end of it.

"What are the effigies for?" David asked. Some were covered in black and others in yellow. Parchments were pinned to the effigies with names written on them.

"They represent heretics who have died in prison, and cowards who ran away." They will burn the ones covered with a black sambonito.

Searching the prisoners' faces and listening to Mariano speak at the same time, David's eyes were drawn to men and women with rope tied around their necks and twisted into knots. "Those are the filthy bigamists and imposters," he heard

Mariano say. "They wear as many knots as the lashes they are to receive."

Some of the prisoners were howling loudly and tearing their hair out as they walked. David wondered if their suffering was due to the biting cold weather, their humiliation, or the fear of being given a harsh sentence ... He didn't think they were weeping because of their so-called offences against God.

Finally, David saw his father. Juan, walking with his head bowed, was wearing the yellow sambenito. A surge of hope lifted David's spirits. His father had not been sentenced to death. Not death! "Papa, I'm here!" he shouted to him, but his voice was drowned by the beat of a drum and the thick humming of the crowd.

Mariano, nudging David, seemed surprised. "Your father is a *reconciled*? Then he has confessed. Only heretics who have admitted to their sins are being sentenced today."

Ignoring Mariano's smug observation, David focused his eyes on the women, just coming into view behind the last of the men. His mother, near the front of the line, hobbled like an old woman, and every step she took seemed to cause her great pain. Tears rolled down her cheeks as she searched the faces in the crowd. "Mama, I'm with you!" David shouted, but again his voice was lost.

A few rows behind his mother, a woman cried out in distress. For a brief second, David saw her eyes, which were so wild, feverish, and filled with so much terror that he felt it too. Still watching her as she passed, he saw her trying to rip off her black sambenito. When her hands were slapped away by a man-at-arms, she threw her red cap to the ground. The same man-at-arms picked it up and placed it back on her head ... and then David lost sight of her.

God was not responsible for this, he thought. He would not want to see his children suffering in this way. This fanatical insanity had been instigated by a man-made church, for want of power and dominance over its worshipers. Religion could go to hell, for it seemed more suited to the devil's work than God's. He was finished with prayers and penitence.

Fixing his eyes on the Dominican monks and priests following behind the prisoners, he inadvertently sniggered with scorn. Did these so-called pious servants of God think that they would see the gates of heaven when they died? Did they believe that God would welcome the Catholic Church's clergy, guilty of burning and torturing its flock? His little pinky God would!

"Is this what you travelled so far to see? Good people, like my mother and father, humiliated and disgraced for the rest of their lives?" he hissed at Mariano.

"It is God's will that heretics be punished," Mariano answered, looking astounded that he should be asked such a thing. "How can you even question the Holy Office? They are doing glorious work for God, and it is our honour to witness it ..."

CHAPTER FIFTY-FOUR

David pushed his way through a horde of people blocking the entrance to the Roman theatre and pulled Mariano, the man he had met earlier, behind him. He wasn't enamoured by the man's devoutness to the church, but he would be useful, David had thought, when Mariano offered to guide him through the auto-de-fé.

The Roman amphitheatre sat within a dip in the land below the south-east gate, next to the ruins of Diana's temple. Monumental in scale and decoration, it and remained an impressive sight, even to those who had lived in the town all their lives. Semicircular in shape and with rows of raised seating, it had been well plundered by Sagrat's rulers. And over the centuries, many of the stone steps once housing spectators had been transported and used to build parts of the castle and some of the town's houses.

David wanted to take in every detail and every moment. After all, he thought, this would be a day he would remember and detest for the rest of his life. Casting his eyes towards the galleries overlooking the ancient arena, David saw that there were still plenty of empty spaces. No one would want to sit on the higher levels, for they wouldn't see much or hear anything from there. Noting the sections which had long since been chiselled away and dug out, he deduced that during the Roman occupation, the theatre might have been able to accommodate up to eight thousand spectators. Not even half that amount of people would find a seat today, but there was still plenty of room for those wanting to rest their arses and have their macabre curiosity satisfied by the goings-on in the arena.

Forging through the crowd to a good position amongst one of the front rows of spectators, David now had a good view of the two scaffolds which had been erected in the centre of the arena. The smaller of the two was decorated with an altar bearing gold chalices and candles. The larger, packed with men, was adorned by lengths of red material hanging above and behind the scaffold, presumably to shelter the occupants from the biting cold.

David had not seen the dignitaries arrive, but he observed them now, seated comfortably on red velvet thrones on the largest scaffold. The inquisitor sat like a king in the centre. The man sitting on his left was also an inquisitor, David believed, judging by his thick purple robes embroidered with gold threads. They were almost identical to the robes worn by Gaspar de Amo. A man who appeared to be an important nobleman was dressed in an even more decorative mantle than the two inquisitors, and he was the only man who had not removed his hat, which sported tall multiple-coloured plumes. He sat on De Amo's right.

And then David saw the duke's head of brown curls. As one would have expected, Peráto was not sitting right next to his most important guests or the inquisitors. He was tucked in the row behind them and barely visible.

"Who is he?" David asked Mariano, pointing to the elegantly dressed nobleman to the right of De Amo.

"He's the viceroy of Valencia, a fine man, a man of vision, and almost as rich as the king. They say the monarchs have given him free rein to rule Valencia."

That was not surprising, David thought. King Ferdinand rarely set foot in Aragon.

Facing the scaffolds were two rows of ten wooden benches, which is where the prisoners sat. The men sat on one side of the aisle and the women on the other. David searched for his parents. His mother's agony as she'd limped by him was engraved in his mind. And his father's stoic yet resigned expression made David want to kill every one of the smug aristocrats sitting on that grand podium. He couldn't see them, but he knew they were there. He'd watched them traipse into the arena with the other penitents.

Feeling his chest tighten with nerves, he asked Mariano, "What happens now?"

Mariano stroked his goatee, peppered with grey, and smiled with what could only be considered malignant joy. "Now we will celebrate Mass and listen to a sermon. Then a notary will come forward and call out the prisoners' names one by one. The penitents will raise their candles at the mention of their names and say yes to confirm their presence."

After the Mass, just as Mariano had predicted, the notary read out every name on his long list. David listened intently but wasn't able to hear a word of what was being said. When the notary sat back down, the bishop and Father Bernardo passed through the rows of prisoners and made the sign of the cross twice on each forehead. "Receive the sign of the cross, which you denied and lost through being deceived," David managed to hear the Bishop say to a penitent wearing the black sambenito.

Looking up at the spectators in the gallery, David wondered what satisfaction they were getting. They certainly couldn't see what he was seeing or hear a word of Mass or the sentencing to come. "What now?" David asked again.

"The moment you have been waiting for has arrived," Mariano said gleefully. "The prisoners will now be given penance, and you, lad, will learn your parents' fates." Mariano, who had not uttered a word since the beginning of Mass, seemed to be in a state of elation. With his rosary beads perpetually turning in his fingers, he looked as though he had just been taken up to heaven and was savouring its ecstasies. David wanted to slap the pious man, but instead he nodded in understanding and kept his feelings to himself.

He was desperate to find out his parents' fates, but he was also terrified of what he might do should their sentences be anything other than exile. "My parents were accused of refusing to eat boar meat. What do you think their sentence will be?" David asked.

"Oh, lad, that's the sign of a Judaist if ever I saw one. You say they are not wearing black sambenitos or marked for the lash?" Mariano asked, pensively stroking his goatee again.

"No, they are wearing yellow tunics, and there are no ropes knotted around their necks."

"Hmm. In that case, they could perhaps be sentenced to four or five years in prison, which, in my opinion, does not seem harsh at all."

Wanting to hit him, David said, "Really?"

"Yes, really. I've heard of many prisoners being incarcerated and then being transferred to a hospital or monastery because the prison was overflowing. There are even rumours of penitents being sent home before their sentence has been completed! But back to your parents … Hmm. Your father may be sent to the king's navy to row in the bowels of one of his galleys. Or both might be ordered to wear a tunic of shame."

"What's that?" David asked, dreading the answer.

"A white sambenito emblazoned with a red cross on the front and back. It is worn by the penitent for an entire year, in private and in public. And every townsperson must shun such sinners when they walk past them."

"God give me strength," David couldn't help but hiss with anger. "And what other sentence could they receive?"

"Well, they might be exiled from this place, but no matter where they go in Spain's realms, they will never again be allowed to hold certain positions."

David's heart leapt at the thought of exile. They had been planning to leave before their arrest. Lifting an inquisitive eyebrow, he asked, "What does 'certain positions' mean?"

"It means that none of the penitents here today will be able to become shopkeepers, moneychangers, vegetable or fish merchants, or hold any official post whatsoever. And they will never be permitted to wear silk, the colour scarlet, or any jewels. If they break any of these rules, they will be burned. And no matter what their punishment is this day, whether a public lashing or shaming by the wearing the sambenito for a year, they will have to go in processions for six Fridays; they will discipline their bodies with scourges of hemp cord, bare-backed, unshod, and bareheaded; and they will fast for those six Fridays.

Dear God in heaven! There had to be a way to help his parents, David thought. No, he was a fool to think he could do anything, he then told himself. He had a dagger hidden on his person, but what use was it? What did he think he was going to achieve? Get them to safety using a short blade? Run with them through the crowd unnoticed?

CHAPTER FIFTY-FIVE

Just as the first penitent rose from the bench to hear his sentence, a volley of arrows and longbow darts flew over the spectators' heads towards the scaffold. A nobleman pinned to his chair by a dart, which had gone through his chest and into the upholstery, died instantly. The Inquisition's magistrate, standing at the edge of the platform with documents in his hands, was also killed by an arrow that pierced his throat and came out the back of his neck.

Luis, in relative safety because he was shielded by those sitting in the front row, leapt from his chair and crawled until he was at the back of it. Crouching on his knees, he covered his head with his arms. De Amo, slow to move, was struck in the stomach with a longbow dart. Crying out, he fell to the floor and lay there moaning, his fingers wrapped around the length of dart, protruding from his belly. The viceroy, appearing to be unhurt, had also leapt from his chair and was running down the scaffold's steps with two other visiting noblemen.

Inquisition men-at-arms, Paco, Tur, and the duke's entire escort leapt onto the platform and shielded their masters with their bodies. The inquisitor's familiars, positioned right at the edge of the scaffold, were more exposed than the duke's militiamen, who were situated behind the second row of chairs and took the brunt of the attack with only their buckler shields to protect them.

Paco, looking up at the eastern part of the small hillock, which was only a few feet taller than the theatre's highest seats, was blinded by the sun just clearing its crest. Squinting in the brightness, he managed to see men's heads bobbing up and down and the steel arrow tips in their bows poking above the top of the rise. He was just about to shout his observations to Tur, but instead he held his breath as the scaffold's wooden floor rumbled and shook under the weight of men now on it.

Seconds later, most of the platform's wooden beams and supports collapsed and crashed to the ground ten feet below. Although it was not a great distance, the splintered wood, chairs, and sheer number of men tumbling through the scaffold's floor at the same time caused serious injuries to those who had landed first. Soldiers and nobles mingling together in a messy heap, winded and engulfed in a thick fog of dust, lay dazed for a moment. Some cried out in pain, whilst others were pinned down and couldn't move or utter a sound.

Paco's eyes rolled upwards. His head was spinning. Spitting, he tried to clear his mouth of dirt. Pain shot up and down his right arm. He looked at it and pulled a splintered piece of wood from his lower forearm. Freeing his legs, which were trapped by a thick beam, he crawled away from the mound of men who were also beginning to untangle themselves from the heap.

He looked dazedly at the scene and gasped in horror. People were screaming and howling like beasts while surging uncontrollably towards the theatre's exit. There were hundreds of them running down the spectators' stone steps, being trampled on or struck by arrows by attackers who were no longer hiding but standing on the ridge and training their bows directly at the scaffold.

In the arena, people were being trodden on by those callously running over the fallen bodies as though they were a bridge. The arrows and darts were still raining down on the area where the dignitaries had sat, trapping the noblemen and clergy, who were crouching or lying on the ground.

Paco caught a glimpse of the penitents. Only a few remained. Some were dead where they sat. Others cowered between benches, and for some strange reason, they were not even attempting to run away. The air grew heavy, with a grey mist rising up from the other side of the hill. Paco's nose followed the smell of burning, and his eyes found the wall of smoke.

The soldiers and men-at-arms, partially shielded by the debris, concentrated on freeing their masters and getting them to safety. The visiting inquisitor and the viceroy were unscathed, apart from a few cuts to their faces, legs, and arms. Paco could hear the viceroy screeching like an old woman, "Get me out of here!" The visiting inquisitor was shouting for his merciful God to save him from the devil. The duke was demanding to know if De Amo lived, and he sent a man to check on his condition. De Amo was alive but unconscious. The longbow dart in his stomach had snapped in the collapse, and only a ragged inch or so of its length protruded from his skin.

Paco, shielding Peráto's body with his own, kept his eyes peeled on the hill. Militiamen and men-at-arms were climbing the stone steps towards the top of the arena's back wall but were being pushed back by spectators trying to descend. The arrows had stopped flying. The glinting arrow tips and marauders had disappeared from sight.

Observing the chaotic scenes in the arena, his mind searched for a reason. Was this an attack on the Inquisition, the duke, or a rebellion? Had it been an assassination attempt? No, no assassin would use so many men to kill one in such a public display. Were the attackers targeting the viceroy? Was this the work of the duke and Garcia's marauders?

"Paco! Morales, listen to me!" Tur shouted, jolting Paco from his thoughts. "We have to move now. Escort the duke and his guests to safety. I'll remain here with the men."

Luis, cowering behind his escort, sat up and gave Tur a furious look. "Captain, my entire escort will accompany me back to the castle, all twelve of them. Your only concern is to make a safe path for me, my guests, and the Inquisition council."

"The people need our protection," Tur shot back. "Would you have us leave them to a terrible fate?"

Paco glanced at Tur's bright red face, looking as though all his blood were about to burst forth from his skin. He was studying the theatre's exit. People were still bolting towards it. Paco guessed that Tur was considering the chances of getting the dignitaries through the mob of citizens.

"Captain, your orders?" Paco asked tentatively.

"You will not ask your captain for orders! You will listen to me!" Luis shouted, looking at his guests and their men strewn on the ground. "Hear me, every soldier and man-at-arms. These are your orders. "Take your masters to my castle. Protect them with your lives. Move aside every person blocking your way, by force if need be!"

"Your Grace, you and your guests have enough soldiers between you to see you safely to your door," Tur insisted. "Leave me here with my men. We must protect the townspeople from further attack."

"You will follow my orders, Tur," Luis said angrily. "Or by God, I will have you for treason! How can I serve my people if I am dead, you fool!"

"How can you serve a town when it has been burnt to the ground?" Tur countered.

"Still your tongue or I will have it cut from your mouth. I am your duke!"

"You're no more a duke than the boil on my arse!" Tur shouted. "You're a disgrace!"

CHAPTER FIFTY-SIX

David looked briefly at the soldiers attempting to climb the first level of the spectators' steps towards the marauders. He opened his mouth and gasped at their useless attempt to reach the assailants' positions. At least a thousand people were trying to get into the arena from the galleries. Those in the higher seats were pushing against the people beneath them, causing the panicked crowd to tumble over each other in a stampede to get to the bottom. The sound of people screaming was deafening, but David could only imagine that they were panicking not because of the threat of arrows but because they were being trampled on. "God help them!" he uttered. God help them all!"

He flicked his eyes back to the arena. The scaffold's platform was overcrowded. Just about every soldier on guard duty was either on or positioned around its base. He spotted Tur, Paco, and his other brothers-in-arms. Then he gasped in horror as the scaffold collapsed and the men upon it dropped to the ground as though they had all fallen through a trap door.

He rushed forward against the flow of escaping prisoners, looking like a swarm of bees in their yellow and black tunics, and in their midst, he saw his father and mother. His father was carrying his mother in his arms, struggling to hold on to her as others pushed and shoved them out of the way.

After reaching them, David's first reaction was to rip the yellow sambenitos from their bodies and toss them to the ground. Then he took his mother from his father and carried her like a sack of wheat over his shoulder. There was no time for embraces, instructions, or to tell his parents that he loved them.

For the moment, the soldiers were preoccupied with marauders and noblemen, but soon they would regroup and focus their efforts on recapturing the penitents.

David looked at a wall of people trying to leave. They were like a pack of rabid animals surging towards a prey. Prisoners still wearing their telltale tunics rushed alongside townspeople and visitors to Sagrat. A large contingent of Dominican monks, tripping over their habits as they ran and seemingly dismissing the idea of helping the aged or infirm, demanded a path be made for them. And there was not a longbow man, pikeman, or single swordsman guiding or protecting the terrified crowd.

With his mother balancing precariously on his shoulder and his father behind him, David continued to push his weight against the crowd. Not caring who he shoved aside, he pushed his powerful body like a barrier ram against all those in his way, until the crowd thinned and he caught sight of the road outside the arena.

When they had crossed to the other side of the stone path, David stopped for a brief moment, flicking his eyes in all directions. One day a week, a public grassland situated next to the Roman theatre was used as a livestock market. This day it was filled with closed and open carriages, carts, horses, and mules belonging to people attending the auto-de-fé.

David observed the chaos and saw that some spectators had already found their animals and were riding at top speed down the hill. He looked at his parents' exhausted faces. His mother's mouth was ulcerated. Her lips, ragged and blistered, were twice their normal size. His father's eyes, sunken into his cheekbones, were filled with pain. But as much as he wanted to, David could not give them any kindness. There was no time for rest or the indulgence of a drop of water.

They wouldn't get far on foot, he thought, leading them through a maze of animals and transports. His mother, now hobbling uncomfortably behind him, moaned with pain as though she had suffered an injury. He looked back at the Roman theatre and felt his heart punching the wall of his chest. Again he considered that it would not take the Inquisition long to regroup and then send every man-at-arms and those under orders from its Holy Office to hunt down the prisoners and bring them back; those unfortunate enough to be caught would be sentenced to death.

"Mama, I know you have never sat on a horse's back," David said hurriedly, "but you will today. You will ride as fast and as far as you can, and you will hold on for dear life and not fall off."

"I would sit on the back of a black wolf if I thought it would get me away from this hell," Isa sobbed.

Halting abruptly, Juan looked for a brief second down the hill towards the centre of town. There was a wall of flames stretching in a straight line all the way from the south-east to the north-east section of the hill. From where he stood, he could see the fire partially obscuring the church's spire and almost all of the municipal palace's dark grey roof tiles. "*Hijo*, the centre of town and road to the plain might be blocked by flames. We won't get through them," he shouted to David, who was striding towards tethered horses.

"You must, Papa. You must!" David's voice boomed over his shoulder.

Two young boys, about twelve years old, held horses' reins. David stared again at his father and mother's worn-out faces. His father had never looked so scared or vulnerable. His mother wouldn't be able to walk farther than a few paces. Drawing his sword, he strode towards the two boys and planted a furious scowl on his face.

"If you don't want to be bled like goats, you will hand me the reins and move out of the way," he said to the youngsters.

Seeing the sword, David's great height, and the fury on his face, neither boy hesitated in handing the reins to him.

"Stand aside!" David shouted at them for good measure.

"You must come with us, son," Isa begged. "You cannot stay here!"

"Mama, there's no time to argue," David said, lifting her onto the horse's back. Putting her feet into the stirrups, he saw her burnt feet. "The inquisitors can bugger each other," he cursed.

"David, come with us!" Isa insisted again.

Looking at Juan, David said, "I'm staying to help my brothers-in-arms. I must do this. Papa, listen to me. Bad people did this to you. They are a hundred leagues away from any Christian God or humble charity, and they *will* burn you if you don't set off down that hill right now!"

"David will find us," Juan said, looking nervously about him. "Isa, we must leave now, before we're trapped by the fires."

David said, "Just outside Valencia, with the sea to your left, you will find the Convento de los Ángeles. No more than a thousand paces from there, you will see an abandoned farm. You will recognise it because its house no longer has a roof. Diego and Sinfa are there waiting for me."

"When will you come?" Isa asked, crying. "I cannot lose you."

David took off his cloak, handed it to his mother, and then reached up to caress her cheeks gently with his fingertips. Staring into her face, he engraved it in his memory. "Soon. I'll join you soon," he said. "Go now. Ride through the flames if you have to – and don't stop until you can no longer see the town behind you … God has sent us a miracle this day. Papa, don't get caught," he said, slapping the horses' flanks and sending them bolting off.

Taking one last look at his parents clinging to the horses' backs, he wondered if he would ever see them again.

CHAPTER FIFTY-SEVEN

Alejandro's assault on the municipal palace had been met with very little resistance. Arriving at its doors with two closed carriages and four of his regular men, he had counted on Luis's assurances that only two guards would be posted in the main hall and another two in the basement, where the treasury's vaults were situated.

"I will make sure that most of my men are held back behind the castle's walls and that *all* the townspeople, including the Jews and visitors, are well entertained in the Roman theatre," Luis had said confidently. "I will also advise the dignitaries to have their personal guard beside them at all times. The inquisitor's men-at-arms will not be a problem. They will be in the theatre, flanking the scaffold and the penitents' benches. I'm taking a great risk, Alejandro," Luis had added. I will be on that scaffold. I should be safe enough hidden behind the others, but there is still an element of danger ..."

Alejandro and his men dispatched the surprised militiamen with swift thrusts of blades to their chests and abdomens. Then Alejandro opened the treasury vault with the keys Luis had given him. "The duke has not disappointed us," he said to Jóse, his second in command. "The town square and surrounding streets are deserted."

"True, he kept his word, but even so, we don't have any time to waste," Jóse said, staring at the chests.

Alejandro's most trusted men were with him, men he had known for years and who had lived with him in the caves these past few months. Like him, they had left their hiding place only to rob and whore when their urges to poke a woman overshadowed the need to hide from the authorities. Outside the building, another five men, not well known to Alejandro, stood watch, armed with crossbows and pikes. They guarded the two closed carriages, which would be used to carry the loot, and they'd been ordered to kill anyone entering or leaving the square or to alert Alejandro if there was a problem too great for them to deal with.

Observing the size of the chests filled with ducats and maravedis, Alejandro conceded that getting them to the carriages outside would take longer than Luis's calculations. "Christ's blood!" he cursed to his men. "We won't have time to take the three of them. They're too big and fat. It'll take all of you to carry one."

"What about our share of the money?" José asked. "If we can't take the third one, our purses will be lighter."

Staring pensively at the chests, Alejandro said, "If there's less money to go around, it seems to me that we might have to get rid of some of the men I employed."

"And it seems to me that if we're going to kill some of them, we might as well kill all of them," José suggested. "They're common thieves. They won't be missed."

Alejandro looked again at the chest he would have to leave behind. He should get rid of the newcomers, he thought. This important robbery would be talked about for months to come. The fewer people who knew about it, the better.

"Yes," he agreed. "Sacrifices will have to be made."

The seventeen unfortunate men in question were those Alejandro had acquired only a week earlier in the bustling streets that sat next to the River Turia, in the heart of Valencia's capital city. Employing the right men, however, had taken longer than he'd anticipated. He was supplying the weapons, but bugger the devil if he'd been able to find men who knew how to shoot arrows!

Eventually, he'd scraped together an army of impoverished beggars with swords for hire. There were also old soldiers living on charitable handouts and carrying nothing on their persons but parchments inked with recommendations and thanks for their service to the king. They'd jumped at the chance to earn decent money, but Alejandro had not divulged any details about how the robbery was to take place, only that they were to meet him half a league from Sagrat on the night before the auto-de-fé. It was a daring, risky, and dangerous endeavour, Alejandro admitted, but the prize was an unimaginable treasure that would see him live like a lord for the rest of his life.

Luis's plan had been sound. Alejandro's best bowman would accompany nine hardened ex-soldiers to the top of the small hillock banking the Roman theatre. Only Alejandro's regular man knew that his job was to target and kill the inquisitor. The others had been ordered to shoot their arrows in quick succession at the scaffold and into the arena, but without aiming to hit anyone. Their objective was to foment fear, instil panic, and to trap the townspeople and dignitaries inside the amphitheatre so that Alejandro had the time he needed to rob the treasury. When the men saw smoke rising from the fires set by three others in the group, they were to halt their assault, ride as fast as they could from the town, and regroup at the meeting place, halfway between Sagrat and the sea.

Cowering under a hail of arrows, it would take awhile for authorities and people to react. And Alejandro's other men, setting fires in the streets running parallel to the town square, would delay the town's militiamen from reaching the lower part of the hill and, more importantly, the municipal palace. Sniffing the air, he allowed himself to smile. He could already smell smoke drifting down the stairs to the vault. Everything seemed to be going according to plan.

Stepping into the town square, Alejandro encountered a thick grey fog covering the entire area. The men who had been with him inside the vaults had already put the chests inside the carriages. The five men who had been placed on guard outside the building stood in a group beside one of the carriages. Alejandro signalled to his regulars, who drew their swords, and within minutes, the unsuspecting men were dead in the surprise attack.

Panting, Alejandro cleaned his sword and looked at the bodies. "We have to leave, but before we do, bring the dead militiamen out here and put bloodied swords in their hands. Lay them with these thieves. Let the people think they died fighting for their duke and their town."

Alejandro looked at the dead men again, stabbed hastily but with precision. Ideally, there would be honour amongst thieves, he thought. But this was not an idyllic kingdom ruled by fair-minded authorities, and he was not an idealistic man. Life was challenging, and only the strongest and most hard-hearted lived decently in these feudal lands. He had long since chosen an affluent life over an impoverished one, with honour that mattered to no one.

"That's five less we have to share the loot with," he said to his men after they had staged the bodies. "We ride to the caves. Sagrat is as hot as hell. Let the devil take it."

"You're not going to the meeting point?" Jóse asked. "Those nine men will be waiting for their coin."

Alejandro laughed. They could wait forever. He wasn't going to meet them or pay them. "We can't kill all of them, my friend. Best we just let them wander the plain looking for us. They'll never find the caves, and they are in no position to ask questions about me."

When the carriage had reached the plain and was heading north, Alejandro stuck his head out of the window and took a last lingering look at the burning town. Flames were rising. Houses were crashing to the ground. A bright orange ribbon of fire streaked across the entire length of the bottom half of the hill like an uncrossable gorge to all those situated above its line.

Resting his head against the carriage wall, he wondered whether the bowmen had done their jobs properly. Had his man managed to kill the inquisitor as ordered? If De Amo was dead, the king would send an army to rain hell down on Valencia … He shrugged and pleasured his eyes with the sight of coins inside the chest at his feet. So what if he did send his army? There were not enough knights or soldiers in all of Spain clever enough to catch the man who'd emptied a treasury.

Relaxing his body with a long-drawn-out sigh, he rested his eyes on José, sitting opposite him. "After we've moved the chests into the caves, I want you to hide the carriages. Militias will be swarming the countryside."

"I hope we don't have to stay in those cursed caves much longer. My arse forgets what a soft mattress feels like," José said.

Alejandro was thinking the same thing. It had been a long six months. He was tired of living like a rat underground, waiting for Luis's orders, which at times had seemed altogether too personal and senseless for his taste. The trivial whims of dukes and varlets never ceased to amuse and astound him. "Patience. After I conclude my business with the duke two days hence, our mission will be accomplished and our months of hardship at an end." Alejandro smiled. "We can put up with another week or two in that squalor for such a prize as this, don't you think?"

CHAPTER FIFTY-EIGHT

The smoke from the fires covered the hill, and from a distance, the castle looked as though it were sitting above a grey-blanketed sky.

Sagrat's visitors ran through the streets and alleyways like a charging army, dodging flames, falling timbers, and masonry. Few remained behind to help put out the fires, and many of them blatantly ignored cries for help from desperate townspeople valiantly trying to save their houses. Not knowing the best route to take, some of the travellers were blocked by steep rocks and deep crevices. Others ran all the way to the most northern part of the hill, where there were no fires, and started their descent from there.

More than a thousand men, women, and children had arrived in Sagrat filled with morbid curiosity and virtuous desires to see heretics being punished in the name of God. But it now appeared that their sole aim was to leave the town as fast as they could – and by any means possible.

The townspeople, casting aside their fear of marauders and invisible bowmen, fought to control the flames from reaching La Placa Del Rey. The church of San Agustin, the monastery, and municipal palace were the town's most beloved buildings. The square itself was Sagrat's heart and soul. If destroyed, it would never be resurrected to its former glory. It would be a treasure lost forever to a sordid event in history, and no one wanted to be associated with such a shameful legacy.

David, alongside men from the neighbourhood, stood knee deep in an open sewer which ran vertically down an incline at the edge of Calle Sandunga. The old and young rushed to the sewer with empty buckets in their hands. They were not hopeful of dousing the fires, for Valencia was still in the grip of a drought. The rainfalls two weeks previously had been welcomed, but there had not been a large enough deluge to seep through the hard-caked soil and fill underground reservoirs or town wells. Even if the wells had been full, there would still not be enough water to kill flames which were taller than the buildings.

David was handed one empty bucket, pan, and chamber pot after another. As he filled them up to the brim with pee and shit and passed them back to the people, he turned his anger towards the duke. Where were the militiamen, the Inquisition men-at-arms, and the dignitaries' guards? Why had the duke not sent them to help his town? It was bad enough knowing that *he* had not put in an appearance or lent his support to the people trying to save Sagrat ... but to leave his citizens to fend for themselves without the militia's leadership was unpardonable.

Luis stood at the sleeping chamber's door, hiding his disappointment with a sympathetic frown on his face. He wanted to say to the inquisitor, "I paid a lot of money to have you killed, yet there you lie, alive and well." Instead, he clasped his hands and joined the bishop of Valencia in a prayer of thanks.

De Amo had a slight injury. Wearing thick armour underneath his robes had stopped one longbow dart from ripping through his body and killing him. It was a shallow cut, and not much more than the length of the dart tip had pierced his fat belly.

After the physician and bishop left, Luis was made to wait at the door until De Amo summoned him to the bedside. All he could hope for now was his father by law's support at the next election for viceroy. "It's a great relief to see you recovering," he said. "Josefa was worried about you. This news will make her very happy."

"It was God's good grace that saved me. He knows I have work to do. As for my Josefa," the inquisitor said sadly, "we cannot deny the truth forever, Luis. She no longer knows who I am. I presume she no longer recognises you either. She has a disease of the mind and will die soon. You know this, and so do I."

Surprised by this admission, Luis nodded in agreement, wondering how De Amo's revelation might be of use. Diseased of the mind, De Amo had said. She was a witch, and her father knew he wouldn't be able to hide her heresies for much longer. He was afraid.

Looking furtively towards the door, Luis whispered, "I fear she might be possessed. I don't know how we can hide this. I will find the very best physicians in Valencia and bring them here."

"That promise does not placate me one whit. There is no cure for what ails her."

Pausing, Luis's face crumpled as though he were about to cry with grief. "She deserves to have the best care. Perhaps we could send her to a convent? I would care for her here, but the town is burning ... I cannot. Sagrat has bankrupted me ... I don't have the means to rebuild. It's a disaster."

A spark of sympathy sat in De Amo's eyes, but then it was gone. Lifting his arm and waving his hand dismissively in Luis's face, he said, "This is not the time to talk of your needs. See to your town. God has sent his wrath upon Sagrat for all the evil that has taken place. Bury your dead and mourn them. I will recover and so will your cursed town. This tragedy happened because you are an incompetent leader. The burden must fall on your shoulders."

"I am not responsible for criminals that roam this kingdom," Luis retorted. "Maybe we should look to the king and ask him why he spends all of his time in Castile instead of in the land of his birth." Remembering who he was talking to, Luis tried to gain control of his breathing and his temper. "Forgive me. I am distraught."

De Amo groaned as he turned over onto his side. With his back to Luis, he said softly, "Leave me. You will rebuild, even if you lose your entire wealth doing it. Your town will be cleansed, but as duke, you must answer to God for the wickedness that has infected it."

Standing on the battlements, Luis watched the town burn. His plans had gone awry, but only slightly off course. The inquisitor's death would have meant a great inheritance for Josefa. The money would have come to her husband, for she wouldn't have been aware of its existence. It was ironic. It would appear that the inquisitor would outlive his daughter and that when he eventually died, his money would go to little Gaspar.

Looking at the town, he couldn't help but feel a tinge of sadness. He wiped smoke and ash from his eyes as he questioned his decision to torch the town. He had not intended to have fires set, at least not in the beginning. Alejandro had conceived the idea at their last meeting. Luis recalled how the conversation had begun ten days previously in the secret chamber. "Your father was a good man, Luis, but he mismanaged his coffers. And thanks to his obsessive desire to fund the king and your soldier brothers, he left you a pauper.

"Your brothers are wealthy knights with more men under their banners than you will ever be able to afford. They were given estates in Castile and wealth far beyond your own, whilst you received the remnants of a great town wallowing in decline. You have the title, but what good is it when you are forced to live in a damp castle with walls that crumble at the slightest touch? Burn Sagrat. The houses are old, and half of them are falling down anyway."

"And what do you think will happen when Sagrat is in ashes?" Luis had asked, shocked at the very idea.

"It will be resurrected, of course. The king has close ties to Sagrat and your family. He won't allow such a tragedy to go unanswered. He'll be duty-bound to fund its rebirth. And you, Luis, will no longer be in the shadow of your father's failures. You will fill your vaults with the king's coin and build a magnificent town, worthy of a viceroy."

Luis spoke in a soft, unthreatening voice, informing Tur that he was to be forgiven for his mutinous protests earlier in the Roman theatre. Having reflected on what he should do about the captain, he decided that Tur would be much more useful as an ally than as a prisoner locked up for treason, so he had swallowed his pride.

"I hope we are clear, Captain. I will not tolerate such behaviour in the future. If you ever question my orders again you will be severely punished. Is that clear?"

"Yes. Your Grace is very generous," Tur said.

Luis leaned against the battlement wall and stared at Tur, trying to gauge his mood. Finally, he said. "Take your men. Tell them to aid the townspeople in whatever way they can."

Tur nodded. "And when do we go after the marauders? They stole two chests of coin. That amount of money will have to be transported in carriages. My men might yet find the opportunity to capture the thieves, if we ride after them now."

"No, the town needs to see the militia out in force. Have them patrol the streets all night. There will be homeless people to attend to. All the townspeople must help their neighbours. I will ask the viceroy's soldiers to hunt the vermin."

For a moment, there was silence, and then Luis straightened himself and puffed out his chest in a show of authority. "I have another task for you. This is a job for you and you alone. I want you to find David Sanz.

"And when I do?"

"You will kill him, quietly and without witnesses. There is evidence to suggest he may have had a hand to play in these fires and the assassination attempt on the Inquisitor's life."

Tur appeared to be stunned. Luis lifted a sinister eyebrow. "You have something to say, Captain?"

"Why would he perpetrate such a crime?" Tur managed to stutter.

"Revenge for being thrown out of my militia by his ear, of course … Why else?"

"There is no evidence against him..."

Luis turned his back on Tur and stared at the town below. "Report back to me when it is done. That will be all, Captain."

CHAPTER FIFTY-NINE

David gazed at the gaping empty tract where six tightly knit streets used to stand and shook his head in disbelief. It was as though a huge rock had been tossed to Earth from the heavens and had blown everything away.

Smouldering within the rubble were bodies of men and women who had lost their lives trying to retrieve their most precious possessions. Every person had an ash-coated face and smelled of burnt timbers. Every straw and wooden roof had disintegrated. Walls made from stone had tumbled, and shells of houses left standing were black and so hot that they could blister a hand if touched. There was no sky, no white clouds. The entire town was engulfed in a black and grey fog, smelling like the devil's breath.

David heard his name being shouted. He stopped what he was doing, wiped his eyes with his forearm, and looked into the crowd of people who, like him, were stamping out the remains of the fire. The militia had finally arrived, too late to be of much use here, David thought, and then he saw Captain Tur.

Tur ordered his men to work and then turned his attention to David. Taking stock of his filthy clothes, he said, "Sanz, you stink like a strong wind in a shit storm. I've been looking for you. Come with me."

"I no longer take orders from you, Captain. What do you want with me?"

"I'm not ordering you to come with me, Sanz. I'm asking you," Tur answered.

"I can't imagine why we would have business together," David said, unwilling to move. Trepidation grew, but with one eye on Tur and the other on the militia, who had already begun to sweep and dampen debris to make sure it would not reignite, he concluded that Tur was not tricking him or deceiving him. Tur was an honest man. If he had come to arrest him, he would have done it with force. He looked at Paco, who was watching from a distance. Paco shrugged his shoulders as if to say, *I don't know anything.* At last, David nodded. "At your service, Captain," he said sarcastically.

Tur led David through the smouldering streets, saying nothing until they were inside the Roman theatre. It was strangely quiet and clean. There were no dead bodies. The platforms' remnants and timbers had been removed, as had the penitents' benches. No arrows were strewn on the ground. It looked as it did every day, a deserted old monument.

David's heart thumped as a thought struck him. Was he going to be asked to rejoin the militia? He wouldn't, of course, but for some reason the notion excited him. "Captain, you have my attention," he said, not knowing what else to say.

After sitting down on a spectator's step, Tur drew his sword and laid it beside him on a stone. "Sit," he said, motioning David to the spot beside him.

Once David was seated, Tur said, "I lost five good men today."

"Who?" David asked, saddened by this news.

Tur reeled off the names in a voice that shook with a mixture of anger and sorrow.

"My condolences. They were good men. I should have been serving with them," David said.

"A soldier prays for a good death in battle, not to be murdered," Tur went on, staring at the empty arena. "There has been too much murder done in this town. Too much suffering and grief ... and loss."

The conversation was civil, David thought with some surprise. But where would it lead? Should he speak up or say as little as possible? He felt cold spread through him and the hairs on his arms rise and tickle his skin. "Yes, there have been too senseless killings," he found himself saying. "How many people died in here?"

"Twenty five. It could have been much worse, but I don't think the marauders wanted to kill innocent people. They seemed more intent on killing the dignitaries on the scaffold." Waving his arms in the direction of the arena, Tur asked, "Do you know who is responsible for what happened here and for all the other terrible crimes plaguing Sagrat?"

"No. How could I know anything?"

Tur grunted and then sneered with disgust. "This is the question I have been asking myself for weeks. What is David Sanz's involvement? Why does he seem to be at the heart of every matter."

"I am not involved in anything or with anyone," David protested, but his voice shook with guilt.

"One would think not. After all, you're a pup with no credentials, yet on the very night a young family was slaughtered and your farm was attacked, you were in the duke's private chambers having dealings with him. I watched you leave the castle with Garcia and speak to him in whispers, and then you disappeared. You left your watch post and did not return until morning. Where did you go?"

A cool head was needed, David thought, but for the life of him, he couldn't think of a single thing to say. "I don't know," he eventually muttered. "I can't remember."

"Is that so? I think you remember very well what happened that night."

"What are you implying?"

"I imply nothing ... I know."

"If you know, you should get to your point," David said gratingly.

"Not yet. There are still pieces of the puzzle that leave me baffled. I'm hoping that you will give me the answers I'm looking for."

"What are you looking for? It seems you already have all the answers."

"If I had, you might already be dead. I would have done to you what I did to our dear departed lord treasurer."

David gasped loudly. Instinctively, he rose from the step.

"Sit on your arse!" Tur's voice hissed.

Paralysed with fear and his mind frozen with questions, David sat back down, stared at Tur, and saw a murderous intent in his dark eyes that terrified him. He did it ... Tur, a man who went to Mass every day and carried a rosary. "Why? Why did you kill him?" he asked, so softly spoken that the words were barely audible.

Seemingly confident that David was not going to make a run for it, Tur sat back and rested his elbows on the step above him. "Had I let him live, he would have gone to the duke. I would have been killed the next day, and Peráto would not have to answer for his crimes. That hardly seems fair."

David's ears rang. Holding his breath, he waited for the words that would condemn him and the punishment that would follow them.

"Now back to what I know, Sanz," Tur continued with not a hint of malice in his voice. "Garcia lied to me on the night he left the castle with a prison cart and came back with two men disfigured, in agony, and unable to whimper their innocence. Perhaps he thought me dim-witted when he made those blunders. You see, the lord treasurer has no power to arrest citizens. The arrest warrant in his possession was signed by the duke, yet only the magistrate has that authority. I was suspicious, so I investigated.

"I heard from witnesses at the port that a scar-faced man and his cohorts, using the prison cart that Garcia took, abducted Miguel and Ignacio and killed their friend. I also found out that on the night of the Immaculate Conception, Miguel and Ignacio were in the port's taverna and that both had consumed enough wine to put a horse to sleep. They could not have killed that family or raised fires … so who committed those crimes? I asked myself.

"After Miguel and Ignacio were arrested, I kept a close eye on Garcia. At the burnings, I watched him approach you. I saw the hatred on his face when he gripped your arm and whispered in your ear. I also heard about your sword fight with a man who had a scar running down his face. That's when I knew you and Garcia were connected."

David's mouth was as dry as bone. He swallowed painfully and said, "No." Labouring to keep his breathing steady, he looked at his options. Say nothing and be tortured; admit everything and be burned. Fight Tur? Kill him?

"Sanz, I have dedicated my life to soldiering. I have seen guilt written on men's faces after they have killed in battle, and I saw it on yours when the men were burned. The shame was emblazoned in your eyes, as though you felt personally responsible for their deaths …"

During a strange pause in which Tur seemed to want to give David the opportunity to rebut his statement, David found himself unable to deny what had just been said. Sighing wearily with defeat, he kept his mouth shut.

"I waited. I bided my time, looking for an opportune moment to question Garcia," Tur continued. "I knew he had the duke's ear and that it was a dangerous pursuit, but I came to believe that Garcia and the duke were connected to a terrible crime and that somehow you were also involved. Unfortunately, Garcia proved to be elusive, but on the night before the High Mass, I saw him leave the south-east gate alone. I followed him. I confess I was torn ... What would happen to me were I to accuse our illustrious treasurer of being complicit in the murder of an innocent family? And *why* were they killed? I could not find any possible reason."

"But you decided to ask him anyway?" David asked, finding his voice. He could feel droplets of sweat run down the side of his forehead and into his hairline. "Well, did you?" he asked again.

In the silence, Tur's face took on a satisfied expression, as though he were remembering a pleasurable experience. "I waited until he was almost at the municipal palace. I put a knife to his throat and led him here, to this very spot. I tied his hands and feet with hemp cord. Every time he raised his voice louder than a whisper, I nicked him with my dagger.

"I began by asking him who had ordered the arrest of two innocent men. Of course, I didn't want to believe it was our duke, but Garcia was quick to offer me Peráto like a pig's head on a plate. I told Garcia that I knew who had killed the young family but that I needed him to tell me why. I suppose he must have believed me. Or perhaps he was terrified of being tortured further and wanted to keep some skin on his bones. To this day, I don't know what possessed him to tell me about the duke, the baby, and you, but to my surprise, he did. He sang like a canary and begged for his life.

David could almost hear his own heart beating. He had imagined dying in many different ways in the past weeks. At times, he thought that death might be easier than trying to stay alive. But faced with it now, he realised that he wanted to live. He wanted to see Sinfa again and to be given the chance to redeem himself. "Garcia spoke the truth," he said, crushed. "I followed the duke's orders after he threatened to kill my family. I have been living in fear ever since that terrible night."

"Fear is what that young family must have felt when you slaughtered them!" Tur stopped speaking. His jaw tensed, twitching the muscles in his cheeks.

David could feel the captain's rage. "If you're going to kill me, do it now."

"You followed orders." Tur, sneering with bitterness, ignored what David had just said. "Valencia is full of men who follow orders and hire their swords for money. They kill not out of necessity or pleasure but because it gives them a living. You are not the only soldier to follow a foul order from a bad leader, Sanz. And had you not killed a little girl, I might have given you a head start before I implicated you in that shit of a crime.

"You'll get your death soon enough. You sicken me. There is no filthier scum than a man who murders a child, so before you face justice, you will take me to the child's grave and you'll dig up her body. She will be given a Christian burial."

As Tur's words raced through his mind, David's breath felt as though it was being sucked out of his body. He gasped for air, panicking at his inability to say what he wanted to say. "No … no," he finally managed to utter. "I could never harm a child. I had to kill the parents. Had I not ended them, Peráto would have sent another man in my place – or another infant would have been stolen and his family killed, perhaps in a house with even more occupants than the one I chose, but I swear to you, I would rather be gutted alive than kill a child."

A cry ripped from Tur's throat. His mouth remained open, and for a second, a spark of approval sat in his eyes. "You had better not be lying to me," he whispered in a broken voice.

"I'm not. I swear to you. After I delivered the infant to Garcia, I carried the girl from the town and hid her somewhere safe."

Pensively but with the hint of a smile, Tur nodded. "God is indeed merciful."

David felt a spark of hope ignite and dared to ask, "Captain, why did you wait so long to confront me?"

"I needed time to find solid evidence to use against the duke. Who is going to believe an old drunk like me? What man or priest is going to accuse a duke of such a wicked crime without irrefutable proof?"

"Do you still mean to kill me?"

"No."

"Then let me serve you," David begged. "I'll give you your proof."

Tur stood up. "Lad, I mean to see this through. If you remain in this town, you will be arrested."

"I know," David nodded, knowing he couldn't run away from this. "I will stand by your side... I give you my oath."

CHAPTER SIXTY

The old farmhouse sat in the middle of a field which had not been ploughed for years. Pampas grass the height of a man swayed in the soft afternoon breeze and obscured the overgrown path that led to the dilapidated building.

David walked in front of the horse with the reins held loosely in his hand and picked his way through the dirt trail littered with sharp-edged rocks and potholes. At the farmhouse, he tied the horse's rope to a tree and edged his way towards an opening in the stone walls. This was the right place, he thought. From the road, he had seen the convent's tower in the distance, just as Diego had described.

There was no roof on the house, apart from a sparse covering of branches belonging to an overhanging eucalyptus tree, exactly as Diego had said it would look. Yet there was no mule or cart and not a sound or a face greeting his arrival. It was late afternoon, and being January, it was already growing dark. There were still streaks of light in the sky, but the enclosure within the walls was as black as a boar's mouth. Standing perfectly still, he took a closer look, stared at the run-down structure, and then walked doggedly towards it. "Is there anyone there? Hello?"

A twig snapped. Diego appeared at the opening and sighed with relief. "Thank God," he said. "Thank God, David."

The first thing David saw when he went inside was Sinfa, propped up against the back wall like a dark shadow. His heart filled, but his mind was racing with questions, diluting this rare happy moment. Blinking, he adjusted his eyes and looked about him again. "Where are Mama and Papa?" he asked Diego. "They should have arrived here hours ago."

"They were set free?" Diego asked, gripping David's shoulders.

"In a manner of speaking. They're fugitives," David said. "They escaped from Sagrat yesterday morning, along with hundreds of other prisoners. They were riding two good horses. Christ's blood! Where did they go?"

"What do you mean, 'escaped'? What happened in Sagrat?"

Sinfa struggled to her feet like a half-starved dog. "No one has come near this place, only foxes," she said in a weak voice. "It's so quiet here that we can hear the rats gnawing at the date palm outside. If only there were dates," she said, getting emotional.

David looked at her and then lightly touched her face. "There you are," he said, smiling. "I have food and water."

"Where are Mama and Papa?" Diego insisted, but his sunken eyes were looking greedily at the bread David had retrieved from the sack he was holding.

David didn't know where to begin. "Eat and drink, and then we'll talk," he said.

Diego tore at the bread with his teeth, and with a full mouth, he mumbled, "I swear to God, I never thought time could march so slowly. We tried to make the food last, but we finished the last of the bread yesterday morning. There's a river not far from here, but it's as dry as a bone. We won't survive here another night here."

In the brief silence that followed, David watched as his brother tried to swallow a lump of bread. God help them, they were starving, he thought. His mind turned to his parents. How long would Diego and Sinfa be able to wait for them? He'd seen for himself that there was nothing here but dry weeds.

"I tried to get here as fast as I could," David finally said. "I don't have much water, but I do have more bread and a little cheese. There should be enough food to last you a couple of days."

"What about you?" Sinfa asked.

Not able to answer her, David said, "We'll talk about me later. We have to find Mama and Papa. Papa must have taken a wrong turn, although it's a straight road all the way here. Diego, where is the mule and cart?"

Chewing on the bread, Diego pointed and muttered, "There's a patch of grass out back. The mule is grazing." Diego grew thoughtful. He stopped chewing and asked, "Why did you not travel with them? Why did you allow them to flee without you?"

Hesitating to speak in front of Sinfa, David motioned Diego outside. The less Sinfa knew, the better. If he had anything to say about it, she would never find out what he had done.

After telling Diego about the ambush in the arena and the fires raised by the marauders, David finished by saying, "Captain Tur knows everything. I have given him my word that I'll return with the little girl. I'm going to help him bring Peráto to justice."

David searched Diego's watery eyes and saw the tears ready to slip from them. Putting his hand on Diego's shoulder, he said, "Brother, listen to me. The future looks bleak, but it's not lost. I will live through this. Tur will protect me. I have the promise of a full life."

"Yes, you have, if the authorities don't decide to burn you at the stake. Tur's plan could be shot to hell for a number of reasons. To accuse a duke of a crime is like accusing the pope of sinning! It will be the end of you both."

"You're right. If Captain Tur and I fail to convince the authorities that the duke and his marauders are to blame for everything, I will be arrested and tried for murder. I might not come back. But don't grieve for me just yet." David smiled.

"Why are you smiling?" Diego asked angrily. "You don't have to do this. You're free now. Can't you leave Sagrat behind you? Come with us!"

David shook his head. Captain Tur had given his word that he would do everything in his power to make sure both of them came out of this ambitious and perhaps foolhardy plan with their hides still intact. And he had given Tur *his* word that he would see this through to the end, no matter how grim the outcome looked. "I can't do that."

"You care more about your own redemption than you do about your family," Diego said petulantly. "Have we not grieved enough? Have you not caused enough harm?"

"That's enough! Turn your thoughts to our parents. They must be your priority," David said, irritable, tired, and running out of time. "As soon as I leave with the child, you will search for Mama and Papa. Their stay in prison weakened them, and they're probably sick with hunger. They could be resting somewhere close by or they've taken a wrong turn in the road and are completely lost."

"And if I find them? What then?"

"When you find them, leave this place. Don't wait for me. Travel southwards towards Castile. Beg for food and shelter if you have to and don't stop until you are no longer in this kingdom. An army will soon be scouring Valencia, looking for escaped prisoners."

"How will you find us?"

David's heart broke. He had rarely seen his brother cry. "I will follow your route along the coast. I've heard there's nothing but a barren wilderness and impassable mountains inland so don't go there. I will find you before you reach the edge of Spain. I give you my oath. I won't stop looking for you."

Darkness had fallen. Enough time had been spent talking, David thought. "We should leave for the convent. I need to get the little girl back to Tur," he said.

"I pray she's still there."

"She will be. If the nuns were kind enough to take her in, they wouldn't have thrown her out after a few weeks. Just be your charming self and get her out of there as quickly as possible. Beg for water and food. They won't turn you away empty handed."

Diego nodded in agreement.

"Get the mule and cart ready. I want a moment alone with Sinfa," David said.

"You're going to leave again, aren't you?" Sinfa said when she saw him.

David paced aimlessly for a moment and then stopped in front of her. All he could see was her outline against the wall's stones. "I'm returning to Sagrat. I don't want to leave you, but I have something important to attend to. I gave my word to someone," he told her, and then he held her hand. "Before I go, I wanted you to know that I have often thought about a life with you by my side. You're very dear to me," he said.

A tiny sob left Sinfa's mouth ... and then another. "David, I am in your debt, and I will never be able to repay your kindness," she whispered hoarsely. "You saved me in that prison and took me from it, at great risk to yourself. But ..."

"But what?" Confused, David followed Sinfa's eyes. Behind him, Diego stood with his head slightly downcast and eyes averted. He seemed unwilling to return David's questioning gaze. David stared again at Sinfa and back at Diego, and then he let out a painful sigh. "You have affection for each other?" he asked stupidly.

"We're in love," Diego said.

"In love? You've only known each other for five minutes."

"And you have known her for six," Diego parried back.

Sinfa touched David's arm. He recoiled and shook his head. "You love my brother. You feel nothing for me? We held hands ... The way you look at me...?"

"You are my saviour!" Sinfa choked. "Forgive me, David. Diego and I have spent every waking moment together for weeks. I have come to care deeply for him. He fills my heart. Please understand. Tell me I have not hurt you."

David felt his heart being pummelled to dust, leaving him with a gaping hole that was consuming all rational thought. Sinfa had filled his mind with dreams of love and a future worth fighting for, yet Diego filled her heart. Diego ... He had everything. His soul was untarnished. His ambitions were still intact. He had the love of a wonderful woman and the promise of joy. For a moment, he was stunned by the hatred he felt, not to mention the urge to punch his brother's face, which was glowing with smug victory.

"I entrusted Sinfa's safety to you. It seems to me you took your task seriously," he said sarcastically.

"You did not declare your affections," Diego answered defensively.

David wanted to scream, "I was not afforded the time or the opportunity to declare my love for Sinfa. I fed you both, covered your escape from Sagrat, suffered our parents being sentenced in a public display of filthy lies, and remained to help put out fires. And you, dear brother, have been well aware of my affections for weeks!" Instead of speaking, he hid his feelings and swallowed the retort.

Walking to the entrance, he smiled weakly at Sinfa. She had just shattered his dreams, yet he still thought her the loveliest, most adorable creature on God's earth. How could he face her again? He could barely breathe with the pain of losing her, although he realized eith sickening clarity that he never truly had her. Glancing scathingly at Diego, he caught a flash of sympathy.

"We have to leave for the convent. It's growing dark," he said. "The sooner I leave this place, the better."

CHAPTER SIXTY-ONE

Soft flames from a campfire were visible even before David had turned off the road by the river. Driving towards the ruins, he looked at what was left of his father's farm. It was a pitiful sight. Patches of ground were still charred, even after the recent rains, and everywhere he looked, black tree trunks looking like ugly sculptures marred the land.

Before he got to the where the fires were, he gazed at the child lying in the back beneath thick layers of hemp sacks. He lifted a sack and, watching her sleep, was reminded of the day he'd met her grandparents, Eduardo and Alma. "Our granddaughter's name is Ángelita," they'd told him. "She is our little angel."

Halting the mule with a saw at the reins, he glanced to his left and saw Captain Tur. Behind him were eight militiamen. Tensing, David looked at them one by one, feeling a mixture of envy and fear. He remembered the weight of his helmet, shield, and sword; the feel of armour on his body; and the pride of being a part of something bigger than himself. The men reminded him of days he wanted back ... But he recalled the last time he had seen his brothers in the castle's courtyard, when he'd been stripped of his pride and led away in shame.

He hadn't expected Tur to bring his men, although it had crossed his mind that Tur might decide to punish him after he got the girl back. Putting what might happen to him aside, he looked at the men's expectant faces and realised that the little girl was so well hidden that no one would ever guess she was there. Motioning to the back of the cart, he said, "She's asleep under that pile, Captain. Her name is Ángelita. She's well."

Tur peeled away a couple of sacks, and for a moment, he watched his men gaze at the child as though they had never seen one before.

"She's no worse off for her ordeal," David assured the men again.

"I would not have believed it, were I not looking at her with my own eyes," one of the men said, seeming deeply affected by the child, who had stirred and was trying to sit up.

"It's a miracle," another added.

Tur, still staring at Ángelita's face with eyes kinder than anyone had ever seen them, pulled back the sacks completely and touchingly held her hand. Her face crumpled, and at her first soft whimper, he again displayed a rare glimpse of emotion by hushing her with a soft melodic voice. "There, there, little one, everything's going to be all right." He looked at his men with an austere expression back on his face, and said, "She is the only light in what's been the darkest of days for Sagrat. She makes what we are about to do worthwhile."

The men nodded.

Now that he had delivered on his promise, David wondered again about his own fate. As the men continued to coo over the child, he took a quick look around. There were two closed carriages sitting a short distance away. Three horses were tethered to a tree stump. Longbows and pikes were lying beside shields, and beside them was the duke's flag, lying carelessly in a muddy pool. What he didn't see were prisoners' chains.

"Did you catch the marauders?" he asked Tur.

"We've not been looking for the marauders," Tur surprised him by saying. "We left the town last evening, but we came straight here. We've been waiting for you all night."

Glancing at his men, he added, "But as far as the authorities in Sagrat are concerned, we've been on patrol, searching for the whoresons who destroyed our town."

Looking at the two carriages, David asked. "What are they for?"

"One is for the little girl. The other is carrying the body of one of the marauders we found dead outside the municipal palace."

A look of confusion crossed David's face.

"He still has his uses, which is more than I can say for you, Sanz."

David stared at Tur and the men, and then his hand instinctively went for a sword he no longer had.

Tur looked amused, and for a brief second, it appeared he might smile. "Were you thinking about fighting all nine of us?"

David lowered his eyes. "What are you going to do to me?" he asked no one in particular.

Tur was pensive for a moment, as though thinking about how to answer. Lifting Ángelita from the back of the cart, he turned to the man standing next to him, and said, "Take the child to the carriage. Sit with her and keep her happy. We'll be leaving in a minute. As for you," he said to David, "you're free to leave."

"I can go?" David's eyes brightened. He wasn't sure what was going on, but suddenly all the hope he had suppressed now flooded through him. "Don't you need me to testify?" he asked, surprising himself.

"No, you're no longer a militiaman, and your presence here will hinder us, not help us." Tur looked at the mule and cart. "I won't even ask where you got that. Take it. Go now – and don't show your face in Sagrat again."

David looked again at the men. He was still sceptical and unclear about why he was being set free. Remembering Tur's words in the Roman theatre, he had to ask what he was thinking. "If the authorities find out about my involvement, will you come after me?"

Tur cocked his head to one side. "There is only one person who might accuse you of being complicit in the murders. The other was Sergio Garcia, and he's not coming back from the afterlife to talk. As for the duke, *if* he accuses you, he'll be admitting his own guilt. Of course, he might be interrogated and squawk, like a canary, in which case the council will order your arrest. I will send my men to look for you north of Sagrat. You must go south. Leave Aragon – do you hear me?"

David nodded. He felt exhilarated with a burst of energy he hadn't felt in a while. He was free. It was over, and he still couldn't quite believe it. He watched a man put water, a sack of bread and cooked kid meat in the back of the cart.

"You have a long journey ahead of you. Make the food last, young Sanz," he said, patting David on the back.

Tur handed him a purse filled with maravedis. "When you were dismissed, you didn't get paid what was rightly owed to you," he said matter-of-factly. "This is from your brothers."

"Thank you for giving me my freedom, Captain," David said, his voice cracking with emotion.

"I'm not doing this for you. As I told you, you'll only complicate matters further. I just hope to God you're right about the infant's birthmark."

"I am."

In another rare moment, Tur stretched out his hand and placed it on David's shoulder. "Make amends to God. No man is truly free when his soul has been damaged and his conscience weighs heavy."

Watching Tur and the militia leave, David reflected on Tur's words and was unable to comprehend fully what had just happened. He had not been able to say goodbye to Paco, who'd been absent, or to ask why the dead marauder's body was being used in Tur's plan. Everything had occurred with the speed and twisted logic of a dream.

Before leaving, he visited Juanjo's grave a short distance from where the cart stood. He said a Jewish prayer, uttered his goodbyes, and then left Sagrat without once looking back.

CHAPTER SIXTY-TWO

The sun had risen, promising another day of dry, mild weather. Having had no rain, the stale smell of smoke hung over the town square, looking oddly barren without the trees and shrubbery that had given it shade in the summer and a touch of colour in wintertime.

Fortunately, the fires had not spread as far as the Jewry, Roman theatre, and prison, situated higher up the hill, but the six streets which had sat directly behind and to the right of La Placa Del Rey no longer existed. Stone steps which had once bordered streets packed with houses looked oddly out of place now, like superfluous decorations, but they were the only reminders of the homes and the people who had lived and worked in the once bustling area.

A carriage carrying the marauder who had died outside the municipal palace and another with the child inside it, were but ten paces from where Tur stood outside the municipal palace. His soldiers were ready. He was ready, yet he hesitated. Beads of sweat glistened on his forehead. His hands and legs were shaking, and he couldn't seem to stop clenching and unclenching his fists. He looked at his men, standing at ease but encircling the carriages with strict orders not to allow townspeople to get too close to them, and sensed their nervousness.

He was not one for speeches, he thought, gathering his militia around him for a final briefing, but if ever there was a time to bolster his men's courage, it was now. "You're all here of your own accord, but I understand your worries," Tur said with an unusually quiet voice. "And you're right to be

377

concerned. There are risks, but do I need to remind you that we've just buried five of our brothers?"

"Peráto insisted that most of the men be left at the castle on the day of the auto-de-fé. That was a deliberate ploy to leave us vulnerable to attack. He also refused to double the guard at the municipal palace, and after the ambush, he scurried back to his chambers, leaving the townspeople without protection. He dismissed my request to go after the marauders because he wanted them to get away ... and don't forget that he robbed two chests of coin from his own vault.

Watching the men's anger growing, he carried on. "I will not even talk about that poor young murdered couple or about their babies being abducted ... You all know Peráto's responsible. Our duke is a deep festering boil on this town, allying himself to marauders who have terrorized our people. And who is going to replace the stolen money, eh? We are. We will pay with higher taxation. Our earnings will be cut in half. And whilst we're suffering, our duke and his marauders will be sharing their blood-covered coin." Pausing for a moment, Tur clenched his fist, fighting the rage festering inside him. "Luis Peráto has done more damage to Sagrat than an invading army ever could. He has hurt those he swore an oath to protect. I want to see him executed."

One of the men said, "As far as I'm concerned, the sooner the better. I won't serve that bastard anymore."

Nodding with approval, Tur added, "I hear the inquisitor wants the king to send an army to hunt for Sagrat's escaped heretics. Well, I say let them see to their business, but we will remind the inquisitor that Sagrat's biggest heretic is his own son by law." Pausing, he searched the faces clustered around him. "All you have to do is back up my story as we discussed. But if any of you are having second thoughts, you have my permission to leave now."

Nobody moved, and Tur turned his attention back to the mission. Gesturing to two of the men, he said, "Go. Bring them here now." To the rest, he repeated his order that they wait by the carriages until he came back out of the municipal palace, either walking or being dragged in chains for treason.

The two militiamen guarding the double doors to the council's meeting chambers stood aside and greeted Tur with a weary nod of their heads. "Captain, the meeting is still going on," one of the men said. "There are a lot of angry voices in there. Even Father Bernardo is shouting about something or other. If I were you, I wouldn't disturb them."

"Since when do you give your opinion so freely?" Tur asked, scowling. "Is the duke with them?"

"No, the council have been asking for him, but His Grace has not arrived yet."

Good, Tur thought. Peráto would have been a hindrance. It would be much easier to make the accusations without him sitting there denying the charges.

"Open the doors," Tur ordered the two men.

The town council members were holding an emergency meeting with the clergy and the viceroy, who had remained in Sagrat to lead the investigations into the town's recent murders. The men sitting at a long table stopped talking when the thick double doors swung open to admit Tur. Glaring at him, the magistrate stood up. Looking Tur over from head to foot, he seemed disgusted by the filthy clothes and dirt caked armour. "What's the meaning of this, Captain? Who gave you permission to interrupt us?" he asked gruffly.

Tur faced the men, swallowing painfully with a mouth as dry as Sagrat's wells.

Casting his eyes over the members in the chamber, he saw the viceroy, sitting farthest away from him at the head of the table. Father Bernardo sat next to him. He had just been appointed as *comisario* after being selected to help the Inquisition on administrative matters, and he looked as proud as a peacock.

"My apologies for the intrusion, Your Mercies," Tur said in a loud voice. "I have just returned with my men from the northern plains, and I bring news about the marauders who ambushed the auto-de-fé. I have also brought a treasure of greater value than what was lost in the robbery."

After the mumblings had died down, the magistrate said, "Go on."

Tur felt every pair of eyes boring into him. Their jaws would drop with the story he was about to tell them. "During the night, we came across the remains of the marauder's encampment. The thieves had fled before we got there, but they left behind an injured man and a little girl …"

"This child – who is she?" the viceroy asked with an intrigued tone.

"She is the little girl who was abducted from her home in Sagrat one month ago."

Tur stood perfectly still, listening to the murmuring voices heighten in a hurried discussion.

"This cannot be true, Tur," the magistrate said. "You are mistaken."

Tur looked at him and at all the other faces turning white with shock. "A dying man usually speaks the truth, Your Mercy," he said confidently.

Father Bernardo gazed at him with feverish eyes that would raise gooseflesh on the bravest of men. Shaking his waxy index finger at Tur, he spluttered, "Whatever that man said was a lie! The two men we executed confessed to killing her, along with her infant brother and parents … The child cannot be Ángelita Casellas. It is impossible."

Tur narrowed his eyes with disgust. He'd lost faith in the clergyman. For two years, the padre had been his confessor, and three times a week, Tur had offloaded his sins to the priest. But since taking up his new position, Father Bernardo seemed to have forgotten what God wanted from him. It would appear that serving his own political ambitions had become more important than being of service to his flock.

"You arrested the two men we burned, Tur," the magistrate said accusingly. "Are you telling us that you arrested the wrong men?"

"I arrested no one. Sergio Garcia captured the two men without my knowledge or yours," Tur said pointedly. "I simply transported them to the prison on his orders. I do not presume to question my betters."

The viceroy banged his fist on the table, obviously disturbed by the sound of raised voices and what they were talking about. "Someone had better tell me what's going on here. I've never witnessed such a disorganised body of authority in my entire life!"

"This is a misunderstanding, my lord," the magistrate said, giving Tur a scathing look. "Captain, continue with this absurd story of yours and you'll find yourself in trouble with this council."

Tur was undeterred. "After I persuaded the dying marauder to talk, he perfectly described the child's house, the way in which her parents were murdered, and what happened to the two babies."

Surrounded by loud objections, Tur's voice became louder and louder, until he was shouting above the noisy threats and insults. "There is no doubt in my mind that Garcia, and the marauders who had left the man and the little girl to die on the plain were responsible for all of Sagrat's troubles! Your Mercies, you must listen to me!"

"And where is she, then, this child you say you have?" the magistrate asked angrily.

"She is with my men outside, but before you see her, there is more you should know … It concerns the duke."

CHAPTER SIXTY-THREE

Tur stood in the hallway outside the council chamber after they told him to wait until they had made a decision concerning the matter. His head was pounding, and his ears were still ringing with Father Bernardo's threats of incarceration and excommunication from the Catholic Church. He craved water to ease his burning throat, and he was irritated to the point where he wanted to smash the door down and tell the council not to waste any more time.

He had done everything he could to convince the shocked men in chamber that the duke was the head of the snake that had reaped havoc on the town. And he had not even mentioned the suspicious death of Saul Cabrera, the physician who had once been a council member. Unfortunately, the facts he'd laid before them had been met with grunts of disgust aimed at him and not Peráto. They would sooner believe in a flying goat than in their duke being a murdering thief!

Relating David's account of the night of the murders and abduction of the infant and his older sister had been a simple matter of using David's words and details and replacing his name with the now-defunct marauder lying in the carriage outside. "The marauders were the duke's mercenaries, paid with his coin," Tur had informed the open-mouthed men." He told them that they had acted on his orders to acquire an infant, his own son having died at birth. Peráto had also ordered the attack and burning of the town and probably knew where the two stolen chests from the treasury were hidden. Tur wasn't sure if this assumption was accurate, but his gut feelings said it was, and he believed his instincts, sharpened by years of soldiering.

"So you still insist that the duke is guilty of all these monstrous crimes?" the magistrate asked, facing Tur again.

Tur chose his words with the utmost care. "No, I insist that the marauder we found accused the duke of those foul crimes before he died."

"You want us to believe that the duke's son does not carry his father's blood?"

"I am not asking you to believe anything I say. I am simply telling you what was told to me."

"All the saints above," the magistrate murmured, rising to his feet to pace the room. "Do you really expect us to stride up to the duke's door and arrest him because you say he's guilty? We need proof, Tur. Real proof!"

"I took the liberty of bringing the little girl's grandparents here. They are outside as we speak. They will confirm that she is their granddaughter," Tur said, becoming even more irritable at the magistrate's scepticism. "Will you at least speak to them?"

"Even if it is the missing girl, we cannot connect her to the duke. There's nothing to be done," Father Bernardo said to the others.

"Nothing," another council member agreed.

"I say we arrest Tur for heresy," Father Bernardo then suggested for the umpteenth time. "He is bearing false witness against His Grace."

"The grandparents also have information about markings on the infant's body. I think you'll all agree that's something only family members would know about."

The viceroy, who had been conspicuously silent, finally stood up and tapped his knuckles on the tabletop. "I'm wondering whether you men are afraid to learn the truth or if you're fearful of the consequences it will bring you. What if everything Tur says is true? Is it not our duty to investigate such horrible crimes to the fullest extent of the law, no matter who the suspect is? Padre, am I not correct in thinking that God judges all men equal in station when it comes to sinners?"

"Of course ... but we are talking about a respected Duke."

"We are talking about a duke accused of murder and mayhem. Tell the guards outside to bring the grandparents and the child!" the viceroy shouted. Looking at Tur, he added, "You, Captain, don't move more than one pace from where you stand."

After intense questioning and witnessing during which Ángelita clutched a handful of her grandmother's hair and snuggled into her shoulder, the council reluctantly agreed that she seemed to be familiar with Alma and her husband, Eduardo.

On the viceroy's orders, Tur led the group of men outside, and when they reached the carriage, he opened its door and said, "Your Mercies, the dead marauder I told you about is inside."

The magistrate took a quick look and then just as quickly turned away. The others stood back, being able to smell the man's rotting flesh from where they stood. Covering his nose with a kerchief, the magistrate asked Tur, "When did you say he died?"

Tur's eyes were steady. A man less hardened by war and even more devoted to religion than he was would have found this a difficult lie, but he was fighting for his life. "A few hours ago," he said calmly enough.

"He stinks."

"Dead men usually do."

The magistrate gestured to Father Bernardo and then said to Tur's militiamen, "Do you men swear to tell the truth in front of your priest?"

The soldiers nodded without hesitation.

"So will you all attest to seeing this marauder alive and of hearing him accuse the duke and the late lord treasurer of murder and abduction as well as other crimes?"

One by one the men answered, "Yes, Your Mercy."

"You'll all go to hell if you're lying," Father Bernardo warned the men with a look of sheer disgust.

The viceroy nodded. "Captain Tur, assemble your men." And addressing the magistrate he added, "I have decided to investigate this matter. Your council can debate this all day if they want to, but you and Father Bernardo will accompany me to the castle.

CHAPTER SIXTY-FOUR

The inquisitor, recovering from his shallow wound, sat in a cushioned chair in front of a blazing hearth fire and gazed at his grandson with love and a measure of suspicion. Feeling sick to his stomach, shocked, and outraged, his mind fought against the alleged facts being laid before him. The allegations were too evil even to contemplate, and he was still unwilling to believe a word of what he was hearing. Lifting his eyes, he stared again at the magistrate, Father Bernardo, and the viceroy, standing before him in a line. No doubt they were waiting for him to explode with outrage or weep with inconsolable sorrow.

His silence was palpable. He accepted that a viceroy and priest would not be there were they not fully convinced that their accusations held merit. Likewise, a magistrate never accused a person of any crime without having some credible evidence or witness at hand. Yet he could not bring himself to do what they were asking of him. Lowering his eyes, he stared lovingly at Gaspar. How could he live without the grandson he had come to love above all else? He would never have another, he reminded himself. He would soon lose his only child, and when Josefa died, his line would be at an end. It was unimaginable and unacceptable.

"As if the accusations against my son by law were not absurd enough, you say you want me to strip my grandson naked and allow you to inspect his body?" he questioned angrily.

"It is the only way to know for sure, Your Excellency," the viceroy said.

De Amo tightened his hold on the baby. "No, I won't do as you ask. This is my daughter's child. I see the resemblance between them."

"Inquisitor, I have done you the courtesy of coming to you first. We have not questioned your daughter or the duke, and we will not if we can disprove the grandparents' claim," the viceroy insisted. "If you don't comply, I will be forced to make this investigation public. I was asked by Sagrat's council to come to the town because of its present troubles. Your son by law's inability to keep order in this town has already reached the king's ear in Granada, and I will be writing a full report on what I have seen and experienced here. No one is above the law, not even your family."

"Have a care! I am the inquisitor! My office has a long reach, Viceroy, and I have a long memory."

"Let me remind you that my arm is just as long and as powerful as yours."

De Amo's chest tightened with fear. Without insulting the viceroy, there was no way to avoid doing as he was asked. Being inquisitor gave him power and privilege, but the Inquisition had to walk hand in hand and in close cooperation with the civil authorities. Without that mutual respect, there would be no order. He was not afraid to arrest a count, a duke, or even a clergyman, but the viceroy of Valencia was out of his reach.

Reluctantly, he handed the infant to his nurse and then rose painfully from his chair. "Wait outside. Let the nurse unwrap the baby in private. When we have him prepared, I will call you," De Amo said, without looking at the men.

"We will be outside the door. Please do us the courtesy of being quick about this," The Viceroy said curtly.

"The mere suggestion that you have all believed the lies of a dying thief makes my blood run cold," De Amo said bitterly as they were leaving. "But I will do as you ask, and after it is done, I will expect an apology from all three of you... And you will arrest the accuser."

Five minutes later, the viceroy, Father Bernardo, and the magistrate were invited back into the inquisitor's chamber. The naked baby lay on the bed on top of a white cotton sheet. De Amo threw a look of disgust in the direction of the three men and then ordered the nurse to lift the infant and hold him in the air with his back to the visitors.

The oval-shaped dark red birthmark was situated in the centre of the baby's back and covering part of the long spinal bone. De Amo watched the men's reaction with an impassive expression. After a minute or two, he ordered that the baby be laid back down and covered up with the sheet.

"You can see that there is indeed a mark on the baby's back," De Amo said quite calmly, "but I would like you to listen to what the nurse has to say before you come to any ridiculous conclusions about my grandson's heritage." Nodding to the nurse, he continued. "Tell them what you told me."

The nurse, a small rounded woman wearing a headscarf and thick white apron over her dull dress, flicked her eyes nervously at the three men and then couldn't seem to stop herself from taking an anxious deep breath. "I was present at the infant's birth, your mercies," she began. "I helped the physician bathe him just minutes after he came into the world. I remember seeing the red mark on his back because it was so distinctive. I thought at the time that I had never seen anything like it on a baby's body. I assure you that this is the duchess's child, borne from her womb ..."

The viceroy was granted a private audience with De Amo, whilst Father Bernardo, Tur, and the magistrate were ordered to wait for further instructions in the great hall. Fear tore through

Tur's body as he sensed an invisible rope tightening around his neck. Standing some distance away from Father Bernardo and the magistrate gave him time to observe them and to think about how he was going to save his hide from an arrest, which was looking increasingly more likely.

The priest wrung his hands and sat staring at one particular spot on the wooden table. The magistrate, on the other hand, flicked his eyes around the hall, jumped at the slightest sound, and continuously bit his lips. Neither looked Tur's way, nor did they speak to each other.

Tur wondered if they were as scared as he was and if perhaps they were regretting making the accusations against Peráto. Powerful men literally got away with murder and every other sin spawned by the devil. Accusers were more likely to be murdered for opening their mouths than the noble being accused of perpetrating a crime. And to point a finger at a member of the Holy Council for covering up a crime was unheard of, he reminded himself. Heads would roll, maybe even the viceroy's, should any more accusations against the inquisitor's family be pursued further. It made sense that his head would roll first.

CHAPTER SIXTY-FIVE

Appearing worried and seemingly indecisive, the viceroy paced up and down the great hall and repeatedly refused Father Bernardo's request that he sit down. His arms were crossed in a defensive position. His hands lay on each forearm, and his fingers tapped his skin, making an irritable noise which sounded like dripping rainwater. Despite all his intentions, Tur couldn't drag his eyes away. His heartbeat had quickened the moment the viceroy had walked into the great hall, mumbling under his breath and continually pushing his hair back from his forehead, even though it wasn't unruly.

Staring angrily at the magistrate and Father Bernardo, the viceroy finally said, "There is no more to be done regarding the infant. We can neither prove nor disprove the claims that have been made by the grandparents or the nurse. It would seem we are at an impasse. The inquisitor will never give the baby up to us."

"My Lord, the birthmark!" Tur inadvertently cried out. "The grandparents knew about it? Is that not proof enough?"

"No, it is not, Tur," Father Bernardo said hurriedly. "Workers in the castle often tell tales about what goes on here to their neighbours. There are gossiping shrews in every street. Perhaps the nurse spoke to people about the mark."

"I'll wager my little pinky that that's not the case, Padre," the viceroy said impatiently. "Magistrate, what do you have to say about this?"

Strangely pensive, the magistrate seemed to be either wavering in his opinion or was perhaps too afraid to call the inquisitor a liar. Shaking his head as though searching for the right words, he answered. "I believe it's time we either speak to the duke or leave."

"I think we should go now. Arrest Captain Tur and his militia and put this sordid matter to rest," Father Bernardo said in an agitated tone. "The town has suffered enough."

Tur was becoming increasingly alarmed by father Bernardo's demands, and only the certainty of being in the right gave him the strength to carry on. Bringing himself up to his full height, he found this the perfect time to get the men to focus their attention on the duke. "Your Mercies, begging your pardon, I have been informed that the duke's valet has been trying unsuccessfully to get into His Grace's chamber since early morning. My men have tried to open the door and have banged on it repeatedly, but there has been no answer from within."

"Then he is out somewhere or he does not want to be disturbed," Father Bernardo said harshly.

"I don't believe so, Padre. The doors cannot be locked from the inside unless someone is actually in the chamber."

"Lord above in heaven, it's possible that this is becoming the most unsettling affair I have ever had to deal with," the viceroy said, slamming his fists on the table. Without waiting for the others, he strode from the hall, shouting to Tur over his shoulder as he went. "Show me the way to the duke's chambers, Captain. I will not leave this castle until I have an answer to something or other!"

Tur knocked loudly on the door. When there was no response from within, he waited a minute or two and then thumped the thick iron-studded wood with his fist. "Your Grace, His Excellency, the viceroy, is here on urgent business!"

"Open it," the viceroy said when there was no answer the second time.

It took time, but eventually a ramming device comprised of a smooth tree trunk on two wooden wheels was brought and placed in front of the doors. Tur gave the order to strike, but the doors were built to withstand a major assault, and it took some time for the wooden bar on the inside of them to finally crack and then snap into two pieces.

After drawing his sword, Tur entered, followed by the three dignitaries, the duke's valet, and Paco, who had been one of the men banging on the doors earlier. The chamber was empty, and for a moment, all of them stood mystified and in silence. Going to the long, narrow shuttered window, Tur noticed that it was also barred. Not that anyone would be foolish enough to jump out of it, he thought. Frowning at the mystery, he asked the valet, "Is there any other exit?"

"No, the only other room in here is the wardrobe, where the duke's clothes are kept. It's behind that curtain."

Tur walked into an anteroom and looked around. All he could see were stacks of tunics, breeches, cloaks, boots, hats, and all other manner of clothing. How could one man wear everything in here in a single lifetime? he couldn't help but wonder. Then directing his oil-lit torch to one particular cabinet, he saw the partially hidden hole beside it.

The viceroy stood behind him, and behind him the magistrate and Father Bernardo, who was clutching his rosary at his chin and kissing the wooden crucifix attached to the beads. Without words, Tur slipped into the hole. Seeing the stairs, he shouted for the others to follow, and then he descended to the bottom.

Tur stood open-mouthed, stunned, and panting with shock. Feeling as if he'd been struck dumb, he could only manage to point to the duke's dead body lying on the ground.

Father Bernardo moaned like a man in agony. The viceroy gasped and instinctively put his hands to his throat. The magistrate clamped his hand over his mouth. His eyes widened and looked as though they were about to pop out of his head, but neither he nor the others seemed to be able to utter a single word.

Tur tried to concentrate on the scene. His mind knew what he was seeing: Luis Peráto, the duke of Sagrat, had been murdered in a secret chamber and was lying beside the two chests of coin that had been stolen from the municipal palace on the day of the auto-de-fé. The words sounded ridiculous in his mind, and they would sound even more fanciful if he were to say them aloud. But it was true.

"Holy Mother of Jesus," the viceroy said, breaking the silence.

"God have mercy on us," the magistrate uttered under his breath.

And Father Bernardo wept.

Tur managed to calm himself enough to focus on the rest of the chamber. An opening on the wall covered by an iron grill, which was open, drew his attention first. Getting on his knees, he poked his lit torch inside and saw that a tunnel stretched as far as his eyes could see. "Crawl into that tunnel and follow it to its end," he ordered Paco.

Watching Paco's figure disappear into the darkness, Tur thought, *If that tunnel comes out on the hill, I'll feel ashamed for not knowing about it, and so I should.* "I knew nothing about this tunnel or this chamber," he said sheepishly to the viceroy.

The viceroy ordered the valet to send for more soldiers and asked Tur, "What can you tell us about his death?"

Studying Peráto's body more closely, Tur answered, "It would appear that the duke died of a single slash to his throat, and I can see no reason to believe he put up a fight. There are no defensive wounds or signs of a struggle."

"He does look surprised," Father Bernardo said, getting on his knees to pray. "God have mercy on his soul!"

The magistrate stared at the two chests of coin and shook his head as though his mind was denying the sight of them. "It's impossible. How did he manage to get them in here?"

Bending down, Tur pointed his torch's flame into the hole in the wall. "My man should be back soon. He'll tell us where this tunnel leads." Staring again at the chests engraved with the duke of Sagrat's family seal, he said in a grim voice, "It might be wide enough to take the chests, but the duke would have needed a lot of help to pull them in here. He certainly didn't get past my men outside the chamber's doors …"

The viceroy, looking furious but with not a hint of sympathy for Luis, said, "I care not a whit how or why he did what he did. He was obviously demented. I am only concerned with what I now believe to be true." Taking a last look at Luis, whose eyes were wide open and staring up at the ceiling, he added, "He played with the devil and got burnt, I'll wager. Tur, I am presuming that his marauder friends killed him, turning on him like the dogs they are."

"It would appear so, my lord."

The viceroy then said, "I don't think we need to investigate this further. It's obvious to me that the duke colluded with thieves and murderers to rob the municipal palace, murder innocent people, and set fire to this town. These," he said, wagging his finger at the chests of coin, "are all the evidence I need to write a formal report to the king, in which I will charge the duke with atrocious crimes. I will demand that the Peráto family and their heirs lose their claim on the dukedom and that their name be stained … Now get me out of this stinking hole and take me to the inquisitor!"

Jana Petken

CHAPTER SIXTY-SIX

The inquisitor winched and breathed deeply as his chamberlain eased the coarse tunic over the bleeding wounds criss-crossing his back. He shivered. The pain was excruciating, yet it brought him comfort amidst the chaos. Listening to the commotion outside his chamber, he could somehow picture exactly what was happening. His daughter was screaming at his men- at-arms, who were trying to lift her out of her bed. Other familiars, grunting with exertion, were currently removing her belongings from the castle. And Josefa's ladies-in-waiting, crying with helplessness, were running away from their duties and their duchess.

He sat for a moment to pray and reflect. In a short while, his carriages and entourage would leave Sagrat. He had come to this town with high expectations for success. How could he not triumph? he'd thought. His son by law was the duke! He had expected exalted praise for his good works, yet here he was, leaving weeks earlier than planned, with a tarnished reputation and the memory of a failed mission. The auto-de-fé was supposed to have been a glorious occasion, the pinnacle of his career, but instead it would be remembered as the day the devil walked into Sagrat and stole God's thunder. He would never recover from this humiliation.

Outside in the courtyard, De Amo stood by a carriage, saying nothing when Josefa was unceremoniously bundled into it, kicking and biting whatever flesh her teeth could find. Taking a long, lingering look at Luis Peráto's castle, he forced back the anger and bitterness that twisted like a knife in his gut. His eyes went to the baby he cradled in his arms. His grandson would not become a duke, live in this castle, or be entitled to the king's favours. No noble would forgive the Peráto family, not in his grandson's lifetime. They would talk about Gaspar not as a duke's son and grandson of Aragon's inquisitor but as an imposter stolen from his rightful family.

Sitting in the carriage, he told his chamberlain to close the curtains. He would not look at the burnt streets or succumb to the suspicious gazes of common people judging him. They were judging him! He was seething with resentment. Luis Peráto had destroyed his ambitions and had left him fighting to hold on to his position as inquisitor. An inquisitor did not lose over one hundred heretic prisoners and survive …

Militiamen had set to work blocking the tunnel's entrance and exit holes. The duke's body had been taken to the castle's chapel; the two chests of coin went to the municipal palace vault.

Tur stood inside the watch tower and looked out over the plain. Somewhere marauders were wandering free, too far away now to be caught and probably too clever to ever return to Sagrat. He was baffled. He would always be at a loss to understand exactly what had transpired in his town – why the marauders had not taken the two chests of coin and their reasons for killing the duke were two burning questions that would probably remain unanswered until the day he died.

"Sagrat will heal now," he remarked to Paco, who was standing beside him.

"The burnt tracts of land will scar this town for years to come, but yes, we will heal," Paco answered.

In silence, Tur watched the Inquisition's caravan kick up dust on the plain as it headed south towards Valencia. His mouth spread in a rare smile, and in another rare gesture, he placed his hand on Paco's shoulder.

"Morales, the Inquisition will return one day to terrorize and burn people in malignant displays of faith, but it would appear that this particular inquisitor is no longer interested in Sagrat's errant flock."

"What will happen to the incarcerated in our prison?"

Tur shrugged. "I imagine they will remain there until the Inquisition comes back to interrogate them."

"That could be months … years," Paco said angrily.

"Then we shall be patient," Tur said.

EPILOGUE

Cartegena, Spain
June 1492

The port of Cartagena sat at the edge of a great plain and was bordered at the north and the north-west by pre-coastal mountain ranges. The town, limited by five small hills with an inner sea between them, was not affluent or pretty, and to the dismay of its people, it had been allowed to fall into decadence and decay ever since the king annexed it to Aragon.

Near the Roman amphitheatre, where the sea met the land, a gathering of Jews prayed with soft voices and with one eye open for the militia, who wouldn't waste a minute in scattering them. The noisy port behind their backs was congested with boats of every type, from basic punts which moved with agility even in shallow water to the larger, more imposing merchant ships with trapezoid sails that navigated the open seas.

Cartagena was also congested with Jews being exiled from Spain. The expulsion decree, issued on the last day of March in Granada, had been made public less than three months after the Catholic monarchs' victory against the Muslims in Granada. The Jews had half expected the announcement. The Christians had defeated the Moors, and now they wanted to get rid of the Jews and unite Spain under one faith.

David stood amongst the congregation celebrating a brief Shabbat service, which would be, for some of them, the last they would ever attend in Sefarad, the Jews' name for

Spain. He wondered what the congregation was thinking. Were they concentrating on the prayers or were they, like him, swathed in sorrow and still trying to come to terms with the cruelty being directed against the their race?

He would never forget that terrible day in April, when he, Diego, and Sinfa had happened upon a public reading of the king's edict regarding the fate of all Spanish Jews. The memory of the callous words read by a rabbi barely able to speak, and with grief drowning his voice, would haunt him until the day he drew his last breath.

Forgetting where he was for a moment, he grunted with disdain and then quickly snapped his mouth shut in embarrassment. The Jews, given only four months to convert to Christianity or leave the country, had been promised royal protection and security until the day of their departure. That had turned out to be the king's first false pledge, David thought.

Looking at a wealthy Jew he'd met only that morning, standing with head bowed next to the rabbi, David wondered how the man would take to a new life without money, servants, or familiar comforts. Jews, in accordance with Their Majesties' declaration, were being allowed to take their belongings with them, with the exception of gold, silver, minted money, and other things prohibited by the laws of Castile and Aragon. In other words, they could take nothing of value.

Listening to the rabbi speak brought vivid memories of his earlier life in Sagrat, when Shabbat was as important as avoiding the fish stalls at the end of a hot day. Life was full of ironies, he thought, glancing at a woman who reminded him of Sinfa. On the journey south, Sinfa had repeatedly refused to convert to Christianity, preferring exile from the country of her birth to baptism. But when Diego had pointed out that he would not leave Spain, not even for her, she had cast aside her reluctance and had been baptised in the next town they had come to.

Standing there amongst Jews reciting prayers from the Torah, David accepted that the three years in which he had lived as a Christian now felt like a fleeting experience, one he wouldn't miss or regret losing. Smiling at a little girl tugging at his tunic, he believed that it mattered not that he was a Jew again. Being part of a religious body was one of life's necessary evils. Cities destroyed, countries fractured, and lives lost to hatred were what religions had offered the world, as far as he knew. The Jews had shown him kindness since leaving Sagrat. They had been more benevolent that any Christian spouting pious devotions whilst killing members of their flock. Although he didn't truly believe in God insofar as the way organized religion depicted Him, the Jews made him feel that he belonged.

Turning his head, David glanced briefly at the waves lapping against the harbour's stone wall. An image of Diego and Sinfa waving goodbye to him one week previously at the water's edge rushed into his mind with such clarity that he felt as though they were with him. He would never see his brother or Sinfa again. After a disagreement about which route they should take next, Diego elected to remain in the fishing town of Los Alcazares, sitting less than three leagues north of Cartagena. Sinfa was tired of journeying, Diego had pointed out. It was time for them to settle down. Feeling alone and defeated, David had watched them walk away, yet his chest had swollen with pride, not anger or bitterness.

Had they seen him become a man, his parents also would have been proud of Diego. But they had not been in Los Alcazares. They had disappeared into thin air, like the smoke that had hovered over Sagrat. Looking at the people praying, he forced himself to believe that the Inquisition had not recaptured them. Many had, according to some people he had met, yet others had been sure that only a few had been led back to prison after that great escape.

Thinking about the long journey he, Diego, and Sinfa had taken brought David a mixture of sadness and relief. For months, they had travelled southwards, using their instincts and gut feelings to guide them. They had searched for their parents in every port and town they had passed through, and not once did they give up hope of finding them alive and well, until that day at the water's edge, when they had said goodbye.

Sighing softly, he shifted his weight from his right to his left foot and at the same time shuddered with apprehension for the future. He, Diego, and Sinfa had been fortunate on their journey. They had sold the mule, cart, and horse early on, after deciding that food was much more important than the comforts transportation could bring. But knowing that Jews were being expelled, the buyers had offered a pittance in money. Everywhere he looked, he saw Jews trying to sell their worldly possessions to unscrupulous people taking advantage of Jewish vulnerabilities and their need to sell everything they owned quickly.

Studying the worn-out faces around made him think about the struggles he and his travelling companions had overcome on their way south. They had suffered cold, hunger, and had been lost at times. But they had also met hundreds of Jews along the way and had been touched by their generosity.

Recalling an incident which had occurred a few weeks previously brought a smile to his face. They had been travelling along a particularly difficult road that had no rivers running by it or vegetables in the fields bordering it. Starving, parched with thirst, and moving like snails, they had come across a carriage with a broken wheel. He and Diego had repaired it for the wealthy Jew who owed it, and afterwards the man had been charitable, allowing Sinfa to travel on the carriage beside the driver and sharing his food and water with all three of them.

At another stage on the journey, they had wandered onto someone's land and had managed to remain there for weeks after they were employed to plough and seed the soil for the elderly farmer. Yes, they had been fortunate, but there had been times on that journey when he'd wondered if they would ever get to their destination in one piece. There had also been times when he thought his heart would break. Watching Diego hold Sinfa in his arms, her eyes lovingly gazing at Diego, and the stolen kisses between them, had been torturous to watch.

Looking absently at the Jews praying with him, he couldn't help but recall some of the conversations he'd overheard in the past few days. Fleeing Jews were being murdered. Rumours of Jews swallowing gold and diamonds had spread like a plague, and many had been stabbed to death by brigands hoping to find treasures in their stomachs, some Jews had openly stated, convinced that they spoke the truth. And earlier that day, he had listened to a Jewish husband and wife who had just returned from North Africa. Their account of what happened when they arrived in the Maghreb had filled him with so much fear that he'd thought about running all the way back to Diego and Sinfa, farther up the coast, and to hell with being a Jew again!

"We arrived in North Africa and were pillaged before we had even left the dockside," the traumatised husband told a crowd of Jews at the port. "Two men who had been travelling with us on the overcrowded boat had their throats cut. Others were dragged away alive. We had coin hidden on our persons, and they stripped us of all our clothing and took everything of value from us. It would seem that God's hand was against us. He allowed some of our brothers and sisters to starve, be killed by the sword, and sold into slavery ... How could anyone witness the sufferings of the Jews and not be moved?" David had asked them what they were going to do. The man had answered resolutely. "We are going to the nearest church to ask for baptism and to be accepted into the Christian faith. That's what any sane person should do, and that's what I advise you to do."

Staring at the array of ships at anchor, David wondered which of them would take him across the water. The Maghreb was not a great distance by sea, yet it was, according to many, a strange new world ruled by Muslims and Ottomans, who didn't seem to be much more enamoured by Jews than the Spanish Catholics were. Sensing the little girl's eyes on him and feeling her pull again at his tunic, he looked down at her and was amused by her earnest expression.

"You should be praying," she whispered, craning her neck to look up at him. "You will be in big trouble."

"I *have* been praying and thinking and wondering," he said, smiling. He then squeezed her hand.

He was not alone, he thought just then. These people would be with him. They would all be strangers in a new country. They would need each other. And if there really was a God, he would forgive the past. He, David Sanz, a sinner, a man who had done unspeakable harm to people and who'd caused suffering to those he loved most in the world, had been punished – maybe not enough in the eyes of the Catholic Church, but in no small measure. He had no family by his side, and no Sinfa. They had been taken from him forever, and not one day would pass that he wouldn't wonder what had happened to them or where they were … That had been God's wrath. He would not fear the future or the dangers it might hold, he thought, gazing out to sea again. The future existed in this moment, ever evolving with each breath taken and with every thought passing through his mind like a river rushing downstream. He was alive and well right now, and he *was* fortunate. He had been given a second chance, and he was not going to waste it, not one minute of it.

About the Author

Author of the critically acclaimed epics, The Guardian of Secrets and The Mercy Carver Series.

Jana Petken is Scottish but resides on the East Coast of Spain. She is ex military and has travelled extensively, studying conflicts and the after effects they had on the population. She is a fulltime writer but says her hobbies include, walking great distances and painting in oils.

Thank you for taking the time to read The Errant Flock. I would be honoured if you would leave a review on Amazon. Word of mouth recommendations are gifts for authors.

www.janapetkenauthor.com
@AuthoJana
On FB, Author Jana Petken

A recommended thriller for you

Major Jimmy Wilson, late of the Royal Engineers, has been obliged to leave the rapidly shrinking British Army. He needs a job but they are thin on the ground even for a highly capable Army Officer. Then he is offered the chance to go to Northern Germany to search for the last great secret of World War II, a hidden U Boat base. Once he unravels the mystery he is asked to help to spirit two submarines away from under the noses of the German government, to be the central exhibits in a Russian museum. But then the betrayal begins and a seventy year old horror unfolds.

Part one of a trilogy. On Amazon, worldwide.

12352914R00245

Printed in Great Britain
by Amazon.co.uk, Ltd.,
Marston Gate.